ECHOES
OF A
GLORIED
PAST

Ken Lozito

ECHOES OF A GLORIED PAST

ISBN: 978-0-9899319-2-2

The author greatly appreciates you taking the time to read his work. Please consider leaving a review wherever you bought the book, or telling your friends about it, to help us spread the word. Thank you.

Published by Acoustical Books, LLC

KenLozito.com

Edited by: Jason Whited jason-whited.com

Cover Design: Alexandre Rito

Discover other books by Ken Lozito

Safanarion Order Series:

Road to Shandara (Book 1)

Echoes of a Gloried Past (Book 2)

Amidst the Rising Shadows (Book 3)

To my sons, Tristan and Brendan, for listening to me read the early drafts of this story and for never ceasing to ask questions. All of these stories are for you.

Table of Contents

Chapter 1
HYTHARIAM

Time passed as Aaron slipped in and out of consciousness, occasionally awakening to the muttering of voices, both familiar and not. The steady rise and fall of the airship as it rode the winds was gone, replaced by a soft bed. He forced his eyes open again, ignoring their determination to remain shut. Sunlight and a gentle breeze oozed their way in through the balcony doors on the far side of the room. The harsh burning on his back where the Ryakul clawed him had faded to a dull ache. Stretching his neck, he slowly turned his head, trying to wake up. Stiff limbs quickly yielded to movement as he sat up in bed, rubbing the sleep from his eyes. He was almost naked except for where his wounds had been cleaned and dressed. The skin of his arms and legs was dotted with the remnants of faded bruises. A brown robe hung near a metallic chest across the room. The rune-carved staff rested on the wall near the chest along with his medallion, which sparkled in the sunlight, sending hazy dragon emblems upon the smooth walls. He swung his feet to the floor and bit his lower lip, wincing at the burning pain along his back that flared at his movement. The tiled floor warmed beneath his feet. He took a steadying breath and slowly rose. The more he moved, the less his body seemed to protest.

Aaron crossed the room and pulled the robe on, tying it off at his waist. Its silky fabric felt cool on his skin. His mind still felt muddled, as if he were still waking up. He stepped out onto the balcony into the warm sunlight, allowing it to caress his face. He slowly stretched his arms out to either side, feeling the tender skin protest at first and then give way to the slow movements of his arms. Birds chirped nearby, and a few hawks circled high above him. As he glanced to the side, he saw the outlines of white buildings, which appeared more like pods joined together than the grandeur of the architecture of Shandara. He reached out and ran his fingers along the outer wall, and where his fingers met the surface it turned black. Aaron removed his hand, and the color returned to white. He ran his fingers along the outer doorframe, watching as the surface went from white to dark and back again.

More technology, Aaron thought to himself, and then his thoughts turned to Sarah. She was out there somewhere, under the influence of the Drake. Images of the battle flashed in his mind like lightning. He closed his eyes and tried to draw the energy into himself, but felt as if he were trying to grasp something made of smoke. He couldn't reach out to her. How could the Drake control her so easily? He suppressed a shiver, remembering her baleful yellow eyes looking back at him. With a gasp, he held onto the balcony railing and opened his eyes, filling his vision with the clear skies to keep from seeing her that way, but his last image of Sarah was burned into his mind. He hadn't anticipated the Drake taking a prisoner. Instead, foolishly believing that its only aim was to kill him. His pulse quickened while his hands clutched at the railings.

"You're awake!" Verona said, coming into the room through a metallic door that slid silently into the wall. "They said it would be another day." He poured some water and handed the cup to Aaron.

"Thank you," Aaron said, taking a sip of water. "How long have I been out?"

"Three days. It was touch and go there for a while, my friend. The Ryakul's claws are quite poisonous," said Verona.

"Sarah?" Aaron asked, fearing the answer in his friend's eyes.

"I'm sorry, but we haven't seen her or the Drake since Shandara," Verona said.

Aaron nodded slowly, expecting as much. He sipped the water, tasting the faint hints of cinnamon, and felt his stomach tighten for a moment.

"It's medicine that will help purge the remaining poison from your body."

Aaron remained standing and allowed the queasiness to pass. "Where are we?" he asked.

"We're with the Hythariam, north of Shandara in a place called Hathenwood," answered Verona.

"Is everyone… Did everyone else make it?" Aaron asked.

"Yes." Verona smiled. "Some bumps and bruises and a few

shallow cuts, but the Hythariam helped with those as well. The repairs to the Raven will be complete in the next day or so, and the Hythariam are installing some extra things that will help against the Ryakuls," Verona said.

Aaron sighed and felt his shoulders slump in relief. He stretched his neck and rolled his shoulders, still feeling the effects of the medicine. He needed a clear head, and the medicine didn't appear to be helping with that. "I'd like to take a walk."

Verona frowned for a second before giving a small nod. "There is clothing in there," he said, pointing to the chest. "I'll give you a few minutes to change, and then we should get some food in you."

Verona left the room by placing his hand on a pad near the door, and the door slid silently into the adjoining wall. *More technology,* Aaron thought. He walked over to the chest, which didn't have any handles. He placed his palm on top of a pad similar to the one on the door, and a drawer extended from the bottom. The clothes were loose fitting and, like the robe, felt good on his skin. He pulled on black boots that molded themselves to the contours of his feet. He stood up and noted how comfortable they felt while being both sturdy yet almost weightless at the same time. They were a clear improvement over the hiking boots he had brought with him from Earth. He hung the medallion around his neck and grabbed the rune-carved staff. It was a good walking stick, after all.

Aaron exited the room into a quiet hallway where Verona waited. His stomach rumbled noisily, giving Verona the audible clue he needed to lead the way. As they made their way down the hall, a Hythariam appeared, heading in their direction. His golden eyes flashed briefly in surprise, then with a nod to each of them, he turned back the way he had come.

"We've had you on constant watch since arriving the other day," Verona said. "Eric and Braden had only just left your door earlier at my insistence." After Aaron nodded he continued, "I know you want answers, and you'll get them, but I must tell you that it's really good to see you awake, my friend."

"Was it that bad? The poison, I mean," Aaron asked.

"Lethal to most people almost immediately. Even the Hythariam will die if they don't get help in time."

"Colind?" Aaron asked.

"Will be anxious to see you. He's been all but locked in a room with Iranus, Vaughn, and several other Hythariam. I haven't seen much of them since I kept Eric and Braden company."

"Thanks," Aaron said and swallowed a lump down his throat as the image of Sarah's smiling face flashed in his mind. They walked in silence, and the more he moved, the better he felt. Aaron could tell that Verona was holding something back and guessed he didn't want to overburden him. The rune-carved staff proved to be a good walking stick, even on the smooth metallic gray floors. The farther they ventured from his room, the more Hythariam they came across. Most nodded in friendly greeting, but some looked at him with worry in their golden eyes. Those eyes were so similar to the Drake, it was disconcerting.

"Is it much farther?" Aaron asked.

"Not much. We can rest if you need," Verona answered, gesturing toward one of the benches along the wall.

"I'll be fine," Aaron said, waving him on.

The corridors echoed of people walking, and muffled conversations could be heard throughout the place. Wherever they were, there was a bustle of activity. They turned down another corridor, and Aaron smelt food, making his mouth water. He just needed to eat, then he wanted answers.

Verona took him to an open courtyard filled with tables and benches, which was a cross between a garden and an outdoor cafeteria. People took plates of food from several buffet stations strategically placed throughout. Aaron selected food by Verona giving either a nod of approval for some or a vigorous shake of his head for things to avoid. He stuck mostly with vegetables and meat, preferring not to experiment with things he couldn't readily identify.

The Hythariam still glanced in their direction, with some whispering to their companions, and others nodding in friendly greeting. Aaron had never seen so many golden eyes and was surprised to see green ones as well. They were very similar to humans except that their eyes were just a bit bigger and had an almost feline quality to them. They wore clothing of the same quality as he had been given, which Aaron found quite comfortable. Nothing too colorful, and all could have blended easily in a forest if needed. The occasional cyan-colored scarf adorned some of the women, and similarly colored cords were tied around the arms of the men.

They ate in silence, or more like Verona watched as Aaron devoured his meal. The moment the first bite passed his lips, he was filled with an overwhelming need to eat. He was starving. They washed down their meal with water, and Aaron felt his mind clear and more of his strength return.

"You're looking more human now," Verona said.

"Feeling like it, too," Aaron answered.

They were approached by a tall Hythariam with raven hair and green eyes. He had the bearing of a soldier though he was out of uniform. He gave a slight bow to them both and said, "Hello, I am Gavril. Iranus sends his greetings and asks for you to join him and Colind, if you are able."

Aaron shot to his feet, ready to follow Gavril, and Verona rose as well.

"It's not far," Gavril said and led them down a short corridor lined with glass doors. Behind each of the doors appeared to be oval-shaped rooms that hung suspended over tracks heading in different directions. They stepped into one of the rooms, and a panel opened on its far side. Gavril keyed in some of the buttons on the holographic touch screen. "The tram will get us there much faster than on foot," Gavril said, and the door quietly shut behind them.

The tram shot forth, following one of the tracks leading outside. Verona looked delighted, and Aaron reached immediately for something to hold onto before he realized that while they were moving quite fast, he hardly felt as if they were moving at all. Aaron figured the trams must have some type of dampeners to suppress the forces that would put them off balance. Gavril studied their reactions and nodded to himself.

The tram took them outside, and Aaron looked out the window at the complex of buildings from which they left. Some were similar to the style he had seen in Shandara but more modern by comparison. Where Shandara had buildings and gardens complementing each other in their design, the complex of the Hythariam buildings seemed to be more sparse and functional rather than built for appearances. After a few minutes, they approached another set of buildings mostly hidden by the trees, but Aaron saw a few metallic towers strategically placed around a central octagonal dome that peaked over the tree line. The tram entered one of the tunnels near the dome, and Aaron watched the track disappear behind them into darkness. They exited the tram, and Gavril led them away from the platform.

Aaron was growing tired but refused to give in, and he straightened up when he felt himself start to stoop. Gavril pressed his palm to a panel, and the metallic door quietly hissed open. Colind and Vaughn turned immediately and came over to greet Aaron.

"You should not be up and about yet," spoke a silky voice behind him. Aaron turned to see a beautiful raven-haired Hythariam reach inside her pocket and pull out a device. She held the device inches away from his head and slowly scanned down his back.

"Aaron," spoke an older Hythariam, "please forgive my daughter, Roselyn. She is a healer first and person second. Do you remember me? I am Iranus, and I'm most pleased to see you recovering so quickly."

Aaron remembered Iranus, with his long white hair contrasted by his golden eyes. He had been among those on the ship that rescued him when he fell. "I do remember you," he replied.

"Since you're here and not resting in your bed where you should be, give me a moment to examine you," Roselyn ordered and ushered the others away.

The others quickly moved to give the healer room to work, save Verona, who stood rooted in place for once but was clearly at a loss for words. Roselyn raised the device to Aaron's eyes and slowly scanned downward.

"Can you give us a moment please?" she said to Verona, snapping him out of his reverie.

Verona joined the others across the room, giving them some privacy, but he kept glancing back in Roselyn's direction.

Roselyn focused her attention on Aaron and asked him a few questions about the Ryakul wound on his back.

"You're a remarkably fast healer, Aaron," she said sternly. "You don't realize how close to death you were."

"You'd be surprised," Aaron answered quietly. "But thank you."

"Indeed," she said and then leaned in so only he could hear what she was about to say. "You have friends here, Heir of Shandara, but be careful, as all is not what it seems, and the answers given may not be complete in their truthfulness. Some would see the return of the Alenzar'seth as a very grave threat."

Aaron gave a slight nod, and Roselyn moved away.

"He's recovering well. Do not keep him long," she said, looking sternly at Iranus.

"Thank you, my dear. Won't you please join us?" Iranus asked, motioning for them to sit in one of the nearby circles of chairs.

Aaron sat down, and after everyone else was seated, all eyes drew toward him. "First, I'd like to thank you for your help and for giving us a place to stay."

Iranus held up his hand. "No thanks are necessary. It was the least we could do."

Aaron nodded. "Second, where is the Drake, and what did it do to Sarah?"

"We don't know where the Drake is now," Iranus said. "As for what it did to your friend, I need to know exactly what you saw."

"What I saw… " Aaron began, and the image of the Drake holding Sarah up by her neck invaded his thoughts. "It blew some kind of green vapor into her face, forcing her to breathe it in. Then she began to writhe in pain, and after only a few moments her eyes turned yellow like his. When I called to her, she pulled away as if she didn't recognize me. It was like one moment she knew who I was and the next she wanted to kill me. Then the Drake called to her, and she went with it… I could…I could still see… her, but at the same time she was different," Aaron said. "I know, it doesn't make much sense, but that's what I saw."

"It makes perfect sense," Roselyn said and then turned to her father. "The Drake is using a biological delivery agent to spread itself. We suspected, but no one could confirm before now."

"What is it delivering exactly?" Aaron asked.

"A way to control its victims," Iranus said.

There were a few moments of silence until Colind cleared his throat. "Tell him the rest."

Aaron divided his gaze between Colind and Iranus, expectantly.

"I had hoped to give you more time to recover before burdening you with this," Iranus began. "We have observed your world. Where you were raised."

"Earth," said Aaron. For a second, he thought of his sister, Tara, and how he would have liked for her to meet Sarah someday.

"Yes, I've no doubt you are familiar with machines?" Iranus asked and continued when Aaron nodded. "We've developed machines that are smaller than the finest grain of sand. They can live in our bodies and group together to form larger machines to perform any number of tasks."

"We have something similar. We call it nanotech," Aaron said. "It deals with manipulation on a molecular level." His response drew a frown from Verona, but Colind, he noted, didn't look at all out of sorts.

"Excellent, I suspected you would be familiar with the concept," Iranus said. "The Drake used a gas to deliver the Nanites into your friend. It was the Nanites and not the gas that caused her to change."

"But what do the Nanites do exactly?" Aaron asked.

"By themselves not too much, but networked together they can perform complex calculations, including probability, and can adapt to a number of situations. They can form tiny power plants to recharge. Within an organic host, they can convert the movement of the beating heart into energy. When they were first developed, they were coded with a prime directive to keep the body healthy. They worked with the brain and the body, observing the body's reaction to infection. After some analysis, they would help eliminate infections while allowing the body's natural immune system to still function. This was essential so we didn't lose our natural immunity to diseases. We also equipped them with the ability to communicate with other nanotech so knowledge and methods were shared. This went a long way, ultimately eliminating the visible signs of sickness altogether."

"I think I understand. Like a cold, once you start feeling the effects of the cold, you're already sick," Aaron said.

Iranus smiled slightly. "Correct. So, by all outward appearances we 'cured' most diseases entirely, but in truth, the Nanites enabled us to resist them before they were even felt by the body."

"I understand the concept of Nanites, but that doesn't explain what happened to Sarah," Aaron said.

"I'll need to delve a bit into our history to help you understand better," Iranus began. "Particularly how we came from our home world of Hytharia to Safanar. The Nanites' ability to keep the body healthy was only the beginning of their capabilities. We could also use them to manipulate the biological blueprints of a living organism. We learned how to alter the genes for aging, to increase brain function, thus stimulating growth in our ability to calculate, and even increase our bodies' durability and strength."

Iranus paused, allowing for what he said to sink in. The gravity of such a momentous advance in technology was not lost upon

Aaron.

"The moral implications of those advances must have been profound," Aaron said after a few moments' thought.

"That's putting it mildly," Roselyn said, speaking up for the first time since she had examined him.

"Aging?" Aaron said. "So, you were able to stop aging entirely? Didn't that lead to overpopulation on your world?"

"Much more than that," Iranus said evenly. "When people live too long, they lose perspective. Organisms such as ourselves were not meant to evade death entirely. So yes, we were able to heal ourselves and delay aging, allowing for the possibility of a fuller life, but some wanted to live forever, believing that since we could, in theory, live forever, that we had a right to do so."

"That doesn't sound so bad," Verona said.

Iranus's lips curved in a knowing sort of way. "It sounds wonderful, does it not? But imagine this, if you will. A whole society that doesn't have to fear death or growing old? You would amass a multitude of knowledge but without wisdom—without the certainty that you were allowed a finite time in this life. People became unmotivated, and their fundamental values changed. Instead of bringing people together into harmony, it drove them apart into chaos. Essentially, we took away the things that made life worth living."

"What did you do?" Aaron asked.

"We decided not to stop aging altogether, but simply slow it down to acceptable levels," Iranus answered.

"How did you decide how long one should live?" Aaron asked.

"We voted on a range and agreed on 200 to 225 years, lifestyle permitting. To prevent constant lobbying in our courts, an agreement was put into place to revisit the age range every 50 years," Iranus said.

"I can't imagine deciding as a society how long one should live," Aaron replied.

Iranus pursed his lips in thought for a moment. "Is it so foreign a concept to you? If you live a healthy lifestyle, you have a better chance to live longer. People, no matter their origin, have this balance, and ours was the next logical step with the resources at our disposal. We were able to manage the genes for aging so that it still took place, but at a much slower rate."

"Still," Aaron said, "even with a majority vote, conflict or even outright war must have been inevitable."

"Yes," Iranus replied solemnly. "There are those who worked in secret to thwart the council's efforts to maintain peace. War, as you said, became inevitable. The precious gift stemming from the Nanites became a weapon. You've glimpsed the remnants of Hytharia through the portal. You've seen firsthand the result upon our world."

"Why Safanar?" Aaron asked. "Couldn't you open a gateway to another world instead?"

"I'm sure they tried, but opening a door doesn't mean you're going to like what is on the other side."

"That's not really an answer, now is it?" Aaron replied.

Iranus smiled. "No, it's not. Safanar was the first successful connection to a habitable world we were able to make. But to understand why we came here, I must explain the situation on Hytharia. Our planet was dying." Iranus began addressing everyone in the room. "In developing our technological prowess, we all but exhausted our natural resources. Something happened to our sun that caused it to age faster than we had originally projected. The lifespan of our star should have ranged in the billions of years, but was eventually reduced to thousands and then hundreds of years. Even then, it should have been enough time for us to find a suitable world to colonize. We utilized every means possible in the search. Sending out probes through space as fast as possible, but these things take time.

"The search for another home became a cycle of destruction for us. Those in power used the impending crisis as a way to justify reckless decisions that eventually put the stability of Hytharia in jeopardy. Super volcanoes killed millions, and a war for the remaining resources necessary for survival reduced our numbers further. Amid all the death and destruction, we found Safanar. Our beacon of hope. A short distance, relatively speaking, but it still took our probe thirty years to find this place. We could never build ships with enough resources to take a significant number of our people here, so we had to find a different solution, but at least we had a target to reach for. This gave us hope and brought the factions of our society back into harmony...for a time.

"The probe continued to send us information and landed on the surface not far from where we are sitting right now. With all the hope that a new home brings, war all but ceased as efforts were focused on viable solutions to get us here.

"The most brilliant scientists of the age were brought together, along with a specialized branch of Hytharia's remaining military factions. They acquired the resources we needed and gave us a place to work."

"Us?" Aaron asked. "You mean you were one of the scientists?"

"Yes," Iranus answered. "Many of us here were part of the original group. It wasn't just scientists, though, but our families as well. We focused on opening a portal between our two worlds. At least that was our end goal. All great things have small beginnings, and we were eventually successful. The calculations involved just to open a portal on the same planet were impressive. Imagine trying to hit a moving target across an enormous expanse of space. What we were able to achieve was startling to say the least, but it did come with its fair share of failure and risk. Now, given the discussion, I won't go into the details of the intricacies of bending space-time. There is simply not enough time for that. So, I will continue." Iranus paused for a moment. "After our first few successful trips to Safanar, we were happy to report that this world was beyond our wildest expectations. We studied the people here and came in contact with one of your ancestors, Aaron. You carry his staff with you here in this very room."

"Daverim," Aaron gasped, his mind flashing back to the abandoned temple he had come to when he first arrived on Safanar. He traced his hands along the rune-carved staff. "But that's…"

"Eighty years ago, yes," Iranus said with a small smile, his eyes growing distant as he remembered his first meeting with Daverim.

"Full of life to say the least," Iranus continued. "He was a good man. We allied with the kingdom of Shandara, because the ideals of that kingdom closely matched our own, before the harshness of survival sapped some of our morality from us. In exchange for their help, we agreed to share our technological advances and knowledge. There was actually quite a bit we learned from one another, and we started bringing our people to this world. Shandara was a buffer for us from the rest of Safanar, but it was always our intent to work with all of the kingdoms here.

"When we brought our proposal to our leadership council, a new general was appointed to oversee the whole effort. His name was General Morag Halcylon."

Aaron looked around the room and regarded the cold, expressionless looks of the other Hythariam as confirmation of the sinking feeling he felt.

"We proposed what was in our mandate, which was to find a way to bring survivors from our dying world to Safanar. To live and interact with the people of this world. But others had a different plan," Iranus said bitterly. "They wanted to conquer and rule what they perceived as lesser people. We didn't realize the extent of the ruthlessness of our leadership and the measures taken to provide the resources we needed. They simply took what was needed from others of our home world. Leaving them exposed and in some cases murdering whole cities. I began researching any information I could find about the new general and cursed my ignorant self. General Halcylon was among the most ruthless of our military, who thrived under the guise of survival at the cost of the soul of our people. Most of the council cowered in fear of him, and those that did not were aligned with the means by which he accomplished his goals."

Aaron felt the bile rise to the top of his throat as he tried to imagine what the collapse of a proud civilization like the Hythariam looked like. He realized that like Shandara, nothing in his wildest imaginings would come close to the shadowed horror that lived within the gazes of people who had actually witnessed these events.

"What did you do?" Aaron asked.

"I didn't want to believe it," Iranus began. "We were supposed to be better than this. All of our accomplishments as a people pointed to us being more enlightened than the barbarism being committed. But as great as we were in the good things we did, they were outweighed by the evil done. Evil that was born in the name of desperation under the guise of the good for the many. With my illusions shattered, I alerted others to what was happening and began formulating a plan to get people through the portal to Safanar, people who did not want to bring war to this world."

"Civil war?" Aaron asked.

"Not at first, but yes," Iranus said, his golden eyes becoming steel. "All war is evil, but a war among brothers and sisters is a different kind of evil entirely. We resisted where we could, bringing people through the portal without notice as best we could. At the same time, we didn't want to alert the Shandarians to what was happening for fear that the doors to Safanar would be closed. Daverim, however, suspected that things were deteriorating on Hytharia, and after meeting General Halcylon, he discovered the true intent of the general. He later said that one didn't need to travel so far to know a tyrant when he saw one. After that meeting, Daverim confronted me about the state of Hytharia, and I told him everything. I left nothing out, and he simply listened. Together, we worked on a plan to get as many people as we could off of Hytharia before the portal was to be blocked.

"General Halcylon underestimated the people of Safanar, dismissing them as undeveloped, which couldn't be further from the truth. Where we were strong in science to enhance ourselves, they were strong in their connections to the world and its undercurrents of energy. It's something we've never seen. We used inventions like the Nanites to enhance our bodies, while the Shandarians could do similar things by drawing energy into themselves.

"The plan was to organize a large wave of our people through the portal then block the passage for those who would ravage this world. We had been bringing people through in small groups and were setting up living space with the help of the Shandarians. Daverim came up with a way to block the portal while keeping it open. My job was to see to it that the likes of General Halcylon couldn't open another portal when this one became blocked. We compiled a list of targets so that our work couldn't be followed after we were gone."

"Did it work?" Aaron asked.

"Yes and no," Iranus replied. "There were many sacrifices, and many good people died so that we few survived. We brought as many over as we could, but once those in power finally discovered what we were doing, they moved quickly to thwart us. We had some help on the council from like-minded people. Daverim kept the portal under constant watch along with the Guardians of the Safanarion Order," Iranus said, looking to Colind. "When the fighting appeared on this side as troops came through, Daverim created the barrier."

"How?" Vaughn asked.

"He used the bladesong evoked from the Falcons," Aaron answered. He couldn't help but sympathize with Iranus, who was clearly pained to bring up so many tragic memories, but he needed answers—they all did. The people of Shandara had paid a heavy price in blood to give aid to the Hythariam.

"Yes, that is correct," Iranus said. "Daverim used the bladesong to align the energy from beneath the ground into a barrier that essentially locked the portal open, yet allowed no one through."

"I'm not as well versed on this subject as some," Aaron began, "but my understanding is that what you're describing requires an active connection. How was Daverim able to do this?"

"He was able to connect to the energy deep beneath the ground. That connection is maintained by a living member of the house Alenzar'seth, a secret known only to a few. There is a life energy in this land that is tied to the portal, which forces it to stay open," said Iranus.

"Then how was it maintained when my grandfather and mother

left Safanar?" Aaron asked.

"I'm not sure, to be honest," Iranus answered. "Do you know, Colind?"

Colind pursed his lips together in thought, "His soul was able to return to Safanar when he died, so I think it's safe to say that part of him remained connected."

"How does the Drake fit into all this?" Aaron asked.

"The being you know of as the Drake is not of Safanar, but of Hytharia," Iranus said. "We believe that some of Halcylon's people made it through the portal prior to it being locked and were able to send him information."

"How?" Aaron asked.

Iranus looked up to the ceiling. "They couldn't use the portal, but there was nothing stopping them from sending a signal through space. It would take years to reach Hytharia, but it is possible. We didn't find evidence of the Drake until Shandara fell. It appears that those left on Hytharia were able to develop a new weapon to open the portal to this world."

The room was silent for a moment. "You were hoping to wait them out," Aaron said, the pieces fitting into place in his mind. "That was the plan. Block the portal and wait for them to be destroyed with the death of your sun. Except they were able to reach across the stars to get you."

Iranus nodded. "We later figured out that the Drake is a construct of Nanites with a prime directive to open the portal to Hytharia, but these Nanites were different than any we've encountered. Normally, Nanites can be turned off with a kill command, or have their programming rewritten, but not these. They are the perfect sentinels, because they contain all the benefits of normal Nanites, but are able to manipulate the brain on a molecular level, rewriting certain parts, memories for instance, turning love into hate."

Aaron felt his stomach drop out from under him. If what Iranus said was true, Sarah was in more danger than he originally thought. "How long does she have?"

"It's hard to say, but we've seen the process take as little as a few weeks, depending upon how much the subject resists," Iranus answered solemnly. "So, you see, she may already be gone."

"I don't believe that," Aaron said, standing up.

"Wait, what do you mean? How is Sarah already gone?" Verona asked.

"The Drake can rewrite your brain so that you are no longer you anymore," Roselyn answered him.

"She'll fight," Aaron said.

"I'm sorry, Aaron, but it is a fight she cannot win," Iranus answered. "Even if you go to her, which is exactly what the Drake wants, what will you do? We've tried to remove the Nanites, but it always resulted in the death of the person we were trying to save. We've tried augmenting our own to seek and remove them, but the results are the same."

"I won't abandon her," Aaron said.

"I know you won't, Aaron, but you must see reason. What if they're right? What if she's gone?" Vaughn asked gently.

"No!" Aaron slammed his fist onto the table. "I refuse to believe that. I know I can reach her. The Drake doesn't control her fully."

"She left you, Aaron," Colind chimed in. "This is what the Drake does. It turns those that you love against you. It's how it hunted down all of the Alenzar'seth. The ones it wasn't strong enough to stand against, it defeated using cunning and strife to weave a perfect web of destruction, using their greatest strength against themselves."

Aaron's body was rigid, and his muscles rippled with the clenching of his teeth. "I'm not them."

"You think to defy what has been proven over and over by sheer will alone? It's not going to be enough. The Alenzar'seth were once many, but those that survived the fall of Shandara weren't able to stand against the Drake," Iranus said. "I say this not to be cruel, but because I want you to live. Playing the Drake's game is the surest path to meeting your demise. Even for you."

Aaron regarded the Hythariam coolly. "Not playing its game will cost me more than I'm willing to pay. Haven't you been hiding long enough? Convinced it was the best course of action? Tell me, did you stand idly by while the Alenzar'seth were hunted down, slaves to a terrible fate because they refused to yield? Even in the face of death, they fought. They didn't hide in the shadows, nor abandon the ones they loved...neither will I."

Iranus's golden eyes were ablaze with anger. "Do you know how to make war, Aaron?"

"No," Aaron replied, "but I can fight, and it will have to be enough. I will fight for the parts of Sarah that will never submit to the Drake, no matter what technology your people have created.

However small, it's worth fighting for."

Colind sighed, "Will you at least consider that Sarah may be beyond your reach and that the person you love is gone?"

Aaron shook his head, feeling the stirrings of the bladesong within him. Sarah's beautiful blue eyes looked back at him when he closed his. I will always come for you. He looked up, his gaze sweeping across the men in the room. Verona stood up and came to his side. Colind returned his gaze evenly, and Iranus's golden eyes narrowed.

"Colind," Aaron said evenly, "I have considered it, and know this. I will never abandon Sarah, not for anything. Not for your war," he said dividing his gaze between Colind and Iranus, "and not for this world."

"She wouldn't want you to sacrifice the world for her," Vaughn said.

"I know, Vaughn, and I won't need to," Aaron said. "That army on the other side of the portal is coming no matter what we do. Whether I live or die, that is one thing that you can count on. The barrier between worlds will fall. If you don't believe me, return to Shandara and study it. Things are wildly out of balance. Now, instead of focusing ourselves on keeping things as they've always been, we should be focused on moving forward."

Aaron felt his energy drain and leaned on his staff, beginning to hunch over. "You can't run from the wind," Aaron muttered to himself.

"What?" Colind asked.

Aaron swallowed, and looked up. "My father used to take us

sailing when we were younger, and sometimes we'd be caught out on the water when a storm came. As a child, I was so afraid. All the big waves and wind tossing our boat mercilessly. 'You can't run from wind, son,' he would tell me. 'Trim your sails and face what's ahead.' And he was right. A storm is coming, gentleman, whether you want to believe it or not." Aaron turned and left the room with the dull thumps of the rune-carved staff trailing in his wake.

Roselyn rose and silently followed.

Colind looked at the door and sighed. "He is right. The barrier was always just a temporary measure. We need to prepare."

"He doesn't understand what will be unleashed if the barrier fails. And to abandon all to pursue the Drake..." Iranus said, biting off the last.

Verona cleared his throat. "Without Aaron, none of you would be here. He was lost when I first met him, teetering on the brink of darkness that has claimed many a man's soul. Sarah was the one thing that gave him hope. The one thing that brought the light back in his eyes and gave him some semblance of being whole. So, he cannot do as you would want him to, despite the certainty of the science that supports *your* reasons. They are not his reasons. Your war has cost him almost everything before he was dragged into it. Are you really surprised that he won't follow the path that you've laid at his feet? Should not a strong leader forge his own path, and we, as his friends and comrades, support him as he would for any of us?" Verona asked, his gaze sweeping the room. "You've had more time than he has been alive to do things your own way. Perhaps it's time for a different approach, because to go against Aaron on this would risk…much," Verona said, narrowing his gaze. "If you can't help, fine, but don't tell him that what he intends to do is impossible, because my friend has a knack for doing the impossible." Verona glanced pointedly at Colind, then rose and left the room.

***

"Aaron, wait," Roselyn called behind him.

"Is this what you warned me about?" he asked, leaning on the staff heavily.

Roselyn's eyes narrowed as she caught up to him. "You need rest. It's only been a few days."

"No, Sarah needs me now," he replied stubbornly, and specks of darkness invaded his vision. Aaron sank to the floor, the last of his strength leaving him. I won't abandon you.

"She has time," Roselyn said gently.

Verona came up silently behind them, but said nothing.

"Don't charge off like the others," Roselyn said. "I believe you are right. There is a way to stop the Drake. We just need to put our heads together, but first you need to recover your strength. You're no good to her like this… "

Aaron felt himself slipping further away, Roselyn's voice growing distant, until he couldn't hear anything at all as the last vestiges of his strength left him.

CHAPTER 2

HIGH KING'S WRATH

Mactar expected the others to underestimate the Heir of Shandara, but not himself. The broken window cast a fragmented light as his fingers drummed the now-clutter-free desk in his quarters onboard the airship. He dismissed the mess on the floor, having given his pride a small part of its due. His heart pumped with the excitement of a new challenge. A worthy adversary. Despite this setback, the growing power of the Alenzar'seth put him closer to his goal. In fact, their return drew out the true gatekeepers, the Hythariam. He had witnessed the battle with the Ryakul from afar and had little doubt that the Drake's first battle with Aaron had been enlightening. His lips lifted at the thought of Sarah's betrayal of one Aaron Jace. He was sure he could find a way to turn it to his advantage given some time, but for now he set the thought aside.

Mactar's journey back to Khamearra with Darven, the former Elitesman, and the young Prince Rordan, the High King's remaining heir, was swift and uneventful, even somber. The fact that travel crystals couldn't be used within Shandara's borders still perplexed him. It was as if Shandara was out of phase with the rest of Safanar. Once they were beyond its borders, they were able to use the crystals to shorten their trip. Rordan had been in a fragile state since the battle. Something he had seen had shaken him to his core, and Mactar was going to have to draw it out from him.

The palace of the High King loomed ever closer, and the twin tower of the Elite stood on the far side of the city. The capital city of Khamearra was truly a sight to behold. The busy traffic of airships dotted the sky, and the construction of a bustling city could be heard below. Mactar preferred to have a few moments to himself prior to facing the wrath of High King Amorak once he learned of the death of his son. Primus was such a fool. He allowed petty rivalry to poison his mind. It was never part of his plan to kill Sarah, but he supposed her betrayal by aligning with the Alenzar'seth had pushed Primus over the edge. Rordan, he noted, hadn't spoken of it.

"My lord," Darven spoke quietly. "It is time."

Mactar turned to his loyal companion. "Indeed it is."

Darven's eyes narrowed. "Is there cause for concern? Perhaps we should wait before meeting with the High King?"

Mactar smirked. Darven didn't understand his relationship with High King Amorak. For all Amorak's talk of killing him, there was no escaping the fact that Amorak needed him, which wasn't about to change anytime soon.

"No," Mactar said. "It would be unwise to keep him waiting."

Now the fun begins." For all intents and purposes, Darven was his apprentice, but he still had much to learn. The vehemence with which Reymius's heir had singled out Darven was another matter to consider. That was yet another tool at his disposal. A worthy adversary indeed, this Alenzar'seth, Aaron, turned out to be.

They were joined on deck of the High King's airship by the remaining Elitesmen and Rordan. They withdrew their travel crystals and activated them. Teleporting with crystals was much like having the ground pulled abruptly away, only to be plunged into darkness, and then emerge upon the other side.

They landed in the Great Hall of the High King's palace to the immediate hush of all those in attendance. Mactar preferred to make an entrance. The High King, perched on his throne, regarded them coolly as he narrowed his eyes. Amorak rose from his throne and was before his son in an instant, but Rordan wouldn't meet his father's gaze.

"Where is your brother?" the High King asked.

Rordan looked up at his father, his chin trembling. "He is dead," Rordan whispered.

The High King's eyes darted to Mactar.

"It is true. He was killed by the Alenzar'seth," Mactar said.

"Is that what you call it?" Rordan said shakily, his eyes growing distant. "There is no honor in doing battle with someone that can't be beaten. No one can move as fast as he. This Aaron, scion of Alenzar'seth, is a match for any Elitesmen. Primus never stood a chance. If I had faced him, Father, you would have two dead sons instead of just one," Rordan said, hanging his head low in shame.

The High King said nothing, but the air grew colder around him.

"He is Ferasdiam Marked, my lord," Mactar said. "Like you."

The High King nodded and stuck his hand out, gently raising Rordan's head. "This is not your failing, Son. I have sent you out there ill prepared. Something I can remedy."

Rordan's tear-stricken eyes burned with a cold anger. "There is something else. Sarah stands with the Alenzar'seth. She fought by his side."

The High King remained motionless for a few moments, allowing the silence to gather. Mactar felt a torrent of energy gather itself then suddenly the High King lashed out, surprising the Elitesmen. He struck down the Elite Masters who had failed him. Though the High King was unarmed, they were no match. The High King moved with the blurring speed of a shooting star, and the blood of the Elitesmen gushed forth onto the pristine floors of the Great Hall. Amid the carnage, the High King's body glowed with a luminescence of its own, and the attendees in the Great Hall fled in terror until only Rordan, Mactar, and Darven remained.

"Failure is not to be tolerated!" the High King's voice echoed, his face awash in the blood of his victims. "No heir of Khamearra need fear the Alenzar'seth. It is time for your training to begin, my Son, and together we shall rid the world of the taint of Shandara once and for all!"

Mactar waited a few moments before speaking. Now that the High King's rage had found its victims, he thought it was safe. "There is more, my lord. The Hythariam have come out of hiding.

They were at Shandara, while the Drake fought the Alenzar'seth."

High King Amorak smiled wolfishly. "To be expected. I think you'll find we're better prepared for the likes of the Hythariam than we were when Shandara burned. But come, I want you to tell me everything," he growled.

They followed the High King as they stepped over the bodies of the fallen Elitesmen. Amorak, as a council member, could dispense judgment upon the Elitesmen as he pleased without any repercussions. Mactar followed, preparing for what was to come, but as he stepped from the room, something caught his eye. A shadowy reflection of pale skin and black eyes regarding him with pure hatred.

Tarimus?

CHAPTER 3
SECLUSION

The rocky ground bit into Sarah's side as the Drake deflected her attack. The days blurred together, split apart by bouts of consciousness. The Drake was always there when she woke, hovering over her like a storm cloud. The cycle was always the same. Upon regaining consciousness, she would attack. The Drake never took any of her weapons and easily thwarted her attacks. It loomed over her, peering at her with yellow eyes filled with a deadly promise. She had felt Aaron reach out to her and wanted to go to him, yet at the same time the very thought of him repulsed her. Her thoughts twisted into a hatred so intense that it yearned for his death. She pictured stabbing him through the heart. The thought filled part of her with a heated joy, while another part of her cried out in denial of such dark thoughts. She would never hurt Aaron.

What was happening to her? Every thought of her love for Aaron became warped into something maddening and sinister, but she still felt him along the fringes of her thoughts. The warmth of his love surrounded her, which part of her embraced while another part pushed away as one would recoil from a poisonous viper.

KILL HIM! a sinister voice bellowed in her mind, followed by images of Aaron suffering by her hand. He would look at her in betrayal with helpless regret, and the euphoria that followed sent her mind spiraling. She denied the images from the confines of her mind. *I would never hurt you, my love.*

The images only intensified with her resistance, and the pain unfurled, spreading from her head to deep inside her muscles. Where warm memories of their time together should have shielded the walls of her heart, instead it only fueled the fires that commanded his death. She cried out at her shattering heart, every waking moment plunging her deeper into a cycle of madness until only bitterness remained. A hate spurned within her from the betrayal that her love for Aaron had caused her. How could he leave her like this?

She heard the cries of a little girl whimpering, and she opened her eyes, frantically searching for the girl. Surrounded by mountain peaks, the frosty air stung her throat, causing her eyes to tear. She was alone except for the Drake, who sat across the way, its yellow eyes watched her mercilessly. Waiting... Expecting …

Sarah drew her sword and charged. She attacked with the ferocity of a cornered animal, abandoning years of training. The Drake wielded about, bringing up its armored forearm to block her attack. She pulled from the energy buried deep in the mountain and hammered at the Drake. The Drake blocked her attack, and as she glimpsed the stump of its arm, Aaron's face flashed in her mind. Her body crumpled to the ground in agonizing pain. The Drake did not attack; instead, it rose steadily to its feet, watching her. She lay helplessly before it, struggling just to breathe. She shook her head to clear it and concentrated on keeping her mind blank. Behind her, she heard the deep rumbling growl of a Ryakul. She sprang to her feet. The beast sat back on its haunches, with its long neck swinging slowly from side to side, licking its chops. The Ryakul blew a tuft of air from its nostrils as Sarah inched closer.

The Drake screeched a warning, snapping Sarah's attention. The Ryakul unfurled its large bat-like wings and in a colossal whoosh, launched itself into the air. The Drake leaped upon its back and took off into the air, leaving her stranded at the top of the mountainside.

Sarah's elation lasted only seconds as the Drake landed farther down the mountain, blocking her only path. If only she had kept a travel crystal. She looked back down at the Drake as it watched her from below. The Drake was toying with her. She could wait up here and die of exposure or head down in the direction of the Drake. Her thoughts drifted to Aaron, wanting to reach out for the ever-present connection she felt. The bout of pain and nausea followed by images of his demise became the only things she saw. There was a part of her that knew the images were a lie, but they felt so real. She began to yearn for the sickening pleasure that followed the images of Aaron dying. The sick pleasure spread through her like a plague, as all the conflicting feelings fractured her mind. She felt the person she was being systematically stripped away. She turned from the Drake's expectant eyes and stepped toward the edge, seeing the dizzying heights below. The barest hints of a promised release urged her forward. She drew in the energy from the depths of the mountain and launched herself away from the edge, hoping the rising peaks below would claim her so the madness would stop. The wind roared past her face and she closed her eyes, welcoming the end of her suicidal leap. Her body jerked to the side as a Ryakul's claws snatched her from the air and away from the death for which she yearned. She pushed against the beast's claws that held her, and when that failed, tried to reach for her knife, but she couldn't grasp it.

The echoes of her screams bounced off the mountains as the Ryakul deposited her in a heap at the Drake's feet. She knelt there powerless and alone, with her shoulders slumped in defeat. Nothing in her life had prepared her for this. She couldn't trust her own thoughts, lest they dwell upon the one thing the Drake was taking away from her. She looked up with bitter defiance as the yellow hue that circled her vision became more prominent.

Her face was wet with tears as she squeezed her eyes shut.

No! she screamed in her mind, momentarily throwing off the shackles she could neither see nor touch but were firmly in place. A shaft of sunlight peeked through the clouds, and its warmth caressed her face for the span of a single breath. Her connection to Aaron pushed to the furthest reaches of her mind, shimmering, calling to her. She drew strength from it. Without hesitation, she reached out to hold onto it with all her might, despite the cost.

Aaron! she called out from within and without, her voice going from a scream of defiance to a cry of pain across the rooftops of the world. For a moment, she heard his gasp of breath across the expanse between them. The plunge into pleasure and pain was swift, and as her mind split apart, she held grudgingly to the thought that she had reached out to him, and that he had heard her.

***

Aaron awoke crying out Sarah's name. His body was drenched in sweat. He opened his eyes to a room where the walls were blackened as if they'd been burnt except for a solitary spot where Colind and Verona huddled behind a barrier of light.

"Sarah," Aaron gasped doubling over. "I could feel...her pain. So much pain," he said, wincing as he wrapped his arms around himself.

The barrier disappeared, and Colind and Verona rushed to his side. Colind ordered Verona to bring some water.

"Easy now," Colind said.

Verona quickly returned and offered Aaron a cup. He took a sip and looked around the room. "Did I do this?" Aaron asked.

"I'm afraid so, my friend," Verona said. "You were thrashing about, and I was trying to restrain you when Colind barged in and hauled me out of the way. Just in time, I might add."

Colind nodded back to Verona and turned toward Aaron. "What did you see?"

"The last thing I remember was collapsing in the hallway. Then I woke up and heard Sarah calling out to me, and for a second I felt the pain she was in. It was unlike anything I've ever felt. It was her, but at the same time it wasn't."

"It's the work of the Nanites. She is fighting their assimilation," Colind said.

"She's fading. I have to find her. There must be a way to fight them," Aaron said, rising to his feet.

Colind sighed. "Iranus doesn't believe so, and he's not the only one. He wasn't exaggerating when he said they tried everything after the fall of Shandara."

"The Hythariam would have me abandon her, which is something I won't do," Aaron said.

"Everyone will pay the price if you fall now. You're all that stands between the horde and this world," Colind said.

"So Iranus says, but I get the feeling they aren't telling us everything. The only thing I do know is that the Drake has Sarah, and I won't abandon her to that fate."

The door to the room opened, and Roselyn stood in the doorway, looking at the ruined room. "What happened?" she asked.

Aaron was about to answer when he realized that he didn't know what had really happened, and looked at Colind questioningly.

"What I think happened," Colind began, "is you experienced a backlash of energy from your connection to Sarah."

"But how is this possible?" Aaron asked.

"You brought Sarah back from the brink, and used your own lifebeat to feed into her, keeping her alive while her body repaired itself," Colind said. "Extremely risky, as you both could have died or worse—such as being trapped in a world of shadow."

"Some risks are worth taking," Aaron replied.

"Indeed they are," Colind agreed.

"A backlash of energy emanating from a person caused all this?" Roselyn asked, her voice trailing off as she tentatively reached out to the blackened wall. "These walls are resistant to your average fire and heat. Nothing short of a plasma bolt could scorch these walls in such a way, and even then a bolt would only affect a concentrated area. The fact that all of these walls are burnt to such a degree is a testament to the amount of power this 'backlash' unleashed." Roselyn looked at Colind. "Do we need to move him away to a more secure location, away from others?"

Colind shook his head. "No, I don't think so. I'll stay close for the time being and will be able to protect this place and him, should the need arise."

Roselyn nodded. "Very well. I would like to speak with Aaron alone."

"We'll be right outside," Colind said as he and Verona left the room.

Roselyn waited until they left before speaking. "Is your friend always so quiet?"

The question caught Aaron off guard, and it took a few moments to realize she was referring to Verona. *Quiet? Verona?* "Sometimes," he answered.

Roselyn shook her head, dismissing the subject. "I've been speaking with Garret, and he's been telling me about the travel crystals that the Elitesmen use."

Aaron's eyes lit up. "They use them to teleport from one location to another. Do you think they could help with the Nanites?"

"Possibly," she said. "I am thinking that they could cause the Nanites to reset."

Aaron frowned. "What good will that do?"

"It will give us time," Roselyn answered patiently. "Remember, the Nanites are machines. They are doing what they were programmed to do. I'm not familiar with these travel crystals, but I am familiar with the concept of teleportation, and in order for it to work, they must break down our living tissues and reassemble them somewhere else. I believe that this process could reset the Nanites to the state they were in when Sarah first became infected by the Drake."

Aaron perked up at the thought. "Can we get them out?"

"No," she said, "there are too many, but I'm hopeful that we can make them dormant, and then the body will absorb them as it would any foreign agent."

"So we turn them off," Aaron said thoughtfully. "But what about the damage they are doing, can it be reversed?"

Roselyn looked at him with sympathy. "I don't know, to be honest. The measures that we tried in the past were from a distance and had almost no response. This was before we realized that these Nanites were different from what most Hythariam have in their systems. They were designed to be self-sustaining and to help people stay healthy. Not...this."

Aaron swallowed his disappointment. "It's okay. This is a start and is more than what we had before." His back still ached, and he still felt weak. He needed to be outside and breathe in fresh air.

"We have a device that may help with the Nanites," Roselyn said. "It's meant for taking readings from them, but it can also give instructions."

Aaron rose to his feet. "Why are you helping me?" he asked.

Roselyn's golden eyes searched his for a moment. "I've seen enough suffering and heartache at the hands of the Drake. My people have lived in fear of the barrier since it was first sealed. It has taken a toll on us. The decision to withdraw from the kingdoms of this world was not an easy one, nor agreed by all. We came here seeking refuge, and we brought death and destruction in our wake. Some would say we're responsible for all that you've suffered and for the fall of Shandara."

"I don't think that at all," Aaron said.

Roselyn's lips curved into a slight smile. "That is very kind of you to say, but if helping you in some small way atones for some of the wrongs my people have brought here, then it is a worthy cause."

"I appreciate your help," Aaron said. "But the barrier is not going to last. Your people should be helping this world prepare for the horde and General Halcylon."

"We have been, but through subterfuge as opposed to outright alliances. My father was devastated when Shandara fell. He and Reymius were quite close."

"Subterfuge? I hope it's enough. Your father would have me abandon Sarah," Aaron said, unable to keep the bitterness from his voice.

"He is doing what he believes is right. Would you do any less?" Roselyn asked.

"No," Aaron said, "I wouldn't."

He began dressing himself.

"What do you intend to do?" Roselyn asked.

"I'm going after Sarah. There is something I want to try before going after the travel crystals, and I need to be outside to do it."

Roselyn couldn't keep the shock from her voice. "You're leaving? Now? But you're still recovering from the effects of the Ryakul poison."

"Soon, yes. The longer I wait, the less of a chance there is to save Sarah," Aaron replied. "I need to talk to the others. Do you think they will try to stop me?" Aaron asked, thinking of Iranus, who had let fear guide him for too long. *Is brash bullheadedness any less of a folly?*

Roselyn's golden eyes narrowed. "Possibly," she said quietly.

Aaron nodded. "I appreciate your honesty."

He finished dressing in the clothes provided by the Hythariam and strapped on his swords. He still felt a weariness within the depths of his bones, but he didn't have time to wait for a full recovery. Time waited for no one, least of all him, and he wouldn't sit idly by while the woman he loved suffered at the hands of the Drake.

CHAPTER 4
INTENTIONS

Aaron left the blackened room to find Verona and Colind waiting outside for him. Verona looked as if he were about to say something when Roselyn came through the doorway. He watched as his friend stared helplessly at the beautiful raven-haired Hythariam. Colind suppressed a slight chuckle and bowed in greeting. Roselyn nodded to each in turn and hurried down the hallway while Verona all but sighed as she left.

"Enjoying the view?" Aaron asked, reducing his normally eloquent friend into a sputter of sounds that could scarcely be called words.

Verona nodded, but said nothing.

"I need to get outside. Someplace discreet would be preferable," Aaron said.

Colind nodded. "I know of a place."

"Verona, would you mind gathering the others, including Captain Morgan?" Aaron asked. For some reason, he couldn't bring himself to address the Captain by his first name, Nathaniel.

Verona nodded and set off at a trot down the hallway.

Colind and Aaron continued down the hallway, letting the silence build until Aaron couldn't take it anymore.

"Don't try to talk me out of it. I'm going after Sarah."

"Why would you think that I would try to talk you out of it?" Colind asked.

"I don't know. I just figured you would."

"Aaron, you've brought me back from the world of shadow. I'm not about to stand in your way," Colind said. "I will help you in any way that I can."

Aaron gathered his thoughts for a moment. "But surely, you have an opinion."

"I do indeed have an opinion, and I would surely share it with you if you ask it of me," Colind replied.

"Will I always need to ask?"

"No." Colind chuckled and then grew serious. "Everyone will pay the price if you fall now. You're all that stands between the remnants of the Hytharia military, the horde if you will, and this world."

"So Iranus says, but I get the feeling they aren't telling us everything. The only thing I do know is that the Drake has Sarah, and I won't abandon her. Doesn't it matter that the barrier is already failing?" Aaron asked.

"It matters, but we will need the Hythariam before this is over," Colind answered.

Aaron frowned. "Of all the things Iranus said, he glossed over some important details regarding the Drake. Like how it got here in the first place. It couldn't have broken through the barrier. They couldn't have opened another portal to this world. So that leaves one other possibility," Aaron said as they stepped outside into a small valley. Colind merely looked back, waiting for him to finish. Aaron pointed to the sky, drawing Colind's gaze toward the heavens. "Now do you understand?"

Colind pursed his lips, considering. "You've given this a fair amount of thought, I see, and I agree with you. They must have sent a machine to Safanar across the great expanse of the heavens."

"Which also means that there could be something much worse on the way right now. Waiting is not an option. These people need to prepare themselves," Aaron said.

Colind nodded.

"It's not just us, but the people of this whole world need to be united to face this threat," Aaron said.

Colind took a long look at him. "Vaughn was right about you. For one so young, you have an uncanny ability to see right to the heart of matters."

"There is something else I need to tell you," Aaron said. "Tarimus is alive."

Colind's eyes hardened for a moment. "What do you mean?"

"I mean he is back in Safanar," Aaron said, and he told Colind what had transpired prior to his rescue—about how he had to free Tarimus in order to bring Sarah's soul back to her body.

Colind shook his head. "Well, it appears that all the pieces are on the board. If I know Tarimus, he will go after Mactar. My advice to you would be not to trust him."

Aaron nodded, laying his pack and staff on the ground, then drew his swords.

"What are you going to do?" Colind asked.

"I'm going to reach out to Sarah through the bladesong," Aaron said. "We're connected somehow. I can feel her connection to me, but it's almost like being connected to two different people."

Colind thought about it for a moment then nodded.

Aaron removed his shoes and knelt upon the ground, opening himself up to the energy that surrounded him. He drew it in as easily as one draws a breath. He came to his feet and began to wield the Falcons, releasing the harmony of the bladesong. The melodious tune that was his own rode along the air. The connection to Sarah lay among the furthest recesses of his mind, and Aaron focused his attention there.

He rode along the currents of energy, following the connection to its source. He couldn't tell where she was, but he knew she was there. She was diminished somehow, and it occurred to him that she might be sleeping. But the energy appeared erratic as though two opposing patterns sought to cancel each other out. She had been able to reach out to him before, and he was hoping to do the same. He watched unobtrusively for signs of the Nanites that he knew were in her system, focusing on the patterns of energy and looking for some telltale sign of something artificial. Then he saw it. A pattern that seemed to only react to other patterns of the whole. It took no other actions otherwise. These had to be the Nanites affecting Sarah.

Aaron reached out to block the connection from the Nanites in an attempt to shield Sarah. A spike of energy flashed before him and sent his mind reeling with pain. At that same moment, he heard Sarah's voice cry out in his mind. As if suddenly aware of his presence, she withdrew from him like a scurrying animal avoided a predator. Aaron tried again, only this time both the Nanites and Sarah reacted with vicious certainty, sending shocking pain that jarred his concentration. Aaron tumbled to the ground, and the bladesong left him. He gasped for air. *I can't even reach out to her.*

Colind came to his side. "Can you hear me?"

Aaron nodded as he slowly came back to his senses. "It's like she is there but not completely. I think I made it worse by trying to reach out to her."

"Her time is short, but by all accounts she is very strong. There is still time," Colind said.

Aaron came to his feet as they were joined by the others. Vaughn and Garret, followed by Sarik, Eric, Braden, and Verona. Even Jopher came and nodded shyly to Aaron. It was good to see them all, and after their greetings, Aaron told them about his discussion with Roselyn.

They were joined by Captain Morgan and Roselyn, along with several other Hythariam he didn't know. Then Iranus walked out.

"Are you proposing to journey to the heart of the Elitesmen Order in Khamearra and steal a cache of travel crystals?" Vaughn asked, unable to keep the shock from his tone.

"Not all of us. I think we need to divide our efforts," Aaron said.

"This ought to be good," Garret said. "Never a dull moment, is there?"

Aaron smiled a bit at the comment. The bladesong had invigorated him. "This threat that we're facing affects everyone on this world. This is not my fight or even the Hythariam's fight. This is our fight. We must unite whomever we can. At some point, the barrier is going to fall. It is already weakening." Aaron explained his theory that the military from Hytharia were able reach Safanar through means other than the portal. Considering that the natives of Safanar had no previous concept of space travel, they were very accepting of the idea.

"The Drake first appeared about twenty-five years ago?" Aaron asked.

"That is our best guess," Iranus said.

"At some point, the faction on Hytharia must have realized that the Nanites didn't work, or at least developed an alternative plan. How long before they could send something else?" Aaron asked.

Iranus exchanged glances with the other Hythariam, all of whom looked shaken by Aaron's question. They spoke quickly in a language that Aaron couldn't understand until Roselyn hissed at them.

"I would say a year at the most," Iranus answered.

"Depending upon when that was, and if they had waited an entire year to prepare something else to reach Safanar to open the portal, when would it arrive? Your best guess," Aaron said. He had them now. Iranus now realized that his tactic was flawed and that all of them were in real danger.

Iranus's eyes grew wide. "About three months from now."

The other Hythariam gasped.

Aaron looked at Colind and the others before addressing Iranus. "Are you able to confirm that? Do you have a telescope or something that can see if there is, in fact, something heading for us right now?"

Now you see, Aaron thought to himself.

The Hythariam conferred among themselves, and one tapped a device above his ear and spoke.

Iranus seemed to nod to himself. "I didn't see it. I didn't see this coming, but hearing it from you, even without the confirmation, I know the truth before my eyes."

"Will you help the people of this world?" Colind asked. "Will you help them stand against the horde that would take their homes from them?"

Iranus glanced at the others, who slowly nodded their approval. "We will stand with you."

"We need to start coordinating with the other nations—" Aaron stopped with a slightly amused expression. "I just realized that I don't know about all the nations of this world, but I think starting with Rexel and— " Aaron motioned to Jopher to step forward, "—will you return to Zsensibar and inform them of the threat to this world?"

Jopher brought his fist over his heart. "It would be my honor." He looked like he was about to say more but remained silent.

"What is it?" Aaron asked.

"It's just that I will need help convincing people of the threat,"

Jopher said.

Aaron chewed on his lower lip in thought. "He's right. Iranus, it's time for the Hythariam to step back into the spotlight."

"What do you suggest we tell them?" spoke a Hythariam man whom he didn't know.

"I would suggest telling them the truth," said Aaron. "They will find out soon enough if they don't heed the warning."

Colind raised an eyebrow. "Who did you have in mind to travel to Rexel?"

Aaron smiled. "You and Vaughn. Probably Garret," Aaron paused. "And Jopher. Colind, yours will be the voice the Hythariam need to validate their story."

The others protested, but Colind's gaze remained fixed upon Aaron. "I can help with the other 'nations' as you put it, but what will you be doing while we travel?"

An immediate hush swept over the crowd as they waited for his answer.

Aaron glanced at Verona, who nodded back to him. "I'm going to Khamearra to infiltrate the Elitesmen Order."

Verona actually laughed and looked excited. Eric and Braden gave him challenging looks, daring him to leave them behind. Sarik looked concerned for a moment before Verona clamped his hand on his shoulder and whispered something in his ear. Sarik looked back at him and nodded. The others all shouted their protest, save Colind, who called for silence.

"Please explain to the others the rest of your plan," Colind said calmly.

"I'm going to steal a cache of travel crystals," Aaron began. "Then track down the Drake and escape with Sarah, using the crystals. Roselyn has a theory that using the travel crystals will confuse the Nanites in her system, allowing us to make them dormant."

Iranus snapped his golden-eyed gaze toward his daughter. "Theories," he spat.

"Yes, Father, worth a try I think," she replied.

"One doesn't simply trek into the capital city of Khamearra and knock on the doors of the Elitesmen Order," Vaughn said.

"One doesn't walk into Shandara, but we did," Aaron replied.

Vaughn took a deep breath, gathering his patience. "I'm on your side, Aaron. I want you to succeed. I want to help Sarah, but what you propose is…suicide."

"Suicide missions are our specialty," Verona answered. "Hit the enemy where he thinks he is safe. I believe you taught me that, old friend."

Vaughn shook his head. "I don't believe this," he said to Colind and then looked at Aaron. "As powerful as you've become, you are not unstoppable. Everyone has their limits."

"I know I'm not unstoppable," Aaron said softly. "What wouldn't you do to protect the people you love?"

"It's not as simple as that," Vaughn replied.

Of course, not everyone has the strings attached that I do, Aaron thought bitterly. People were looking for him to lead this fight and raise Shandara from the ashes. "I know what's at stake, and I won't debate my leaving with anyone else," Aaron said, sweeping them all with his gaze, thinking of the family he lost to this damned war. *I won't lose Sarah, too.*

Vaughn nodded. "Okay," he conceded. "How long do you think she has before whatever these Nanites are doing to her have finished?"

Aaron glanced at Roselyn, who shared a brief look with Iranus when another Hythariam dressed in a strange metallic armor whispered something.

"A week," Roselyn said. "Two, at the most."

A week?

He recalled the map of Safanar he had seen in the map room on the Raven. Khamearra was almost across the continent. It had taken them about a month by airship to journey to Shandara. Aaron looked around at his friends and saw the same conclusion reflected in all their eyes. His plan was hopeless. There was no way he could make the journey in time, but it was even worse than that. He intended to return to Shandara with Sarah, this part of the plan he kept to himself. Aaron brought his gaze to Iranus, who immediately knew what he was going to ask.

"I need your help," Aaron began. "You have the means at your disposal to travel faster than what is considered normal here. Khamearra is almost on the other side of the continent."

Iranus appeared thoughtful for a moment. "I know there will be no dissuading you from this."

"I'm going with him," Roselyn interrupted.

Iranus's golden eyes flashed angrily. "No."

"Don't try to stop me, Father," Roselyn replied, and then she softened her gaze. "We owe our aid to the Alenzar'seth, whose shelter of protection we've lived under for these many years."

Aaron watched as Iranus weighed his options, and he could tell that there were none that he liked. Iranus glanced at Colind, who cleared his throat.

"This is what I intend," Aaron began. "For you to provide a way for a small party to accompany me to Khamearra. We will infiltrate the Elitesmen stronghold and use the travel crystals to return here quickly. We will also attempt to make contact with the Resistance in Khamearra."

Colind narrowed his gaze thoughtfully. "What Resistance?"

"Sarah was working with a faction that is looking to overthrow the tyranny of the High King," Aaron said. "A faction loyal to her mother. This faction sent a lone protector, who was loyal to the old order to the Elite. This man trained Sarah. After he died, she returned to her father's court and saw it ruined by the corruption. We may be able to find help there along with the most abundant source of crystals. It makes it a worthy target."

"What if you can't get into the Elitesmen stronghold?" Colind asked.

"Then I will take out as many Elitesmen as I can and take their crystals," Aaron said.

Colind shrugged and glanced at Iranus. "It's not a bad plan."

"Who will be in this 'small' party?" Iranus asked.

Aaron had anticipated the question and shared a brief look at his friends before answering. The fact that he didn't even need to ask touched him. They would follow him anywhere, because they believed he would get them out of any hell that his path took them through.

"Verona, Sarik, Eric, Braden, and Roselyn," Aaron said. He wasn't sure about Roselyn, but he knew the others could hold their own against the Elitesmen. He hadn't been able to reach Eric and Braden with the bladesong as he had been able to with Verona and Sarik, but hopefully there would be time enough.

"I will go as well," spoke a Hythariam in metallic armor that Aaron recognized from the day before. "I am called Gavril Sorindal," he said, bowing his head slightly. "I assure you that I will be an asset. I am formerly of the Hytharia military. My rank would translate to colonel."

Aaron took a long look at Gavril, who had the confident stance of an experienced leader, but he wondered if Gavril would be more of a hindrance than an asset.

Gavril stepped before Aaron and extended his hand. "I was a friend to Reymius and fought by his side at the fall of Shandara." Aaron nodded and shook his hand firmly as Gavril continued. "I would like to bring one other of my crew. A specialist. He's got experience sneaking into impossible places," Gavril said, sparing a glance at the others.

"Just seven of you?" Iranus asked, barely keeping the shock from his voice.

Aaron grinned. "Seven is considered a lucky number where I come from."

"Well, you are certainly going to need a lot of it," Colind said dryly.

"You as well," Aaron replied. "Any thoughts on how you will convince people of the danger they are in?

"I've had a few thoughts, and Iranus will help with the rest," replied Colind.

Aaron turned to Iranus. "I'd like to leave as soon as possible."

"Indeed," Iranus said. "It would be better to wait until nightfall. We should be able to get you near Khamearra by morning. Could I have a private word with you?"

"Of course," Aaron said, and the others left with the exception of Verona and Colind.

Iranus walked farther into the meadow. "Safanar is a beautiful world, don't you think?"

"I do," Aaron said, and his thoughts returned to Sarah dancing with the other women around the bonfires on the night of the choosing. He had lost the laurel crown she had placed on his head. It was on board the Raven... "Did Tolvar contact you?" he asked, remembering his encounter with the old man before they had reached Shandara. Tolvar had been able to shield them from the Ryakul until the Raven had caught up to them.

Iranus nodded and smiled. "Yes, that is how we knew you were in Shandara."

"I know you don't think much of my chances for saving Sarah," Aaron began, but Iranus held up his hand.

"No, we've both made our points, and you're right. It's time to move on. I wanted to talk to you about my daughter," Iranus said.

"She appears to be able to take care of herself."

"Yes, she can, but it doesn't mean I'm not worried about sending her off," said Iranus. "It is the burden of fathers, I'm afraid."

"I will look after her as best I can," Aaron promised. "I've faced impossible odds at Shandara with Verona, Eric, and Braden, and we would not have survived if we hadn't watched out for one another. In fact, the others will attest that I try too hard to bear the burden myself."

Iranus looked at Aaron evenly. "Desperation has a way of grinding the honor out of most. I don't know you well enough to be a fair judge of your character in that respect, but it is a lesson we learned from our dying world. Desperate people take desperate measures. I just want you to try to be clear-headed about this. None of this is fair, especially for you, but like it or not there is great importance attached to your survival. The people of this world need you."

"Sometimes one can only do the best with the time that one has," Aaron said. "And decide when or where to make a stand."

Iranus's face broke into a smile. "You sound very much like Reymius," he said and then his face turned solemn. "I know what he sacrificed to save your mother and therefore you."

"I didn't know it at the time," Aaron began, "but I saw the emptiness he felt and the scars he had. I don't think he was equipped to deal with the Drake."

"It's worse than that," Iranus said softly. "The form of the Drake you faced was once your grandmother, the Lady Cassandra, Princess of Shandara. It's an unfortunate part of what the Nanites do. Not part of their original programming, I can assure you, but around the fall we came close to creating a true artificial intelligence. That is what I suspect the Drake is, in part. It was sent here to ascertain the barrier and remove it. When it figured out that the barrier was linked to the Alenzar'seth, it conceived this twisted cycle that you are part of now. You have no idea how much it saddens me that one of our most remarkable achievements could be perverted into something so vile and repulsive."

My grandmother? Aaron's mind reeled at the thought. "My grandfather couldn't have known. He wouldn't have left otherwise."

Iranus gripped Aaron's shoulder. "He did," Iranus said gently. "I know because I was there. I helped him escape to the planet you call Earth, but you will never see it in our night sky."

"Why not?" Aaron asked.

"Because Earth is on another dimensional plane than Safanar," Iranus answered. "While we were looking for a way to escape the destruction of Hytharia we figured out a way to open a doorway to another dimension. Same place just in a different universe. In each dimension we were able to open, Hytharia was already destroyed. There was nothing there. When it became apparent that the Drake could not be stopped here on Safanar, I built a new device. A cylinder that over time would charge enough to open the dimensional doorway, and that is how we found Earth."

"Wait a second," Aaron interrupted. "Are you saying that Safanar and Earth are the same planet but in different universes?"

"That is precisely what I'm saying," Iranus answered.

"But nothing looks the same. The geography is all different. The continents are not in the same place. We have only one moon, and the stars don't even match up," Aaron said.

"Different universes. Different rules. Different everything," Iranus said.

"And the Drake is my grandmother?" Aaron asked, still struggling to wrap his head around this.

"It's better to think of it this way," Iranus began. "The Drake's previous form was your grandmother, but your grandmother is dead. She has been completely assimilated by the Nanites. Sarah still has a sliver of hope to avoid the same fate. There were no travel crystals here at the time that Shandara fell. They came from parts of a comet that grazed the atmosphere primarily over Khamearra."

Aaron didn't know what to think and shook his head.

"I thought you should know and have a better understanding what Reymius sacrificed so that your mother could be saved and you could grow up on a world safe from the Drake. It's the only reason I could think of why he never came back."

Me. My mother. Aaron sighed as he saw his grandfather, Reymius, in a new light. "Thank you for telling me. I just don't know what to say."

Iranus nodded. "I know you have the cylinder in your possession. I would suggest showing it to my daughter and telling her its purpose. Perhaps she can figure out a way for it to help in your journey."

Iranus left him to his thoughts, and Colind and Verona quietly approached.

"Did you know about this?" Aaron asked Colind. "About Cassandra, my grandmother?"

Colind looked at the ground with a pained expression. "I knew the Drake had taken her. At the time, we weren't sure how it worked. We thought of the Drake as a separate entity. Reymius suspected it near the end, but at the fall it wasn't just one thing that caused the destruction of Shandara; it was a maelstrom of events happening all at once. Mactar, along with the High King and the Elitesmen, were able to get inside Shandara with Tarimus's help and bring down the walls from within. Mactar trapped me and … well, you saw the destruction."

After a few moments of silence, Aaron spoke. "Is there anything you can tell me that will help us find what we need in Khamearra?" he couldn't bring himself to think of the Drake as his grandmother. Iranus was right that his grandmother was dead, but part of him wondered if some small part of her was there still. He thought he understood what was at stake for Sarah before, and now...he only had two weeks. Roselyn had implied the longer timeframe was due to her training, which made sense. But he wondered if it was also due in part to the ever-present connection he felt with her. He hadn't sensed it until after he used the bladesong to heal Sarah from her mortal wounds.

Desperate measures. Iranus's warning echoed in his mind.

He had no such ties or responsibilities as his grandfather did. No child of his own to protect. He wouldn't have to make the same sacrifice that Reymius had, but he understood Iranus's fear of events spiraling out of control. Aaron met Colind's concerned gaze and saw understanding mixed with a twinge of fear.

"They need to prepare themselves for war, Colind," Aaron said. "There is no way around this. You must make the leaders of these nations understand this, or they will all suffer the same fate as Shandara."

"I will, Aaron," Colind answered quietly. "Curious word, 'nations.'"

"It is how we refer to other countries or kingdoms," Aaron said, his thoughts drifting back to his life on Earth. He had come to Safanar seeking revenge and to protect his sister, but it had become so much more.

"Verona," Colind said, "listen up. I assume that you will not be leaving Aaron's side for the foreseeable future."

"Your assumption is correct, my lord," Verona answered, joining them.

"Excellent. I will tell you what I know about Khamearra," Colind began.

Across the grand expanse beneath his thoughts, Aaron felt his connection to Sarah splinter. They had precious little time, so he focused on which insights he could glean about Khamearra from Colind.

CHAPTER 5
PARTING WAYS

It was late afternoon when the two groups were making ready to depart. Aaron was grateful for everything the Hythariam had done, but was anxious to leave. Colind had shared a great deal about Khamearra with him that should prove useful. They gathered in a field near one of the complexes of dome-shaped buildings.

The Raven loomed overhead, dark and majestic. The crew scurried about their tasks, getting ready to leave as Captain Nathaniel Morgan spoke with a group of Hythariam. Aaron saw where some additional equipment had been installed, which he was told would augment the crystal-powered engines already on the wings. Sarik assured him the new equipment would make the engines safer as well as continuously propel the ship, which gave it a decisive advantage over any other airship native to Safanar.

Captain Morgan possessed the schematics to build and upgrade the remaining ships in the Rexellian Navy. The advantage wouldn't be long lived, as the Hythariam would share the advances with any other kingdom that would ally with them for the coming war. Aaron was appreciative of the fact that the Hythariam not only provided the proverbial fish, but were now willing to teach the people of Safanar how to fish as well. Colind and Garret assured him that the sharing of knowledge would be reciprocated back to the Hythariam, because as the Hythariam were gifted in science, the native people of Safanar were gifted in tapping directly into energy around them. In Aaron's opinion, it would one day equal the advantage of the Nanites and perhaps surpass them, as he could. Aaron had used the power of the bladesong to finish repairing his body and drive the remaining Ryakul poison from his system.

Captain Morgan descended down the gangplank and strode over. "Aaron, glad to see you looking better. No worse for wear, I take it?" When Aaron nodded and shook his hand, he continued. "I wish you were coming with us, but I understand why you can't."

"I'll miss the Raven. She's a great ship, but not as great as her captain," Aaron said.

"That she is," the captain answered, "and that I am," he said, grinning. "Your Grace," he continued, formally addressing Aaron as he would a royal prince or king. "Despite what you say," he said, holding up his hands, halting Aaron's protest, "you are the Heir of Shandara. A king in your own right. There are many who would flock to the banner of the Alenzar'seth should you wish to raise it, and I would count myself fortunate to be among the flock." The crew around them stopped their activities and turned toward them.

Aaron was stuck in mid protest by gratitude. "Thank you," he said finally.

"This world needs the Alenzar'seth! We need Shandara to rise from the ashes!" Captain Morgan's voice barked, snapping the attention of all those gathered. "We need you, Your Grace," he finished, and sank down to one knee, holding his fist over his heart. The crew around them followed their captain, even those upon the ship. Then his friends followed suit. Even Colind and Vaughn went to their knees.

Aaron's heart thundered in his chest as he stood alone among a sea of kneeling men and women. A lone chant carried throughout the field.

Shandara!

The echoes of each syllable permeated through Hathenwood to the rooftops of the world. The Hythariam looked on silently and bowed their heads respectfully toward him. Aaron was overwhelmed by the outpouring of support and committed to himself (and silently to all the people gathered) that he would honor their faith in him. The crew of the Raven had traveled with him, had bled at his side to get him to Shandara. They witnessed the daughter of the High King fall in love with this lost son of the Alenzar'seth. They had grown to love them both as comrades in arms, and until this moment he didn't fully realize that he wasn't alone beyond his closest friends in this quest to save the woman he loved.

Aaron raised his hands, and the men stood up once more and

waited expectantly for him to say something. How could he not?

"Thank you. Your support means everything to me. Though our paths take us to different places, we are all joined by this moment in time. Hold onto it, cherish each other, and remember that the crew of the Raven stood with the Alenzar'seth and delivered him safely to Shandara.

"Go forth and spread the word. Tell them of the dangers we face. Call upon their honor to defend their homes, to welcome the Hythariam with open arms, and to harbor no ill will toward them. They have sacrificed as much as the people of Shandara and are worthy of our protection. Tell them we are here, and we will fight this enemy with the strength of this world, for we are mighty! We are Safanarions!" Aaron cried out and he was joined by everyone in the field, including the Hythariam, who perhaps for the first time, to Aaron at least, looked upon Safanar as their home. A home worth defending.

The crowd dispersed. Captain Morgan took his leave, and Aaron noticed that all of them stood a little bit taller, walked with a purpose. He didn't know where the words came from and noted he now considered Safanar almost as much of a home as Earth had been. The idea of a king still sickened him, however. It was too much power for one man, even himself, and would be something he would rectify going forward. But if having a king gave these men the courage they needed to walk the path laid before them, then so be it. To himself, he was a man and not a king. A leader perhaps, but no king.

"You certainly have a way with words, my friend," Verona said, coming toward him.

"Funny," Aaron said, "I always thought of you as having the way with words. Perhaps you're rubbing off on me."

A small golden craft flew silently into view and landed a short distance from them. The wings, if they could be called such, were small and barely extended beyond a few feet in length. From its smooth side, a Hythariam emerged from a door that appeared as if by magic. The Hythariam was followed by Gavril, who waved in greeting and motioned them over.

"Do they have machines like this where you come from?" Verona asked.

"Similar yes, but these look better made and more advanced," Aaron answered. "I wasn't in the military, so I can't really comment on how these compare. They are impressive, and it can get us to Khamearra before Sarah is out of time."

They walked over to the golden craft.

Gavril nodded in greeting to each of them. "I would like to introduce you to Tanneth. He will be joining us, and I'm sure you will find that he is quite resourceful."

Tanneth was of medium build with the same golden eyes that marked most Hythariam. He firmly shook their hands and began checking the outside of the ship.

Aaron ran his hands along the smooth golden surface, which was slightly warm to the touch.

"It's a Flyer-class SPT," Gavril said. "Stealth Personnel Transport. It's fast and silent, with some cloaking abilities. We should be able to make the trip to Khamearra in no time."

Aaron was impressed. "Were these the ones you used at Shandara?"

"Yes," Gavril answered.

"How many of them do you have?" Aaron asked.

"We have ten SPTs in working order," Gavril said. "I know the engineers are working to get some more online."

Roselyn joined them, carrying several packs. Tanneth helped her load them onto the Flyer, and Gavril indicated that they could leave as soon as they were ready.

Aaron noted Verona's almost pained expression when looking in Roselyn's direction. "She's extremely beautiful, but are you going to be able to focus?" Aaron asked.

Verona tore his eyes away and looked toward Aaron, but he could tell that Verona fought to keep his eyes from drifting back. "I don't know what has come over me, my friend. I've been bitten, I'm afraid."

Aaron smiled. "I can tell, and so can everyone else. You know you could try talking to her."

"I would if the function of my tongue didn't go awry every time she came near me," Verona answered.

Aaron remembered feeling the same thing when Sarah first came into his life and hoped that his friend would get control of himself soon. Roselyn didn't strike him as a type of woman who looked kindly upon a man who behaved with a boyish crush.

Colind approached quietly. "It's almost time," he said.

"Yes and not a moment too soon," Aaron replied.

"I need to ask what your intentions are regarding the barrier,"

Colind began. "Just so I'm aware."

Aaron calmly returned Colind's gaze. That's what they were all worried about. "I don't know. It's hard to say right now, mainly because we know so little. I'm going to do everything I can to save Sarah though."

Colind nodded slowly in understanding. "Just remember that the people of Khamearra are not the enemy."

"I know," Aaron answered. "But I would think that most people from Khamearra would believe that I am the enemy."

"Some," Colind acknowledged. "There are many factions, but remember they are also a people who live in fear. That is how the High King rules with the Elitesmen working as his right arm. Things were not always as they are now. Remember you may be able to find help in Khamearra." Colind paused, considering his next words. "I wish that I could go with you."

"You are needed elsewhere," said Aaron. "Besides, we'll catch up to you within two weeks," Aaron continued, not voicing what would happen if he failed.

"It seems there is never enough time. May the Goddess's blessings be upon you," Colind said with a slight bow, then pulled Aaron into a quick embrace. "One more thing," Colind began after letting him go. "Remember stealth is the goal. Avoid the High King if you can. He'll be focused on you now, and unlike before, they won't underestimate you."

Aaron understood all too well. "I've killed two of his sons, but it's about time they have something else to think about instead of just hunting me. Where will they stand when the barrier between worlds fails?"

"I suspected that somehow they had been in contact with General Halcylon on Hytharia, but it was never proven," Colind said and went silent as Iranus approached.

"I wanted you to know that we were able to see something heading for this planet," Iranus said. "It's not clear what exactly, but we'll work on it. I can't believe we've been so blind to this threat. We will do everything in our power to help, but, Aaron, I must ask something of you."

"What do you need?" Aaron asked.

"That you return to Shandara," Iranus answered.

"Why? What's there?"

"Up until Shandara fell, we had been working to create a stockpile of weapons to use in the event of the barrier collapsing. We feared they had been lost when the city was all but destroyed. I will send people to search, but I suspect we'll need you in order to find them," Iranus said.

"I'll return to Hathenwood, and together we can search," Aaron said. "I'm just a little surprised that you would need my help with this."

"We're limited by our technology. We, along with your ancestors, decided on this course of action, and it was left to them to hide the weapons as only they knew how," Iranus answered.

Aaron nodded, finally understanding. "They hid it, guarding against an invasion from Hytharia."

"Precisely," Iranus said. "I wish you a quick return, and may fortune smile upon you." Iranus walked away and headed toward his daughter, whom he pulled into a long hug.

"It's time for us to be going, my friend," Verona said quietly by his side.

Aaron nodded and waved goodbye to the others, joining Sarik on the Flyer. Eric and Braden were already on board. He was quickly followed by Roselyn and Verona. I'm coming, Sarah, Aaron thought and turned his attention to the display in the front. The display showed a panoramic view of everything around them. Gavril and Tanneth occupied the pilot and co-pilot's seats while the rest of them sat on the benches along the sides. Aaron barely felt the craft lift into the air. Gavril punched in the coordinates that would take them to Khamearra then turned his chair so it faced them.

"The coordinates are set, and we should arrive in about five hours, making the best speed in stealth," Gavril said, then looked at Aaron. "I hope you've got a plan."

"Verona and I put together some ideas, but much of it depends upon what we find when we reach the city," Aaron answered. "We'll need to take a look around."

Gavril nodded. "Reconnaissance. That's a good start."

"Excuse me," Sarik said, drawing their attention. "But how will you blend in?"

Aaron was wondering the same thing.

"The same as you," Roselyn said. "We have something that will make our eyes look the same as yours."

"I have another question, if you wouldn't mind," Sarik asked. "How come you look so...human? The way I understand it is that you are from another world. I guess I'm just wondering how that could be?"

There was a brief moment of silence as the seven of them regarded each other. Gavril and Tanneth looked toward Roselyn, which made sense to Aaron, as she was a scientist.

"It's a good question," Aaron said.

"Yes it is," Roselyn agreed. "The best we can determine is that we are cousins of sorts stemming from the same tree, but have gone down slightly different paths."

"Cousins?" Verona asked, speaking up for the first time since they came onboard.

"Yes," Roselyn said. "We have the same parts, I assure you. We're made up of the same stuff, to be completely blunt about it. We feel pain as you do, emotion as you do. And..." Roselyn glanced at Aaron, "... some of us even have had children with the people of Safanar."

"Why are you looking at me?" Aaron asked.

"Your grandfather, Reymius, chose to marry one of us," Roselyn said. "Your grandmother, Cassandra, was Hythariam. So you see we are not all that different from each other. You and I are truly cousins of sorts."

"How?" Aaron asked.

"Cassandra was Iranus's sister," Roselyn said. "Iranus is my father," she said, addressing the others on the small ship.

Roselyn was right, they were cousins after a fashion through his grandmother. *And now she is the Drake.* Aaron suppressed a shiver; he wasn't sure to what extent anyone else knew of the real tragedy that had befallen his grandparents, but it did explain some of Iranus's bitterness regarding the Drake.

Aaron eyed Roselyn for a moment. "Cousin." He grinned.

A smile lit up her face. "Cousin," Roselyn confirmed.

"Okay back to business," Aaron said. "Do you have a map of the capital city of Khamearra that you can put on screen?"

The Hythariam's reactions to his question were slightly amusing. They were clearly not used to someone other than themselves possessing knowledge about technology. Gavril nodded to Tanneth, who punched in a few keys. An aerial photograph of the city appeared, which confirmed to Aaron that they either had orbiting satellites or had done their own aerial reconnaissance. Verona and Sarik's eyes lit up at the display.

"That is impressive," Verona said.

"Quite," Aaron agreed. "This will help us immensely. How many satellites do you have in orbit?"

Gavril raised an eyebrow. "Thirty-four. We've mapped the surface of this world," Gavril said. "I'm sorry we're just not used to others knowing—"

"About your little toys," Aaron said with a smile, winking at Verona and Sarik. "Get used to it," Aaron said. "They have machines that fly around the world that can take pictures of the land among other things."

"I was among those in favor of sharing knowledge," Gavril replied.

"Look how big the city is," Sarik said.

Aaron looked at the display, frowning. "We should consider

splitting up to cover more ground. I only want to spend one day at the most looking around," he said, ignoring the painful spike in his connection to Sarah. He wanted to reach across the expanse to her, but was afraid of the pain he would cause her. Aaron knew in his heart that she was still fighting, and he needed to concentrate on finding the travel crystals.

"It may take more than a day," Verona said gently, and Gavril nodded.

Patience, Aaron counseled to himself. "Fine," he conceded. "But no more than two, or we can throw stealth out the window, and I will start focusing my attention on the Elitesmen."

"I suggest we divide the city into sections and pair off to investigate," Gavril said.

"That sounds good," Aaron answered, and glanced at Eric and Braden's challenging glares. "I won't go anywhere alone."

Some of the areas they would be looking at overlapped, but that was only because he insisted on seeing the Elitesmen stronghold for himself.

"I would like to check these areas myself," Tanneth spoke, gesturing to certain areas of the city, including the Elitesmen stronghold. His quiet tone caught Aaron by surprise as it were the first time he had heard him speak. "Meaning no disrespect to anyone here, but I'll do better on my own."

Gavril nodded his approval.

"Okay," Aaron said. "But be careful."

"I would like to go with you, Master Sorindale," Sarik said, addressing Gavril.

Gavril eyed Sarik for a moment and then nodded.

"I will be joining you two gentlemen, it seems," Roselyn said, looking at Aaron and Verona.

"Welcome," Aaron said and was slightly amused as Verona went a little pale. Sarik and Braden glanced at Verona, noting his silence, and Aaron shook his head slightly. Eric, however, could not keep from chuckling and muttered something about Verona being tongue-tied for once in his life.

The discussion turned to more mundane things, which Aaron only half paid attention to. He was focused on the map of the city before him, committing it to memory, especially the Elitesmen stronghold, where he was convinced a cache of travel crystals was stored. They decided to get what rest they could, with some of them dozing off. Aaron couldn't help but think of this moment as the calm before the storm.

***

"Are you sure about this?" Iranus asked.

"Aaron must be trusted to walk his own path," Colind answered. "It was Reymius's last command, and you must admit that Aaron has good instincts."

Iranus rubbed his white beard for a moment in thought. "I'm just afraid. You didn't witness the fall of your civilization. Reymius understood and made the ultimate sacrifice."

"Aaron is different," Colind said. "For one thing, he doesn't have a daughter to protect. He has sacrificed, but there will come a time when a line will be drawn and we must choose whether to stand that line with him. Aaron witnessed the cost of Reymius's sacrifices for the greater good, whether he understood the gravity of them or not. He is quite familiar with the results. At some point, the cost of sacrificing for the greater good is too high for those closest to the fight. Aaron is right to expect that the burden be spread to the people of this world. Either we fight and have a chance at surviving, or we stick our heads in the sand and forgo the right to be surprised when annihilation comes for us."

Iranus nodded. "I don't like it, but I understand, and I even agree with you to a certain extent. The Alenzar'seth have given more than we had right to ask of them," Iranus sighed. "I don't know how they could have survived on Hytharia. Our sun has expanded so much so that Hytharia must have become unlivable."

Colind absently grazed his fingertips along his bearded chin, lost in thought. "I had a friend once tell me that we should only worry about things that we have an influence over and acknowledge the things that we do not," Colind said.

Vaughn smiled. "And only take action upon the things that you can directly affect."

"They were very wise and, of course, correct. Who was your friend?" Iranus asked.

"Reymius," Colind said. "I see the same foundation of wisdom in Aaron. Many that he has come in contact with see it as well. It's why people are so apt to follow him."

"Yes, and he hates it as well," Garret said. "He believes whole-heartedly in people thinking for themselves."

"Exactly," Colind said. "And that's why he'll make a good leader. One that we can look to in these troubled times."

"I agree with you, old friend," Iranus said. "We've got a mountains' worth of work to do and very little time to do it in. Good luck in your journey. Our emissaries will have the means to contact us here in Hathenwood. They will show you how to use the comms device as well, so we should be able to keep in contact as needed."

The group split apart into those going on board the Raven and the Hythariam preparing as best they could for a war they had hoped to avoid.

CHAPTER 6
DISTRICT CAPTAIN

It was supposed to be an opportunity of a lifetime. Moving to the capital city in his beloved homeland of Khamearra. That was how both he and his wife thought of it six months ago. Nolan's wife still believed at least, but he wasn't so sure anymore. He stood in the bathroom, facing a small oval mirror, methodically rinsing his razor in the sink. *Running water.* When they had first moved into the district captain's residence, they had stood around the sink just to see water come from the faucets. This was the first place he had ever lived in that he didn't have to haul water from a well.

Being among the youngest captain of the guards for his city district, he was committed to looking the part. Not that he was all that young, being just past his thirty-second year. The echoes of his children fumbling through the house, getting ready for school, was soothing to his ears. He should feel fortunate that his children could attend school here. Many others couldn't say the same.

They had gone from living in a charming old house in the country, where his duties required him to travel to the surrounding towns to enforce the High King's Writ, to here. His house wasn't lavish by any means and would be considered a country cottage to those of higher rank, but to him it was a piece of heaven. The house was great. It was the job that made him feel shackled for the first time in his life.

"Nolan," his wife called. "You're going to be late."

Nolan quickly finished shaving and washed the remaining gel off his face. A small grin marked his features as he tied back his shoulder-length black hair into a ponytail. Not as stylish as some other captains, but at least he still had hair enough to cover his head, and for that he was content.

He left the small bathroom and came down the hall to the kitchen, where his family had gathered to break their fast. His wife, Arienh, rounded up his son and daughter and got them to sit at the table. Gathering for family meals was of paramount importance to Arienh, which made him sorry for all the dinners he had missed since taking this job.

Nolan could handle the demands of being a district captain, but it was the undercurrents of the city that worried him...and the Elitesmen. The Elitesmen were above the law and could dispense justice to the point of overruling his authority in his own district. He had learned that the hard way. The Elitesmen perception of justice was significantly different from his own.

He had crossed paths with them but a few times, and they were enough. Since then, he had seen them watching his home. Turning up in places where his wife and children frequented. He especially didn't like the attention they paid his eldest child, Jason, who would reach his twelfth year of age this coming month, the age at which he could undertake an apprenticeship. The children of wellborn nobility and ranking officers tried different apprenticeships before settling into an occupation.

Nolan had once broached the subject of them leaving a few weeks back.

"The Goddess wants us exactly where she intends for us to be. Have faith in that, my love," Arienh had said.

Nolan didn't have the heart to tell her of the Elitesmen watching their comings and goings. Arienh loved the city, and he couldn't take it away from her despite the growing unease he felt whenever he walked through his district. The people were kind, but would rarely make eye contact for fear of causing some type of offense. He had witnessed the abuse some captains imposed upon residents of their districts, but he would stomach none of it in his own. People weren't beaten or tossed into his holding cells without good reason, and in the latter case, only in defense of one's self. He had made that as clear as day to his guards his very first week.

After eating a quiet breakfast with his family, Nolan stepped out of the house to head to the station. He brushed off imaginary dust particles on his otherwise pristine black uniform. The silver dragon emblem showed proudly upon his muscled chest. He walked down the street, nodding in greeting to those passing by. The residents that lived closest to his house had long gotten used to his friendly greetings, which were received warily at first but eventually returned in kind. Across the way, his friend called out to him.

"Good morning, Lieutenant Anson," Nolan greeted.

"Same to you, Captain Nolan," Anson said back, but the mirth was short lived, as his normally sunny features grew serious. "The rumor is that Josef is waiting for you at the station."

Nolan frowned. "Do you know what for?"

Anson raised a brow. "I think you know, sir."

"Enlighten me," Nolan said.

Anson was a good man and one of the earliest at the station to give his support.

"An incident occurred last night near the poor quarter, Josef's Lieutenant... " Anson began.

"Captain Commander Josef," Nolan corrected. Despite both their opinions of the man, he still wore the uniform of the captain commander.

"My apologies, sir," Anson replied. "Lieutenant Renke and his squad followed a group of men returning from their work in the crystal mines. They were beating the group of men, claiming that they had stolen crystals to sell for themselves. Our boys were alerted to the commotion and intervened. They said that when they arrived, the miners had submitted to questioning, but Renke's men were still beating them. We rounded the whole lot up and put them in separate holding cells."

Nolan frowned. "Renke and his guards, too?"

"Yes, sir," Anson answered.

Nolan smiled, slightly glimpsing the crap storm that this was going to cause. Regardless, from the sound of it, his men were in the right, and he would back them up even if Renke's boss outranked him.

"All right, I think I get the gist," Nolan said. "Is there anything else?"

"Yes, Captain Commander Josef was accompanied by an Elitesman," Anson said, unable to keep his voice from shaking. The presence of the Elitesmen were enough to rattle the nerves of the most stalwart of men, and Nolan understood Anson's concern.

"Understood," Nolan said and quickened his pace to the station. So much for a quiet morning.

Ten minutes later, he and Anson rounded the corner to the station headquarters for the district. A three-story, white, stone-faced building big enough to accommodate a hundred guards of the watch stood at a main intersection. He took the steps leading up to the main doors two at a time. When he came through the doors, the clerk behind the desk saluted.

"Captain of the watch is on-site," the clerk cried.

Nolan returned the salute and quickly headed for his office. The mood in the station was more somber than normal, which Nolan attributed more to the presence of the Elitesmen than the Captain Commander. Perhaps it was his own nerves.

Nolan glanced back, and Anson was still on his tail. "Stay close."

Anson nodded and took up the post right outside his office door.

Nolan stepped into his office to find Captain Commander Josef sitting in his chair and the Elitesman standing at the window with his back to him. Josef had the look of someone permanently annoyed with everything and anyone that was unlucky enough to cross his path. Of the districts in the capital city, the captain commander's is the most prestigious because it borders included the palaces of the High King.

Captain Commander Josef looked up at his arrival and scowled.

"My Lord, Captain Commander," Nolan saluted.

The Captain Commander narrowed his piggish eyes. "Nolan, you have some of my men locked up in your holding cells."

"Yes, my lieutenant was bringing me up to speed on my way in this morning, sir," Nolan replied, glancing in the direction of the Elitesman who didn't turn around or make any sound.

"Well," Josef growled.

"Sir?" Nolan asked.

"I want them released," the Captain Commander barked.

"They will be released when I review the case and they've been cleared of any wrong-doing," Nolan replied calmly. "I've only just learned of the incident this morning, and it did only occur last night."

Josef's scowl deepened, and his face became an impressive shade of purple. "Are you refusing an order?"

"No, sir."

"Then why won't you release them now?" Captain Commander Josef asked.

"As I've already said, my lord, I haven't reviewed the case nor checked last night's reports—" Nolan's reply was cut short.

"Don't spout these ridiculous reasons. Those are my men you have locked up, and as your superior officer I'm giving you a direct order to release my men or I'll..." Captain Commander

Josef bit off his reply.

"I would caution you against that, my lord," Nolan replied, fighting the urge to clench his fists. "I cannot comply with your order as it would violate our city mandate which is, as you know, to uphold the law of our city. If I were to just release them because of your order, I could be brought up on charges for negligence of duty if any wrong-doing were to be found."

Captain Commander Josef heaved his bulk out of Nolan's chair, glaring menacingly at him. Despite Josef's expanding girth, Nolan knew he had been a brawler in his youth and still enjoyed a good fight. Nolan kept his cool despite Josef's outward display.

Just then, his office door burst open and Lieutenant Anson stepped inside under the guise of delivering reports from the night watch. Anson wore a shocked expression as if he didn't realize anyone was in the room.

"My Lords, I'm sorry for interrupting," Anson stammered, but Nolan knew better. Anson stood, waiting with the files in his hand.

"Thank you, Lieutenant," Nolan said and gestured for him to place the files on his desk.

Anson placed the files on his desk and winked at Nolan before leaving the room.

"Release the commander's men," said the Elitesman, speaking for the first time, slowly turning from the window. "And the miners." His voice didn't hiss, but it still reminded Nolan of a snake.

The Elitesman's icy stare sent shivers down Nolan's spine. He couldn't argue his way out of this, and the Elitesman knew it.

"At once, my lord," Nolan said, bowing his head, knowing that the miners in the holding cell were doomed to a cruel fate.

The Elitesman nodded and turned to address Josef. "Captain Commander, I trust that should satisfy you. Deliver the miners to the Citadel."

The Citadel was the stronghold of the Elitesmen, and there was little chance that they would ever see the light of day again. Nolan felt a pang of regret for the miners settle into the pit of his stomach. *Do something. Help them,* a small voice urged, but there was nothing he could do. The Elitesmen's word was law, and to challenge it often turned out badly for the challenger.

There were rumors spoken in hushed corners about a man who openly challenged the Elitesmen, but he put little stock in them. Who could ever challenge the Elitesmen? Those miners were as good as dead, which is where he would end up if he tried to help them. But he wanted to help. The stink of the Elitesmen autonomy gnawed at him. He was a district captain, and he should be able to protect the citizens in his district and uphold the law.

The Elitesman turned back to Nolan and dismissed the Captain Commander. Josef left the room, still glaring at him. The Elitesman moved closer to him, and Nolan had to fight the urge to grab the sword at his side. He was an expert swordsman. Most captains were, but he had seen some of the things the Elitesmen could do, and he had no desire to test his mettle against any from that order.

"Whenever you're ready, Captain," the Elitesman said.

Nolan nodded. "Lieutenant."

Anson stepped back into the room and saluted.

"Release the captain commander's guards at once. Take a squad and escort the miners to the Citadel," Nolan said.

As Anson saluted, the Elitesman cleared his throat, narrowing his gaze.

"Do we have a problem?" the Elitesmen asked quietly.

"No, sir," Nolan replied.

"I said for the captain commander's men to escort the miners to the Citadel, not your men."

Nolan clamped his jaw shut. He was hoping that his interpretation of the Elitesmen orders would be over-looked. "My apologies, Elitesman," Nolan said.

"You've been here six months, is that right?" the Elitesman asked.

"Yes, my lord," Nolan answered.

"This isn't the first time your 'interpretation' of our orders has almost put you in direct conflict with our will," he hissed.

Nolan swallowed. "My Lord, I was thinking of the well-being of the miners. My only concern was to deliver them safely into the care of your brethren at the Citadel. I meant no offense."

"Perhaps it is my *will* that the miners suffer," the Elitesman spat. "Would you have issues with that?"

The Elitesman knew damned well he would have an issue, and the look in his eyes confirmed it.

"No, my lord," Nolan answered numbly.

"I see," the Elitesman said, striding about the room before

turning to face Nolan again. "I would like your men to escort the miners to the Citadel. See to it that they are properly cowed by the time they arrive."

Nolan fought down the nauseous feeling in his sinking stomach as his mind leaped ahead to not only what he was being ordered to do to the miners, but what the cost would be to the men under his command. The spark gave way to the flame of his anger despite his fear of the Elitesmen.

"As you wish, my lord," he said softly.

"I want them driven like livestock through the streets, and I want you to personally oversee their transfer," the Elitesman sneered, his gaze unwavering.

Nolan's hand itched to reach for his sword. He couldn't do this. This was an order he couldn't follow.

"Captain," the Elitesman prodded, "we're very interested in your son. We've watched his progress and have noted his special talents."

Jason! They know!

He had tried to keep Jason's talents secret, but the boy was twelve. No, not my son. Nolan's hand hardened around the hilt of his sword, much to the Elitesman's delight. Nolan stood there for a moment, upon the precipice of openly rebelling against the Elitesman and certain death. The Elitesman, he noted, delighted in his struggle as a spider mercilessly spins his web around his prey.

How could they know about Jason?

"We are keen to get him into the academy of the Elite when he comes of age. That's next month, is it not?" the Elitesman asked.

Nolan nodded, not trusting himself to speak.

"Excellent, I look forward to his training," the Elitesman said in a deceptively sunny tone. "Now I will await you and your men outside. Do not keep me waiting long." The Elitesman finished and left the room.

Nolan stared at the spot where the Elitesman stood until Anson cleared his throat. He released his vice-like grip off the hilt of his sword.

"Lieutenant, gather a squad of men and bring the miners to the front of the station," Nolan said evenly.

"But, Captain, we can't do this," Anson said, his eyes wide with fear.

I have no choice. They are coming for my son.

"We have our orders. Tell the squad to… " His voice faltered. "Bring the whips," Nolan said, turning to face his friend. The look of betrayal nearly broke him as much as the threat to his family had. Almost. There was a line between protecting his friends and comrades and protecting his family. Anson was about to voice another protest. "You have your orders, Lieutenant!" he shouted.

Anson saluted and bowed stiffly. "It shall be done, My Lord Captain."

Nolan felt something break inside him as Anson left the room. Could he really have been so naive to believe that he could have changed things here? The Elitesman had played him as a master swordsman played with a fresh recruit that had never held a blade, and the sting of it burned him inside. The Elitesman was waiting for him outside, and their plan finally dawned on him.

For him to drive the miners through his own district like a bunch of animals would prove to all its residents that he was no different than any other district captain that had come before.

CHAPTER 7
STRANGERS IN KHAMEARRA

The arrival at Khamearra was uneventful. They had decided to split up and enter the city at different entrances, using the Flyer's stealth mode to drop them off at strategic locations. The sky was beginning to grow brighter as dawn approached and the city began to awaken. The capital city was grand in size, easily four miles wide, and went on a good distance beyond that to the river after. Airships dotted the sky as they went to and fro. The walls of the city were slate gray, a stark contrast to Shandara's pristine white walls. There were houses and other buildings beyond the walls. A grand palace to the western side of the city. *Sarah's home.* Toward the eastern edge was the Elitesmen stronghold from which two dark towers spiraled toward the sky, easily as high as the towers of the palace proper.

Before setting off, Gavril once again emphasized the importance of stealth and that they should focus on reconnaissance only. They had planned to meet at an inn near the center of the city, and Gavril handed out small comms devices about six inches long and thinner than a pencil, but quite durable. They had a range of ten miles and were networked through the Flyer SPT's on-board computer, but they could also communicate back to Hathenwood through the satellite. This gave them some small measure of reassurance that they could at least speak to one another if they needed to, and that help would be on the way if someone were to get into trouble.

Tanneth had all sorts of small devices hidden within his long leather jacket. While not exactly native to Khamearra, its appearance wasn't exactly foreign either. They bid farewell to the others as Aaron, Verona, and Roselyn watched the silent Flyer leave them behind.

Roselyn brought her hands up to her eyes for a moment, and when she took them away, the Hythariam's golden eyes had been replaced with brown eyes matching Aaron's own. She couldn't hide the exotic beauty of her facial features, which were accentuated by her rich dark hair, but that's what hoods were for.

"This should be interesting," Aaron said, beginning to walk down the road to the western gate.

"I agree, my friend. Interesting indeed," Verona said, coming up behind them.

They walked up the road, silently approaching the houses along the outskirts of the walls. The people that were outside took note of their approach with a pointed indifference. The occasional few offered a friendly nod, but most went about their morning tasks, seemingly not to invite attention. They passed through the gates under the wary eyes of the guards in black uniforms with the silver dragon emblems on their chests. Aaron felt a momentary surge of anger at the sight of the uniform. When they were out of earshot of the guards, Roselyn asked him what was wrong.

"I've had a few encounters with men who wore the same uniform as the guards here," Aaron answered, keeping his head low as they passed yet more guards. He had to remind himself that simply because they wore the same uniform these were not the men who burned down his home or murdered his mother and father.

The streets became more crowded the farther they ventured into the city. Whenever there was a group of guards or a passing nobleman, a path instantly opened through the throng of people. The city fully awakened from its slumber and took on a life all its own. It was markedly different from the quietness of Hathenwood or sailing the skies on an airship. Try as he might, Aaron couldn't help but feel out of place among these people. He tried his best not to think of them as the enemy, which became easier the more he observed the silent interplay between the citizens and the guardsman. Not all the guardsmen gave the open appraisal of what could they take from you as they walked by.

Aaron turned his head to the side at the sounds of a struggle to see a man being dragged through an alleyway by a group of guards. The guards occasionally threw the poor sod to the ground, giving him a few kicks for good measure before hoisting him to his feet again.

Verona seized Aaron's arm and shook his head slightly.

"I know what you would do my friend, but we can't make

everyone's business our own. Not here."

Aaron nodded reluctantly, unable to decide which bothered him more—seeing such brutality occur in broad daylight or watching the city's denizens go about their way, ignoring the scene. Another group of guards passed, heading toward the alleyway, shouting for the path to be cleared. Aaron quickly got out of the way, but watched as the guards approached the group, carrying the almost-unconscious man. The two groups stopped while the leaders conferred. Aaron noted that the men of each group had their hands upon their swords. After a few terse words that he couldn't hear in their entirety, the new group of guards took custody of the prisoner.

"You see they must take care of their own," Roselyn whispered.

Aaron was glad for the intervention of the guards, but his impression of the city was gravitating toward one of a powder keg, where a single spark would set all aflame.

"How does anyone live like this?" Aaron asked quietly.

"Look who rules these people," Verona said. "They are caught between the tyranny of the High King and that of the Elitesmen."

As if by magic, two figures in dark cloaks moved fluidly through the crowd, making their way like the opposing forces of a magnet. Aaron sensed the gathering energy and knew that these were Elitesmen. He wanted to quell the arrogance right out of them. Sheer will alone kept Aaron from attacking the Elitesmen as they passed. Will and knowing that Sarah's life was in the balance if he failed. He wondered if they sensed him. If only he could sense whether they had a travel crystal with them.

Aaron turned to Verona. "Can you sense them?"

Verona's brow furrowed in concentration and after a few moments. "Yes," he whispered, sounding surprised.

"Good," Aaron said, pleased. Both Verona and Sarik had been practicing the slow forms for meditation while he had been unconscious, and they were slowly increasing their ability to sense the life energy around them. Very soon, they would be able to pull the energy into themselves.

"You can sense them?" Roselyn asked quietly.

"Yes," Aaron answered.

Roselyn frowned and held up a small device in her hand. "I get nothing," she said, putting the device away. "Nothing beyond body heat. I don't think they have any travel crystals on them."

Aaron nodded, knowing that it would have been too good to be true if it were that easy. He turned his attention to the people again and finally understood why Sarah had held them all at arm's length in the beginning. He had assumed she was slow to trust, given the things she had to deal with during her childhood, but now he understood all too well.

Seeing the place she called home put things in a clearer perspective. He knew she aided an underground resistance, but he had no idea how to reach out to them. Aaron felt a cold shiver run the length of his spine and turned to see an Elitesman staring squarely in his direction. *Not yet.* He turned in the opposite direction and headed down a side alleyway away from the droves of people at the market place.

A short while later, they made steady progress toward the

Elitesmen stronghold. The massive dark towers stretching their clawed crowns toward the sky loomed ever present in their view. Through strings of conversations and asking seemingly harmless questions, they learned that the city was divided into districts, each run by a captain who then reported to the captain commander.

Despite the oppressive power of the guards, the vibe from each of the districts was vastly different from one to the next. Aaron couldn't determine where the borders of one district ended and another began. The district they were in now was cleaner than any of the others so far, and the people were not quite so downtrodden. Even the guards they passed seemed friendly and stood with pride rather than a challenging stance bent on trouble. He was almost starting to relax when a guard called out to them.

"You three," the guard said.

They all turned to the guard, none of them volunteered to speak first.

"I don't believe I recognize you. Are you lost?" the guard asked.

Verona recovered first. "Yes, my good sir. We have newly arrived to your wonderful city. We are heading toward the central market square. Would it be too much of a bother if you could point us in the right direction?"

The guard stepped closer to them, his eyes lingering on Roselyn, who slowly pulled off the hood of her cloak and returned the guard's gaze in kind.

The guard's eyes flashed admiringly and looked respectfully toward Aaron and Verona. "Yes," the guard said. "Head up this way for three blocks until you come to Main Street East and then turn right. You can't miss it, but it will be eleven blocks whence you turn."

Verona nodded appreciatively, "My thanks to you, good sir. We'll be on our way then."

The three of them walked in the direction that the guard indicated. To do otherwise would arouse suspicion.

"I see you've found your voice," Aaron said quietly to Verona.

"One rises to the occasion," Verona replied with a grin, but the grin faded as his eyes drew toward Roselyn, who walked in front of them. She pulled her hood back up and tucked away her silky black hair. "I don't suppose I could trouble you for a bit of advice?"

"Why not," Aaron grinned, he had been expecting this.

"For the first time, words escape me, my friend," Verona began, still staring longingly at Roselyn's back. "It's stupid to bring this up. Forget I said anything," Verona said quickly and began to walk away.

Aaron grabbed his friend's arm. "It's not stupid. The world doesn't stop simply because of one's problems. I am your friend as you've been to me ever since I arrived here. If I can help, even if it's just to listen, then I will."

Verona smiled. "Thank you, my friend. I know we have bigger things to be concerned about than my boyish crush on our beautiful, fair, and exotic traveling companion."

"Is that all it is then, a boyish crush?" Aaron asked.

Verona was silent for moment, and Roselyn glanced in their

direction to be sure they were still following. "No," Verona answered, "it's not."

"Good," Aaron said, "because if it were, I'd thrash you for wasting my time," he said, giving Verona a playful shove.

Verona laughed. "What do I do?"

"You could try talking to her," Aaron quipped.

"What would I say?"

Aaron swallowed a chuckle, because Verona was completely serious and he didn't want to offend. "I suggest being honest and listen. Listening to what a woman has to say is good place to start."

"What if— " Verona stammered, "what if she doesn't feel the same way?"

"There is only one way to find out, but I would suggest picking your moment and taking small steps with a word here and there." Aaron grinned, and Verona shoved him back. That was good. Verona must have it bad if he was asking him these questions. What did he know about women?

Roselyn waved them over. They had come to Main Street East. The sounds of a crowd grew steadily louder, beyond the normal rabble of city life, and they quickened their pace. A large crowd gathered at the intersecting streets, and the closer they got, Aaron could hear the sharp crack of several whips and screams of pain. He pushed his way through the crowd to get a better look. Roughly fifteen men dressed in filthy rags stumbled through the street. Blood stained their backs. He counted twenty guards forming a circle to keep the crowd at bay, while three guards carried long leather whips dripping with blood. They were followed by a grim-faced captain who looked as if he were about to be sick. The grisly group was still a block away from where Aaron stood and approached rapidly. Aaron's hands drifted to his swords as he glanced across the street and saw children interspersed amid the angry crowd.

Aaron noticed the captain glance behind him at the two cloaked figures that followed. *Elitesmen,* he thought, utterly disgusted with the display. Aaron was about to step out into the street when Verona pulled him back.

"Look at them," Verona said. "The guards."

Aaron turned back and studied the guards. They all appeared grim faced and frightened despite the horrendous actions of which they were a part.

"They are afraid," Aaron said. It hadn't occurred to him until this moment that the guards themselves would feel powerless against the Elitesmen. He underestimated the hold that the Elitesmen had upon these people. His first encounter was in a small town remote from any cities; he had assumed the awe of the townsfolk had been exaggerated when he took down the Elitesmen. Now he witnessed a mob of people in a city cowed by merely two Elitesmen. He couldn't absolve the guards entirely in his mind. How could anyone do that to another human being?

"I can't walk away from this," Aaron said to Verona and Roselyn. The latter looking as if she were about to protest, but stopped when Verona gently put his hand upon her shoulder and shook his head slightly.

"I'll be right back," Aaron said, pulling up the hood of his cloak. Then he grabbed a swath of black cloth and tied it so that only his eyes showed and disappeared into the crowd.

"What will he do?" Roselyn asked.

Verona guided her to the outskirts of the crowd so they had a clear view. "I'm not sure. Remind me to tell you about how Aaron and I met at a small town called Duncan's Port. In the meantime, let's watch and help if we can."

Roselyn nodded, and they waited while the poor men under the whips were driven forward.

***

Crack!

The harsh snap of the whip struck the miner's back, sending droplets of blood flecking into the crowd, with some hitting Nolan's cheek. Anson wouldn't make eye contact with him now. When they had first left the station, Nolan had ordered the men to drive the miners along using the whips to crack the air. More of a theatrical display than anything else. He had hoped that the display would satisfy the Elitesmen, but he had been wrong. Dead wrong, and five of his guards had paid the price with their lives. The side of his head still throbbed from where the Elitesman had thwarted his attack, while another raised his hand, sending a searing blue orb into his chest. His chest still burned from where the orb struck. A warning, the Elitesman had said. The next one would not be aimed at him, but at his wife and daughter. His son, Jason, was too valuable an asset to waste. Jason they would simply take.

Nolan spat the blood from his mouth where he had bit his cheek. The remainder of his squad hardly glanced back at their captain, who had failed to protect five of their number. Though Nolan had only been their captain for six months, he had made it a point to know the men under his command, and he knew that there were some with families whose husbands and fathers would never again come home. His hand lingered upon his sword. How he wanted to lash out and kill the Elitesmen in a torrent of righteous fury, but deep down he knew he would only hasten his own death and doom his own family. He buried his emotions and continued to drive his men forward mercilessly. Let them hate their captain if they could. He would bear the burden of what the Elitesmen had done to all of them in this display of barbarism. Deep within the foundations of his inner core, Nolan knew that he could never absolve himself of the actions taken this bloody day. He turned back to the Elitesman who stared back at him impassively.

Nothing. There is nothing I can do to stop this.

Nolan's hand drifted toward the knife in his belt, toying with rebellious thoughts.

Throw it! a voice in his mind ordered. At the same moment, Anson glanced his way, noting where Nolan's hand had strayed. Nolan looked back at his friend, and Anson nodded back with his own hand tapping his knife.

I'm sorry, Arienh.

It would be a good death. Nolan pulled his knife free and hurled it at the Elitesman, with Anson matching his movements in perfect unison.

The Elitesman's movements blurred, sending both his and Anson's knife harmlessly to the side. The Elitesmen growled and drew their swords, and Nolan did the same. Behind him, he heard the sounds of numerous blades hiss free of their sheaths, and he risked a quick glance to see that all his guards had drawn their swords, grim faced and determined. It appeared he would be testing the Elitesmen's mettle this day.

A dark figure slammed upon the ground between them, startling the advancing Elitesmen. The figure stood tall in silent waiting as a hush swept over the crowd. The Elitesmen lashed out with their blades in a blur, and the dark figure moved equally fast, whirling his staff and blocking their attacks.

***

Aaron squared off against the two Elitesmen. The bladesong coursed through him, but he did not draw his swords. He held the rune-carved staff steady in his hands and patiently waited for the arrogance of the Elitesmen to win over. They fed upon the fear of those around them. They would contend with someone who could stand against them today.

The Elitesmen attacked as a pair, perfectly coordinated with lethal accuracy, their blades racing to meet him. Aaron shifted through their attacks, drawing upon the energy around them and moving faster than they ever could. In a quick burst, he sent one of the Elitesmen to the ground with a blow from his staff. The other Elitesman, lighter on his feet, danced deftly out of reach, coming to a stop in the middle of the rabble of men the guards had been trying to clear out of the way. Aaron's eyes caught the captain's as they flashed in alarm. He swung his staff in a wide arc, catching the Elitesman that approached from behind. He followed up with a crushing blow to the head, and the Elitesman moved no more.

With a nod to the captain, Aaron drew upon the energy around him and leaped into the air, closing the distance between himself and the remaining Elitesman. The crowd scattered, and the Elitesman snatched a fleeing child attempting to run past him and turned to face Aaron with a wicked gleam in his eyes.

Aaron stopped in his tracks and held his breath. The end of his staff touched the ground next to his feet, and the runes glowed faintly. The Elitesman held his blade to the child's throat. *Why do they always go after the children?* The energy practically crackled down his arms and legs, eager to be released. Aaron saw something move along the crowd's edge, and the Elitesman's sword arm jerked away from the child's throat. Aaron released the energy built up within him and moved so fast that the world stilled around him as he blurred into action. Grabbing the Elitesman by the scruff of his neck, he launched himself into a powerful jump, clearing the buildings around them. Aaron slammed the Elitesman down upon the roof of a small nearby tower. Before Aaron could deliver the final blow, the Elitesman reached inside his pocket and disappeared.

Aaron clenched his teeth, looking toward the dark towers in the distance. Then he slowly leaped down to the street below and headed to where Verona and Roselyn would be waiting.

***

"Who was that?" Anson asked, coming to Nolan's side.

"I don't know," Nolan said, grateful for the help of the stranger. "Release them and help them get to safety," Nolan said, and the miners disappeared into the crowd.

"What about him?" Anson asked, gesturing toward the dead Elitesman.

"Take the body and burn it," Nolan said. "I want all evidence of it to be destroyed."

Nolan said a silent prayer to the Goddess, rubbing his hand in a small circle upon his brow in a customary show of respect. Anson, who had caught the gesture, stepped up to him and handed him a leather pouch pulled from the Elitesman's pocket, which Nolan stuffed into his own. The crowd, which had been an angry mob before, began to dissipate.

The guards gathered around after carrying out his orders. Most looked shaken by the events that had taken place. Twenty men looked expectantly at him for orders. Nolan looked at them all with a mixture of sympathy and pride. They had stood with him, ready to defy the injustice of the Elitesmen, knowing full well it would bring them wrath. Some, like himself, had families.

"It was an honor to stand by you on this bloody day, my friends," Nolan said. Friends they were, for from this day forth they could be nothing else. "I fear that the ire of the Elitesmen will be swift. None of us are safe. The Elitesmen will not stop with us.

They will visit their retribution where we live. The lives of our families and loved ones are in danger. The city is not safe for us."

"Where can we go?" one of them asked.

Nolan looked back at them helplessly. Where could any of them go now? He couldn't answer the question because he didn't know himself. Anson cleared his throat and gestured to the ground. In the dirt was a sketching of a dragon cradling a rose, with one clawed hand raised before it.

Some of the guards gasped their protests, while others hastily looked around to see if anyone else had seen. Anson quickly brushed away the image.

Nolan looked at Anson, unable to keep the puzzlement from his face.

"The Resistance. We should seek their aide," Anson said. "You're new to the city and don't know how widespread they are."

Judging by the men's reactions, he could tell that more than a few were quite familiar with them.

"We shouldn't talk about this here out in the open. Let's meet in fifteen minutes," Anson said and gave them a location to meet. The guards split into groups of twos and threes and departed.

Nolan looked at his friend. "I need to get my family to safety. Out of the city, if possible."

"I'm not sure if that will be possible. We should be able to get them into hiding," Anson said, leading him down a set of streets farther away from the crowded parts of the district.

They came to an older section of the city where the stonework appeared almost ancient with a lost elegance. Nolan had the distinct feeling that they were being followed, but each time he looked, there was nothing there. Chalking it up to nerves, he kept following his friend. Eventually, they arrived at an old rundown building with a dome-shaped roof that had collapsed in a few places.

They entered the building, which appeared to be as dilapidated inside as the outside except for the pristine fountain with a statue of a woman standing resolute, her gaze sweeping the entranceway. Anson brought his hand to his forehead and made a small circular motion with this thumb and forefinger. It was just the two of them.

"I had hoped to bring you here eventually. You are different from the other captains," Anson said, his gaze lingering upon the fountain. "Better."

Nolan watched his friend. "What are you saying?"

Anson was about to answer him when the other guards arrived. After all twenty arrived, Anson called for quiet.

"My friends," Anson began, "at this point, if you're here, you've accepted that things have gotten so bad that we cannot go back to our old lives. You can, of course, go your separate ways, but after this moment when you learn what you're about to learn, there is no going back, and it would be a danger for us all to allow it."

"What do you mean?" Nolan asked.

"I am a descendant of the De'anjard, Keepers of the Watch. Shields of Shandara," Anson said with his fist across his heart. "We are the heart of the Resistance here in Khamearra. Our main objective is to bring down the Elitesmen and the High King wherever and however we can. Captain Nolan had no knowledge of this and has not participated in any of our activities. He's simply a good man. One that they will never let live because of his commitment to the law and to treating people with a sense of decency."

Nolan's mouth fell open. The De'anjard were the remnants of the Shandarian Army. Many took refuge into neighboring kingdoms, but to learn that after all this time they had kept fighting in whatever way they could was astonishing.

"We can hide your families and your loved ones," Anson said.

"At what price?" one of the guardsman barked.

"Service," Anson said. "To our cause would be ideal, but if you find that you cannot allow yourself to do so, then we will still help you leave the city."

Some of the guards murmured among themselves.

"Was that one of your people who helped us today?" Nolan asked.

Anson shook his head. "No, while there are some older Elitesmen who indirectly serve our cause, none were present today. How could they be? I didn't know we would be transferring the miners. I'm not sure why the Elitesmen wanted those miners brought to the Citadel."

"They wanted to make an example out of me," Nolan said. "This was about their asserting control, but perhaps you are correct. There may be more to their methods than what we are being led to believe."

The guards murmured their agreement, but fell silent when

Anson spoke again.

"I'm not the leader of the De'anjard, but I do have the authority to speak for them. Time is short. We can help you escape the injustice of the Elitesmen, but I urge you to take up the cause. If not us, then who will stand up and fight for those who cannot fight for themselves? Give voice to those who cannot speak," Anson leveled his gaze at all of them. "Give shelter to those who wish to escape the storm."

Nolan raised his hand to his friend. "You have my sword. Just help me get my family to safety."

Anson shook his hand. Others spoke up, and they agreed to join the Shandarian Resistance in the home city of the High King. For the first time in months, Nolan felt a sense of pride that could only come from hope. He might die in service to this cause, but knowing that his family would be safe and that he could be of service to a good cause was worth dying for.

Anson split them up into groups of four, giving a different set of instructions to each. He gestured to Nolan to come with him to the various groups. Each group was given a passphrase and a specific action to take at a certain location, the purpose of which was to alert others of the Resistance that they were in need of aid. Help would be provided to gather those with loved ones in need, and after the former guardsman of the High King left, it was just Anson and himself in the old temple.

"Yours will be the riskiest of actions," Anson said.

Nolan raised an eyebrow. "Why is that?"

"Because we need for you to stay in your current place, serving as district captain."

"But," Nolan began.

"Your family will be hidden and eventually smuggled out of the city, but your position as district captain is one we can't hope to pass up. We can come up with some type of cover story for their absence."

Nolan's mind raced. He could see Anson's point. "I agree. I'll help you."

Anson smiled, clearly relieved. "I'll be there with you, my friend. We will protect you as best we can. Now, let us go for there is more work to do before this is done."

"What about the man that helped us?" Nolan asked.

"That's one of the things we need to find out," Anson said, with a wink running his hand through his unkempt brown hair.

As they left the temple, Nolan glanced back at the statue of the Goddess and thought of his wife's words to him when he broached the subject of them leaving the city.

The Goddess wants us exactly where she intends for us to be.

With a respectful nod in the statue's direction, Nolan left the building.

Dawn approached, and the sun peeked through the clouds. The air was crisp being so close to the mountains near Hathenwood, but since Colind had been released from his prison, he never missed an opportunity to witness the sunrise. The first rays of the sun caressed his craggy old face. Having been deprived of the sun's warmth for a score of years, it was these small quiet moments that made him feel as if he was being born again.

He sat on the deck of the Raven with a large bucket to capture the wood shavings from his carving. A good sharp knife and a couple of other tools gave his hands something to do, whittling away the block of wood. Carving wood was something he hadn't been able to do in a very long time, and it still surprised him how much he missed the simple pleasures in life. He ran his fingers along the fine grain, feeling the density of the old block of wood. Much like himself, he mused. He would often whittle wood to think through a problem, and there was no shortage of those.

His eyes drew east to the horizon where Khamearra was many

miles from where he sat. Aaron had occupied much of his thoughts, and despite his preconceptions of the boy, he had grown genuinely fond of him. Boy. He smiled. At Colind's age, anyone younger than fifty was considered a boy. Aaron had shown a remarkable sense of wisdom when dealing with the Hythariam. That's not to say he thought much of his chances of succeeding in his quest, but he understood and agreed with his reasons for trying. Not that Aaron needed or required his blessing, but he still found himself yearning to go with the boy and lend a hand.

"You're up early," Garret said.

Colind looked up at Garret and nodded in greeting. A man well into his fifties, so not a boy. His gray hair had been cropped short, and his eyes were so blue they bordered on silver.

"I've been asleep a long time," Colind said. "In my imprisonment I was unable to enjoy the shine of the sun." His tone was friendly enough, but the terror of being pulled from the shadow back into the world of the living was all too real for him. Mactar had trapped his soul, separating it from his body, leaving it slightly out of phase with reality. He brushed thoughts of Mactar aside lest his mind stray into the reckoning that he would visit upon that evil man in a thousand different ways.

"I wonder how they are getting on," Garret said, glancing to the east.

Colind shifted in his chair. "I'm sure they are fine. They've only just arrived in Khamearra and haven't had enough time to stir up trouble. The boy has quite a following, won't you agree? Present company included."

"That he does. To be honest, I found myself wanting to go with them. What are the odds of them succeeding?"

"I wouldn't bet against Aaron if that's what you mean," Colind said. "I'm not sure, to be honest, based upon everything I've seen and knowing how the Drake hunted the Alenzar'seth. But as Verona put it, Aaron has a knack for doing the impossible," Colind said and raised his hands as living proof to validate the claim he just made.

"I see your point," Garret said. "If there is anyone who can pull off something like this, I believe it's him. He would have walked to Shandara to find the answers he sought. That is the measure of his conviction. He will do no less for Sarah and probably a great deal more."

Vaughn joined them. "It's what he wouldn't do to save Sarah that concerns me."

Colind sighed. They had been over this, and still they came to the same subject yet again. "I think we need to accept the fact that Aaron will do what he needs to do. If those actions bring war to this world sooner than we had planned, then so be it. The Alenzar'seth have sacrificed enough. They gave us almost a hundred years to prepare for this. Besides, Aaron makes a compelling argument, wouldn't you agree?"

Vaughn's bearing changed. He wrapped his arms around himself. "Indeed, he does. I feel foolish for not having thought along similar lines myself, and I know I'm not the only one."

Colind shrugged his shoulders. "None of us did. A fresh perspective is worth its weight. He managed to convince Iranus, which is a monumental feat in itself."

Soft chuckles released the tension. They were all frightened by the looming threat from Hytharia and dealt with their fear in different ways.

"I hope he succeeds," Vaughn said. "I hope he is able to save Sarah. They were good for one another."

An unexpected smile appeared on Colind's face, which was then mirrored on the others' faces as well. This was Aaron's gift, getting people to care. "I never realized you were such a romantic, Vaughn. Can an old dog learn new tricks?"

Vaughn laughed. "Not according to Verona."

"Those two in Khamearra," Garret chuckled. "Now if that doesn't spell trouble for the High King, I don't know what will."

"Eric and Braden will look after them," Vaughn said. "And Gavril seems quite sensible, which leads me to the reason why I sought you out in the first place."

Colind sat up. "Which is?"

"The Hythariam ambassador," Vaughn said.

"Tersellis," Colind said. "I've only just met him, but he seems to be a sensible sort."

"He is quite intelligent," Vaughn replied. "He has been spending quite a bit of time speaking with Jopher."

Despite Aaron's lack of enthusiasm with princely types, Colind knew they were key in preparing for this war. Prince Jopher Zamaridian of Zsensibar, no longer the petulant child, showed the makings of becoming a good man in his own right and would be an asset toward aligning the kingdoms. At least Jopher would be able to bolster their position and lend some credibility in convincing his father, the King of Zsensibar, of the impending invasion.

Colind wouldn't be too surprised if Iranus requested that he resume his place as Guardian of the Safanarion Order. They were an order of extraordinary people whose primary focus was protecting the lands of Safanar and her people. At the peak of their influence, they had members from every kingdom spanning their corner of the world. That is until the fall of Shandara. There wasn't time to reach out to see how many of the old members were even still alive. While the Safanarion Order was aligned with no particular kingdom, they were founded in Shandara, and with his own imprisonment, he suspected the others had faded quietly into the background to avoid being hunted by the High King and the Elitesmen. Most had assumed that Colind had died all those years ago, but perhaps there were more members like Garret, who stumbled across Aaron's path and followed him in the off chance that he was somehow still alive.

The Order was founded by Daverim Alenzar'seth shortly after meeting the Hythariam. The ruling family of Shandara was always striving for the betterment of people as a whole, but Daverim's genius was in founding an independent group that wasn't tied to any kingdom. Perhaps he should think of them as nations? A term he had heard Aaron use to describe the kingdoms here.

Colind now believed that Daverim had suspected that the Hythariam left on their dying world would find a way to reach

Safanar, but he and Reymius had been too preoccupied in their youth with changing the world that they lost sight of the looming threat hidden among the shadows. Colind had spent much of his time in the dawn of his imprisonment wondering if the Hythariam that were left on their home world had a role in the High King's rise to power. There was nothing he could prove, but the itch to find out was still there, and he meant to scratch it if he could.

Then there was Mactar, the master architect in the fall of one of the most powerful kingdoms in the history of Safanar. He was going to need an entirely different block of wood to whittle if he were going to crack that nut. He shoved thoughts of Mactar aside, another time for that one.

"Are you still with me?" Vaughn asked.

Colind shook off his reverie and nodded for Vaughn to continue.

"Tarimus," Vaughn began, "we don't know where he is or what he is doing at the moment."

"I know," Colind said. "I think we've got enough to contend with for now. I've spoken with Aaron at length about this. For now, I believe Tarimus is focused on seeking retribution from his jailer. Something I wouldn't necessarily want to get in the way of."

"My Lord Guardian," Garret spoke, "we cannot lose sight of Tarimus, not this time."

Colind sucked in a deep breath and released it. "What would you have me do?" he asked. "We have more pressing matters and cannot afford to go traipsing around the continent after Tarimus. I'm not proposing that we forget about him altogether, but just for the moment while we work to unite the nations of this world. Also, do not believe for a second that I have forgotten Tarimus's role in Shandara's destruction. He will be brought to justice, I assure you."

They grew silent as Jopher arrived on the far side of the deck. He laid out a staff and sword before him. They watched in silence as he practiced the slow forms that Aaron had taught them. The same forms that both Vaughn and Garret practiced when time could be spared. As for Colind, he was too old and had too little time to contend with that. He could draw upon the energy around them without the help of the slow forms.

Colind turned his attention back to Vaughn and Garret. "How do you think Cyrus will react when he learns that our good captain has pledged himself to Aaron?"

"I wouldn't be so naive as to say that he would be overjoyed at the idea," Garret said. "But I don't think he will have a problem with it either. In fact, the more I think about it, the more I think he might ultimately embrace the idea. Rexel has ever been aligned with Shandara."

"And he understands what is at stake," Vaughn said. "He has been quietly preparing for war since we left. With Rexel's central location, I'm sure there will be other leaders there that the ambassador will be keen to meet with."

As if they had summoned him, Tersellis joined them on the deck.

"Good morning, gentleman," Tersellis said. Having learned of their plans to help align the kingdoms of this world against the looming threat from Hytharia, Tersellis demanded to be the one to work with the other kingdoms. It was Colind's understanding that Tersellis was historically passionate about engaging the people of Safanar to share knowledge with them, but the motion was voted down. The sharing of knowledge would be a good thing, but Colind couldn't fault Iranus, and the others of the elected council, for voting to wait. Colind shuddered to think what would be done with the Hythariam technological wonders in the hands of the High King and the Elitesmen.

"I'm glad I found you all together," Tersellis said.

"How are the engines coming?" Colind asked.

Tersellis smiled. "Very good. Their engineer, Hatly, is a quick study. I knew that once we showed the Safanarions how the engines worked, they would be able to build their own in short order and, I suspect, improve upon our design. But don't tell the others I said that," he finished with a wink.

"Excellent," Colind said.

Tersellis's face grew somber. "It seems as if the world has been holding its breath building up to this moment. And now we're finally able to go out into the world and hopefully bring these people together. It shames me that the threat from my homeland is the catalyst for such actions."

Tersellis was not a young man, but it was so hard to tell with Hythariam. According to Iranus, Tersellis was well over a hundred years old. Old enough to bear witness to fall of Hytharia.

"It is what it is," Garret said.

The Raven lurched forward, gaining speed rapidly. The thrust from the engines gave a quiet whine instead of their normal roar, something in the way that they utilized the energy from the crystals to recycle themselves. Colind expanded his senses and saw the gleaming currents along the wings of the airship. The large balloon keeping the ship afloat in the air now had smaller cone-shaped engines on the sides and one on the top.

Tersellis's wide smile infected them all. "At this speed, I would expect we should be able to reach Rexel by the end of the day."

They had long left Hathenwood behind them and skirted the borders of Shandara, which allowed for little chance to encounter the Ryakuls. The landscape sped by as the engines churned the airship onward until Colind noted the tall spires of Rexel's palace in the distance. A trip that had taken Aaron almost a month, they had been able to make in a day, which was truly a marvel. He felt his chest tighten as the sight of Rexel loomed closer. He and Reymius had been close in age and full of reckless abandon in their youth, and Cyrus, too, later on. A single tear paved its way down Colind's cheek then became lost within the stubble of his gray beard.

Rexel was full of activity, but the presence of so many airships caught Colind's attention. They had built the first airship in Shandara before the fall, and it gladdened his heart that not everything they had worked for was lost in the fires. The Raven flew faster than any other airship, even when they slowed their approach as they came closer to the city. The crew of the Raven waved proudly to the crews of the other ships as they approached the airship yard to the east of the palace. The return of one of their own was greeted with great enthusiasm, but the presence of the guards armed to the teeth could not be missed. There was a city of tents outside the city proper, with fields cleared where temporary barracks were erected for the troops training nearby. Vaughn was right—Cyrus was taking the return of the Alenzar'seth seriously. Cyrus was no fool, and for that Colind was grateful.

The guards on duty at the airfield directed the Raven to a secluded spot on the far side. When the Raven finally landed, the ship was surrounded by a sea of dark-blue-uniformed guardsman adorned with silver hawks upon their chests. Colind's eyes took note of the banners along the way and was surprised to see the flag of Shandara raised with Rexel's own silver hawk. Cyrus was not being too subtle about his alliances.

As they got closer to the city, Captain Morgan flew the flag of Shandara with the dragon emblem grasping a single rose in one of its claws.

"What does the rose symbolize?" Jopher asked.

Colind smiled. "Life," he said. "The Alenzar'seth have always been fond of making statements."

Jopher nodded silently.

"My Lord Prince, if you will," Captain Morgan said from the gangplank leading off the ship. By tradition, the senior ranking nobleman was afforded the honor of disembarking first.

Jopher stood to the side and bowed his head to Colind. "My Lord Guardian," he said.

Many of the crew, including the captain, bowed in respect and voiced their approval. Colind bowed back in return. *It appears that more of Aaron's traits have rubbed off on you, young one.* Colind descended the gangplank to the wide open gaze of Prince Cyrus.

"Am I dreaming?" Prince Cyrus asked. "For if I am, I wouldn't want to wake up for anything." The Prince wrapped his arms around Colind in a firm embrace. "It's good to see you again, old friend."

"You, as well," Colind said.

"I see our mutual friend succeeded in reaching Shandara," Cyrus said. "Where is he?"

"We have much to discuss," Colind answered.

They were joined by the others, who all bowed in respect toward the prince. Captain Morgan saluted with all the practiced formality of having been in the military for the length of his life.

"Your Grace, I must humbly ask to be released from your service," Captain Morgan said.

Prince Cyrus narrowed his gaze and then looked up at the colors flying on the ship. "Why, Nathaniel?"

"I've pledged my service to the Alenzar'seth," Nathaniel Morgan said. "He has saved this ship and all of our lives a number of times. I appreciate everything you've done for me and my crew, but in this I must follow my heart, and it tells me to serve Shandara."

Prince Cyrus put his hand upon Nathaniel's shoulder. "In this we are aligned, my friend, and know that you always have a place here in Rexel." Cyrus glanced up at the ship. "The Raven looks different whence she left?"

"Yes, Your Grace," Nathaniel said. "The engines have been upgraded with the help of our new friends, and that's not all. I have the plans so we can perform those upgrades to the rest of the ships in the fleet. You see, I come bearing gifts," he finished, gesturing toward Tersellis and his two Hythariam bodyguards as they came to join them.

Prince Cyrus's eyes widened as he met the Hythariam's golden-eyed gaze and bowed respectfully.

"Peace be upon you, Gate Keepers of the West," Tersellis said. "We have much to discuss, but know this. The Hythariam are proud to ally with the people of Safanar."

"Peace be upon you," Prince Cyrus said, returning the formal greeting. "Please join me so that we may take our ease and discuss the important matters that must be addressed."

They were escorted by a group of soldiers dressed in plain, dark blue uniforms.

"My friend, why do these soldiers appear different than the Rexellian Corps?" Colind asked.

"That is because they are not Rexellian," Cyrus answered. "Some of them are, but the soldiers you see in blue are made up of different kingdoms who have agreed to take up arms in our cause. And a number are formerly from Shandara or direct decedents of those that are."

Colind frowned. "Our cause?"

They came to a plain room a short way from the airfield, big enough to accommodate all of them. Spreading around the room, some chose to sit in the proffered chairs, while others including the Hythariam remained standing. Only when Prince Cyrus sat did Tersellis take his seat, which Colind nodded at in approval.

"Yes, our cause," Cyrus answered. "War is coming. If we know anything, it's that the heir of Alenzar'seth would be the herald for war returning to these lands."

"I see," Colind said. "You are, of course, correct. War is coming, but our enemy is not only the High King and the Elitesmen. It's time you learned the truth of why Shandara fell and why it's critical that it be reclaimed."

There was a small commotion from the doorway to the room as an older woman entered, dripping of authority, as most bowed in her direction.

"Sebille, please join us," Cyrus said. "My wife," he said to the Hythariam.

The Lady Sebille stopped, her steely gaze swept the room and widened in shock as it came upon Colind. She slowly circled the room until at last she came before Colind, who stood waiting and took her hand.

"My Lady," Colind said and placed a small kiss upon her hand. Though the years had been many since he had last seen her, he was happy to see her grown into the woman she had become.

"Uncle," Sebille whispered into a hushed silence then turned to Cyrus, who smiled. "Uncle," she cried and pulled him in for a hug.

Colind smiled, hugging her in return. "Back from the dead, little flower."

He watched as his niece sat next to Cyrus and took his hand in hers. It gladdened his heart to see them both happy and alive. He had missed so much because of his imprisonment, but he denied the dark thoughts threatening to intrude upon this happy moment.

The Prince's gaze found Vaughn, and he motioned for him to come forward. "I think we need to start with what happened after you left here."

Vaughn stood up and motioned for Garret and Jopher to join him in the center of the room so they could address the crowd. They each recounted the events that brought them to Shandara, inserting their own take where appropriate.

Colind found himself marveling at the profound impact that one man, Aaron Jace, had upon all of these men before him. By all accounts, Jopher had been the equivalent of a petulant child, only to become a man on this voyage thanks to Aaron's influence. Aaron himself was barely more than a boy, with the attitude of a much younger man when last he saw him on Earth. The trials of fate had not been kind to him, but they had forged him into the leader that Aaron had become. Men from all walks of life were lining up to follow the lost son of Alenzar'seth, and while some surely were endeared to the family name, there were a number of powerful men in this room that were attached to the man behind the ancient and powerful mantle of Alenzar'seth.

The Prince silently listened to their tale and looked at Jopher with a knowing smile. "A touch of humility can be medicine for the soul," Cyrus said.

Jopher's face flushed for a moment. "Indeed it has, Your Grace."

Tersellis quietly came to the center of the room. "I would like to speak for my people at this point."

Prince Cyrus nodded and thanked the others for recounting events. Colind decided to join Tersellis on the floor as he sensed he would be needed.

Tersellis swept his golden eyes around the room. "As you know, we Hythariam withdrew from the world shortly after the fall of Shandara. We aided the Shandarian refugees as best we could, and then our leadership voted to withdraw ourselves from directly interacting with the outside world until such time as it became necessary to return. I would like for you to understand that this was by no means a unanimous vote and one that our people continue to struggle with. However, recent events and the resurgence of our old alliances have forced a change within the Hythariam. I am honored to say that the time of seclusion for my people is over, and we are proud to stand along the side of men once more to whatever end we may meet. "

Colind listened as Tersellis spoke at length of the origins of the Hythariam and how they came to be on Safanar. For the most part, the room remained quiet as all of them listened to his every word. They were joined by the visiting ambassadors from neighboring kingdoms who were already allied with Rexel. Some were learning the depth to which the Alenzar'seth had shielded their world from an invading horde, including Cyrus, who often glanced in his direction. He and Reymius had planned to bring Cyrus into the Safanarion Order with the knowledge of the Hythariam and their true origins. So many plans executed and so many that didn't see the light of day. He did feel as if he had returned from the dead. Waking up to a world at times only vaguely familiar and not at all like the one he had left all those years ago.

"My Lord Guardian," Cyrus said.

Colind looked up. "Yes?"

"I think many of us would like to hear your take on these events."

"They are true," Colind said. "As real as I am who stands before you. You've all been privy to knowledge that was once only known to a select few, myself, and the Hythariam being the last. None of us were prepared for the High King's attack on Shandara or the betrayals leading up to it. Betrayals by Tarimus, my son, who let the snakes into our beloved city and ultimately led to its destruction." Colind stopped as the murmuring of the men grew in pitch. "Enough! We can talk about the past, or we can prepare and take hold of our future. There is an army on the other side of the barrier, waiting to invade your homes. It is my belief that the promise of power taken from the Hythariam is what motivated the High King to attack."

Cyrus frowned. "It is common knowledge that Khamearra and Shandara have always been at odds, but how could they have known, and who could have made such a promise?"

"They were not always at odds," Colind said. "Just recently."

"Agreed," Cyrus said, "but the actions taken by you few, one could contrive as provoking. The balance of power shifted between Shandara and Khamearra. Some would speculate that the Hythariam were the cause, but Shandara was a place of innovation. The first airships were made there."

"I see your point," Colind said. "It was always our intent to share the knowledge of the Hythariam with the resident nations of Safanar."

"Nations?" Cyrus asked.

"It's a term that Aaron taught me," Colind said. "It's another word for kingdom or empire. I prefer it because it implies a people as a whole rather than a few key individuals."

Cyrus nodded knowingly. "I see the young scion of Shandara has had a profound effect on you, my old friend."

Colind chuckled softly. "He is quite passionate, but it was Reymius who first sparked the flame within me. I see you've begun preparations. There are a number of troops gathered outside the city here."

"Yes," Cyrus said, stroking his beard. "After the Elitesmen showed up here, breaking the treaty we had with the High King to get to young Aaron, I knew the time had come. I had advised Aaron to seek out the Hythariam and hoped that his path would cross theirs in his travels. The High King and the Elitesmen grow more bold with each passing year, traveling through any of the kingdoms they choose, dispensing the *High King's* justice. Reports of their appearance occasionally come from the more remote towns, but for them to come here in my city, I knew that war was only a matter of time. I would have expected to see Aaron and Verona with you, but clearly they are not. Where are they?"

Colind swallowed some water. "They are in Khamearra, attempting to infiltrate the Citadel of the Elite."

Pandemonium.

"It is true," Colind's deep voice rang out, silencing the chaos. "It was not my idea but Aaron's, and as Vaughn and Garret can attest, once the boy sets his mind to something, there is no dissuading him from it. Regardless, in this case I agree with him. He is exactly where he needs to be. Many who once called Shandara home will flock to the Alenzar'seth's banner, and as word spreads that number will grow. The High King will not sit idly by and allow this threat to go unchecked. Cyrus was right to see the signs once he believed that the Alenzar'seth had returned to Safanar. It falls to us to help prepare this world for an invasion of unknown proportions."

"You would have us fight a war on two fronts?" asked an ambassador whom Colind didn't know.

Colind fixed the man with a hard stare. "If it comes to it, then yes, because we have no other choice. Surrender is not an option. We only suspect that the High King is in league with the Hythariam on the other side of the barrier. The very same faction that sought to rule this world."

"How do we know if things haven't changed on Hytharia?" the ambassador pressed.

"They have not," Tersellis said. "Tell me, would an ally send a beast such as the Drake to your lands? Would an ally send the infestation such as the Ryakul?"

The ambassador grew silent, and Colind continued, "Khamearra is not united behind the High King nor are the Elitesmen. There are those who are allied with the old regime. I've been told upon good authority that Amorak's daughter, Sarah, has been involved with the Resistance in Khamearra."

"Good authority?" Cyrus asked.

"The best," Colind said. "From Vaughn and Garret, who heard it directly from Sarah herself."

"Your Grace," Vaughn said, "you've seen her, but I don't think you realized who she was as she was in disguise. Think back to when the Raven left the castle. A lone figure in black lent their aid to Aaron to help us escape and get you to safety."

Colind watched as the memory came to Cyrus's eyes.

"Ferasdiam," Cyrus whispered.

"Is Sarah with them in Khamearra?" Cyrus asked.

"No," Colind said. "The Drake has taken her prisoner." He had no wish to divulge any more information regarding Sarah and the Drake, and he hoped that Cyrus wouldn't press him right now. Something unspoken passed between the old friends.

"Aaron is in Khamearra, searching for the source of the travel crystals that the Elitesmen use," Colind said. "His presence in Khamearra will be in direct conflict with the tyranny of the High King and the Elitesmen. I suspect he will be the spark to the powder keg of revolution brewing there. Hitting the enemy where he believes he is safe is a wise strategy."

Cyrus frowned, looking worried. "If it doesn't get him killed."

"I believe your nephew, Verona, put it like this," Colind began. "Aaron has a knack for doing the impossible. I can tell you from my conversations with Aaron that he expects us to fight for this world. He makes a compelling argument that the invading horde is the real threat here. He also says that the barrier between worlds is failing. The Alenzar'seth have sheltered this world from the looming threat for almost a century, and now they call upon us to take hold of our future for ourselves. To do otherwise could plunge this world to ruin, just as Shandara is now."

The room was ghostly silent as no one dared to break the spell. Each taking a moment to gather their thoughts.

"Aaron will fight, on that I have no doubts," Colind said. "It falls to us to gather the nations of this world to fight with him. Though our fear might not pass completely, courage does not occur in the absence of fear, but in being afraid and still taking that first courageous step forward."

The group chewed on this for a moment, and Tersellis once again spoke. "We will fight and share our knowledge with any nation who will stand with us against this most grievous of threats."

"Should Aaron fall," Colind began, "should the Alenzar'seth vanish from this world, then we still need to carry the fight on."

"Excuse me," Tersellis said, and Colind gave him the floor. "I realize we're asking you to take a lot of things on faith, but there are some things that we can show you to prove that our claims are, in fact, the truth."

Tersellis removed a gray box from his pocket and set it on the ground in the middle of the room. He placed a silver sphere in the middle, which immediately began to glow and rise several inches into the air.

"Are you able to dim the lights in the room please?" Tersellis asked. After Prince Cyrus nodded his approval, the guards drew the curtains down over the windows, and Tersellis glided a hand across the glowing orbs, dimming them throughout the room.

Tersellis clicked the remote in his hand, and a glowing image of Safanar appeared, hovering in the air, causing some of the onlookers to gasp. The continents of a vibrant blue world teaming with life was displayed with perfect clarity, and the movement of the clouds shifted as the planet slowly spun upon its axis.

"This is your world," Tersellis said. "Safanar as it is today. This image is built from one of our machines we have in orbit around your world. I can explain more later, but for the time being, accept that what I'm telling you is the truth. The next thing I will show you is Hytharia. Not as it is today, but from our last recording of it."

Tersellis rubbed his thumb across the remote, and the image changed. Where Safanar's blue planet vibrantly blazed a moment before, there was now an image of a tarnished sandy world, almost completely devoid of atmosphere with merely a few splotches of green. Colind watched as Tersellis slowly swallowed the pain of seeing his home world, and his two Hythariam companions looked on with stony expressions. Tersellis let the image of the dying world hang there for a few moments before he rubbed part of the remote again, and the image changed to that of many shining dots expanding the length of the room.

"These are stars," Tersellis said. "Some are much like your sun here in this world." He walked over to one side of the room and gestured to a glowing blue orb. "This is Safanar, and on the other side is Hytharia. We estimated that the ship that brought the Drake to this world took almost thirty years to make the trip."

The moments dripped away until Prince Cyrus spoke. "What is that blinking light there? It appears to be heading for our world."

"We're not sure, to be honest," Tersellis said. "We only just learned of it two days ago. We are fairly certain that it is from Hytharia. We are still estimating the size and gathering additional reconnaissance."

"When will it get here?' Prince Cyrus asked solemnly.

"Three months," Tersellis answered. He retrieved the gray box, and the guards opened the curtains, allowing the sunshine back into the room, but the men scarcely dared to breathe.

"You heard it right, gentlemen," Colind said. "We have three months to prepare ourselves. It is an estimate, but I have the highest faith in the Hythariam, and while the timeframe could be off, it will not be by much."

"What are you suggesting we do?" Cyrus asked.

This was the question Colind had been working toward. "Prepare as you've been doing. Allow the Hythariam and Nathaniel to upgrade the airships so they can move faster. They even have ideas for weapons, but we won't have time to outfit and train all the soldiers in their use. Word will need to be spread to all the kingdoms. All of them, not just the ones that at this point in time you're on good relations with. This must be a burden shared by all."

"Where will this invading army be coming from?" the ambassador who spoke before asked.

"Shandara," Colind said. "The barrier is near the capital city of Shandara. I'm proposing that in two months time we begin moving troops into the city. There are resources that can be used as well as something else. Throughout the city are hidden caches of weapons that were put in place for this very day. They are no ordinary swords and armor, but weapons designed by the great lore masters of the Safanarion Order, based in part upon knowledge learned from the Hythariam. The caches are hidden beneath the city, which there are parts of largely intact."

"Three months isn't very much time," the ambassador said.

"You are correct, but it's the time that we have," Colind answered.

"What about Khamearra?" the ambassador asked. "The High King could move against our homes while we are in Shandara."

"The High King is not interested in your kingdoms at the moment," Colind said. "Khamearra is ripe for a civil war, but the focus of the High King and the Elitesmen will be in Shandara. However, the growing trouble in his own kingdom will put him off balance to a certain degree. We're not going to solve all the problems in this room at this very moment. We will be in contact with our friends in Khamearra, who, I expect, will cross paths with the Resistance." The ambassador was about to ask another question when Colind cut him off. "I'm sorry, but I did not get the pleasure of your name?"

"William of Lorrick," the ambassador said with a slight blush.

"Nice to meet you, William," Colind answered.

William of Lorrick chuckled. "Lorrick borders Khamearra. Perhaps we can offer some assistance to the party in the city."

Colind pursed his lips in thought, glancing at Tersellis, who nodded back. "An intriguing thought. Thank you. I think we'll take you up on that offer." The man asked good questions and seemed willing to help. He had anticipated more adversity, but the kingdoms that would offer the most resistance, like Zsensibar, were not present.

Most of the men in the room, despite not knowing all the details, gave their oaths. It was a small thing, but great things often came from small beginnings. Colind and Cyrus shared a brief nod of understanding. The group spoke in earnest about what could be done in the short amount of time that they had. Colind was surprised to learn that the camps outside of Rexel were mirrored in other kingdoms as well. News of the return of the Alenzar'seth had traveled throughout the land. Zsensibar had not joined their coalition so far and held Cyrus personally responsible for its missing prince.

"My Lord," Jopher said to Cyrus. "I wish to return to Zsensibar and convince them of the threat we face."

"Of course," Cyrus said and looked toward Captain Morgan, who nodded back. "We should get things in order here first then speed you to Zsensibar without delay."

Jopher gave a respectful bow and listened to the rest of the proceedings in silence.

Colind watched with a sense of awe as the representatives from the neighboring nations worked together. Perhaps the groundwork that the Safanarion Order had laid for such a day had not been in vain. Once again, the spark of hope beat a bit brighter from within his chest. Colind glanced out the window to the west and hoped that the small group in Khamearra was safe.

CHAPTER 9

THE RESISTANCE

With the scattering crowd, Verona scanned the area for a safer spot so they could continue to watch the guards. Eying a nearby side street, Verona noted the ladder that led to the roof, a habit instilled into him since his youth, as trouble always had a way of finding him. He gestured toward the ladder, and Roselyn nodded. They climbed up to the rooftop and kept a low profile. Verona watched as the captain conferred with his lieutenant while scanning the area. *The man is smart.* The captain made a small circle upon his brow, paying tribute to the Goddess Ferasdiam, which was all but outlawed in Khamearra. Roselyn appeared to be about to say something, but Verona motioned for silence so he could listen to the captain address his troops. Colind had stated they would find allies in Khamearra, but until now he had doubted the claim. The city lived in fear of the Elitesmen, which included the guardsman that didn't partake in the corruption so evident throughout the city. The captain, while seasoned, looked to be young as far as district captains went. He should know, as he had his run-ins with district captains in most cities he had visited, be it his home in Rexel or some other kingdom. Verona wondered how long the captain had held his post here in the city.

"What sort of captain tells his men they are not safe in their own city?" Roselyn whispered.

Verona didn't make eye contact with her for fear of becoming tongue-tied, as he had been afflicted of late. "A smart one," he answered.

After the guardsmen took the body of the Elitesman away and the miners all but faded into the crowd.

Verona looked at Roselyn, and even with her golden eyes disguised, they still held her fire and beauty. "We should follow the captain," Verona said and glanced behind them.

"What about Aaron?" Roselyn asked.

Verona glanced up the street, looking for his friend, but said nothing.

"Are you always so quiet?" Roselyn asked.

Quiet? Me?

Verona felt his tongue fill his mouth as he struggled to get it under control under Roselyn's disarming gaze. "No, my lady."

Roselyn reached out to him. "Did I do something wrong?"

Verona mustered up his nerve. "Never, my lady," he answered. "I am curious as to how you caused the Elitesman's arm to pull away from the child's throat?"

Roselyn pulled out a small black oval-shaped device that fit into the palm of her hand. "It can pull most metals with varying degrees of strength. I focused the field upon the sword and pulled," she said with a grin that set his heart pounding. Is this how Aaron had felt when he first met Sarah? How could he stand it?

"I'm sure those children appreciated you keeping them from harm's way. That was very brave of you," Roselyn said.

"Only the worst sort use children as leverage," Verona said. "One can expect nothing less from an Elitesman."

They stood upon the roof, watching the guardsmen go their separate ways, but it was the captain and his lieutenant heading down a side street that held his attention. Roselyn gently laid her hand on his arm, and he saw a cloaked figure coming down the street. Try as he might, Aaron often struggled to blend in, but the man stuck out like a sore thumb. One could easily attribute it to his great size, as he was taller than most men, but Verona knew it was his bearing, the proudness of his stance, resembling that of a stalwart defender to the sound of his voice when he spoke. No, there were some things that could not be concealed. Untarnished idealism exuded from his friend and was absorbed by most in his company, causing them to give more than they ever thought they could. Verona was no fool and knew his life had little direction before crossing paths with Aaron. He had spent most of his life stirring up mischief where he went, but he also tried to help those in need.

Verona sought the calmness within, focusing his energy as Aaron had taught, and reached out toward his friend. Aaron immediately looked up to their position and dashed down a side street.

"Did you just communicate with him?" Roselyn asked.

"Yes. It's something that Aaron was able to teach Sarik and myself," Verona answered.

Roselyn's eyes lit up. "But how do you do it exactly? What did he teach you?"

Verona swallowed. If she was going to keep looking at him like that, it would be a wonder if he would ever form a coherent thought again. "He taught us to be able to see the currents of energy all around us. To be able to draw in their power and use the energy within and outside of ourselves. I can't do all of the things that Aaron can, but there are some things that I can do."

"Can you show me?" Roselyn asked.

"I will try, my lady," Verona answered and focused himself. His perceptions immediately sharpened as before. It was getting easier as both Sarah and Aaron promised. He drew in the energy from the air into himself and then reached out to Roselyn. Her lifebeat pulsed in rhythm with her heart, and a golden hue surrounded her form as the rest of the world faded away. He reached out to her, with the yearning in his heart bearing all the beauty that filled his soul when he thought of her. For the briefest of moments, their energies collided and intertwined.

Roselyn's sharp intake of breath broke his concentration, and the energy dissolved around them. Verona's eyes found Roselyn's shocked expression, but the spell was broken when Aaron joined them on the roof.

"Hello," Aaron said.

Curse you, my friend, Verona thought and gave him the perfect excuse not to be looking at Roselyn though he longed to do so. "No worse for wear, I take it?"

"I'm fine," Aaron said. "I think we should head to the Elitesmen stronghold."

Verona frowned. "I think we should follow the captain this way. There have been some interesting developments," Verona said and recounted what they had overheard from the guards below. He watched as Aaron took a second glance at the looming towers behind them and nodded.

"Good call," Aaron agreed. "The stronghold is not going anywhere."

"That's right, and they refer to it as the Citadel of the Elite," Verona said.

They set off, quietly following the captain and his lieutenant from the rooftops, with Aaron leading the way. Before Verona could follow, he caught sight of Roselyn looking in his direction in that disarming way of hers. She still looked puzzled, but the way she watched him left Verona wondering just what he conveyed across their connection, brief as it was.

They tracked the captain as best they could from the rooftops, but keeping out of sight in the middle of the day posed a bit of a challenge. So far, they had been able to evade detection. The buildings became older and in rougher shape than the other parts of the city Aaron had seen thus far, which impeded their ability to follow as closely as he would have liked.

Aaron scanned the buildings ahead and caught a glimpse of a dome-shaped building that reminded him of the temple he had emerged from when he first came to Safanar. Roselyn slipped on a roof tile, sending it sliding to the ground. The captain suddenly stopped and looked in their direction. They hugged the rooftop, hoping that they could remain hidden. After a few moments, Aaron chanced lifting his head.

"We're going to lose them," Verona whispered.

"I think I know where they're going," Aaron answered and led them in a roundabout way toward the dome-shaped roof he had seen.

The roof had collapsed in a few places, which allowed for them to move in closer. The captain and lieutenant were joined by the other guards that Aaron recognized from before. They settled by one of the openings where they listened to the men speak. The lieutenant stepped to the head of the men and addressed them.

"I am a descendant of the De'anjard, Keepers of the Watch, Shields of Shandara," the man said with his fist across his heart.

Aaron locked gazes with Verona, both eyes wide with shock.

"The De'anjard are here?" Aaron whispered.

"Apparently," Verona whispered back. "We should tell Eric and Braden. Perhaps they might know more."

They listened in silence as the lieutenant spoke to the guards, telling them that he was part of the Resistance in Khamearra and how they had been working toward bringing down the Elitesmen and the High King. Aaron was surprised to learn that the captain was ignorant of any of these activities. He couldn't help but glare at the captain. How could the man partake in such actions, even with an Elitesman pointing a sword at his back?

The lieutenant spoke of older Elitesmen who were indirectly involved with the Resistance, and Aaron wondered if they knew they were serving an organization being headed by the former Shandarian Army. He knew the older Elitesmen did not approve of the current regime, or so Beck had told Sarah while he trained her. Thoughts of Sarah made him yearn to touch the ever-present connection with her that he felt in the furthest reaches of his mind. It took all his will not to open himself to the connection. Not for fear of what he would find, but for fear of the pain he would cause the woman he loved. He silently cursed the Hythariam and their technological advances that gave birth to such a vile creation as the Drake. No, it wasn't their fault, he reminded himself. He was dealing with a computer program of sorts, created with a specific task to bring down the barrier between worlds. As complex and advanced as the Hythariam technology was, the core problem the rogue Nanites were sent to solve was the barrier. After having ascertained the problem, the artificial intelligence afforded by the rogue Nanites created the solution that he was now a part of, and one that he hoped to break free of if he could.

Aaron turned his attention back to the guards as they split up into groups and exited, leaving only the captain and lieutenant in the temple. They spoke in hushed tones, but the bladesong burned inside him and sharpened his perceptions so he could hear the men speak as if he were next to them.

Family. The captain had a family. It was not a sword to the back that the captain feared, it was the threat to his family. Aaron felt a mixed sense of loathing and sympathy for the man. Yet, was he any different? Would he not bring down the barrier between worlds if it would save Sarah's life? The question hung there in his mind, tearing his heart in two. He was torn between doing what he thought to be right by giving the people of Safanar a chance to prepare for the coming war and his heart's desire to save the woman he loved. Aaron glared bitterly at the sky as if it somehow had a part in the hand that fortune had dealt him. The barrier was weakening as the land beneath Shandara continued to unravel. Would weeks or a month make a difference in the survival of this world? *Two weeks at the most.* Roselyn's estimation before the Nanites fully assimilated Sarah to the point that anything worth saving would be gone. Aaron turned back to the two men as they exited the building, and his gaze drifted toward the fountain. The statue of the Goddess stood proudly, her gaze staring resolutely forward. *Focus, Aaron,* he thought to himself.

"Are you okay?" Roselyn asked.

Aaron banished his dark thoughts. "I'm fine. Did either of you hear their names?"

Verona nodded. "I believe the captain's name is Nolan, and his lieutenant's name is Anson."

Aaron brought his comms device out from his pocket and clicked the call button for Eric and Braden. After a few moments and hearing a few grumbles from the device, they heard Eric's voice.

"Yes, hello?"

"It's Aaron," he said. "We just learned something that I think would interest you. The De'anjard are leading the heart of the

Resistance here in Shandara."

They waited, hearing the comms device shift hands as more cursing came from the other side. Verona chuckled, and Aaron sighed. They will learn.

"Is there some way you can seek them out?" Aaron asked.

"This is Braden. Eric hates these tiny machines. Did I hear you correctly? The De'anjard are here in the city?"

"Yes," Aaron answered.

"Okay, we'll be on the lookout for the signs. If they really are out there, we will find them," Braden said.

"Good luck," Aaron said, and Braden wished them well.

Verona laughed. "New toys."

"Yeah," Aaron chuckled as he put the comms device away. "This could help us out, if the De'anjard are, in fact, in the city."

"Fate or coincidence, my friend?"

"I'll take what I can get," Aaron answered, glancing back at the statue then turning back to Roselyn and Verona. "Let's head toward the Citadel of the Elite. I just want to take a quick look at the place, and then we can rendezvous with the others."

They made their way back toward the main streets, abandoning the rooftops due in part to the buildings being taller and closer to the looming dark towers of the Citadel of the Elite. The streets were once again filled with people going about their daily lives, but an occasional few glanced at the dark towers with trepidation. There were two dominant towers encased in smooth black stone that could be seen skyrocketing over the fifty-foot walls that surrounded the Citadel. The progression of the walls had an octagonal shape. The wall didn't bother him, as Aaron knew he could clear it if he needed to, but Verona and Roselyn had no chance. He would keep his word despite the urge to charge in blindly, plus he didn't even know if the travel crystals were held within the Citadel walls.

The top of the towers ended in a jagged crown. It was one of the highest structures in the city, rivaling the High King's palace. Between each of the spires were glowing yellow orbs, the purpose of which escaped him. Verona grabbed Aaron's arm and gently pulled him toward the side of the street, and the crowd shifted of its own accord. There were four Elitesmen in their black uniforms along with four teenagers marching among them that couldn't have been more than thirteen or fourteen by Aaron's summation.

"Initiates," Verona whispered.

Aaron clamped his jaw shut and turned back to the group. The Elitesmen strode forward, firm in their authority, followed by their four initiates, who had almost the same arrogant gleam in their eyes. They were followed by a smaller group of younger boys and girls dressed in little more than rags. All looked fearfully at the Citadel of the Elite. Aaron turned toward the gates and saw more guards and Elitesmen upon the towers and along the walls.

One of the boys with dark hair bolted from the group. An Elitesman turned and gestured with his hand, sending a blue orb streaking toward the fleeing boy.

SMACK!

The orb struck, sending the boy down ten feet from where they stood. Aaron felt another set of hands on him and saw Roselyn shake her head helplessly. They couldn't interfere no matter how much he wanted to. Two of the initiates ran over and lifted the boy up. One of the initiates admonished the other for being too rough then carried the scared boy back in line with the others.

A bald man in a dirty white apron glanced in their direction, narrowing his gaze. "New recruits," he said.

Aaron nodded back. "Are they always brought against their will?"

A look of surprise flashed across the bald man's face. "Not to worry, they will soon be like all the rest if they are to survive in there. The Elitesmen Order doesn't tolerate innocence to any degree. Some are used for training and others as targets for future Elitesmen."

The bald man headed back into his shop.

Aaron turned toward Verona. "I had no idea they recruited children."

"Neither did I, my friend."

Roselyn pursed her lips in thought. "Makes sense though, doesn't it? Easier to bend to your will." Roselyn's frosty tone wasn't lost on any of them.

Aaron glanced back at the walls and inventoried all the guards and Elitesmen. "There are so many of them." He summoned the energy into himself and sent it out toward the Citadel. The caw of a crow sounded overhead, and Aaron felt as if the ground were swallowed away beneath his feet. Then the feeling was gone. He glanced back toward the gates and watched as the last of the new recruits went beyond his view. How could anyone let this happen? He was beginning to understand Captain Nolan's predicament regarding the Elitesmen's interest in his children.

"I know that look, my friend," Verona said. "We can't save everyone we come across."

Aaron sighed. "We can't turn a blind eye either."

"What are you suggesting?" Verona asked.

Aaron frowned. "I'm not sure. We cannot do nothing."

Verona put his hand on Aaron's shoulder. "Your heart is in the right place, but we can't do anything about it now. I suggest we circle the walls of the Citadel the best we can. Have a look around and then make for the meeting point with the others."

Aaron stared silently at the gateway to the grounds, refusing to look away, but Verona was right. They couldn't do anything about it right now, but he vowed to himself that he wouldn't abandon those children. The wide-eyed look of the dark-haired boy as the Elitesman's orb struck him was firmly in his mind. There must be a way he could free them. He nodded back to Verona, and they trekked around the walls of the Citadel, noting all the gateways into the complex. Roselyn deftly held a device in her hands that she said would capture images. All things that they could use.

"I wish we could get a look inside," Aaron said.

"We should ask Tanneth or Gavril," Roselyn said. "Perhaps they have something that we could send that would escape notice."

Aaron sent probes of energy into the Citadel, and each time he encountered that feeling of the ground rushing away from his feet as if there were some type of protection in place to guard against his probing. Aaron felt a slight brush upon his senses that was so fast he thought it was a mistake. He turned back, scanning the way they had come with his eyes drawing toward the rooftops, but no one was there. Frowning, he followed the others.

***

Darven clutched to the rooftop. *The Heir of Shandara here in Khamearra?* How could he have traveled here so fast? He knew they didn't possess any travel crystals. No one outside of the Elite and High King carried them. He was the exception, being apprenticed to Mactar. He had idly stumbled upon a presence attempting to probe the defenses of the towers, and he doubted that any of the other Master Elitesmen would have detected it. They sat proudly upon their seat of power, believing they were perfectly safe despite suffering one of the most decisive defeats they'd experienced since the fall of Shandara.

Darven raised his head to watch the distant backside of the man who wanted him dead. He had been there that night on that other world when they had foolishly believed at the time that this boy, Aaron Jace, couldn't be any threat. He was wrong, but where others had died, he had lived. It was a cold comfort to know that the knife he threw that night had killed a princess of Shandara, Aaron's mother. He crept along the rooftops, easily blending in, and followed the Heir of Shandara and his two companions unnoticed.

CHAPTER 10
CRYSTALS

The waning afternoon passed into the early evening hours as Aaron and the others made their way to the inn. Despite having memorized the main thoroughfares in the city, they had to rely upon Roselyn, who showed them that the comms device also functioned as a GPS.

"Something else you are already familiar with?" Verona asked.

"Yes," Aaron answered. "But like you, I didn't know how these worked until Roselyn showed us."

They had learned a great deal about the Citadel of the Elite, but without a look inside, Aaron knew they were still flying blind. Roselyn for the most part was quiet, but Aaron caught a few glances in Verona's direction when his friend wasn't looking. Something must have happened between them while he was gone, but he couldn't dwell on it because he still had that nagging feeling of being watched.

"Still have that feeling?" Verona asked, echoing his thoughts.

Aaron nodded. "Yes, but it's so slight that I can barely feel it. It has been with me a while though."

Verona nodded, and Roselyn checked the comms device and shook her head. They came to the inn, and Verona spoke as he was the only member most comfortable with the currency used in Khamearra. Something Aaron hadn't had the time to learn, but thought it important to do so. He scanned the modest first floor of the inn, and after Verona passed the innkeeper a silver mark, he showed them to a private alcove located on the second floor.

Sarik and Gavril waved in greeting, with Gavril looking relieved to see Roselyn, then he nodded to Aaron.

"Safe and sound as promised," Aaron said.

"As promised?" Roselyn asked, glancing at Gavril and himself.

"Roselyn, forgive me, but I promised Gavril and your father that we would look out for you," Aaron answered.

The fire seemed to spike through Roselyn's eyes. "As if I'm the one who needs looking out for."

Gavril held up his hand. "If not your father then how about a beloved uncle?"

The fire flared less brightly in her eyes. "Fine."

Aaron recounted their day's events as Verona went quiet again. Shortly after, they were joined by Eric and Braden. One of whom had a large bruise on his left eye.

"Are you okay?" Aaron asked.

"I'm fine," Braden answered.

"We ran into a small spot of trouble looking for our friends," Eric said.

Aaron nodded silently, agreeing that it was probably not a good idea to speak of the De'anjard in so public a place.

"Were you able to find your friends?" Aaron asked.

"Yes, but they weren't exactly welcoming," Braden said.

"I think we scared them," Eric said. "The sect that came to this city has grown into a very secretive bunch. It took us some time to figure out how to find them, but once we did, we saw signs of them all over the city."

"How?" Verona asked.

"Quite clever actually," Braden answered. "They've stripped down the emblems that were associated with the De'anjard and Shandara. Instead of using the whole family crest, they broke it into pieces. A dragon claw here, a rose there, and sometimes a white tree. We managed to stumble upon one group, which was a mix of normal-looking citizens and some of the city guards. They didn't like that we found them, but before we could identify ourselves, they chose to run or attack. Not a full-out attack. Mostly they were buying the others time to get away. We let them go, but not before one threw something at my head."

"A horse-shoe," Eric chuckled, slapping his brother on the arm.

Aaron smiled. "Good work. Do you think you could find them again?"

"Yes," Braden said.

Aaron turned his attention to Gavril. "Have you heard from Tanneth?"

"No," Gavril said, shaking his head. "I'm not concerned. At least not yet. I expect he will check in via the comms device at some point through the night. Young Sarik and I checked the area near the High King's palace. The place is well protected as one might expect. Being the governing seat, the activity seemed normal. I tried to take energy readings where I could, but there are only small readings coming from inside the palace."

"I have some readings as well," Roselyn said. "Some parts of the Citadel of the Elite were extremely active, and then there were some areas that were quiet. Too quiet, as in no readings at all, as if the place simply weren't there. I've never seen anything like it."

"Is there a way we can get a look inside the place?" Aaron asked.

Gavril nodded. "Tanneth brought some equipment that could work. I'll send him a message. Let me do it because if he is in a position that requires stealth, I don't want to give it away." Gavril brought out his comms device but held it beneath the table and after a few moments, nodded. "Tanneth will do as you ask, but he is asking if you will meet him later tonight."

"Me?" Aaron asked.

Gavril smiled knowingly. "I would say he expects that you will be out and about this evening."

Aaron glanced at the others, seeing slightly surprised looks from some and not from others. "I thought I'd take another look around," he admitted.

Gavril nodded. "I thought as much. We couldn't find any sign of travel crystals in the palace. That is not to say there aren't any there, just that we couldn't detect any. I think focusing on the Citadel of the Elite is our best bet. We did hear about some commotion in that part of the city. Care to enlighten me about that?"

Aaron told them about the events involving the guards and their prisoners and his standoff with the Elitesmen. Then moved on to how the Resistance in the city was being led by the De'anjard, cleverly referred to as Eric and Braden's long-lost friends. He finished with the Elitesmen's recruiting practices that they had witnessed.

"I hate them," Braden said. "I knew they were malicious and cruel, but to take children…"

"I'm with you on that one," Aaron said. "I don't understand how people can just go along with this."

"Do you even know how to keep a low profile?" Gavril asked. "You need to keep a cool head even in the face of what you've seen. A smart warrior knows to make a stand on the battle ground of his choosing."

"I couldn't stand by and let those men be beaten," Aaron said.

"And the children?" Gavril asked.

"If I can help them, I will," Aaron said.

Gavril grimaced. "Okay, perhaps we can help. But please try to remember that we can't fix all the problems with this city in the short amount of time we are to be here. I applaud your idealism, Aaron, I really do, but there are others that are depending upon you. If we are to be an effective team, we need to function as such, and that includes not charging off, leaving the others exposed."

Aaron thought about Gavril's words for a moment and sighed. "I understand. I'll try to keep that in mind, but someone needs to wake these people up. Who will stand up for them if they cannot stand up for themselves?"

Gavril listened patiently. "I know your intentions are good, and my instincts agree with you, but there is a time and a place to make a stand. We're in hostile territory, and our enemy has us outmanned. If we must strike, we must use the element of surprise. How long do you think it will take them to figure out that you are somewhere here in the city? Outside of overwhelming odds, you are the only person in a generation to go toe to toe with these Elitesmen."

Aaron struggled to get his thoughts in order and took a moment to digest what Gavril was telling him. Other people's lives were in his hands now, and he had to take that into consideration. "Perhaps my being here is the best way to put them off balance. Hit your enemy where he believes he is safe. Regardless, Gavril, I will keep what you've said in mind."

They ate dinner and made plans for the next day. Throughout all of it, Aaron kept seeing the dark-haired boy being struck by the Elitesman's orb and falling down in a heap before him. The sting of being powerless to help had affected him more than he thought. Tanneth was right. He would be going back out into the night, and if he could free those children tonight, then he would.

"Gavril, a word if you please?" Verona asked.

Aaron had just left them, much to Eric and Braden's dismay, himself included, but he understood why Aaron needed to go back out there, and it frustrated him that he couldn't keep up with his friend. Not yet, at least. He and Sarik shared a determined look. They had been practicing everything that Aaron taught them and experimented with things that Sarah had only hinted at. They had come a long way since the decks of the Raven, but Verona knew that they were quite a bit away from being as adept at these abilities as Sarah and Aaron. No, he and Sarik had a long night ahead of them. He glanced longingly at Roselyn, who had followed Aaron out, but said she would be back.

"Verona?" Gavril asked.

"I understand that you believe Aaron's actions to be reckless and even fool-hardy at times," Verona said.

"I just want him to act with a bit of caution," Gavril answered.

"He carries the weight of his decisions quite heavily, I assure you," Verona said. "He blames himself for failing to protect his family back on Earth. Part of him realizes that there was nothing more he could have done, but he still feels responsible. He lost someone important to him there. A mere flicker compared to the blaze he has with Sarah, but the dead weigh heavily upon him. He understands how precious a gift life is. It is something that I don't think he can suppress because it comprises the very fiber of his being."

Gavril took a sip of his ale, and his eyes appeared haunted for a moment. "I understand, more than you can realize. I, too, was a boy thrust into a harsh world of danger and sacrifice."

Verona nodded and sipped his ale in silence. "Perhaps if more did as Aaron and made a stand against injustice, then a situation like what we have here in Khamearra could be avoided."

"If only life would cooperate in perfect little pieces. Most people just want to survive and be left alone. But I do agree that at some point enough is enough."

***

Aaron stepped out from the inn through a side entrance. The air was growing cooler in the night, but the skies were clear. His staff rested easily in his hands though he didn't think he would need it. This would be a night for the Falcons.

"Aaron," Roselyn said, "a moment before you go."

Aaron faced the beautiful raven haired Hythariam and inclined his head attentively.

"Must you go alone?" Roselyn asked. "Couldn't one of us come with you? Verona perhaps?"

Aaron smiled at the mention of his friends name on her lips. "I'll be able to move better on my own tonight, and I don't want to put you in anymore danger if I can avoid it. There is something you can help me with though." He reached inside his pack and pulled out the chrome cylinder. It still glowed with a faint bluish light at his touch. "Your father thought I should show this to you. This is how I was able to travel from Earth to Safanar."

Roselyn's eyes lit up. "A Keystone Accelerator."

Aaron smiled. "Do you know how it works?"

"In theory, yes. This one is still charging as it requires a certain amount of energy to open a dimensional doorway. This is my father's design," Roselyn said, holding it up and examining the device.

"He said as much," Aaron replied. "Do you think you can take a look at it? It's been used twice that I know of, one of those times by me, but I'm wondering if it can do more."

"More?" Roselyn asked.

"Just a thought regarding the Nanites and whether the keystone could help," Aaron said.

Roselyn's eyes narrowed. "What are you saying?"

He should have known his intentions wouldn't escape her notice. "Let's keep this between us, but I've been thinking about the Nanites. In the simplest of terms, they are machines with a purpose to fulfill. It just so happens that the purpose they are fulfilling is grotesque, but ultimately they either need to return to Hytharia or the barrier must be destroyed. It's the only thing that makes sense to me, otherwise a dumb machine would have found another way to achieve its primary programming. The Nanites were created specifically with the barrier in mind. It's a scary kind of intelligence if you think about it."

Roselyn swallowed and nodded. "I see what you mean. Focusing the Nanites upon the barrier wouldn't allow for them to create another craft and journey back to Hytharia through space. So you mean to go through the portal to Hytharia? I'm not sure if what you're asking for is possible with a device this small."

Aaron returned her gaze evenly. "Only if there is no other choice. Could I use the keystone to come back to Safanar?" He was taking a chance by telling her even this much. "Will you help me?"

Roselyn divided her gaze between himself and the keystone she held in her hands, considering. Aaron's heart thundered in his chest as he waited for her answer. She slowly lifted her gaze to him and nodded wordlessly.

Aaron sighed in relief. "Thank you," he whispered and put his hand on her shoulder giving it a slight squeeze.

Roselyn put the Keystone Accelerator away. "Be safe. I know many will flock to the name, your linage that is, but there are those of us here with you that truly are your friends."

Aaron nodded and launched himself silently to the rooftop of the building. The sky was dark, and the shadows were many despite the bright lights of the city. He squatted down and scanned toward the direction of the Citadel of the Elite. The bladesong churned within as he drew in the currents of energy around him, strengthening his muscles beyond the capabilities of bones and sinew. His perceptions sharpened, and although the night descended upon the city, he could see clear as day. He picked his target—the top of a taller building along the path to the Elitesmen's fortress—and launched himself into the air using his augmented muscles and the wind to push him along the great distance. His black cloak dragged behind him, rippling through the wind, and he spread his arms to slow his descent as he landed upon the stone building.

Aaron scanned the area again and launched into the air, once more relishing the freedom. To keep from a bone-jarring landing, he aligned the many particles hidden in the air to slow his descent. He landed with barely a sound and without damaging the rooftop upon which he now stood. Quite the difference from his clumsy trek through the forest with Sarah. He'd give anything to be back in the forest with her. The next jump brought him close to the Citadel of the Elite, and as he approached, he got his first look at the interior of the fortress grounds. To the far right was an open arena clearly visible by the ring of orbs circling the different levels. He pulled out the comms device, noted the rendezvous point to meet up with Tanneth, and headed that way to wait.

The dark towers loomed overhead, and Aaron stared at them, unable to guess as to how tall they really were. The area nearest the Citadel was quiet, even on the inside as far as Aaron could tell. His grip hardened on the staff as his gaze bored into the Elitesmen's fortress trying to rationalize a likely location for the travel crystals. A sharp pang pierced the walls in his mind through his connection with Sarah. She was in pain again, and the knowledge grated along his nerves. His hands clutched his staff, and the runes glowed softly. Not being able to head straight to her and ease her pain tore at his chest. Unable to resist his need to know, he reached across the expanse and followed the sickening pain toward its source. He dared not go any closer for fear of causing Sarah more pain. He couldn't read her thoughts exactly; it was more like feeling the undercurrents of one's intentions and what he saw in Sarah was a tangled mess of a mind at war with itself.

He recalled the time on the Raven when he tried to open the others to the energy around them, where he had become lost in Sarah's golden blaze that caressed every crevice of his skin. His mind purred at the memory for a moment before another bout of pain snapped his attention.

The tangled mess before him now was a mixture of black and gold, and he watched in horror as the multitude of golden strands comprising Sarah's lifebeat slowly turned black. The Nanites were visiting a fate worse than death with their assimilation of the woman he loved. Twisting her very love for him into its most potent weapon.

The knowledge that the woman he loved was fading before his eyes sent his own core into shambles, breaking his concentration. He opened his eyes, and the runes flared brilliantly under his white-knuckled grip. His anger wound up like a coiled viper yearning to be released. Aaron drew in the energy around him, feeding it into the rune-carved staff. He faced the direction where the Drake was sure to be and brought up the staff.

He stood poised, longing to unleash all the energy he hoarded within him and quench his thirst to kill the Drake. In this moment, he didn't care who the Drake had been before. There was something animalistic inside him that demanded he protect the woman he loved and the ever-mounting frustration of not having done so grated away at him. Growling, he turned back to the towers of the Elitesmen and pictured himself launching headlong in their midst, bringing fire and destruction in his wake. The vision fed the beast inside him that craved to make the world bleed for his suffering. And then he saw Sarah's deep blue eyes that seemed to drink up his soul, staring imploringly at him. The firelight caressing her face dissolved his rage to an angry hiss, and Aaron collapsed to his knees, tears streaming down his face.

I'm so sorry, my love. Each moment you are in pain is my failure.

Aaron wept as he had not allowed himself before, until the tears would no longer come. He knelt with shoulders slumped, giving into the darkness that threatened to overwhelm his heart into hopelessness. Time slipped by as he knelt there in the shadow of the Citadel of the Elite. The moons had risen, claiming the night sky above him. Aaron sucked in a breath, planted the knuckles of his fist into the ground, and rose slowly to his feet. He would not allow himself to fail. He chanted it in his mind like a mantra and drew strength from it. He was here, and there was still time. He pushed aside the despair he'd once given into. Now, he would do what must be done.

Aaron felt a presence off to the side and saw Tanneth patiently waiting. The young Hythariam's golden eyes met his in silent understanding. Tanneth had seen the whole thing.

Aaron strode over and sat next to the mysterious Hythariam that Gavril had vouched for. He did say he had a knack for getting into impossible places.

"I hope you have some good news," Aaron said, still shaking off the remnants of his despair.

Tanneth's lips curved into a slight grin. "Take a look," he said, holding a small black sphere about half the size of a baseball. "These are our recon drones. As you can see, they are quite small, and I deployed several of them earlier today. They have active cameras so we can see everything they are seeing. Plus, they record where they've been. We can track their progress through our comms devices. Here, watch," Tanneth said, bringing up his own comms device as a small video feed showed the drone hovering along the Citadel grounds.

Aaron couldn't help but be impressed. "This is great."

"I thought you might appreciate it, but the drone's capabilities go beyond video," Tanneth said, and he flipped through the different modes, some of which Aaron recognized as infrared and others he didn't know at all.

"I've found something," Tanneth continued. "The base of the far tower is broken out into separate chambers, which are mostly being accessed through an underground network of tunnels that lead away from the city."

Aaron frowned. "The mines would be my guess," he said, thinking of the miners that the Elitesmen were so keen to take into custody earlier.

Tanneth nodded in thought. "That actually makes sense for some of these. There is a chamber higher up where I see some strange activity."

"What do you see?"

"Well, it's some type of momentary spike in energy, only it has a pattern that I'm not able to measure. The spikes occur seemingly at random," Tanneth said.

Aaron kept looking between the display on the comms device and the tower of the Elite before them, his brain making the leap. "Random you say. Were you able to get in there and see what's in the chamber?"

"Things have quieted down now," Tanneth said. "I wasn't able to get a drone in there earlier because of all the activity in the area, but perhaps we'll have better luck now."

Aaron frowned for second. "Were you able to physically get inside?"

Tanneth nodded. "Only for a short while. I was able to get inside through that structure over there."

Aaron's gaze followed where Tanneth pointed. "The arena?"

"Yes," Tanneth said, and then he asked, "Arena?"

"I'm only guessing at the name. We have structures like those where I come from, but they are often referred to as an arena or coliseum," Aaron said.

"Interesting," Tanneth replied. "I have a drone heading back to that chamber right now. Let's see where it is and hopefully what's inside."

They were already in an alcove off to the side of the street. Tanneth hit a button, and a small holographic display appeared above the device with the image of a dark hallway. The drone hovered a few inches above the ground. Aaron winced as he saw people walk down the passageway, believing they would see the drone, but surprisingly they passed right by.

"The drone is cloaked, and in the waning light they are almost impossible to see," Tanneth explained.

Aaron nodded and continued to watch the display. The drone zoomed down the hall and curved around several stone staircases. The inside of the tower was sparsely furnished, and looked to be more of a work area than a place where people actually lived.

The drone approached a wooden door and paused for a second. Waiting. After a few minutes, Aaron realized that the drone couldn't exactly open any doors. He glanced at Tanneth, who shrugged his shoulders. The drone moved along and came to an open landing near the very center of the tower. There were copper tubes along the walls, running in different directions that reminded Aaron of pipes used for plumbing, only these were about six inches in diameter. Tanneth was about to recall the drone after it had circled around looking for an alternative way into the room, when Aaron noticed something along the ceiling.

"Do you see that opening up there along the ceiling? I can't tell if it is a shadow or an actual hole," Aaron said.

Tanneth saw it and directed the drone toward it. As it closed in, they could tell that it wasn't a shadow, but some type of ventilation shaft that ran inside the walls. The opening had a small screen blocking the entrance. Tanneth brought up a smaller secondary display that held symbols that Aaron didn't recognize. Tanneth entered a sequence into the comms device, and then there was a small flash from the display as the drone cut a perfect hole into the metal screen.

The drone squeezed its way through and headed down the dark airshaft. The display was plunged into darkness for a few moments before a soft purplish glow appeared in the distance. The drone sailed along until it came to another screen, but they could still see the room beyond. In the center of the chamber was a large purple crystal jutting from a black boulder sized rock. The rock was pock marked with channels and holes. Aaron assumed it to be a meteorite that had crashed into the planet at some point. The purple crystal looked to be about ten feet tall and had offshoots protruding in different directions.

The drone used its laser to burn a hole through the screen, and it slowly moved inside the chamber. Secured above the purple crystal was a smaller yellow crystal that reminded Aaron of the crystals that powered the Raven. Along the wall there was a large window with metallic shutters, which were all closed, but Aaron suspected they opened to allow sunlight in to power the focusing crystal. The purple crystal flashed in a momentary brilliance as its discharge was sent to the smaller yellow crystal above and then dissipated. Along the floor were containers filled with different-colored crystals. Aaron noted one filled with crystals that were black, and he recalled when Sarah had shown him her blackened, spent travel crystal as a sign that she had no intention of leaving him.

"Jackpot, Tanneth. See the dark ones there?" Aaron pointed to the container with the black crystals. "Those are spent travel crystals, and I'll wager that this one here has fully charged crystals, considering they're all glowing purple. You did it, Tanneth. You've found the source of travel crystals that the Elitesmen use."

Tanneth nodded, muttering that it was nothing, "More luck than anything else. Now comes the hard part."

Aaron frowned, "Getting inside—"

He was cut off as the drone suddenly went dark. Tanneth frowned and tapped a few commands, and the video feed played back the final seconds before the drone went dark. They couldn't see anything, so Tanneth changed the display to a panoramic view of everything around the drone. There was a movement in the shadows, only revealed from the glow of the crystals. Tanneth paused the feed at the drone's final moments. A silver, blurred image showed something destroying the drone.

A blaring shriek sounded off from the towers, and the inside of the Citadel spawned to life before their very eyes. They shared a brief look and fled down the street away from the Citadel.

***

Nolan collapsed into his chair at his desk, utterly exhausted, but at least his family was safe, even if a little confused. The agents of the De'anjard were able to move quickly and intercept them all to keep them from harm's way. Part of him was a bit uncomfortable with of how easy it was to convince his wife and children to follow the agents of the Resistance simply because they donned a guard's uniform. He shuddered at the thought of what would have happened if the Elitesmen had reached his family first. He hadn't been able to see them, but Anson requested that he write his family a note, which he hastily did, informing them that they were in danger and to trust the people they were with. It wasn't elegant, but it got the point across.

"I'm sorry, Nolan, but it's not safe for you to go to them now," Anson said quietly.

Nolan sealed the letter and handed it to his friend. He was placing an awful lot of faith in the man. The very lives of his family were in his hands, but he understood. "I know. I just don't like it."

"They've already been to your house," Anson said.

Nolan sighed, wishing he had a pint of dark ale in front of him instead of water. "What is to stop them from coming here and taking me by force?"

"Isaac, for one," Anson replied. "He is right outside the door. He was part of the faction that left the Order of the Elite when

Shandara fell. He survived the culling, and it was not because he was unskilled."

Nolan glanced toward the doorway to his office and saw the shadow of the quiet old man that stood outside it. Isaac wore a dark leather duster concealing a heap of weapons beyond that were carried by ordinary Elitesmen. What made the hairs on the back of his neck stand on end was the fact that people appeared to ignore Isaac's presence, as if his imposing form wasn't standing there in front of them. He found Isaac's presence unsettling to say the least.

"Are you sure about him, Anson?"

"As sure as I can be. I've worked with Isaac before, and if he didn't want to be here to help, he wouldn't. You can trust me on that."

Nolan nodded. "I don't really have a choice now do I, but you already know that. I gave you my word. I'll do what I can."

Isaac gave a soft knock on the door, and they both looked up as a messenger from the captain commander's office came in. The messenger gave Nolan a salute, retrieved a sealed envelope from his satchel, and handed it to him. Nolan took the letter and read it silently.

"Tell his Grace I will mobilize the guards at once," Nolan said to the messenger, who then left the room.

"What is it?" Anson said.

Nolan reread the letter just to confirm. "Something big is happening. They're mobilizing guards from three districts to converge at an inn. We're to surround the inn and capture all those inside. The Elitesmen will be on site, and we are commanded not to move in until they have arrived. We have fifteen minutes to get there."

Anson nodded and followed him out of the office as Nolan gave orders for the night watch to gather in front of the station. The letter didn't explain much, but Nolan had a sinking feeling that this night was about to get a whole lot more complicated.

CHAPTER 11
SACRIFICE

Verona sat at the table talking quietly with Sarik and Eric. Braden left them, heading to one of the rooms they had rented toward the back of the Inn. Gavril stayed with them, occasionally surveying the room. He visibly relaxed when Roselyn joined them. She looked a little upset, but shook her head at Gavril's questioning glare. Instead, she turned to Verona, and for a moment his heart thundered in his chest and he felt the heat rise to his face.

"My Lady?" Verona asked.

"Your friend is something else."

Verona snorted. "He tends to have that effect. What has he done this time?"

Roselyn shook her head, and Verona drank in the sight of her black hair cascading down her shoulders.

"Nothing yet, but he's gone off, so I'm sure we're in for an eventful night. You'd never believe he nearly died a short while ago." She turned to Eric. "Would you mind moving to sit right there, please?"

Once Eric heaved his muscular bulk into the chair, Verona noticed that the view of their table was sufficiently obscured to keep most casual onlookers from observing. Gavril sat forward, waiting. Roselyn pulled a shining cylinder from her pocket, and Gavril gasped.

"Is that...?" Gavril asked.

"Yes," Roselyn answered. "Our absent friend had it. It appears this is how he was able to travel to Safanar in the first place."

"What is it?" Verona asked. He was becoming quite proficient at not stumbling over his tongue when Roselyn spoke to him.

"It is called a keystone accelerator," Roselyn said. "It opens a doorway to other dimensions. In this case, from Aaron's Earth to Safanar."

"I thought Iranus couldn't account for its whereabouts," Gavril said.

"It was a prototype," Roselyn said and looked around at the patrons in the common room. "I'm going to my room to take a look at it in private."

She nodded to all of them, her gaze lingering for a moment on Verona who failed to still his beating heart.

"You, too?" Eric asked after she left.

Verona sighed and glanced back at the men around the table. "What did Aaron say about being fortune's fool? That is what I've become."

Gavril was about to say something, but Verona's gaze snapped to the front of the inn the same instant as Sarik's did. He focused himself, drawing in the energy around them, and stretched his senses away. Verona surged to his feet as he felt the presence of many men surrounding the inn. The rest of the men came quickly to their feet.

"What's wrong?" Eric asked, gripping the sword on his belt.

Verona glanced behind him in the direction that Roselyn had gone. "We're surrounded."

The front doors burst open and men in black uniforms all bearing the silver dragon emblem of the High King poured in. Eric flipped the nearest table, scattering the men in front of them. Verona heard Roselyn scream from behind him, and he dashed down the hall as the common room erupted into chaos.

"Shandara!" Eric bellowed, bringing the shield of the De'anjard to bear as he drew his sword.

Verona nearly collided with Roselyn as she fled down the hallway.

"There are too many that way," she gasped.

"Up the stairs," Verona said.

They took the steps two at a time and came to the landing above the common room. Eric was in the center, drawing the attention of all the High King's guards, using his shield to knock them back two at a time. Sarik was pinned down by a group, and Roselyn gasped as Gavril went down. He had to help them. Verona unslung his bow and smoothly fired an arrow taking down one of the guards holding Gavril down. The Hythariam joined Eric in the center of the fray, fighting the guards hand to hand. There was a growing number of wounded guards littering the floor.

"Go!" Gavril shouted up at them.

Verona grabbed Roselyn's wrist and turned to flee. There were three flashes, and immediately before him were three Elitesmen with their weapons drawn. Verona swung his bow and hurled himself into the Elitesman, knocking one of them off the landing. The other two spun out of the way and shot their hands in front of them. Two blazing metal bands appeared and closed around his wrists and feet, collapsing him into a heap. He heard Roselyn fall to his side. Verona growled, struggling to free himself from the bonds, but there was nothing he could do.

Eric was being overwhelmed as Braden came to his side, tackling three guards at once. The Elitesmen danced amid the men, immobilizing them as they went. First Gavril and then Sarik. Eric saw the oncoming Elitesmen and pushed Braden through a window out the side of the inn.

"Live free, my brother," Eric yelled and faced the Elitesmen.

The forward Elitesman thrust his hands forth, hurling an orb. The orb bounced harmlessly off the shield of the De'anjard back toward the Elitesman. Eric roared and charged forward, launching himself into the air while bringing his shield down upon the first Elitesman and swinging his sword toward the next.

The Elitesman caught his wrist with glowing hands, and Eric came to his knees, crying out in pain as he dropped his sword. The Elitesman sneered over him, and the other rained down blows upon his exposed back. Eric heaved to his feet and swung the Elitesman that held onto his wrist into the other one and brought his shield down in a crushing blow to the man's neck, killing him.

Eric roared as he charged forward, plowing through the guards and shoving them aside. A third Elitesman appeared at his back, and Verona cried out as twin daggers plunged into Eric's side. Eric collapsed to his knees, unable to draw breath as the daggers pierced both his lungs.

Verona strained against his bonds as he watched his friend collapse stiffly to the floor, blood pooling at the Elitesman's feet. The Elitesman looked up in his direction. Their eyes locked, and Verona pulled in the energy around him, wanting for the first time to lash out using what Aaron had taught him. The room darkened until he could only see the sneer of the Elitesman and Eric dying at his feet. Verona projected his rage-filled scream into a thrum of force that sent the Elitesman sailing through the wall of the inn. The last thing Verona saw was an armored fist that knocked him unconscious.

***

Nolan's men had arrived at the Blue Lantern Inn on the heels of Captain Commander Josef's men. The captain commander sneered in his direction and sent him to cover the back of the inn and alleyways, while his men made ready to storm the front.

"Stop any of the people from escaping. We are to capture these patrons, as they are believed to be the cause of dissidence and destruction near the Citadel of the Elite," Josef said, then waved them away.

Nolan deployed his men to the back of the inn, which itself was a three-story wooden building at least a hundred feet across, including a covered porch. The smell of a smoking hearth laced

KEN LOZITO | 171

the air. He was pleased to see so many of the guards that they had met with in the temple of the Goddess return to the station and accompany him tonight. They made up more than a third of the men he had brought with him, and it was those men that he kept closest to him, knowing that he could trust them.

"Do you know anything about this?" Nolan asked Anson in hushed tones after deploying the men to cover the alleys leading away from the inn.

Anson shook his head, and Nolan didn't have time to ask any more questions as they heard the captain commander's men break through the doors of the inn. He kept his men outside, as their orders were to lend support if needed. Screams came from inside the inn, and several patrons attempted to escape out the back. His men took them into custody, and he was pleased that they didn't use an excessive amount of force.

From the commotion inside, it sounded like the captain commander's guards were being met with heavy resistance. A dark shadow crashed through a window and into the middle of the alleyway. Nolan's men retrieved the bear of a man that laid unconscious, struggling to carry him even this far.

After a few minutes, the sounds of struggle died down from inside, and an Elitesman appeared in the doorway.

"You there, Captain," the Elitesmen said. "Take your detainees and interrogate them. If anything appears out of place, you are to send them to the Citadel immediately. Is that understood?"

"Yes, my lord," Nolan answered.

They gathered the people they had captured and slung the

unconscious form over a horse and headed back to the district headquarters.

***

Aaron and Tanneth quickly navigated the rooftops heading away from the Citadel when both their comms devices started blinking red. They stopped, and Aaron scanned for signs of pursuit while Tanneth opened his comms device.

"They're in trouble," Tanneth said.

"Where?" Aaron asked.

"They're still at the inn," Tanneth said.

"I can go faster myself," Aaron said.

Tanneth plunged his hands into his pack and pulled out a golden rod a little more than a foot in length. Tanneth clicked a mechanism on the side of the rod, which fanned out at the points to form discs. He placed it down in front of him and stepped onto the discs, bands extended over his feet. Tanneth keyed a sequence on his wristband and hovered off the ground.

"I think I can keep up with you," Tanneth said quietly.

Aaron smiled and nodded, then launched himself into the air, heading back toward the inn. He glanced back a few times to see Tanneth skating across the air, keeping pace with him. Aaron nodded back to him and really turned on the speed, using the air to propel himself forward, and skipped along the rooftops of the sleeping city. They stopped at a building near the inn. The Blue Lantern where they had agreed to stay for the night was crawling with guards in black uniforms. The silver emblem of the dragon caught the light from the orbs that dotted the street below.

"How could they have found them?" Tanneth asked.

Aaron shrugged his shoulders. "I'm not sure." He didn't think they had been followed, but then his stomach sank. He had that nagging feeling along his senses and cursed himself for not paying more attention. "We may have been followed, but I couldn't be positive, and there wasn't enough evidence..."

Tanneth grabbed his arm. "You couldn't have known. We're in enemy territory. We should assess the damage and decide from there."

Aaron nodded and turned back to face the inn. They moved in closer to get a better look. There were many guards mixed in with a few Elitesmen.

I shouldn't have left them.

People were filing out of the inn, and Aaron saw the unconscious forms of Verona and Gavril, followed closely by Sarik and Roselyn, who huddled nearby.

The energy of the bladesong churned inside him as he drew the Falcons from their sheath.

"No," Tanneth said, grabbing his arm. "If you go down there you will kill them all."

The words of Tanneth penetrated the walls of his anger, but his body was poised to spring.

"You're right," Aaron said, tensing his jaw.

A few moments later, they watched three Elitesmen approach their captured friends, and in a flash of light, they were all gone. Aaron could guess where they were taking them and glanced back at Tanneth.

"We'll be heading back to the Citadel sooner than expected."

"Where are Eric and Braden?" Tanneth asked.

A horse-drawn wagon pulled up, and the guards piled up dead bodies carried out from the inn. Two guards struggled with a large body, and Aaron felt a cry freeze in his throat.

Eric, no!

Aaron struggled against Tanneth's grip. Eric was dead. He scanned the crowd, looking for Braden, but couldn't find him. Aaron refused to believe that Braden would abandon his brother. An Elitesman reached into the wagon and took something from Eric's body.

Aaron sheathed his swords and drew his small curved ax.

The shield of the De'anjard extended in the Elitesman's hands, showing the Alenzar'seth coat of arms emblazoned upon it.

Aaron was poised to unleash the ax and kill the Elitesman holding the shield. The very same shield that Eric unearthed in Shandara with an enormous sense of pride. In a flash, the Elitesman was gone.

Aaron secured the ax to his belt.

"I don't see Braden. Let's circle around and see if he is in the back," Tanneth said.

Aaron nodded, and they circled to the back of the inn. Aaron took grim pleasure at the number of dead and injured guards, knowing full well that Eric had fought to the bitter end.

They said nothing more as they came to the back of the inn. Aaron immediately recognized the district captain from earlier and saw his second in command hovering near an unconscious

Braden lying across the saddle of a horse. Aaron sighed in relief as he realized that Braden was breathing and took a small amount of comfort knowing that Braden, for the moment, had escaped the Elitesmen.

"I can't let them take Eric's body like some piece of meat," Aaron said.

Tanneth nodded. "I'll take care of it."

The Hythariam slipped silently away and returned a short while later. "We have a few minutes. Then we should be away from here."

Aaron nodded. The captain was leaving with Braden in tow, and they decided to follow. They would free Braden first before going after the others. A loud explosion painted the street in an orange blaze, and a plume of smoke rose into the air. The streets echoed the cries of the guards at the front of the inn. Captain Nolan, Aaron noted, did not look back but kept heading away from the inn. With a grim nod to Tanneth, they followed Braden's unconscious form amid the guards and the rogue district captain.

CHAPTER 12

AN ALLIANCE

Nolan snapped his head back at the sound of the explosion and was about to order his men back, but decided against it. The captain commander's men could deal with the cleanup. He motioned to two guards. "Have a look and see if they need aid. If the commander's men are okay, then return to headquarters." The guards saluted and headed off.

"What do you think caused the explosion?" Anson asked.

"Don't know, but I'm glad that none of us were in front of the inn," Nolan answered, glancing at the rooftop. "I think we have a shadow."

Anson nodded, not looking up. "Do you want me to look into it?"

Nolan thought about it for a minute and shook his head. "No, if it's the Elitesmen then there is nothing we can do, but if it's the same man who helped us earlier today, then I don't want to send him off."

Nolan felt the wheels turning in his mind as the pieces slowly slipped into place. He glanced at the prisoners taken from the Blue Lantern Inn and moved closer to Anson. "I don't think he was alone. I think the whole purpose of the night raid was to capture the man's companions. And if he's following us, then it seems that one of his companions is among our captives."

Anson nodded in understanding and took a closer look at their prisoners. After peering at them for a few seconds, Anson turned back to him. "I think you're right, and I would wager that the unconscious man is tied to this. Look at his build. He has the build of a warrior."

Nolan glanced at the unconscious man and nodded. "I won't give him up to the Elitesmen if I can help it. When we get back to the station, I want him secluded away from the others. Be quick and use only men you trust. Treat his wounds, but post some extra guards just the same, because I doubt when he wakes he will realize we mean him no harm."

"Yes, Captain," Anson said and saluted.

Nolan returned the salute and watched as Anson made his rounds among the men and took point near their mysterious prisoner. It took all his will not to look at the rooftops, being both afraid at what he would find and wary of what he couldn't see.

***

Aaron and Tanneth followed the guards from the rooftops, keeping pace easily. They kept silent with Aaron still stuck between disbelief and acceptance that Eric was dead. He tried to deny the guilt within that selfishly demanded that he should have fought by his friend's side and could have turned the tide by allowing them to escape.

He gave grief's guilt its due then allowed reason to slowly push those thoughts aside, only to have it start again. Sarah had tried to tell him that he couldn't be everywhere at once, nor could he protect everyone around him, but there could be no denying the fact that they'd been caught in a moment of complacency. Now the Elitesmen had captured all but himself, Tanneth, and Braden. He had thought they could move in the city undetected, but then the incident with the miners occurred. This was all his fault. He had brought the attention of the Elitesmen down upon them, and his friends had paid the price. The blaring truth dragged at the pit of his stomach, making him feel hollow and empty inside. Even though they all knew the risks coming here, Aaron couldn't help but feel responsible. This was the burden of being a leader, and there was nothing he could do for Eric but take the fight to the Elitesmen by striking in the very place where they thought they were safe. He would prove them wrong. He vowed to make the Elitesmen fear the shadows.

Tanneth motioned down to the street, and Aaron noticed that the lieutenant had taken up point nearest to Braden. They must have realized that Braden was somehow connected to him. His thoughts were confirmed when the lieutenant brought Braden into the district headquarters through a side entrance by a small number of guards broken off from the main group.

"Do you have any drones left at the Citadel?" Aaron asked.

Tanneth nodded. "I didn't pull them out. I just had them shut down after we tripped the alarms."

"We need to find out exactly where the others are being held if we're going to have any hope of a rescue," Aaron said.

"What are you proposing?" Tanneth asked.

"I want you to have the drones look for the others. We know that there is a way into the Citadel through the arena, but what if there is another way? I will go and get Braden," Aaron said.

"By yourself?" Tanneth asked.

Aaron shook his head. "I think I have a friend on the inside. They are part of the Resistance and could perhaps mobilize the De'anjard remnants in the city. I won't know until I go down there."

Tanneth nodded and then frowned. "Do you intend to just walk in there?"

Aaron's lips lifted into a small grin. "I thought about it. Just walk in there and ask to see the district captain."

"What makes you think they will let you in?"

"I'll think of something. If things go badly then I'll try and get Braden out by force," Aaron said.

"You're right, we need to divide our efforts if we are to have any hope of success," said Tanneth.

"Thank you for agreeing," Aaron said.

"Let me show you how to call up the video feeds from the drones. I will highlight the important finds in a way that will be easy for you to find," Tanneth said and began showing him the sequences to bring up the video feeds. It was actually quite easy. The Hythariam designed their interfaces for simplicity rather than complexity, which Aaron appreciated.

"I think you have it," Tanneth said after Aaron went through the sequence a few times on his own.

"Be safe," Aaron said.

"Safe journey to you as well," Tanneth said, and then he melted into the shadows, heading back toward the Citadel of the Elite.

Aaron studied the district guard headquarters. The bustle of activity had died down as the night drew on. He could try sneaking in through the side entrance, but dismissed the thought because he didn't want to cross swords with people who could be allies. Going through the front door in this case was the best approach. He leaped down to the street and walked purposefully toward the building, saying a silent prayer for the safety of his friends, hoping that fortune had not entirely forsaken them this night.

The district headquarters with its marbled facade and polished columns appeared more impressive from the street than the rooftops. Aaron walked calmly up the wide staircase without any of the guards giving him more than a passing glance.

He pushed open the metallic gray doors, which yielded easily and required very little force once he engaged the handle. The air had the faintest hints of a musky leather aroma mixed with the sweet smell of a smoking pipe. The inside was swept clean and held the inner trappings of a police station with a duty clerk sitting behind the counter, grumbling to himself. Behind the clerk was a room filled with mostly empty desks. A few guards were stationed throughout, with some polishing their armor or sharpening a blade. More than a few glanced in his direction.

Aaron approached the desk slowly, and the clerk looked up at him.

"Can I help you?" the clerk asked.

"I'd like to speak with Captain Nolan please," Aaron said.

The clerk narrowed his gaze and then glanced at the clock hanging on the wall. "A bit late, isn't it?"

Aaron glanced at the clock and then back at the clerk. "I have some information for him."

The clerk did not look impressed and frowned. "You can leave it with me, and I'll pass it along to the captain. He's quite busy at the moment."

Aaron silently cursed the clerk in his mind and kept his eyes from rolling in annoyance. "I understand that he is busy. I can wait for him, if that will suffice. Can you tell him that I know his family isn't safe and I'm here to help him with that?"

The clerk took a long look at him, seeming to judge whether Aaron was a threat. After a few seconds, he sighed. "You can have a seat over there," he said, gesturing to one of the empty wooden chairs on the far side of the room.

Aaron went over and sat down. The clerk waved over one of the guards and whispered something. The guard nodded and headed toward the back. The minutes dripped past, and Aaron wondered whether his message was being delivered or if they were simply gathering more men to try to arrest him.

After about ten minutes, the captain came around the clerk's desk and stopped mid-stride. His uniform held the golden tips of an officer's wings on his collar, and his dirty blond hair was tied back into a ponytail. The captain looked to be a few years older than himself, and his hazel eyes held an edge to them as they noted the rune-carved staff in Aaron's hands with a flicker of familiarity.

They each appraised the other for a few moments before the man smiled in greeting. "Captain Nolan, at your service."

"Aaron Jace. I appreciate you taking the time to see me, Captain. I know you must be busy. Is there someplace where we may speak privately?" Aaron asked.

The captain nodded. "Of course, if you will follow me," he said and led Aaron through the building toward the back.

They came to the captain's office, and as they entered, Aaron saw an older man off to the side. Without thought, Aaron brought his staff up, and the runes flared faintly.

"Elitesman," Aaron spat, but much to his surprise the older man made no move.

Nolan held up his hands. "It's all right. He is with us and not with the faction you've faced."

Aaron drank in the sight of the old Elitesman in his dark leather duster and his shocking blue eyes alight with energy. They both stared at the other ,scarcely daring to breathe.

The Elitesman slowly held up his hands and bowed his head. "I could hardly stand against one such as you, Ferasdiam Marked. You have nothing to fear from me. I do not stand with the Elite Order, not as it is today. Not since they betrayed the Shandarian masters of the Safanarion Order."

Aaron's breath quickened, and he held the energy within him, waiting for the inevitable betrayal that must come from any Elitesman. It was then he thought of Sarah and the Elitesman named Beck who trained her. Beck couldn't be the only one of the old order of the Elite who did not hold with the current regime's ideals.

"There are none here who can stand against you, but you look to be in need of aid regardless," the Elitesman said.

Aaron stood poised with his staff ready, but he couldn't sense any malice in the Elitesman, nor the superior arrogance that was ever-present in the others he had faced. He relaxed his guard, but kept a firm grip upon the bladesong within.

"I do need help," Aaron said. "You have my friend held captive here, and your Elitesmen brethren have taken the rest."

Nolan cleared his throat. "Your companion's wounds are being treated, and I will take you to him momentarily, but there is something I must know. Were you the man who fought the Elitesmen earlier?"

Aaron slowly nodded.

Nolan's eyes widened. "How?" he whispered.

Aaron glanced at the Elitesman before returning his gaze to the captain. "I am the only living scion of the house Alenzar'seth."

"Ferasdiam," the Elitesman whispered.

"Isaac?" Nolan asked.

The Elitesman Isaac ignored the captain. "The rumors are true. You are Reymius Alenzar'seth's heir. Why would you come here to Khamearra?"

Aaron took a long look at the Elitesman and decided to take a chance. "Did you know a man named Beck?"

The Elitesman's eyes widened in shock, and he took an involuntary step forward. "Yes. He and I were part of a smaller group who broke away from the Elitesmen."

Nolan frowned. "How is it that no one has ever heard of this rogue faction before?"

"We stayed out of sight and let the Elitesmen be, and they stopped trying to hunt us down. But now…"

"Not all of you stayed on the sidelines," Aaron said. "Some of you have worked with the De'anjard here in the city, and the daughter of the High King was too good an asset to let slip through your fingers."

"You know Sarah?" Isaac asked. "We've not had word from her for over a month."

Aaron swallowed. "I know her, and she is the reason I'm here in Khamearra."

"She is in Khamearra?" the Elitesman asked.

"That's not what I said," Aaron answered, but was surprised to hear the note of concern in the Elitesman's voice. "She is the reason I'm here."

The silence hung in the air for a few moments before Nolan said quietly, "I will take you to your friend now."

Aaron followed the other two men from the room after silently insisting that the Elitesman go first. He would be damned if he was going to let an Elitesman at his back no matter what their current allegiance happened to be.

The captain led them down to the lower levels of the building through several hallways to an almost deserted part of the station. Nolan, it appeared, wasn't taking any chances. He stopped before opening the door.

"We moved him here because I wasn't sure when the Elitesmen would return. We were to question the patrons of the inn and report anything suspicious. Having been witness to how the Elitesmen treat their prisoners, I was intending to keep him hidden for his protection."

Aaron nodded. "I appreciate your efforts, Captain. We overheard you and your lieutenant speaking earlier today, and I know the Elitesmen were threatening your family."

Nolan clenched his teeth. "They did, but they are relatively safe for the moment," he said, and then he opened the door.

Braden lay on an old bed in the dusty room, still unconscious. A pitcher of water was by the bedside, and a man in a brown shirt was rubbing a damp towel on his forehead. To the side was the lieutenant.

"Sir," the man in the brown shirt said. "He has minor wounds, and the blow he took to the head just happened to be in the right place. I think he will be fine and should wake up soon."

"Thank you," Nolan said and looked at Aaron. "He's our resident surgeon."

Lieutenant Anson saluted the captain upon entering the room, but Aaron ignored the man as he approached the bed where Braden appeared to be sleeping.

"Do you know what happened to him?" Aaron asked, checking him for any signs of wounds.

The lieutenant shook his head. "We found him in the alleyway next to the inn. He was thrown forcefully from the window. He has not regained consciousness, but as our surgeon said, he will be fine."

Aaron nodded and gently shook Braden, who remained unresponsive. He sent a tendril of energy to Braden and saw that his lifebeat was greatly diminished. Aaron focused the energy around them, pulling it through him and fed it into his friend. The body, as always, was an effective conduit. Something seemed to awaken within Braden, as he felt him grasp at the energy being fed. Braden had become more open to the process as of late than when they had tried on the deck of the Raven a few weeks before.

Braden shot upright in the bed, sucking in a loud gasp of breath and shouting his brother's name. Then he sank back down and looked at Aaron in surprise, still gasping for breath.

"You're going to be fine. Just take it easy," Aaron said.

"The Elitesmen attacked us. The others..." Braden said, his voice trailing off questioningly.

"The others were captured," Aaron said.

Braden rubbed the top of his head. "When I find Eric, I'm going to teach him a thing or two. He threw me out a window."

Aaron felt his lips curve into a smile for a split second despite the lump in his throat. "Braden, your brother was killed in the attack."

Braden looked back at him dumbfounded, as if he hadn't heard him right. Aaron met his gaze and watched as Braden struggled to his feet, shaking his head.

"Dead?" he whispered.

Aaron nodded back, and Braden sank to his knees. His body slumped then immediately went rigid as fire sparked in his eyes. Aaron felt the bladesong churn within Braden as never before. Braden's eyes slowly scanned the room before they settled upon Isaac. His eyes widened in rage, and he lunged for the Elitesman. Aaron caught him in midair.

"No!" Aaron said, struggling against Braden's muscular bulk. "He is not with them." He had to repeat it two more times before Braden stopped.

Braden relaxed enough for Aaron to let him go, but kept a wary look on the other men in the room.

"They saved your life, kept you hidden from the other Elitesmen. Otherwise, you would have been captured with the rest," Aaron said, and this seemed to penetrate Braden's fog of grief. He nodded in appreciation to the other men but still kept a wary eye on the Elitesman. "We need to get into the Citadel of the Elite to rescue our friends. Do you know a way inside?" Aaron asked.

The captain and lieutenant shared an incredulous look, while Isaac the Elitesman looked slightly amused.

"They are no doubt in the holding rooms where new prisoners are taken," Isaac said. "But if they know that they are associated with you, then they may take them to a different place inside the fortress. Probably one of the towers to the Grand Master's Hall. As for getting inside…" Isaac's voice trailed off as he glanced back at the captain. "We'll need the help of the Resistance, which will take some time. I wouldn't advise to go charging off tonight."

"But the others," Braden insisted.

The Elitesman's eyes became cold and calculating. "You stand the best chance at a rescue if we do some planning first. If you charge off at this moment, the only thing you will accomplish is getting them killed, and yourselves, too, for that matter. Have no doubts they will kill them all in the blink of an eye if it means keeping you from getting to them. The Elitesmen are no strangers to ruthless tactics, and right now your friends' worth is in their knowledge about you," he said with his gaze settling on Aaron.

The breath caught in his throat, and Aaron unclenched his jaw to speak. "What are you proposing?" Aaron asked, activating the comms device in his pocket in hopes that Tanneth or even Gavril would be able to overhear them.

"There is still time," Nolan said. "They took everyone from the inn, which was easily over a hundred people."

Isaac kept his gaze upon Aaron. "We use the Resistance to create a distraction throughout the city to draw their attention. They know that you will be coming. There can be no doubt about that. What they don't know is when or how. They've underestimated you up until now, but that luxury is gone. They will send their very best and most dangerous recruits after you."

"I've faced your Elitesmen before," Aaron said.

Isaac nodded. "I believe you, but have you by chance seen how they bring in new recruits?"

Aaron's mind flashed to the children he saw earlier being driven to the Citadel. "Children?" he whispered.

"What's this?" Captain Nolan asked.

"Children," Aaron said firmly.

Isaac nodded, his face grimly set. "They will send the Elite Masters to you, but they will also send their crop of specialized recruits. The ones honed for their ability to work with the energy in ways no sane person would ever think to try. This requires a younger mind more easily manipulated. They can boil your blood from the inside until your veins burst. Trick your eyes into seeing things that aren't there. They are lethal killing machines and not children, despite whatever their appearances are. Are you prepared to face that?"

Aaron swallowed the bile that inched up his throat. "I will do what I must. I will never abandon my friends. And the only thing keeping me from charging off to the Citadel of the Elite is the chance that you may offer a better way to get inside while minimizing the risk to my friends. I don't trust any Elitesman, and if I so much as suspect a hint of foul play, there will be no force on this planet that will keep me from seeking retribution. Rest assured that we may not be able to save our friends, but you can be damned sure we will avenge them."

Isaac searched his cold eyes for a few moments. "Yes, I believe you will," he said, then looked at the others. "Tomorrow night, or rather tonight since dawn is approaching, is when they will be initiating the new recruits at the arena. The Elitesmen will gather there with the new crop of recruits to test them to see if they are worthy of the Order."

"What kind of test?" Captain Nolan asked.

Aaron sensed the fear mixed with relief, as the Elitesmen had been targeting his son for such a fate.

"A series of trials that will allow for the assessment of their physical capabilities, but give light to their cunningness and ruthlessness in their bid for survival," Isaac replied.

"And the prize is induction to the Elite Order at the sacrifice of their innocence," Aaron said, unable to keep the sneer from his voice. He wanted to lash out at the Khamearrans in his midst, but their shocked looks gave knowledge to the fact that none of them had known of the practice.

"I can send word to the Resistance," Lieutenant Anson said. "They will rally, but they will need targets."

"No innocent lives are to be caught in the crossfire," Aaron said.

Anson fix him with a stony gaze. "We hold with the ideals of the De'anjard, my lord. Defend the helpless. Stand the watch. Honor your brothers of the shield. Sacrifice for the many."

Braden brought his fist to his chest as the words of the De'anjard were spoken. Aaron nodded, and Isaac cleared his throat.

"The best distraction is for you to appear in the arena at precisely the right moment. If the Elitesmen believe you to be there, then they will let their guard down, further allowing for a small group to infiltrate the Citadel."

Aaron thought about it for a second, granting that the Elitesmen had a point. "Who will go inside to free our friends?"

Isaac's craggy face lifted into a small grin. "I would offer myself, but somehow I don't think you would allow that."

"I'll go," Captain Nolan said, drawing everyone's attention.

"And since you're here to protect me," he spoke to Isaac, "then it looks like you'll have to come with me."

Isaac nodded.

"I will go with them. They will need to see a face that they can trust," Braden said in a tone that did not invite any arguments.

Aaron glanced at Braden, concerned for a moment that his friend was too hot-headed for this, but who was he to judge? They were all here because of his need to find the travel crystals. Aaron looked back at the old Elitesman. In what world would he have ever thought to trust the lives of his friends to one of them? But what other choice did he have? The Elitesman's plan made the most sense and was certainly better than shooting from the hip and making it up as he went.

"There is another thing I would like to ask you," Aaron said. "Travel crystals. Do you know where I can find them?"

Isaac's gaze narrowed for a second. "I know they are charged in one of the towers. Why do you ask?"

"I need them," Aaron answered. "I need to know how I can get inside the tower and what guards them."

Captain Nolan cleared his throat again. "I think we'd be more comfortable if we use my office for this. This way. We can use some of the maps to help in the planning."

Aaron looked back at Braden, who nodded. "That sounds like a good idea. Thank you, Captain."

"Please," the captain said. "Call me Nolan, Your Grace."

"Nolan, please call me Aaron."

Nolan nodded and led the others from the room. Once again,

Aaron brought up the rear, but allowed the men to get far enough ahead to bring out the comms device.

"Were you able to hear all that?" Aaron whispered.

"Yes," Tanneth answered. "The plan has merit. And I agree that there is nothing we can do tonight. They have that place locked down tight. I'll continue to have the drones recon for us, and you already know how to access the feeds. If I find something worthy of your immediate attention then I will let you know. But there is one more thing."

"What's that?" Aaron asked.

"Be wary of one of those men with you. I'm not sure he is being entirely forthcoming," Tanneth warned.

Aaron nodded. "I know and thanks. Be careful. I trust your reconnaissance more than another man's knowledge at this point. Were you able to reach Gavril or Roselyn?"

"I don't want to draw unwanted attention to them, but I can tell you that Gavril and Roselyn are still alive. If they can reach out to us, they will. I'm betting that Sarik and Verona are alive, as well."

Aaron frowned. "How do you know about Gavril and Roselyn?"

"Through the Nanites in their system."

"Understood." Aaron put the comms device back into his pocket and caught up to the other men. There was work to be done.

CHAPTER 13
RUMINATIONS

This was the longest Mactar had taken up residence at the fabled High King's palace in recent memory, and he hated every second of it. The furnishings were beyond compare, but all the pandering from the pathetic creatures that resided in the palace were beyond his contempt, and distracted him from the real work that required his attention. His scowl deepened at passing servants that knew better than to make eye contact with him. It only took a few examples to convey that he neither needed nor wanted anything a servant had to offer. People were meant to be ruled; subservience had been bred into them for thousands of years. The weak were ruled by the strong and the cunning.

The plush and pomp setting of the High King's court served its purpose for the masses, but the true rulers of Khamearra were the Order of the Elite who functioned as the High King's right hand. High King Amorak allowed them the illusion of a council, which he could squash at a moment's notice. Like all tools, the council served a purpose, unlike his current efforts, but some goals required certain sacrifices. The task of overseeing the training of Prince Rordan, the High King's remaining heir, with the exception of the Lady Sarah, didn't qualify as worthy of his time. The thought of Sarah brought a frown to his face before he could quell it. Sarah alone held true potential, and it was a bit of a shock to see her aligned with this Aaron Jace, the sole heir of the House Alenzar'seth.

Sarah's whereabouts were unknown, even to him, but there could be no mistaking where her loyalties lay. It was terribly vexing to be outsmarted by the likes of Reymius Alenzar'seth. The destruction of Shandara should have been enough to satisfy the ambitions of any man, but now that the Alenzar'seth had returned, the victory over Shandara had become hollow and unfinished. The resilience of the Alenzar'seth was worthy of even his respect.

For all the High King's might, he lacked the intelligence and foresight that would put him on equal footing with the Hythariam. The fact that Amorak was also Ferasdiam marked was truly an accident of fate, by his reckoning. Aaron had proven to be a worthy adversary and would be a rallying cry for the kingdoms of this world to unite behind. Not even the power of the Elite Order would be enough to bring them into line. No, Aaron was the real threat. Having no ties or ambition beyond immediate survival gave him the freedom to act in such a way that even he himself had underestimated. Their confrontation at Shandara was illuminating to say the least. His thoughts drew back to the events as they replayed in his mind.

What connection was there between Sarah and Aaron, he wondered.

Then he saw it. As Aaron transitioned from the crossroads back to this reality, he scanned the battlefield and immediately went to Sarah's side where the Elitesmen were the thickest. Only love would drive one to such lengths as to leap willingly into the fire. Mactar's pulse quickened as the pieces fell into place and a malicious smile oozed its way across his face. It seemed that the princess with the heart of ice had found something in her travels. This was something he could use. Aaron Jace was not as untouchable as it would seem. What were the chances that such a woman would find herself entangled between two Ferasdiam marked, ones touched by fate? There was no precedent for it. Two men, Ferasdiam marked, to shape the world of things to come.

The High King had remained unchallenged since the fall of Shandara, and he still hadn't come to grips with the fact that the Goddess had given her blessing to another. It was true that he himself didn't hold faith with any deity, but it didn't require faith to know the signs of a being with true power. Power that should be his. And yet here he was, observing the young prince with his Elitesman Master to teach him. Rordan had improved, there was no denying that. The Prince could hold his own against most Elitesmen, which in and of itself was an accomplishment shared by few, but in his mind, the Prince would never be a match for Aaron Jace. Reymius's heir had proven to be a worthy adversary and a very grave threat. There was nothing to be gained in not acknowledging the facts before him, and while pride had its place, he would not succumb to its double-edged sword. The window whereby he could take the power of the Alenzar'seth for himself had passed. The one success he could use was the resurgence of the Hythariam. Seeing the land of Shandara had confirmed his theory regarding the stability of the barrier all along. It was failing and it was only a matter of time.

The Drake had the ability to command the Ryakul. This was something he had seen first-hand at Shandara and was something he wanted to exploit. Being able to command a legion of Ryakuls would turn the tide in any war. Mactar's gaze swept the surrounding palace from the practice yard in which he now stood. War was coming, of that he had no doubt. Seeing the Hythariam appear in Shandara with their flying machines only served to whet his appetite of what was promised to him.

"Rordan is making progress," High King Amorak said.

Mactar had not heard him approach, but once the High King let his presence be known there was no mistaking it. "Yes, my lord. He improves every day, but as I have said before, our attention would be better served elsewhere."

The High King kept his gaze upon his son. "You mean your attention? Fear not, Mactar. The call has been sent to mobilize the armies. We will be ready for those who are foolish enough to align with Shandara."

Mactar nodded. "We should continue to hunt the Alenzar'seth and seek out the Drake. I've seen reports of soldiers from various kingdoms gathering in the Waylands near Rexel."

Amorak's eyes narrowed. "Cyrus himself is not a threat, and I believe he has very little chance of uniting the kingdoms of the east against us. Regardless, I have something special in mind for them."

"It's not just them," Mactar said. "The Hythariam have resurged. They are the real threat. They will use the Alenzar'seth as a rallying cry to unite the other kingdoms against us." Partially true, but not something he was especially concerned about.

Amorak turned to him with a raised brow. "I thought you were preoccupied by the fact that Colind's tomb now stands empty? The shadows are lengthening around you, and you are jumping at things that aren't worthy of your attention. Tell me, what is really bothering you?"

Mactar was about to answer the High King when he felt the faintest brush along his senses. A cold touch that hissed at a promise of death, followed by the echoes of a mirthless cackle.

Tarimus!

Mactar pushed out around them with his senses, but the presence was gone. There were times when he thought that madness was indeed consuming him, but at this moment he knew Tarimus had been there. The mirror of Areschel, which had given him dominion over Tarimus, remained closed to him. He had to accept the fact that Tarimus had somehow become free from his prison, but Mactar could not surmise how that could be.

"I felt it, too," Amorak said, glancing around them.

"Now we're both jumping at shadows, my lord," Mactar replied dryly.

Amorak frowned. "I have given thought to your idea about

seeking out the Drake, and I agree. To be able to control the Ryakul is too good an opportunity to pass up."

"I'm glad you agree," Mactar replied.

"I assume you mean to leave as soon as possible," High King Amorak said.

"Yes, but there is something that has come to my attention regarding your daughter."

"Has she returned?"

Mactar noted the lack of concern in the High King's tone. "No, I'm afraid she has not. You have spoken with Rordan at length about the events that occurred at Shandara. I've meditated on the events myself and have come to a realization that not only has your daughter allied herself with the Alenzar'seth, but she has fallen in love with the man."

The High King turned, sweeping his gaze around the practice yard not saying anything, but the air felt to have dropped a few degrees. Mactar would have sworn he saw the slightest of twitches upon the High King's face. So he does still care, or is it a matter of pride and possession? Mactar wondered.

"I allowed her to expend her energies with the so called 'Resistance' at my pleasure, but this…" The High King bit off his last word and graced Mactar with a smoldering gaze. "This is unforgivable. The defiance of my daughter will not go unanswered."

Mactar grinned inwardly, but maintained his composure. "What do you intend to do, my lord?"

"Do?" the High King said, then smiled mirthlessly. "She dug her own grave, and now she will lie in it. My course of action will not change. The Alenzar'seth will die. By my hand if need be."

"And Lady Sarah?" Mactar asked.

The High King eyed him. "You always did have a soft spot for her blonde looks. Very much like her mother."

"She has always been quite gifted," Mactar said, which was an understatement given that she had kept at bay the machinations of her half-brothers, the Elitesmen, and himself.

"She will live," the High King said, "and learn the price of defiance. If she was foolish enough to actually fall in love with the enemy then so much harsher the lesson."

Mactar nodded and was silent as his eyes drifted toward every shadowed corner, looking for Tarimus but not finding him.

"I'm sending Rordan to the arena at day's end," the High King said.

"Then I will plan to leave soon thereafter to track down the Drake," Mactar said.

"And how do you plan to do that exactly?" the High King asked.

"By tracking the Ryakul as well as a few other tricks I know," Mactar answered, growing more anxious for the day to end. He could leave now, but he was due to meet with Darven. The former Elitesman had become an asset and was yet another way to put the young Heir of Shandara off balance. But Mactar was ever watchful to see that Darven did not become overly ambitious. Darven had been with the late Prince Tye when they had attacked Aaron's home in a realm called Earth. Mactar would use any means to ensure victory and survival, which included sacrificing his apprentice to Aaron should the need arise. The real victory for him would be to bring down the barrier and allow the other Hythariam faction their due, letting the glories of war ensue and feeding real innovation with the whole world as his playground.

The High King strode over to his son, and the activities in the practice yard ceased. Mactar's eyes scanned the faces amid the crowd, and he saw a pale face with lifeless black eyes peering back at him, but when he blinked, it was gone. He quickly strode over to the spot, but saw nothing to indicate anyone was there other than the men who were already there.

You will never see me coming, Dark Master, a voice hissed.

Rather than spin about, Mactar kept moving in the direction he was going. He reached out and cast a net of energy all around them, intent upon finding Tarimus. A slight tremor pulled his attention toward the roof. He activated the travel crystal in his pocket and emerged on the roof, only to see the dark form of Tarimus grinning as he melted away before his eyes.

CHAPTER 14
THE PRICE OF CAPTURE

Verona felt a sharp jab of pain on the side of his head. He pushed his eyelids open and groaned as he tried to sit upright. His vision cleared, and the bitter smell of human excrement hung in the air, biting his nose. A gentle hand helped him sit upright.

"Are you all right?" Roselyn whispered.

Verona sighed and shook his head, coming fully awake. They were in a dark holding cell with bars all around.

"I am still breathing, my lady."

A small smile lit up Roselyn's face, and Verona's pulse quickened.

"Have they hurt you?" Verona asked.

Roselyn shook her head. "No. We're all here, but we've been grouped with some others from the inn. You've been out for hours. They've been taking small groups away."

"Eric?" Verona asked, already knowing the answer but dared to hope anyway.

Roselyn's face drew down sympathetically as she wordlessly

shook her head. Verona swallowed down the lump in this throat. There would be time for grief later if they were lucky. He sat up, and his motion aroused the attention of Gavril and Sarik in the neighboring cell. They all looked relieved to see him awake. While all of them appeared bumped and bruised, they were none the worse for wear.

"Is Braden here?" Verona asked.

"The last I saw, Eric had thrown him out of the window. He might have escaped," Roselyn said.

That was something at least. Verona was hopeful that Braden had indeed escaped. "What about—" Verona began, but was cut off as Gavril started coughing and gestured around them. After a moment, Verona nodded. They were not alone and probably being listened to at this very moment.

"They haven't told us what they want," Gavril said and then whispered softly as Sarik coughed loudly, *"Tanneth and Aaron are still free. Neither has tried to make contact which tells me they are planning something."*

Verona nodded and looked up as the doors on the far end of the room burst forth and a hush swept over the people in the cells. Four Elitesmen walked into the room, dressed head to toe in their customary black uniforms devoid of any markings. He sensed the energy gathered within each of them as if they constantly fed upon it. They glided to a halt in front of their cells, and with a slight gesture, the cell doors opened. Ordinary guards followed the Elitesmen and waved the four of them out of their cells. Verona glanced at the others, but did as he was told. Now wasn't the time to put up a fight, but they needed to escape.

One of the guards yanked off Roselyn's hood, and her silky black hair fell down in waves. The guards openly leered and went to grab her, but in the blink of an eye, Verona seized the guardsman's hand and twisted it, then roughly threw the man into the door of the cell where he collapsed to the floor in a heap.

The Elitesmen hissed. Two appeared on either side of Verona and bound his hands tightly behind him. The guardsman rose to his feet and planted a fist into Verona's stomach, and he collapsed to one knee, expelling his breath. He glanced above him and launched into the air, driving the top of his head into the guardsman's face. Blood geysered from the guard's face, and then the man fell stiffly to the floor, his lifeless eyes staring up at the ceiling.

"He's dead!" the guard gasped after checking on his fallen companion. The other guards moved in and drew their clubs, but one Elitesman stopped them with a wave of his hand.

"Enough," the Elitesman hissed. "Bring them forth now."

Some of the guards protested, and the Elitesman grabbed the nearest one by the throat, holding him several inches off the floor. "Do not believe for a second that I value the life of any guard more than these prisoners. You will obey, or we can find other uses for you," the Elitesman said, letting the guard fall to the ground gasping for breath.

Roselyn spared him a small smile that was gone in a flash, and as the growling guards surrounded him, he knew that his actions had been worth it. He would gladly take the beating of a thousand clubs if it spared Roselyn the leers of the prison guards and what followed them.

The guardsmen guided them away from the holding cells, but not without taking a few shots with their clubs. At least they had left the smell behind. Verona focused his mind, continuing to draw the energy into himself, and began feeding it to his aching parts. His body slowly repaired itself, and the aches faded away completely. Aaron had tried to describe the feeling as aligning one's patterns to their correct course, and he now understood what his friend had meant. He was able to draw upon the energy around them with increasing ease, but holding onto and manipulating it was something both he and Sarik continued to struggle with. Aaron had postulated that the reason he was able to achieve so much was that he had spent a lifetime learning to focus his mind without any thought to using life's undercurrents that surrounded all of them. Aaron had faith that in time they would all be able to do the things he could do, but Verona wasn't so sure.

They were brought into an empty room save for a solitary mechanical wooden chair and a table. On top of the table were knives, various steel spikes, chains, and other tools stained with blood. The pit of Verona's stomach sank to his feet.

Torture.

Roselyn! His eyes drew down in shame. He hadn't been able to protect her or get them to safety.

Some hero I turned out to be.

He banished the useless thought from his mind and focused on an escape plan.

The Elitesmen stood to one side of the room where several windows with wooden shutters were tightly closed, allowing only the faintest traces of sunlight in from the outside. Having Aaron and Tanneth show up now would be convenient, but he had no such illusions that it would happen. He wished he knew the time so he had something to measure against how long they would need to hold out until they were rescued, or, better yet, could escape. The others glanced around their surroundings, taking them in. Gavril's face looked set in stone as he regarded the Elitesmen in the room. The air of defiance grew thick around them much to the amusement of the Khamearrians.

The guardsmen gathered to the side, waiting on the Elitesmen, and Verona glanced at Gavril. The Hythariam colonel was completely at ease, and Verona suspected, judging by the impassive look in his eyes, that if Gavril were by himself, he could have escaped anytime he chose. Gavril met his gaze and gave a slight nod toward Roselyn, and Verona thought he understood. For all of Roselyn's tough exterior, she was no soldier. With the exception of Gavril, who survived the last days of civil war on Hytharia, none of them were prepared for what the Elitesmen were about to do to them. The Elitesmen's ruthlessness was known throughout all kingdoms, and despite Aaron's insistence that they were just men, Verona was afraid. He was not afraid for himself, at least not that much. He had faced death before, but Roselyn and Sarik? One so young shouldn't have these weights thrust upon him. Despite surviving the trek into Shandara, Sarik was barely older than eighteen. Verona glanced at Sarik, who stared back at the four Elitesmen with clenched teeth. Though Roselyn appeared to be the same age as himself, Verona knew she was much older, but she was a healer at heart.

The Elitesmen had done nothing but watch the four of them, who were now all bound at the wrists. Verona looked down at his shackles and noted the smooth surface that held neither lock nor clasp. He focused and probed along the smooth shackles, sensing the energy within that kept them locked together.

"One has been trained," an Elitesman hissed.

Verona looked up quickly. The Elitesmen removed their hoods, revealing bald heads adorned with black tattoos. One stepped forward, coming before him. Verona returned the Elitesman's cold gaze and felt him graze his senses, but Verona did not respond. The Elitesman moved on to Roselyn and reached out, putting his hand under her chin to get a better view of her face. Roselyn met the Elitesman's challenging stare, and then he stepped back and closed his eyes. Roselyn shrugged her shoulders at first and then started shaking off something that she couldn't see.

"*Hythariam!*" the Elitesman hissed.

Gavril roared, and in a single motion broke the shackles that held him and launched himself at the Elitesman. The Elitesman stepped back, attempting to use Gavril's momentum against him, but he spun, kicking the Elitesman back toward the others.

Verona stepped forward, but Gavril held up his hand.

"Protect her. Use what Aaron has taught you," Gavril said, then he spun and threw a small object at the advancing guardsmen.

An explosion rocked the room, capturing both the guards and

the Elitesmen by surprise. At the same moment, Verona seized the energy around them and felt Sarik do the same. He projected it outward, shielding them as the flames from the explosion rushed forward. Verona held onto his concentration by a thread, trying to keep the small barrier in place that protected Roselyn and himself. Sarik's barrier sprang up at the same time and merged with his, extending it to protect the three of them.

Gavril went to his knees, bringing his cloak up over him, and the flames bounced harmlessly off him. A strong wind swept through and one of the windows burst open, sucking the flames from the room. The Elitesmen stood unharmed with barriers of their own in place, but the guards that had been in the room were nothing more than smoldering corpses.

The closest Elitesman recovered first and drove his hands forward, sending a blue orb crackling with lightning toward Gavril. He brought up his cloak again, and the orb bounced off harmlessly. Gavril closed the distance between them and fought the Elitesman in a blur of fist and foot.

The other three Elitesmen made no move to interfere, but casually surrounded the lone Hythariam soldier.

Gavril and the Elitesman's arms were locked, each straining against the other. Verona saw the energy gather into the Elitesman, coalescing along his arms.

"This one is strong," one Elitesman observed.

"I think we've seen enough," another Elitesman said.

The Elitesman came up behind Gavril and raised his hand to strike. In a quick motion, Gavril pivoted on his foot and sent the

Elitesmen colliding into each other.

The remaining two Elitesmen appeared immediately at his side. One laid his hand upon Gavril's head, who then collapsed to the floor, unconscious.

Roselyn cried out but didn't move from the shimmering barrier kept up by Verona and Sarik.

One of the older Elitesmen frowned at the barrier that separated them. He turned to one of the other Elitesmen. "Fetch Master Gerric."

"What should I tell him?" the Elitesman asked.

"Tell him that our prisoners are the companions of the Alenzar'seth," the Elitesman said, never taking his eyes off Verona.

Verona's mind reeled. This had been a test. A way to get them to reveal themselves. He glanced at the charred remains of the guards and back at the Elitesman, whose lips curved into a cold smile. The Elitesman had gotten what he wanted. The fact that there were ten dead guards mattered not to him. They had revealed themselves. He didn't know how long he and Sarik could keep up the barrier, but he had no intentions of letting it down.

"Now," the Elitesman said, "we can begin."

The door opened, and several cloaked servants carried a table with three small stone chests on top. Heat ripples appeared over one of the chests, while a cold mist swirled out from the center chest. The third appeared to be plain.

Two Elitesmen heaved Gavril into the chair, striping off his boots to expose his bare feet. One Elitesman nodded to the other, and two bands of energy bound Gavril's wrists behind him. The other Elitesman put his hand on Gavril's head, and his eyes popped open. Gavril struggled against the bands that held his wrists and feet, but they didn't budge. The Elitesman dragged his hand across Gavril's face, exposing his golden eyes, which stared grimly back.

The third Elitesman retrieved metal tongs from the table and opened the chest with the heat ripples above it. The lid of the stone chest opened, and the Elitesman reached inside and retrieved a glowing red crystal. The other Elitesman pulled a lever on the chair, and Gavril's exposed feet shot forth in front of him.

Gavril's eyes shot to the red crystal then to his exposed feet and he closed his eyes. His body sagged as if he were almost sleeping.

Heat ripples radiated from the red crystal, and Verona saw beads of sweat dot the Elitesman's face. The Elitesman casually brought the tongs with the crystal to the bottom of Gavril's exposed foot, and Verona winced as the flesh smoked and turn black. Gavril did not cry out and appeared completely aloof to what was being done to him.

The Elitesman withdrew the red crystal, and Verona's mouth hung open in shock as the burnt tissue on the bottom of Gavril's feet immediate healed itself. After a few minutes, the skin appeared unmarked as if it had never been burned.

The Elitesman repeatedly put the smoldering crystal to Gavril's feet, yielding the same result. The Elitesmen glanced at each other and then put the crystal back into the stone chest. Still using the tongs, the Elitesman opened the centermost chest, and a cool mist oozed out. Verona saw the Elitesman's breath as the room grew cooler around them.

Gavril was still in his meditative state and completely unresponsive despite the Elitesmen's attempts to garner his attention.

The Elitesman stuck the metal tongs into the chest and withdrew a white crystal that dripped with cold vapor. The metal tongs iced along the tips and crept toward the handles. The Elitesman quickly brought over the white crystal, and just as it was about to touch the Hythariam's foot, Gavril's whole body jerked, knocking the crystal to the floor at the Elitesmen's feet. Ice quickly branched out from the crystal and encased the Elitesman's leg, and after a few seconds his whole body was frozen. It happened so quickly that the Elitesman didn't even cry out. The others looked on in shock.

"What is happening here?" a man asked from the doorway. He was finely dressed with golden robes cascading over his tunic. His hair was blond almost to the point of being white with only hints of yellow.

The Elitesmen in the room saluted the man and bowed their heads, momentarily ignoring their frozen companion.

"Elite Master Gerric," an Elitesman answered.

"Go ahead, Sevan," the Elite Master said.

"We believe these four are in league with the Alenzar'seth," the Elitesman called Sevan said. "Two of their number have been trained in the Shandarian way."

The Elite Master frowned and narrowed his gaze at the three

prisoners huddled behind the barrier.

"A barrier?" the Elite Master said, and his mouth almost curved into an exasperated smile. "Impressive."

"We've tried to break through, but have been unsuccessful," Sevan said. "But this one was caught outside the barrier and is a Hythariam."

"You won't be able to get through the barrier. Not directly at least," the Elite Master's eyes narrowed menacingly. "A Hythariam," he said, and walked over to where Gavril waited strapped to the chair. "I've only heard rumors of your kind."

Gavril said nothing, his gaze unyielding to the Elite Grand Master.

"Their healing capabilities are impressive," Sevan said. "He seems to have the ability to both go into a trance-like state yet be aware of his surroundings at the same time."

Gerric nodded and headed for the door. "Proceed as you were. We'll be gathering at the arena. Learn what you can until then," the Elite Master said and left the room.

Sevan whispered something to one of the Elitesmen, who then left. Verona watched as Sevan retrieved the red crystal and held it near their frozen companion, who then thawed as quickly as he had become frozen. Sevan gestured to the remaining Elitesmen who then carried the injured one from the room.

Sevan returned the red crystal to the chest, and a servant entered. The man had on a gray shirt and plain brown pants. The servant's eyes darted around the room and turned as if to run away, but was blocked by another Elitesman.

"Please come in," Sevan said in a sunny tone.

The man entered the room on shaky legs. "Y... Yes, my lord."

Sevan glanced at Verona and smirked, and Verona felt sick.

"Now we can begin," the Elitesman said. "Why are you in Khamearra? Are you here to kill the High King? Cut the proverbial head from the snake? Are you planning to attack the city? Why are you here?"

Verona silently returned the Elitesman's gaze. The Elitesman stepped forward just outside the barrier and divided his gaze among the three of them, his gaze lingering on Roselyn.

"Surely, you must know that a rescue is not possible," Sevan continued. "Why don't you make it easier on yourself and tell me where he is? We know the heir of Alenzar'seth is in the city."

"Don't you mean easier for yourself?" Verona asked.

The Elitesman's head snapped back toward him, and his eyes narrowed, full of hatred for a moment before smiling. "I mean for you. We both know I can't get through your barrier, but I really don't need to," he said, glancing pointedly back at the terrified servant.

The Elitesman drew a small katana from his hip. "Stick out your hand."

The servant looked at the Elitesman and at Verona before slowly holding up his shaky hand. "P-please, my lord don't... "

The Elitesman brandished his blade and looked back at Verona. "Why are you here!"

Verona said nothing and held back the bile creeping up his throat as he looked helplessly back at the terrified servant.

"As you wish," the Elitesman said and immediately swung the katana.

The servant screamed in pain as his left hand was cleanly severed from his arm. Blood spattered to the floor like runny sap, and the poor man collapsed, clutching the stump of his arm to his chest.

"You bastard!" Verona screamed.

He heard Roselyn cry out behind him.

The Elitesman regarded him coolly. "Your silence cost this man his hand. If you remain so, then it will cost him a good deal more until I get the answers I seek."

"You are a fool if you think any of us will tell you anything," Verona said.

The Elitesman seemed unfazed by Verona's defiance. "Have it your way."

Verona was unable to keep the horror from his face as the Elitesman turned to the servant who was now whimpering, crouched upon the floor as he clutched the stump of his arm.

"Get up," hissed the Elitesman.

Despite his pain, the fear of the Elitesmen was too great for the servant to ignore, and he rose shakily to his feet and glanced at the remains of his hand on the floor. Tears streamed down his face as he looked pleadingly to the group behind the barrier.

Verona glanced at the others. Sarik had his eyes closed, his face a mask of concentration. Roselyn returned his gaze with a pained expression, tears brimming in her eyes. For a moment, Verona wanted to tell the Elitesman something—anything—to spare the poor man in front of him further pain, but he couldn't.

"Very well," the Elitesman said and turned back to the servant. "Take your clothes off."

The servant clumsily unbuttoned his shirt with his remaining hand and let it fall to the floor. The Elitesman's baleful gaze ignited when the servant looked at him, and he pushed out with his hand and sent a blast of air that knocked the servant to the floor.

"I said take off your clothes," Sevan hissed.

The servant scrambled to his feet, quickly removed his pants, and stood naked before them.

Satisfied, the Elitesman walked over to the table, his fingers gliding across the instruments of torture as if he were at a market. He then turned back to Verona with a huge smile that split his terrible face. The servant's eyes darted to the door, but two Elitesmen barred the way.

Verona looked back at the Elitesman he wanted to kill and watched as he selected a large spike with jagged edges from the table.

"This will do," the Elitesman said gleefully and stalked, like a leopard, toward the naked man.

The spike glowed for a moment in the Elitesman's hands as he dragged it across the servant's chest. The man flinched from the touch and appeared shocked when nothing happened. Then the Elitesman let the spike linger upon the man's shoulder, and his face crumpled in pain as a growing patch of blackness grew on the skin.

"Stop!" Verona cried over the servant's screams, but the Elitesman refused to stop. The man writhed on the floor while the Elitesman drove the spike deeper into his shoulder and the blackness continued to spread.

Roselyn buried her face into Verona's shoulder, and he brought his arms up around her.

"You want to know why we're here, Elitesman," Verona screamed. "We're here to kill you and all those like you down to the last man. The oppression of the Elite Order will be wiped from the world like a stain. Kill all your servants if you will, but mark me—before this day is done, I will walk over your cold corpse."

The Elitesman looked unimpressed and drove the spike into the servant's thigh next. The echoes of the suffering screams carried Verona out of time until he was a bundle of fury, but he dared not bring down the barrier, because he knew if he did, then the torture being performed upon the poor man before them would be visited tenfold upon themselves.

CHAPTER 15
ANCIENT ALLIES

The hours swept by like a waterfall, and despite the lack of sleep, Aaron felt fine. Anson had left them earlier in the morning to organize the Resistance. Having spent a few hours with the man, Aaron trusted that the distractions created throughout the city would not cause any civilian loss of life. They would target key locations in the most corrupt districts so that it would draw the attention of the Elitesmen and guardsmen alike. Mid-afternoon was the agreed-upon timeframe, and Aaron was impressed at the speed at which the De'anjard Resistance mobilized into action. Anson explained that they already had plans in place to mobilize quickly. Putting the plan into action would be the easy part. They would converge upon the arena after Aaron made his appearance.

Captain Nolan was as good as his word. He kept the less trustworthy of his guards out on patrol or paired with guardsmen either already sworn to the Resistance or loyal to Nolan himself. The privacy was much appreciated. The Elitesman, Isaac, however, was another matter. Maybe it was simply the fact that he was an Elitesman that Aaron couldn't get past, but there was something that Aaron just didn't like. Something in the man's eyes or maybe it was the fact that he had to rely on the Elitesman to help free his friends. Aaron hoped that Verona and the others were able to hold out.

"Why don't we take a break?" Aaron suggested. "I could use some fresh air."

Nolan nodded. "There is a training yard in the back of the building that is normally vacant at this time of day."

Aaron thanked him and nodded for Braden to come with him. A few minutes later, they emerged in a yard that was easily an acre of open space, which this far into the city was truly something to be appreciated. There was a ten-foot wall surrounding the training yard, but Nolan was right, there was hardly anyone here. He and Braden moved off to the side.

"How are you doing?" Aaron asked.

The angry glint had hardly left Braden's eyes. "Anxious to get going. I can't stand the thought of the others being held by the Elite."

Aaron nodded. "Try to keep a clear head. I don't want you to sacrifice your life for revenge."

"Sacrifice is one of the tenants of the De'anjard," Braden replied.

"I know," Aaron said. "Verona and the others are counting on us, but don't let Eric's sacrifice be in vain. He saved your life, and we can't pull this off without you. I need someone I trust to go into the tower."

The jaw muscles on Braden's face flexed at his clenching teeth.

"The Elitesmen will pay."

"On that we can agree, and now you stand a better chance at facing them," Aaron said. "I've felt you open yourself up to the energy. You've hardly let it go since this morning."

Braden's eyes shifted as he scanned around them, then he nodded.

"Use it," Aaron said. "Be aware of your surroundings. Part of control comes, in part, from surrendering to it. The Elitesmen like to use cunning and brutality. Don't let your pride be something that they can use against you."

"The whisperings... The voices are many," Braden said. "How do you know which one to listen to?"

Aaron paused a second to form his answer. "You know when we practice the slow fighting forms or do practice sparring. The movements come from your mind and from muscle memory. I think of them as urges, and they compliment my movements. You will get to a point where the voices or whisperings fade away entirely. Hold true to your core being. You are the embodiment of the De'anjard, the Shields of Shandara. Let that be your compass." He wished that there was more time to practice, but time was not a luxury they could afford at the moment.

Braden was silent for a few moments, lost in his own thoughts. "Thank you, my lord. I won't let Verona and the others down."

Aaron put his hand on Braden's shoulder, squeezed, and then asked, "What do you think of the plan?"

Braden frowned. "I would rather join you in the arena, but I think splitting apart is our best option. The Elitesmen will flock to you like moths to a flame. Are you prepared for that?"

Before Aaron could answer, the comms device buzzed in his pocket. After a quick look around, he withdrew it so that both he and Braden could listen.

"I've found them," Tanneth's voice came from the device.

"Are they all right?" Aaron asked.

"They are alive, but Aaron," Tanneth said softly, "it's grim. I don't know how much longer they can hold out."

Aaron shared a hard look with Braden. "We leave now then. Is there anything the drones can do until we get there?" Aaron asked.

"I'll see what I can do," Tanneth said. "I've also added my own bit of distraction. I would suggest avoiding the northern walls of the Citadel this evening."

Aaron nodded. "Okay. We're moving out now. The Resistance should be starting its own distractions throughout the city."

Without another word, they raced back into the building, heading to Nolan's office.

"We need to leave now," Aaron said. "We have their location."

The Elitesman Isaac frowned. "Where?"

"I'm about to show you something that I don't have time to explain right now, but trust that the information I have is accurate," Aaron said.

He brought out the comms device and keyed in the sequence that Tanneth had shown him, which pulled up a small display. It was a simple map of the levels of the tower, and the glowing point near the middle was where Verona and the others were being held captive. Nolan blinked and moved his hands along the hologram, and Isaac's eyes widened at the display.

The Elitesman Isaac swallowed. "I'm sorry, Aaron. That is where they take captives for...interrogation. If your friends are there then time is short. We must make haste."

Aaron nodded and chose not to reveal Tanneth to the group now, preferring to keep that information to himself and Braden. With the sun beginning to wane, they gathered at the front of the district headquarters. The common prattle of the people on the street seemed deceptively calm considering what was about to happen.

"This is where we depart," Captain Nolan said. "Safe journey to us all."

Aaron shook hands with the captain and nodded to Braden. If all went well then they were to rendezvous at Ferasdiam's temple in the old quarter of Nolan's district.

The former Elitesman, Isaac, regarded Aaron for a moment. "You will mostly likely be walking into a trap, but you already knew that."

Aaron met his gaze. "I know, but I think it will not be enough."

Isaac smiled in a knowing sort of way. "I've never seen anyone with your level of attunement to the energies that surround us. Having faced my share of Shandarians and Elitesmen alike, I know this is not the norm, and I would venture to guess that you are Ferasdiam Marked."

Aaron merely nodded, waiting for the Elitesman to continue.

"The specialist Elitesmen can hurt even one such as you. And I will say this only because I believe that you truly mean to help the Lady Sarah. You are only limited by what you can perceive as possible. Even the specialists have a weakness to unravel. I hope you will survive long enough to figure this out."

Aaron returned the Elitesman's gaze. "If you succeed in helping to rescue my friends, then I won't lump all the Elitesmen together. What will be started today won't end with this day's events, and I hope you are prepared for that, and will remember which side you're on."

Aaron and the old Elitesman regarded each other for a moment and then Braden broke the silence by saying it was time to move out.

Aaron walked to the alleyway next to the district headquarters and brought out the comms device. He needed to see what Tanneth had only hinted about before. The drone hovered near a closed window on an outside wall. The drone's camera showed a translucent frame, as it was in stealth mode. He was able to bring up an image through one of the slits of the wooden shutter and gasped at the bloody mess of the room. Gavril remain strapped to a chair with glowing bindings that joined his arms and legs. The others were hovered behind some type of barrier. Sarik had his eyes closed, his brow furrowed in concentration. Roselyn was crying into Verona's shoulder. Verona's face was a mask of rage and horror at the bloody mess before him. The shadow of the Elitesmen hovered just beyond the barrier.

Hold on, help is coming.

Aaron turned off the comms device and tightened his grip on his staff, and the runes flared. He summoned the energy into himself and launched to the rooftop of the nearest building. Aaron turned to the tallest building closest to him and leaped onto the flying buttress, easily a hundred feet from where he now stood. He squatted down, taking in the view of the city. A gentle breeze pulled lazily at his black cloak. Far to the south, a billowing column of smoke rose into the air, soon joined by others throughout the city. The Resistance comprised of the fragmented remnants of the De'anjard were doing their job well. He heard the pops of explosions, followed by more columns of smoke, and alarm bells echoed in the distance.

Aaron faced the great black towers of the Citadel of the Elite, yearning to head straight there, but he knew his role in the plan. They expected him at the arena, and he would not disappoint. Aaron pulled up the drone's map in his mind. He knew of the tunnel network that ran between the arena and the Citadel. The High King's palace was not connected. He drew in more of the energy around him and felt the medallion grow warm on his chest. He leaped to the very top of the tower and faced the arena, which was still a good distance away. Aaron glanced back at the dark towers of the Elite, knowing where the crystal charging station was and with it, his best chance at securing the needed travel crystals. He released the breath he had been holding and strengthened his body, then leaped toward the arena. The wind roared passed his ears, and he used the particles in the air to push him farther along than any jump had the right to go. His cloak flapped behind him like a cape, and he landed within a stone's throw of the arena. He took a direct path, not caring at this point if anyone saw him. By now the others would be making their way to one of the service entrances to the Citadel to free his friends.

Aaron leaped again and landed upon the top of the arena wall, much to the ignorance of the people below. The twin suns were beginning to set, and their flared brilliance had long settled into a deep crimson that bathed the city in a reddish hue. He settled down to wait and watched as the arena was filling with occupants.

***

Mactar kept clenching and unclenching his fists in a vain attempt to ignore the growing unrest at Tarimus's abrupt appearance. Tarimus had become an unknown quantity, as no one had ever been shifted out of phase between realms for this long. He truly had dwelt between the crossroads of the soul, and it was troubling to know that he was free. He had subverted Tarimus to his will before, and knew that Tarimus would be seeking retribution for his imprisonment. Part of him relished in the challenge of facing Tarimus much like what Aaron Jace was proving to be. Mactar's brow furrowed in concentration as his mind tumbled through the possibilities. Tarimus had been different since his first encounter with Reymius's heir. It was subtle at first, but now as his mind worked backwards with the benefit of hindsight, he saw a pattern that had been hidden before. Aaron had the power to free Tarimus, but what would make him do so? A woman crossed his vision with a swath of golden hair partially hidden in a hood, and the thought struck him like lightning.

Sarah!

What wouldn't someone do for the one they love? Not that he harbored any such attachments. Knowledge and power were what he cared about, that and the thrill of toying with kingdoms while they squabbled and cast their fearful gaze toward the High King. As if the mighty High King Amorak could have accomplished so much without the likes of him. The High King was simply a means to an end for his otherworldly allies. Mactar's thoughts drifted back to Sarah. Primus had tried to kill her and paid the ultimate price. The fool was no match for her. The only way he could have killed her was to come from behind. Not all the pieces fit together because he didn't fully understand how Tarimus came into play, but there was a connection there. He was sure of it even if he didn't know how. Mactar's gaze swept through the arena and momentarily settled upon Rordan's back, who stood a short way off studying the field. The death of his twin brother had shaken the young prince to his core. As if sensing his thoughts, the prince looked at him, and Mactar gestured for him to come over. The sun was setting, and the rite of the initiates was about to begin.

Rordan came silently to Mactar's side and took the seat next to him. It was a mark of the changes in the young man that he kept silent, rather than filling the air with idle chatter. The grounds of the arena were already set with the course that the new initiates of the Elite would have to navigate. The arena held traps for the unwary as well as hidden caches of weapons and other useful items. The arrangement of debris formed a complex maze with enough corners and dead ends to challenge the young recruits.

The center held a wide expanse of open ground where the strongest of recruits would gather. There were many levels of recruits to be tested, from those who had been taken from their homes this very week to initiates who had embraced the order but had not been promoted to full Elitesmen. It had been some time since he had attended one of these events. They were often beautiful in their brutality. One could see what a person was truly made of when stripped away of the preconceptions of civilization. People would conform to a natural hierarchy, giving in to their need to be told what to do, and the illusion of freedom was often enough to satisfy most.

Elite Grand Master Gerric appeared at the podium in a flash of light. Quite theatrical, Gerric never missed an opportunity to convey the power of the Elitesmen. The crowd came to a hush almost instantly, and Gerric raised his hands.

"Bring out the hopefuls," the Elite Grand Master said.

Across the arena, doors opened and a procession entered gathering just inside the entrance. Mactar looked on, keeping the lack of enthusiasm from his face. The new recruits, not more than children in their own right, would be fodder for the more experienced initiates. The practice kept the Elitesmen strong, as the weak would never survive very long in their midst. Only the strong and the cunning would prosper. The only reason he was here was to meet with Darven, who had so far not seen fit to show himself.

"There seems to be more people than usual," commented Rordan.

Mactar glanced at the crowd. The prince had a point. "Perhaps they expect quite a show."

Rordan nodded but said nothing.

"You're rather quiet this evening, my lord," Mactar said.

He watched as Rordan kept his eyes on the arena's occupants. "I'm here, as is required of me."

"Indeed," Mactar said. "Sometimes true insight can be gleaned even if we are in a place we'd rather not be."

"You're speaking in riddles again," came Rordan's terse reply. "Fine, I'll indulge your game. What insights am I about to glean by watching the slaughter of the new recruits?"

While Rordan was more of a leader than his late brother, Primus, he was the more squeamish of the two.

"Patience and maybe we'll both learn something," Mactar replied.

Rordan turned and glanced up, about to reply, and frowned. Mactar looked behind him but didn't see anything out of the ordinary.

"What is it?" Mactar asked.

"I thought I saw something," Rordan said. "I smell a lot of smoke in the air. Do you?"

Mactar sniffed the air and could detect traces of smoke. "A bit, but not enough to concern me. You saw something?"

Rordan's gaze grew distant before replying. "Nothing worth mentioning," he said and turned back to the arena.

Elite Master Gerric brought up his hands again. "Bring out the initiates."

The doors off to the opposite side of the arena opened, and a small group of initiates walked into the arena. The elder recruits melted into the shadows, allowing the new group of initiates to enter.

"Initiates," Gerric said, "welcome to the proving grounds. This is your one chance to demonstrate your worthiness to join the ranks of the Elitesmen. Each of you was invited because of your potential to rise above all others, but that is not a destiny for all, as there is a price that must be paid. Hidden throughout the arena are these white crystals," the Elite Master said, holding a glowing white crystal above them. "Find them, and you survive to the next round. Failure is never tolerated as an Elitesmen."

"I only sense that about half of the initiates have any potential to tap into the energy," Rordan said.

Mactar raised an eyebrow. "They mix the groups. Some may have actual potential and others ... They serve a purpose. Some things can only be awakened through conflict. What would you change? Do not pretend to be so squeamish. I've seen what you've done to people who cross your path."

The young prince narrowed his gaze. "Things change."

Intriguing, Mactar thought. The prince was taking a fresh look at everything he had taken for granted before, but he still sensed something off about the prince just below the surface. He didn't say anything else but glanced around, looking for Darven.

***

Aaron crouched above, watching as the small group of children moved into the arena. He couldn't believe what he was seeing. He had listened to the announcer and heard the undercurrents of what had not been said. Survival was only guaranteed for those able to find the white crystals. He wondered how many of them there were until the cunning brutality of the events about to take place dawned on him as the last rays of the setting sun faded.

"You stand upon a crossroads." The Elitesman's voice echoed throughout the arena, and Aaron could hear him perfectly. "One of the core tenants of the code of the Elite is to sever all ties from your previous life. Tonight, we will help you do that."

The Elitesman gestured, and glowing orbs ignited, revealing a group of older citizens in twelve individual cages. The initiates turned, and some cried out, reaching toward the cages. Aaron's heart thundered in his chest, and his jaw clenched as he realized what the Elitesmen had done.

"I believe you are familiar with the people locked in these cages," the Elitesman said. "Retrieve the white crystals and bring them back to your loved one's cage, and all will be well. Fail to retrieve the crystals in time, and they will die." The Elitesmen paused for a moment. "There are only six crystals in the arena."

Aaron brought the rune-carved staff to his forehead and closed his eyes for a moment. He couldn't risk contacting Braden through the comms device and had to assume they were close enough to sneak into the Citadel by now. He could wait no longer and be a witness to the imminent slaughter of the children and their families. Even the ones who would survive this test would lose part of themselves, and that he couldn't sit idly by and watch.

The runes along the staff pulsed to life as he gathered the energy around him. Aaron looked behind him at the sprawl of the city. The pieces were in place. He saw the smoke of the fires emanating from key locations, and any minute they would gain the notice of the guardsmen.

Aaron stood poised atop of the arena wall and watched as some of its occupants looked in his direction, noticing the glow of the staff. He launched into the air, the glowing runes of his staff streaking across the sky, and then he landed upon the arena grounds.

***

"It's him," Rordan gasped, echoing Mactar's thoughts.

"He is here," Rordan said, rising from his seat. "The Alenzar'seth is here."

Off to the side, Mactar glimpsed a pale white head and heard the mirthless laughter of Tarimus.

The Alenzar'seth will plunge your world into a flaming pit of Hell, Mactar! Tarimus's voice hissed behind him. Mactar twisted around ready to attack, but again there was nothing.

"What's wrong with you?" Rordan asked. "Shouldn't we— "

"We should be patient. Let the Elitesmen cast themselves against the Heir of Shandara. A smart man attacks at a time of his own choosing."

***

Aaron dashed toward the cages, looking for a way to unlock them. The top of each cage held a ceiling of spikes that could at any moment drop and kill the prisoners.

"Leave us. Get the children out of here," a man said from inside the nearest cage.

Aaron was joined by the initiates, none of whom looked more than twelve years of age. He circled the closest cage, looking for a way to stop the spiked ceilings from closing. Everything was enclosed except for the bars.

Bursts of lights surrounded the group as the black-clad Elitesmen appeared. The initiates had spread out to each of the cage fronts, trying in vain to pull the doors open.

The people in the cages screamed for the children to run. Aaron spun around to face the enclosing Elitesmen and summoned the energy into the staff. He swept outwards, sending out a burst of air that blew back the approaching Elitesmen. A lone silver-clad Elitesman leaped to the top of the cages. Aaron hurled himself at him, and the Elitesman launched himself back behind the black-clad Elitesmen.

"People of Khamearra," Aaron's voice boomed across the arena. "I am Aaron Jace, the last surviving member of the house Alenzar'seth. The Lords of Shandara have returned to Safanar. I am not your enemy. I fight the tyranny of the Elitesmen that hold you under their boot!" Aaron planted the rune-carved staff into the ground. A beacon of light surged from the staff, piercing the night sky in a column of pure white.

A deafening clang came from one of the cages. The spiked ceiling had slammed down, killing the prisoners inside. The mechanisms controlling the spikes of the remaining cages shook all at once, and on instinct, Aaron thrust his hands out, summoning the energy around him, wedging the gearing in place. It took all his concentration to prevent the spikes from falling, leaving his back exposed to the Elitesmen behind him.

The gates nearest to them burst open, and grizzly armed men poured through. If he didn't let the spikes go, he would die. The men rushed past him, screaming their battle cry.

"De'anjard! Shields of Shandara!"

Ordinary soldiers were no match for the Elitesmen, but still they poured forth, coming to their aid. The soldiers separated, some stopping at the cages to free the prisoners and the rest forming a line behind Aaron's back. He cringed inwardly as the first of the soldiers died by his side, unable to defend themselves from the blazing orbs being flung by the Elitesmen, but still they came, buying him and the prisoners time with their lives.

As the soldiers freed the last of the prisoners, Aaron turned to the children. "Run for the exit!"

He released his hold, and the spiked ceilings slammed down to empty cages. Aaron howled in rage for the men dying around him and drew his Falcons, releasing a few notes of the bladesong out into the air.

He moved with blurring speed, charging after the surrounding Elitesmen and wielding the Falcons as he went. Aaron thrust himself into the nearest throng, unleashing the bladesong into the night. At one time, the Elitesmen seemed like a mighty foe, but the ones he now faced were nothing more than an annoyance. The bladesong was his window into untapped knowledge that flowed freely from his soul. The black-clad Elitesmen were merely an obstacle that stood between himself and the silver-clad Elitesman.

He moved through them with ruthless abandon, taking them out in droves until he was surrounded by their bodies. None quit the field or ran away. Elitesmen would always choose death over surrender. The silver-clad Elitesman smiled coldly at him before vanishing in the light of the travel crystal.

The surviving solders regarded him in awe, as some brought their fists across their hearts in salute.

"Ferasdiam Marked," was whispered throughout the arena.

Aaron returned the salute. "Run. Go back into the city. Do not throw your lives away. You've helped the children escape. The spirit of Shandara lives on in you. "

More flashes of light emerged around him, and a cold wind blew as the ground rumbled beneath his feet. Eight silver-clad Elitesmen appeared with smoldering red eyes glowering beneath their hooded cloaks. They did not charge, but merely waited. Aaron felt the medallion grow cool against his chest. The bladesong blazed within, surging the energy through him, but he felt something reaching to him.

He was snatched by an unseen force that launched him into the air and slammed him into the ground, drawing him closer into their midst. The medallion grew frigidly cold, almost burning his skin.

"This one is protected," one hissed.

Aaron scrambled to his feet and lashed out with his blades, but his attacks were blocked.

As one, the silver-clad Elitesmen pushed out with their hands, and Aaron leaped into the air as separate bolts of energy singed the area he had been a moment before. He swept his blades out before him, solidifying the particles in the air, and sent them racing into the Elitesmen, startling a few. As he brought up his blades to ward off another blast of energy, he felt his legs sweep out from underneath him. Aaron moved through the sweep, rolling out of the way, and came to his feet. Tendrils of energy latched onto his wrists, attempting to hold him in place. He focused the energy within and, augmenting his strength, pulled several Elitesmen off balance. He dashed forward around another Elitesman who went down to his knees, writhing in pain as his body split open in a hiss. Aaron could spare no more than a glance and was away before he could give any thought to an Elitesman killing one of his own.

He summoned the energy, leaped into the air, and was followed by another Elitesman streaking silver with his sword drawn.

These silver-clad Elitesmen were different from the ones he had faced before. More powerful. A column of flame blazed in the sky around him, and Aaron pushed himself along the air, skating safely out of the way. He landed hard upon the ground, and the crystals in the Falcons blazed white. In a battle such as this, movement was life. With the power of the bladesong, Aaron moved at speeds too fast for the eye to track and then stopped between the Elitesmen, bringing his Falcons to bear. As the silver-clad Elitesmen moved in, he was slowly being overrun.

The notes of the bladesong pierced the air, and all around him glowed white as one voice emerged from all the voices of ancient souls. Aaron pulled the currents of energy from the staff, and a shaft of white light shot forth into the medallion, burning through his shirt. The crystal in the medallion blazed then shot forth the Alenzar'seth family symbol into the night sky. In the heart of Khamearra, home to the High King and the Elite Order, the Shandarian coat of arms of a dragon cradling a single rose blazed upon the night sky for all to see.

A mighty roar streaked through the arena, and the ground behind Aaron thundered and shook, almost sending him off balance.

"We heed your call, Safanarion."

A voice like granite slabs chafing together spoke behind him. The light of his staff reflected off the golden hide of a dragon and washed all in the arena in sparkling brilliance.

The silver-clad Elitesmen hurled orbs of energy, and the dragon exhaled a barrier in front of Aaron, absorbing the orbs. The dragon bounded forth into the midst of the Elitesmen, scattering them, although they regrouped almost immediately. The roar of the dragon shook the ground beneath Aaron's feet, and he charged forward with the Falcons dragging in his wake.

Aaron launched into the air, engaging the Elitesmen, and the ring of the blades echoed throughout the arena. He felt a whoosh of air as the dragon swept out with its tail, pulling him out of the way as it exhaled a blast of energy. The arena lit up as if in the noonday sun, and the rest Elitesmen were caught in the blast and disappeared. The dragon turned its massive head and regarded Aaron with eyes that sparkled of starlight.

"We of the Eldarin honor the one who is marked by Ferasdiam. Seek us

out as our numbers are few and there are things you must know."

The dragon launched itself into the air, moving at speeds beyond that of any beast.

The Eldarin? Aaron wondered as he retrieved the rune-carved staff. The beacon that bathed the arena in light before was now gone. The remaining people in the arena were still scattering, trying to get away. Aaron turned to the dark towers of the Citadel looming to the west and launched himself into the air, leaving the silent arena behind.

Had the dragon sought him out, heeding his call? He landed upon the towered walls of the Citadel of the Elite, putting much distance between himself and the arena. He hoped the soldiers of the Resistance had escaped, and his heart ached for the men who died trying to protect him. He released his hold upon the bladesong, and his strength left him, almost bringing him to his knees.

Aaron took a few moments to catch his breath and centered himself, drawing in the energy from the rune-carved staff to heal his wounds. He would need to eat to replenish what his body demanded now, but he could still function. The lack of sleep was catching up with him. His battle with the silver-clad Elitesmen had left him unsettled. They must be the specialist class of the Order that Isaac had referred to and the ones Sarah had hinted about on board the Raven. The thought of Sarah sent a momentary pang to the pit of his stomach, and it took all his will not to reach across the ever-present connection he had with her. He banished his pain and focused on what he must do next, closing the distance to the Citadel of the Elite.

CHAPTER 16
DENIAL AND ESCAPE

The air stank of blood and excrement, piercing the confines of his nose. The shield that Verona and Sarik had created held against the Elitesmen's attacks, but did not block the air they breathed. They could do nothing for the man the Elitesman Sevan had tortured before them without a hint of mercy. The brutal efficiency with which the Elitesman had taken to the task had shaken him to his core. The Elitesmen saw people as tools to achieve their own ends, and when one tool broke, another would simply take its place, and the cycle would begin again. The fact that he had killed another human being barely registered with the exception of the affect it had upon him and the others.

Verona's hateful gaze lifted and sought out the Elitesman torturer. The bonds of energy were enough to keep Gavril in place, who had long since given up struggling against them. As they each tried to deny the Elitesman Sevan in their own way, he took pleasure in their failings with fiendish delight. The stalemate they were in left them firmly within the Elitesman's power, and Verona wasn't sure how much longer they could hold out. The screams of the tortured man still echoed in his mind.

"I know you want to kill me," Sevan taunted.

Verona looked away, disgusted, refusing to rise to anymore of the Elitesman's taunts. Instead, his eyes found a momentary respite from this very real version of Hell in Roselyn's golden eyes, so much like his own, but with irises like the sun. They mirrored both the pain and bitterness they felt at the Elitesman's brutality, but Verona could tell that her will was eroding, as was his own. He couldn't sit idly by and watch another person be tortured. Something had to give.

The gruesome remains littered the floor at the Elitesman's feet, and Sevan brusquely kicked them aside, making room, seemingly unfazed that they had once been a person.

"Almost time for our next guest." Sevan grinned and motioned to the Elitesmen by the door.

A hunched old woman limped through the doorway, stumbling as if she couldn't see very well. The old woman stepped into the light, and her eyes shone milky white with only hints of the colored irises that should have been there.

The Elitesman Sevan stood stone still in the shadows, his bloodstained hands resting comfortably upon the edges of his shirt over his chest. Sevan's hands shifted slightly while he watched with a dark, menacing gaze as the old woman stumbled over the dead body of the servant. The lighting in the room grew dimmer around them.

Roselyn cried out, and Verona's breath caught in his chest.

"I can't do this again," Verona whispered to Roselyn.

Roselyn turned toward him, her mouth slightly opened, but no words would come forth.

"I'm sorry," Verona whispered.

"It's all right," Roselyn whispered back to him.

Verona steeled himself, coming to grips with what he must do. If he were to meet his end then so be it, but he would be damned if he would be witness to another tortured innocent for an Order that deserved to burn in Hell for all eternity.

Verona looked back at Roselyn and brought his hand to her cheek, brushing away a silky lock of her raven hair. "We've had no time, my lady," he whispered in a voice that echoed the cracks in his broken heart for what would never be.

Roselyn blinked away her tears and brought her hand to Verona's shoulder, gazing into his eyes. In one swift motion, Verona pulled her in and kissed her lips, feeling the press of her body upon his own. For the span of time between moments, he knew true happiness. The elation blazed along every fiber and yearned for more, but it was not to be. He pulled away and met Sarik's knowing gaze.

The hunched old lady stood in the center of the room, calling out, "Is anyone there, my lord? They told me I was needed here." The woman turned about and stumbled. "I apologize, I don't see very well anymore."

The Elitesman Sevan stood behind her with his challenging gaze, daring Verona to act. In the back of the room, the other Elitesmen's attention drew toward the windows for a moment before looking back at them.

Verona focused himself, drawing the energy in while pulling away from the shield they had created, and Sarik did the same.

Sevan stood poised, his hand raised, clutching a large knife whose edge glinted in the dimly lit room. The old woman spun around completely, looking relieved to see the Elitesman.

"Thank you, my lord. Do you need me to help clean up? I would be happy to do that for you, my lord, but please, I could do with some more light," the old woman said and shuffled toward the windows.

The Elitesman's contemptuous gaze swept the three of them. "There is no hope for you. Your friends will never be able to get to you here."

Verona's heightened senses saw as the blade began its decent. At the same moment, he let the shield go and thrust outward, pushing with all his might, sending a shaft of energy that erupted from his outstretched hand. The Elitesman was knocked backwards off his feet.

The window's wooden shutters burst forth with a blinding white light that blazed from a distance into the night sky, startling them all. The room was still for a moment, and Verona stood with his mouth agape, staring at the Alenzar'seth coat of arms emblazoned upon the night sky.

Aaron!

Verona launched himself across the room and grabbed a ragged spike from the table. His eyes never left the Elitesman as he charged, feeling the energy burn inside as the room blurred around him. He planted the spike into the chest of the Elitesman Sevan.

Two flashes of golden light lit up the room, and the two Elitesmen at the door fell in a heap. Verona turned from his crouch over the dying Elitesman to see that Gavril was free and held some kind of device out from his hands. Sarik and Roselyn were at his side.

Verona turned back to the dying Elitesman who glared back with a crazed loathing as blood frothed in his mouth. Verona grabbed the Elitesman by the shirt and twisted the spike in his chest, growling as he did. The Elitesman cried out in pain.

"I can never hurt you enough, Elitesman," Verona hissed.

"You think you're free," the Elitesman said, spitting up blood. "You will never be free of me. I will haunt your dreams long after I'm gone." The Elitesman's words ended in a gurgled sigh, and his face froze with hatred as the life drained out of him.

***

Despite himself, Mactar watched as the battle in the arena unfolded before him. The Alenzar'seth's strength was growing in leaps and bounds. He would soon be a match for the High King, if he wasn't already. The patrons that were not scrambling to leave gasped and cried out as a mighty roar thundered over their heads. The arena was bathed in the golden brilliance of the biggest dragon he had ever seen, appearing as if by magic after the beacon of Shandara pierced the night.

An Eldarin dragon?

Mactar's mind struggled with the truth appearing before his

eyes. What trickery was this? The dragons were all but gone from Safanar. The beacon of Shandara blazed through the night sky and then melted away, taking him back all those years ago to the very night that Shandara fell. The great city burned with an unquenchable fire that spread hungrily, devouring anything in its path. The night echoed of countless voices crying out, trapped amid the flames. There had been no beacon then, nor answering call. *This must be a trick.*

His gaze fell once again upon Aaron, who retrieved his staff as the dragon scattered the witless Elitesmen into disarray. Clearly, the Elitesmen believed a dragon was in their midst. Could it be? He dismissed the thought as soon as it occurred. No one had the ability to summon dragons. Rordan stood poised with his hand clenched upon the hilt of his sword. Mactar looked back at Reymius's heir, who was now facing the Eldarin, and something unspoken appeared to pass between them before they both went their separate ways.

Rordan turned to him and said, "He can speak with dragons?"

Mactar shook his head. "This is a trick. The Eldarin dragons are all gone. They have faded into myth."

"Deny the truth at your own folly, Mactar," the voice of Tarimus hissed faintly.

Darven appeared by his side. "my lord."

Mactar narrowed his gaze at the appearance of Darven, taking it in before asking any questions. His appearance was unkempt and his cloak in tatters.

"How did you find him in the city?" Mactar asked.

"Who?" Rordan asked and then said, "You knew the Alenzar'seth was in the city?"

Darven nodded. "Quite by accident, I assure you. It took every shred of knowledge I had to elude him and quite a bit of luck, I'm afraid. He's more acutely in tune with the binding forces around us. It is like nothing I've ever seen. I managed to send word to Gerric shortly before nightfall, hence the appearance of so many Elitesmen."

Mactar nodded. "You've done well. We will be leaving soon."

Rordan's mouth hung open. "Leaving? You can't leave."

Mactar's mouth lifted into a mirthless grin. "I'm quite certain I can leave, my lord Prince."

"Aren't you going to go after him?" Rordan asked.

"What for? He's not after me. At least not yet, and I have pressing business elsewhere. Surely, the Elitesmen will be able to handle one lone Shandarian," Mactar said, somewhat aloof, and nodded for Darven to follow.

"I think you're wrong," Rordan said. "I'm going after him. There must be a reason why he's here in Khamearra, and I intend to find out what it is."

Mactar nodded. "That you should, my lord."

Rordan stalked off into the fleeing crowd, and Mactar wondered if he would ever see the young prince alive again. Should Rordan throw himself at Aaron, Mactar knew who would receive the shorter end of that particular stick.

"We're really not going after Aaron?" Darven asked.

"I would like to know why he's here," Mactar said, "but at the same time I'm happy for the Elitesmen and the High King to contend with him for the moment. If Aaron is preoccupied here, then others will be slower to rally to his call, and we need some time to help us prepare." The advantage of controlling the Ryakuls was too much of an opportunity to pass up and would give him something else to leverage against whoever rallied to the fallen Shandara banner.

***

A hand gently pressed upon his shoulder, and only when Verona turned around did he realize that he was still gripping the spike in the dead Elitesman's chest. He unclenched his grip, and Roselyn pulled him to his feet. They searched the bodies of the Elitesmen, taking what weapons they could.

The beacon winked out, drawing their attention to the windows.

"That was Aaron," Sarik said. "Do you think he—"

"No," Verona said quickly.

Gavril walked over to the window. "Look at the city."

They were high up in one of the towers within the Citadel of the Elite. The orange glow of fires could be seen throughout the city. The blaze seemed to be concentrated at key locations and not spreading to the other buildings. A thunderous sound rocked the ground beneath their feet, and the sky lit up near them in a blaze of angry red flames.

"That was close," Verona said.

"That was Tanneth." Gavril smiled grimly and went to the table to retrieve the comms device that the Elitesmen had taken earlier. "They are coming. We should head out. Tanneth has more surprises in store for the Elitesmen," Gavril said while his eyes darted across the small screen.

Verona nodded. "Let's go," he said and motioned for Sarik to guide the old woman, who was muttering to herself.

Together, they emerged into an empty hallway, and Verona grabbed one of the orbs and threw it on the ground, setting the room ablaze. Verona took point. They heard men shouting throughout the tower and moved cautiously down the hall. Verona kept the Elitesman's blade ready, but he itched to be rid of it, not wanting the taint of anything to do with the Elitesman Sevan to touch his skin.

You will never be free of me.

Verona banished the Elitesman's last words from his mind and moved forward. They came to a stairwell and stopped when they heard a commotion below them. The ring of steel upon steel could be heard, and Verona's pace quickened when he heard Braden's De'anjard battle cry.

Verona and the others took the steps two at a time until they came to an open landing where they found Braden swinging a large steel hammer in one hand and the shield of the De'anjard in the other. Braden fought with two other men. One of whom he recognized as the district captain they had spied upon earlier. The other man he didn't recognize at all.

Gavril unleashed more blasts of energy from the device in his hand, felling more Elitesmen and earning him wary glances from Braden and the others.

"Braden!" Verona called.

Braden smiled in greeting, but Verona noted that the smile did not reach his eyes.

"Verona, all of you? Good," Braden said. "We were having a hell of a time reaching you."

"You keep strange company these days," Verona said, nodding to the other two men, but his eyes never left the older man with the long leather duster. His eyes widened as he felt the traces of energy gathering around the older man. An Elitesman was helping them?

"Desperate times," Braden answered his questioning gaze. "Come, I'll fill you in on the way."

"Where is Aaron?" Verona asked, following Braden and his two Khamearrian escorts.

"Where do you think?" Braden snorted. "Where he can cause the most commotion. He is the reason why the towers are so empty."

Verona nodded. "What is the plan?"

Braden nodded toward Captain Nolan.

"We're going to get away from here and hide out with the underground Resistance here in the city," Captain Nolan said. "I'm Nolan, by the way."

"You have my sincerest gratitude for coming to our aid," Verona said and then he introduced himself and the others.

"We need to move," the old Elitesman barked from farther down the staircase.

"That one is called Isaac," Braden said.

"Will Aaron be meeting us?" Verona asked, catching up with Isaac.

Braden's answer was interrupted as a group of shadows appeared on the staircase. A young group of initiates burst into the staircase, looking startled to see them. They couldn't have been beyond their mid-teen years. Some of their eyes narrowed suspiciously while most looked on nervously.

Before any of them could do anything, Isaac stepped forward.

"Initiates," Isaac's voice spoke with authority. "Where are you heading?"

The group of boys traded glances with one another before one stepped forward.

"Speak quickly, boy," Isaac said.

"My Lord of the Elite," the boy said. "The alarms have sounded. We're to evacuate the tower immediately."

Isaac nodded as if what the boy said was obvious. "Well, don't let us keep you. Move along."

The boy looked as if he were about to say something else then shrugged his shoulders, nodded to the others, and left.

As the staircase filled with people, Isaac led them away down one of the less crowded corridors. Verona glanced at Gavril, who studied the comms device and nodded back to him. He glanced out of a passing window and saw the arena in the distance. It had grown dark and quiet, and Verona hoped that his friend had not bitten off more than he could chew. A soft hand slipped into his, and Verona turned to see Roselyn behind him. For once, he was thankful that in this moment he didn't have to say anything. The message in her eyes was obvious, even to him. Somewhere in the midst of this nightmare he had earned the attention of his beautiful Hythariam Princess. He knew the Hythariam didn't have princesses, but Roselyn could be nothing else to him, except possibly the queen of his heart.

They came through a small doorway, and the cool night air washed over them. Perhaps there was hope for them after all.

CHAPTER 17
THE TOWER

Aaron quietly circled the towers of the Elite. He had checked the comms device earlier and, judging from the video feeds, knew that his friends were safe. As safe as they could be given that they were escaping from the home of the Elite. The Citadel grounds weren't nearly as populated now as they had been when last he checked. No doubt his own efforts at the arena had proven tempting enough to draw them out. He crept along and headed for the tower where the travel crystals were being charged. He drew in the energy from around him and cast it out to see if he could detect anyone nearby. He tensed up, sensing an approaching presence behind him.

Aaron leaped down from the wall, landing within the confines of the Citadel. People were still pouring out of the tower entrances farthest from him, but where he stood all was dark and quiet. He was torn between moving on and waiting to see who was trying to follow him. He squatted down, deciding that a few moments' caution was a far lesser risk than having someone follow him inside the tower.

The silhouette of a cloaked figure appeared on the Citadel walls and scanned the area. After a few seconds, the figure dropped down to the ground about twenty yards from where Aaron was hiding. The man stopped abruptly and stood up from his crouched position, then he walked purposefully into the moonlight.

"I know you're there," he said.

Aaron stared at the man standing in the moonlight. "No princely titles this time?" Aaron asked, stepping into the light.

They stood twenty feet apart, and even in the shadows Aaron sensed the barrage of emotions roiling through the young prince, the most prevalent one being fear.

Aaron watched as Sarah's brother stood before him, his hands itching to draw the sword at his hip, but clearly unable to decide what to do. For Sarah, he would give Rordan this one chance at reason. "I'm not here for you, Rordan. I'm here for Sarah."

"The last I saw of my sister she was with you," Rordan said.

Aaron leveled his gaze at the young prince. "She is not here with me."

Rordan drew his sword, holding it loosely by his side, and circled around, but Aaron kept his distance. He sensed the energy gathering around Rordan as it would any of the Elitesmen he faced.

"We don't have to do this," Aaron said, keeping his staff ready in case Rordan attacked. "We don't have to be enemies."

"You killed my brother," Rordan said, his voice shaking.

"After he stabbed Sarah in the back with his sword," Aaron countered. "Primus got what he deserved."

Rordan growled as he charged, flailing wildly with his sword. Aaron calmly sidestepped out of the way, but kept his staff ready. The young prince attacked again, but Aaron didn't engage. Rordan was only a few years his junior, but his world had been stripped raw, and Aaron could sympathize with that. To a point, at least.

"Fight me!" Rordan shouted and swung his sword again.

The bladesong hummed within Aaron, but he needed no focus to avoid the pitiful attacks from the prince.

Rordan stumbled and regained his feet. "Why won't you fight me?" he gasped.

"Because she wouldn't want me to," Aaron answered. "That is the only thing that stays my hand."

"Sarah?" Rordan sank to his knees with his shoulders slumped. "She cares nothing for me."

"No, you are wrong," Aaron said. "It is Mactar who cares nothing for you. Tell me, where is he?"

Rordan frowned. "He is not coming. He believes the Elitesmen should be able to handle you."

Aaron took a quick glance around, but there was no one around except for them. "Where is he going?"

Rordan came to his feet, sneering. "Why would I tell you? I can't stand against you, not even with the training of the Elite. But that doesn't mean that I will help you."

Aaron studied Rordan for a moment, debating in his mind what to say. "Then go. You're at a crossroads, and you need to decide what kind of man you wish to become. There is a war coming that will sweep across this land, and if we are to survive then we will need to stand together. You and I don't have to be enemies."

"You intend to raise Shandara from the ashes?" Rordan asked.

Aaron shook his head. "No. There is a threat to this world that none can escape from. The Alenzar'seth have sheltered this world from an invading army. Take a good look around at those in power. Take an honest look at who counsels the High King and then the king himself."

"You mean Mactar," Rordan mumbled.

"Think about what I said." Aaron turned and headed off to the tower. He needed to move on, and he hoped that Rordan would see reason. He rounded the base and jumped into the air, landing on a ledge four stories from the ground. Aaron looked back and saw Rordan standing in the moonlight with his gaze toward the ground. He knew the bonds of family between Sarah and her half-brothers were fragile, but perhaps Rordan would take what he said to heart. Khamearra would be needed to fight the coming war.

Aaron ducked inside the tower to a dark room. He didn't need any heightened senses to tell him that this tower wasn't empty. He came to the door and listened to see if anyone was out in the hall. When he was sure it was empty, he opened the wooden door and stepped through. Even though he had memorized the layout from the probes, there was a difference between what was on screen and actually standing inside the structure. He turned down a corridor and found a group of men heading in his direction. They looked up at him, and in a split second Aaron walked purposefully forward, taking great strides. As he passed them, some bowed their heads at his passing. He didn't take the time to acknowledge for fear that they would call his bluff. Luck had been on his side, as these weren't Elitesmen.

He came to the hollowed interior of the tower where it opened to a great expanse of space. Lighted orbs hung throughout, giving ample light. The place was bigger on the inside than he had imagined, and was made from the dark stone that capped the outside walls.

Aaron was able to continue up several floors without notice, passing people as if he were just another member of the Elitesmen Order. The farther he ventured, the more it grated at his nerves because he knew at any second that they would discover that he was an intruder. It was interesting to see the various faces of the Elitesmen Order. Not all were clouded with the pristine arrogance that had been prevalent with the other members he had encountered. Perhaps there really were factions within the Order of the Elite. Regardless, he had no doubts that the current indifference of the men and women he passed would evaporate if they discovered him. He had to believe that they would stop at nothing to capture him if they knew who he really was. Unless there were more like Isaac, Elitesmen loyal to an older regime.

Aaron was about midway up the tower when he veered off down a corridor and headed toward the room where the crystals were recharged.

"Hold!" a man called out from down the corridor.

Aaron stopped, and his hand reached inside his cloak for one of his throwing knives.

"You there," the man said again, the heavy thud of his boots echoing down the corridor.

Aaron turned slowly, and the Elitesman's eyes narrowed.

"You!" the Elitesman hissed.

Aaron's hand shot forth and sent a throwing knife at blinding speed through the air, which buried itself into the Elitesman's chest. The Elitesman crumpled to the ground, and Aaron fled down the hallway, expecting to hear an alarm at any moment. A few seconds later, a loud explosion from outside the tower shook the entire place down to the floor beneath his feet. Aaron spun and saw a drone hovering in the air along the ceiling. Aaron nodded to the drone and knew Tanneth was keeping watch, but it still bothered him that the interior of the tower held so few guards.

He came to the marked door outside the crystal charging chamber. The door appeared to be made of solid oak with steel bindings. Aaron ran his hands along the door, feeling around the edges. The door had no handles and no visible means of opening it. The door felt solid under his fingertips. He was sure he could get through the door, but was worried about damaging any of the crystals on the other side, not to mention alert whatever was guarding the crystals. Something inside had taken out the drone earlier, and he wasn't going to take any chances. Not when he was so close to getting what he needed to save Sarah.

Aaron reached out with his senses along the door and could almost see the mechanism inside. Only someone like himself or an Elitesman could open this door. He solidified the particles inside the door and forced the gearing to move. The doorway began to swing open. He pushed it the rest of the way with his hands and entered the room.

There was an enormous crystal suspended in midair, pulsating with a glow that lit the area around them in waves. The air felt charged and almost crackled with energy. Aaron felt the edges of the dragon tattoo on his chest prickle, and the runes on the staff glowed dimly. There were crystal deposits throughout the room, pulsing in rhythm with the main crystal. On the far side was a barrel with glowing purple crystals that could only be the travel crystals.

Jackpot!

He stepped inside the room, and the door closed behind him.

Above the giant crystal was a large open shaft that went straight up to the night sky. The shaft was lined with mirrors all the way up. Aaron guessed that the mirrors were used to amplify the light coming from the outside. He moved farther in, cautiously circling the room. There were all types of crystals, some of which he recognized like the yellow ones that stored energy, but most of the others remained a mystery to him. He scanned the room again, which was empty. He stopped before the pile of travel crystals, withdrew his pack, and stuffed them inside.

"So you are here to rob me?" a voice called out.

Aaron spun around, and saw a giant of a man standing to the

side of the charging crystal in the center of the room. The pulsating light distorted his features, so Aaron could not get a good look at him. He quickly closed his pack, now stuffed with the precious purple crystals, and stood up.

The man slowly stepped from around the crystals. He wore a black uniform with a silver dragon emblazoned on his chest that appeared more finely made than any guard's uniform. He wore two katanas on his hips. The set of his high cheekbones and shape of his eyes hit Aaron as if he were kicked in the stomach. Unless he was mistaken, the man before him was the High King of Khamearra, the sworn enemy of Shandara, and Sarah's father.

"You have come here for travel crystals?" the High King asked with a slightly amused expression.

Aaron didn't answer, but stood rooted in place. The prickliness along the dragon tattoo on his chest gained in intensity.

The High King regarded him for a moment, rubbing a spot on his arm. "I don't think we've been properly introduced. I am Amorak," the High King said, but his casual tone did not belie the coldness in his eyes.

"You are Reymius's heir I take it," High King Amorak continued.

"Yes," Aaron replied.

"We went through so much trouble to bring you here to my city, and you up and decide to come on your own. How interesting. Yes, quite interesting, indeed," the High King said, circling toward him.

Aaron sensed the waves of energy exude off the High King in a rigid intensity. "Sarah is in danger," Aaron said quickly, scanning for ways to escape.

"Is she now?" the High King replied. "And how did she get that way?"

Aaron frowned, but kept his distance. "The Drake has captured her."

The High King stepped closer, glowering. "How could you let this happen?"

"I didn't let this happen. We were attacked by your Elitesmen, but you already knew that," Aaron snapped.

"In this you are mistaken," the High King said. "You did let this happen. You brought my daughter to Shandara, and the danger she is in is because of her involvement with you. If you had simply returned with my Elitesmen, she would not be in the clutches of the Drake now."

Aaron clenched his jaw shut, but the truth in the High King's words stung him more than he cared to admit. Curse him, but the High King was right. He was the reason that Sarah was in danger. The seeds of doubt that had been loitering beneath his every action began to firmly take root.

You can't protect everyone, my love.

Sarah's voice echoed within him like a golden beacon, sweeping away the twisted hold the High King had upon him.

"You're wrong. Sarah was there by her own choosing. Primus made his choice when he stabbed her in the back, and I made mine when I took his head from his shoulders," Aaron said and then he leaped into the air, skipping up the shaft emerging into the night sky at the top of the tower. The orange glow of the fires that burned throughout the city dotted his view.

"You didn't think it would be that easy," the High King said, startling him and snatched the rune-carved staff, hurling Aaron to the edge of the tower.

Aaron was on his feet instantly and drew his swords. The bladesong blazed inside him.

The High King smiled in delight. "The Blades of the Alenzar'seth. I have not seen their like in such a long time."

The High King tossed the rune-carved staff off to the side and drew his own dark blades. "Tell me, Shandarian, are you ready to face another Ferasdiam Marked?"

"What do you mean?" Aaron asked.

"Did you think you were the only one?" the High King asked. "You and I are the same, and never before have there been two bearing the mark of Ferasdiam in a generation," the High King said, rubbing his arm. At the same time Aaron felt the sting of the dragon tattoo upon his chest.

"You feel it, too," the High King said.

Aaron kept an eye on the High King, trying to think of some way to escape. "Perhaps it's because you didn't fulfill your purpose that another was required. The land sickens and dies, spreading from Shandara because of what you unleashed."

The High King's face twisted into a sneer. "I crushed your pitiful kingdom and watched as the fires consumed the city."

"Only after Tarimus opened the way for you," Aaron said. "You thought you were conquering a nation, but what you really were was a tool, a blunt instrument playing in someone else's game, and you can't even see it. Mactar used you."

This gave the High King pause. "What are you saying?"

"Mactar isn't loyal to you," Aaron replied.

"You tell me nothing that I don't already know," the High King replied.

"It was only by the grace of the Alenzar'seth that this world wasn't overrun by an invading army from another world. An army that almost won its way to this world except for the actions of my grandfather. It was by his actions and sacrifice that you still live."

"You lie!" the High King howled and lunged for Aaron.

He brought up the Falcons, expecting the High King's attack, and as the blades met, the sky lit up as if lightning had struck the tower upon which they fought. The crystals in the Falcons flared brilliantly as Aaron surrendered himself to the bladesong within. Each movement flowed into the next as a river flows from an icy mountaintop. The bladesong echoed off the rooftops of the towers of the Elite as his blades met those of the High King. Aaron sensed his frustration in their deadly dance. The High King was too used to people falling to his blades, and while he fought with the composure of a master, patient and lethal, he did not expect Aaron to be able to stand against him.

Aaron gave over to the movement that is life, and the urgings of past souls lent their wisdom to his blades. The bladesong churned within, and with it came heightened senses, including those connections he had forced himself to keep at arm's length. The connection to Sarah glowed feebly in his mind, getting weaker and not at all vibrant as it once had been. The brief distraction for the barest of moments was all the High King needed, and Aaron paid the price in blood that ran from a wound down his side. They each broke apart, eyeing the other.

"I'm fighting to save your daughter," Aaron pleaded. He needed to get out of here. This fight with the High King would achieve nothing.

The High King chuckled. "You say that as if your actions, even on my daughter's behalf, would hold sway with me," the High King said, and then his features darkened as if he were standing in a shadow's embrace. "They do not. She is your weakness and will be your downfall. If she was foolish enough to be caught by the Drake, then you were her downfall as well."

Aaron's stomach clenched as if he had been kicked, and from the pit did the fires of his love for Sarah rise within him. He drew in the energy around him, including that from the rune-carved staff, which flared from the ground behind the High King. Aaron launched into the air, sending a great swath of energy from the arc of his blades, knocking the High King back. Aaron was before the High King in an instant and kicked out with the side of his foot, sending the High King into the air, tumbling away from the tower.

Aaron seized the rune-carved staff and jumped in the opposite direction. As his feet left the tower of the Elite, the fires of an explosion rose from the bottom of the tower. Aaron turned in mid-air and watched as the tower of the Elite collapsed in on itself. Where there were once two dark towers now only one remained.

CHAPTER 18
ESCAPE

They emerged from the tower and found the grounds of the
Citadel in complete disarray. The old Elitesman Isaac, as good as
his word, had delivered them from the tower. The night air was
cool and carried the acrid smoke from the fires. Verona's eyes
darted around fearing that the Elitesmen would know of their
escape, but they were swallowed up with everyone else fleeing
the towers.

"Hurry," Gavril said.

Verona nodded. Gavril had whispered to him earlier that
Tanneth was watching over their escape. He glanced up at the
bright flashes of light from the top of the tower across the
grounds. Braden had retracted his Shandarian shield, but kept his
hammer out. Verona wondered how Braden had come by the
hammer. The Elitesmen were gathering on the far side of the
Citadel grounds where most of the order had been restored. Isaac
abruptly changed paths, making a line toward the gates nearest to
them.

A figure in black appeared before them in a flash of light and was joined by two Elitesmen, their eyes burning red, clad in silver cloaks. Verona recognized the Grand Master of the Elite. His eyes narrowed upon them and flashed in surprise when his gaze fell upon Isaac.

"You!" the Grand Master of the Elite hissed.

"Gerric," Isaac answered.

"You're supposed to be dead," the Grand Master said.

"You've run the order into the ground, Gerric," Isaac said. "I'm here to set things right."

The Grand Master of the Elite snorted in disbelief. "You cannot hope to stand against us."

Isaac laughed. "Maybe not, but I think just knowing that there are former Elitesmen like me that stand against you is enough to rattle even your cages and those of your lap dogs," Isaac said. He plunged his hands into his leather duster then threw something at the ground. There was a small flash then smoke billowed up at the Elitesmen's feet.

Verona grabbed Roselyn's hand and pushed her toward the exit. She was followed by Sarik and Braden. Gavril brought up the rear, firing golden bolts into the smoke. They were joined by Nolan and Isaac. A loud shriek came from behind them, and Isaac drew his sword.

Verona looked back at Isaac then drew his own sword.

"No," Isaac said. "Tell the Shandarian that there are more Elite of the old code who don't hold with these ideals."

"We can fight with you," Verona said.

Isaac looked around at the grounds of the Elite in disgust. There were young initiates running to escape the fires. Some initiates helped their brethren while others used the disarray as an excuse to strike.

"Fight for *them*," Isaac said, gesturing toward the initiates of the Elite, and smoke swallowed him up as he leaped through.

An explosion rocked the ground beneath their feet as the far tower collapsed to the ground.

"Run!" Gavril shouted.

The Citadel gates burst forth as a mass of people fled for their lives. Roselyn's hand found his and gave him a gentle squeeze as they lost themselves in the crowd. They had escaped. Verona glanced back at the Citadel. The smoke and dust that billowed into the air was overshadowed by the screams of those within who hadn't escaped in time.

Captain Nolan guided them through the streets, leading them away from the chaos. Verona had managed to get the attention of the fleeing Initiates who were all too happy to have escaped the Citadel. They were young, barely more than boys and girls, and hadn't been inducted into the Elitesmen Order yet. Nolan sent them onward with some of his guards that they had met up with.

Verona frowned, scanning the faces of the men with them. "Where is Eric?" he asked.

Braden shook his head grimly, which was reply enough.

Verona swallowed the lump in his throat, knowing that Eric had died the night before when they were taken prisoner. He gripped Braden's shoulder firmly and shared the promised look of grim resolution. The destruction around them was a cold recompense for the lives lost, both the nameless innocent and those of friends and brothers. He hated the Elitesmen, but through Isaac's sacrifice he grudgingly admitted to himself that they were not all the same. He hoped that Isaac did find a way to survive his encounter with the Grand Master. Hoping for the survival of any Elitesman still left him with a bitter aftertaste. Too much of what that order had done to the people of this world could not be swept away.

Captain Nolan brought them to an abandoned building where they were met by Anson along with other members of the Resistance. Anson reported a resounding victory with none of their number being captured or killed.

"Has there been any word from Aaron?" Verona asked.

"Not yet, my lord," Lieutenant Anson answered.

Verona nodded. He wanted to be out there looking for his friend, but knew that staying in one place was the wise choice, at least for the moment. "You must prepare for retribution from the High King and the Elitesmen," Verona said.

"We are prepared to fight," Anson said. "The rumor throughout the city is that a dragon appeared at the arena. When your friend crashes a party, he doesn't go halfway."

"I'm still concerned for the Resistance, and if the fight becomes too much, you should head to Rexel," Verona said.

Captain Nolan frowned. "Why Rexel?"

Gavril cleared his throat, joining them. "Please, Verona, allow me to share what we know."

Verona nodded, and Gavril proceeded to tell them of the barrier between worlds in Shandara and the invading army waiting on the other side. Gavril was able to quell most skeptics with a few displays of the Hythariam comms device and a demonstration of something he called a plasma pistol.

"According to Aaron, the barrier between worlds is failing, and it is only a matter of time before the armies of the former Hythariam military pour through," Gavril said. "We had hoped that our home would be destroyed and would take care of the military faction that was bent on conquering the people of Safanar, but they must have found a way to survive."

"Was the beacon of light we had reports on throughout the city from the heir of Alenzar'seth?" someone from the crowd asked.

Verona stepped up. "Yes," he answered.

Captain Nolan and Anson shared a look. "Thank you for telling us these things. I will circulate this information throughout the Resistance here and decide what to do going forward. I can't commit either way. Khamearra has become a home for many of us, and some will be reluctant to leave. What started off as vengeance of the De'anjard has grown into something much more."

Verona nodded in understanding. "Don't take too long, as time is growing short."

Gavril continued to answer questions, and Lieutenant Anson stepped away to check whether Aaron had shown up at any of the designated meeting points they had agreed on earlier.

Somewhere during the discussion, Verona noticed Roselyn sitting off to the side, working intently on a chrome cylinder at a small table. She looked up and smiled at him as he approached. She was still shaken, he could tell, and so was he if truth be told.

"My Lady, you don't waste any time," Verona said.

Roselyn nodded, turning back to the cylinder. "This is something that Aaron asked me to look at."

"What is it?" Verona asked.

"This is what enabled Aaron to travel from Earth to Safanar," Roselyn said.

Verona frowned. Earth was where Aaron had called home until coming to Safanar. His friend had told him of the place, but try as he might, it was difficult to imagine. Looking at the small device in Roselyn's hands, it amazed him that such a thing was possible, even knowing what he knew.

"I'm updating some of its functions," Roselyn said vaguely.

"Aaron seeks to protect us all, it seems," Verona said.

Roselyn eyed him with a raised eyebrow. "Do you know what he intends?"

Verona pursed his lips in thought. "Not exactly, but the question really is what wouldn't he do, and I feel the answers lie in that."

Roselyn's eyes narrowed. "Are all men so bullheaded that they must act alone when there are people able to help them?"

Verona shrugged his shoulders. "Sometimes the occasion calls for it," he said and suppressed a smile as she muttered a curse under her breath. "It's okay to take a moment for yourself, my lady."

Roselyn's hands shook as she held the cylinder. "I can't."

Verona sat next to her and put his arm around her shoulders, and she leaned into him, shaking.

"I can't get it out of my head," Roselyn said. "I can't get him out of my head."

Verona gently rubbed her shoulders. He knew exactly what she meant. They were free from the Elitesman Sevan, but the gruesome acts of torture lingered in the back of their minds.

"I know," Verona said. "I... I just..." He couldn't get the words out, and they both took comfort in the other's embrace.

After a few moments, they released each other despite neither of them being able to find the words. Roselyn resumed her work on the chrome cylinder, which she called the keystone accelerator, and Verona stayed by her side. They were soon joined by the others, although Braden sat off to the side, keeping careful watch even though they were with the Resistance. Within an hour, Anson brought word that they had found Aaron. They gathered their things and set off, heading for another hideout to meet up with their friend. Verona just wanted to leave, putting as much distance between himself and the capital city of Khamearra as possible. He fully supported their reasons for being here, but at the same time he wanted it to just be over.

Captain Nolan supplied them with cloaks and uniforms of the guards so they could move throughout the city more easily. That was the plan, anyway. Verona replaced his sword. He was only too happy to be rid of the Elitesman's blade he was carrying. Both he and Sarik carried bows and a full quiver of arrows. He still didn't see Tanneth, but Gavril assured him that the Hythariam was still out there and would help watch over them as they traversed the city.

***

Aaron rested upon the rooftop of a shop in the district's market square. The remaining tower of the Citadel of the Elite was a good distance behind him. Things were quiet for the moment, and the smell of smoke was thinning. The wound on his side ached, and he bit back a groan as he removed his cloak and shirt. He scooped some water from a metal bucket on the rooftop and washed the sword slice down his side. The wound was deep, and Aaron worked to steady his breathing, allowing his mind to focus. He reached out to the energy in the staff, and the runes flared dully. He drew it in, speeding up what his body would do naturally if he had been stitched up and bedridden for weeks. The pain faded to a dull ache until the angry pink scar faded away on his skin. He had been lucky. One lesson he learned from his encounter with the Ryakul was that the ability to concentrate and focus was essential when working with the energy. If he couldn't focus then he would die just like anyone else. He rolled his shoulders, remembering the hot pain down his back as the Ryakuls tore at his flesh. He shook off the memory and put his shirt back on as he took in his surroundings. He was looking for a small shop with the emblem of a tree with clawed roots carved into the door. The subtle references to Shandara that could be found throughout the city of Khamearra amazed him. The Resistance had used pieces from the Alenzar'seth coat of arms as their markings throughout the city. Nothing so bold as the complete picture, but pieces that were just enough to give those who knew what to look for the information they sought to find the Resistance. It was the arrogance of the Elitesmen that allowed for their enemy to dwell among them. Aaron wondered if the irony would be lost upon them as perhaps arrogance played its part in the destruction of Shandara.

Aaron's mind drifted to a history class he had in college, where the teacher pontificated that a smart enemy would strike where you thought you were safe. Mactar and the High King had used this tactic to bring about the destruction of Shandara and here Aaron was, instrumental in doing the same to the Elitesmen Order. He knew the Elite Order was not destroyed, but tonight's events had certainly put them off balance just as the High King had put him off balance. His jaw clenched at the High King's dismissal of his daughter, but his mind refused to accept that a father could so easily disregard that their child was in danger, even if that father was the High King. There were things that just didn't add up where Sarah and her father were concerned, and regardless of his understanding, Aaron would move forward with his own plans. He shook his head in frustration and glanced up at the night sky. Except for the faint orange glow, the night was dark, as the moons were still rising. His hand absently rubbed the medallion under his shirt, and he recalled the image of the beacon of light shooting into the sky over the arena. The dragon referred to himself as the Eldarin. Aaron pressed his lips together in thought. How would he seek out the Eldarin? He had no idea where they were, but knew they were the natural enemies of the Ryakuls. Aaron shook his head and lifted his backpack stuffed full of purple travel crystals. He needed to rejoin the others then find

Sarah. The Eldarin would have to wait. If his faint connection to Sarah were any indication, time was indeed growing short before the woman he loved was gone forever. His grandfather's haunted eyes flashed before him like a silent prophecy of what would happen to him if he failed. Reymius couldn't have known what became of his grandmother, Cassandra, but Aaron *did* know and he would not condemn the woman he loved to the cruel prison of the Nanites.

Aaron snatched the rune-carved staff off the ground and crept along the rooftops, searching for the shop that bore the emblem of a tree with a clawed foot hidden amid its roots. He expanded his search and found the mark upon the door of a shop along one of the side streets away from the main market square. The shop was dark, and Aaron watched silently. The minutes dragged on, but his patience paid off as he saw shadows move from within the shop. Someone was home even if the lights were not on.

He climbed down to the street and came before the door. After softly knocking three times, he waited to the count of five then knocked twice more. There was a soft shuffle inside, but it was the two shadows that silently approached from either side that gave him pause. Aaron turned and was greeted by two men leveling large double crossbows at him.

"I'm sorry to call so late," Aaron said. "But I was told that there are friends of the shield inside."

The older man with gray in his hair regarded him for a few moments, his eyes widening. "Brothers of the shield are indeed welcome, but for the Heir of Shandara I would lay down my life.

It is my honor to be in the presence of the Alenzar'seth once again, Your Grace," the man said, lowering his crossbow and brought a fist over his heart as he bowed his head.

Aaron was about to say something, but the door opened, and the older man brought a finger to his lips, and the three of them stepped inside. He followed the members of the Resistance down a flight of narrow stairs to a storage room that housed long dusty racks. They walked to the back of the room and headed down the farthest aisle. They came to a rack that was covered with old beer steins, and the older man reached toward the back and pulled the top of one of the steins. The wall shuddered for a moment then moved silently back, opening enough for them to easily pass through. The hallway beyond was lit with orbs. They quickly came to an open room that held a few tables and sleeping pallets off to the side. The stone walls were plainly painted, but the air smelled relatively fresh considering they were underground.

The older man turned toward him and regarded him for a moment while his two younger companions waited. They looked to be about the same age as Aaron, and the older man looked to be in his fifties, with a few lines creased upon his face, his beard and hair neatly trimmed. The older man shook his head with half a grin.

"Please forgive me, Your Grace," he said. "I had heard rumors, but to see proof with my own eyes..." The older man went down to one knee with a fist over his heart. "By my life or death I serve Shandara and the ruling house of Alenzar'seth." After a fraction of a second, he was joined by his two younger companions, who repeated the oath.

"Please," Aaron said gently, "don't kneel." Aaron stepped forward and offered his hand to the older man. "I'm Aaron Jace."

The older man rose and took the proffered hand. "I am Nicolas, and these are my sons, Liam and Daniel."

Aaron nodded to each in turn and put his hand out, but it was only with their father's nod of encouragement that they shook Aaron's hand.

"How did you recognize me?" Aaron asked.

Nicolas stood taller, his shoulders back with militaristic precision. "I am a son of Shandara and a member of the De'anjard. I would always recognize the family resemblance of my late Prince Reymius or his daughter, Princess Carlowen."

A proud smile came to Aaron's face, and he nodded.

"I have many questions," Nicolas said. "But I know you're not here to answer my questions. What can I do to help you?"

"I would be happy to answer any questions you have, sir." Aaron replied. "My friends are due to meet up with Captain Nolan and Lieutenant Anson this evening. Are you able to send word to them?"

"At once, Your Grace," Nicolas said and nodded toward Liam, who bowed and left the room.

Daniel approached with a tray of food and water. Aaron thanked them for the food and quickly downed the water.

"I think his Grace could do with something a bit stronger," Nicolas said, and Daniel disappeared down the hallway.

"Please, sir, call me Aaron."

After a few moments, Nicolas nodded, though Aaron doubted he would do so. Daniel returned carrying two steins filled with dark beer.

Aaron raised his stein and took a hearty swallow. "I have things to share with you, but you must have questions for me," Aaron said setting down his stein.

Daniel glanced at his father, who nodded. "Most of my immediate questions surround why you are here in Khamearra and what your plans are moving forward."

"Were you at the fall of Shandara?" Aaron asked.

Nicolas stiffly set down his stein, and shadows from a haunted past glided over his face as he nodded solemnly.

Aaron swallowed. "There are some things I need to share with you, but first I must know—are you the leader of the Resistance here in Khamearra?"

"Goodness, no. In true Shandarian tradition, we share leadership. There are three others besides myself, but beyond that there are very few of the original De'anjard left. Our descendants made a life here in this city, but we've never wavered from our purpose."

Aaron nodded and marveled at the dedication of the De'anjard with their shattered remains spread throughout the world, continuing to fight in their own way. You couldn't buy that type of loyalty, not with all the money in the world.

"I don't know how much you know about the fall, so I ask for your patience—" Aaron began, but Nicolas interrupted.

"You never need to ask for that, Your Grace," Nicolas said then his face softened. "Sorry, Aaron. Part of me doesn't believe that you're sitting here before my very eyes. I was part of the detail assigned with protecting Princess Carlowen, your mother. You have her eyes."

A small lump grew in his throat at the mention of his mother, and while he knew she had been a princess, it was still strange for him to hear of her being referred to as one.

"She lived," Aaron said. "She was happy."

"Was?" Nicolas asked and then reached out and put his hand on Aaron's shoulder. "I'm sorry for your loss."

Aaron nodded, fighting off the bitter torrent of memories. There had always been something to prevent him from properly mourning the loss of both his parents, and it was in rare quiet moments such as these that grief reached out and snatched at him unawares.

Aaron raised his stein. "To those we wished were here and all the lives taken before their time." He took a long swallow from his stein, and Nicolas and Daniel followed suit.

"Well met," Nicolas said appreciatively.

Aaron set down his stein and leaned forward. "There is a looming threat to this world beyond the High King or those seeking retribution for the fall of Shandara..." Aaron told them of the Hythariam and the danger posed by the invading army. How Colind along with ambassadors of the Hythariam were spreading the word and working to gain support from the other nations.

"We need the help of Khamearra against the invading army," Aaron said. "I know there is a small faction of the Elitesmen who have aided your efforts here. You will need their help."

Nicolas looked up alarmed. "Won't you be leading us?"

Aaron knew the question was coming and dreaded giving the answer. "I can't," he said. "To be honest, Nicolas, I don't think I could do anything that you are not already doing, but I will say this. I would much rather see all of the Resistance leave this nation and head to Rexel, where you will find support, than stay and fight the High King and the Elitesmen. We've struck a blow, but they are still powerful, and I wouldn't want you to throw your lives away. I know firsthand how hard it is to leave the only home you've ever known and I realize that many will be reluctant to go, but to not meet this threat head-on could doom this world and give a foothold to an enemy that knows no mercy."

Nicolas gave a small nod and sighed. "You are wise for one so young."

Aaron felt his lips curve into a small smile. "Thank you," he said. "Will you be able to move your people from the city safely?"

Nicolas was silent for a few moments, considering. "There is nothing that can be achieved without risk. Many will need to be convinced. We've moved people from the city before and we do have safe havens setup throughout the land. Some of us always meant to return to Shandara, but—"

"It's not safe," Aaron said quickly. "I wouldn't bring families there, but I fear that this war will take us back to Shandara."

Nicolas nodded. "To where this all began."

Aaron sighed, allowing the silence to stretch between them while he gathered his thoughts. "I don't know where this will end," Aaron said. "I've been to Shandara. We were able to free Colind of the Safanarion Order there, but no one could live there. Not now at least. Perhaps in time the land will heal."

"You have given us much to consider and the events of this night will lend weight to those still in doubt that you do in fact exist," Nicolas said. "How much time do we have before this Hythariam army will invade?"

"It could be as early as three months from now," Aaron replied, and Nicolas's eyes widened in shock.

"Very little time indeed. I'm not sure we could move an army to Shandara in that time," Nicolas said. "We have no time to prepare."

Aaron watched as Nicolas steeled himself to the insurmountable task Aaron was asking him to be a part of. "You will not be entirely without aid. The Hythariam here on Safanar will give aid to any who will join our cause. There are airships being built and augmented with engines that will make the trip possible, but you will have to get your people safely away from the city to meet them. I'm not sure where."

"How will we contact the Hythariam? No one has seen or heard from them, other than rumors, for years," Nicolas asked.

Liam entered the room and bowed his head to Aaron. "Your companions are safe and in Captain Nolan's district. I can take you to them when you are ready, my lord."

Aaron thanked Liam and rose to his feet. He pulled out his comms device. "This is called a comms device and will allow you to call the Hythariam. When we leave, I will give you this one and show you how to use it. The Hythariam have inventions that seem mysterious, but they are not magic. In time perhaps, they will be a commonplace to Safanar."

Aaron activated the comms device. "Tanneth did you get that?"

"Yes, I have their location," came Tanneth's reply. "I will meet you there."

The indicator light dimmed as Tanneth closed the connection, but Nicolas's eyes were wide with shock.

"Mysterious indeed," Nicolas said, rising from his seat. "Let's go meet the others."

They rose, and Aaron watched as Daniel went to the far side of the room away from the entrance. After a moment, a portion of the wall slid away and a dark passageway opened before them. For all the Hythariam technological wonders, Aaron couldn't help but be impressed with the well-hidden secret door as it slid silently upon its hinges, opening the way for them.

"I'm afraid I can't do anything about the smell," Nicolas said. "But at least we will be able to travel through the city unseen. According to my son, the guards are sweeping the city, and regular troops are assembling outside the city walls." He finished attaching a glowing orb to his staff and led the way.

Aaron followed them into the sewers under the city. As they traversed the passageways, his thoughts drifted to his friends. He hoped they were all right. He felt the weight of the travel crystals on his back and wondered if they would be enough to thwart the Nanites. She was slipping. He could feel it and the knowledge gnawed away at him.

Roughly an hour later, through countless turns and passageways, they came to a ladder. Daniel ascended first and gave a series of knocks on the door at the top. A single knock was given in reply, and the door was opened, sending a shaft of light into the dimly lit tunnel. Aaron ascended the ladder and emerged to a crowded warehouse. Curtains hung over the windows preventing light from getting out. There were people tending to wounded soldiers and messengers running about. Nicolas returned a salute to one messenger who greeted them and led them to the other side of the warehouse. As they crossed the way, a hush overtook the people like a wave of silence descending upon them. All eyes were on Aaron, who stood taller than most men. Their eyes lingered on the rune-carved staff and then on Aaron himself. The silence was broken by the sweep of hundreds of feet as all in the warehouse sank to one knee.

"By my life or death, I serve Shandara and the ruling house of Alenzar'seth."

The oath of the De'anjard echoed throughout the warehouse, sending shivers down Aaron's spine. He felt the heat rise to his face, but he let his gaze sweep over those around him. Looking all of these people in the eye was the least he could do considering the loyalty they had shown. His gaze was returned with a proud reckoning in the eyes of those around him. They were a hard bunch and some he recognized from the arena. He nodded to them and they returned a nod in kind. Despite his less than enthusiastic acceptance of being of royal birth, he knew he was something more to these people. A symbol. A leader. And to the smaller group approaching him, a friend.

Aaron leaped atop a small table, feeling that he should say something, and beckoned them all to rise.

"Thank you," Aaron said, his voice traveling through the warehouse. "You honor the spirit of Shandara with your service. I can only stand in awe of what you've accomplished here and at your dedication to the ideals of the Alenzar'seth. Such ideals had merit with my grandfather Reymius. Know that if he were here, you would have had his gratitude, respect, and dedication to the same ideals. I can't imagine what you've had to endure until this day. It is I who pledge to you my life and death to forever serve the spirit of Shandara. The very same spirit I see alive among all of you. The road before us is long, and the battle is not yet won, but we will endure. The spirit of Shandara will endure. The sacrifice of all those before us will never be in vain, for we have something here in this very room that cannot be taken from us."

Aaron paused, his hard gaze sweeping the room as the men and women before him seemed to stand taller. "Honor and courage, never without fear, but always willing to take that bold step forward. These are among the core tenants that the tyrants of this world can never crush. The spirit of Shandara was kept alive because of you and it is you that I should bow to, not the other way around." Aaron knelt down upon the table for all to see and spoke the Safanarion oath. "By my life or death, I serve to protect the world of Safanar and will call brother and sister to all who would take up this cause. Be a shield to those in need. Be an ear for those to listen. Be a voice for those who would speak."

As Aaron spoke, an invisible shroud settled down upon his shoulders. His words had come from the depths of his heart, and he meant every last one of them.

There was a moment of deafening silence until the crowded warehouse erupted with roars of approval. The people stood taller and even those wounded lying in bed held eyes that glimmered with hope.

Aaron leaped down and came face to face with Verona. His friend's eyes held a much harder glint to them, but Aaron was so relieved to see him alive that he pulled him into an embrace.

"Well met, my friend," Verona grinned. "Well met."

Aaron felt as if a fist had unclenched around his heart. Seeing them all alive and safe took a great weight off his shoulders. He glanced at Braden, who nodded grimly in return, and Aaron felt the absence of his brother, Eric, more profoundly than before by the empty spot at his side.

"I'm so glad you're all safe," Aaron said.

"None more so than we are, I can assure you," Verona said with a grin, but his eyes retained the haunted expression that could not so easily be dispelled with a bit of mirth.

Aaron shook hands with Captain Nolan and Lieutenant Anson and noticed for the first time that the Elitesman Isaac was not among them.

Verona sensed his question before he could give voice to it. "He sacrificed himself so we could escape, but he wanted me to give you a message. 'Tell the Shandarian that there are more Elite of the old code who don't hold with these ideals.' When we offered to fight at his side, he looked at the initiates and told us to fight for them. I think the Elitesmen have many factions to their order, and there are some who may join our cause."

Aaron nodded. "I think you are right. Is there any chance that Isaac survived?"

"To be honest, I'm not sure," Verona said.

"We will look for him," Nolan said.

Aaron scratched the back of his head. "It was easier to think of them as all evil, but that is not always the case now."

Verona shook his head, but Braden spoke up. "Most of them are still evil," he said coldly, leaving little room for argument.

Aaron nodded. There would be no easy way forward for any of them. He looked at Gavril. "Tanneth said he would be here soon."

Gavril nodded. "I have no doubts that Tanneth has already taken watch on the roof of this building."

Aaron smiled. Tanneth had done more to help get them this far than Aaron could ever thank him enough for. They sat at a table off to the side and were joined by Lieutenant Anson along with Nicolas, to whom Anson deferred to as one of the leaders of the Resistance.

"It's not safe for all the leaders to gather in one spot, but what is said here will be passed along to them," Nicolas said, and his gaze lingered on Gavril and Roselyn. Both had shed their disguises, and the irises of the golden eyes of the Hythariam shone brightly. "I have not seen your people in a lifetime."

Gavril took the lead and bowed to the Resistance general. "Something we hope to rectify. I will send word to my people, and they will send aid to you." Gavril reached inside his sack and pulled out a comms device. "You can use this to reach our people. Once I show you how to use it, this will help coordinate our efforts better," Gavril said and nodded for Nolan and Anson to come over.

Captain Nolan hesitated for a moment, stopping before Aaron. "Your Grace," Captain Nolan said formally with a fist across his heart. "Many will join our cause, but I wanted to pledge myself to you personally after your actions in the arena and the other day. You have shown me a light worthy enough to beat back the shadows of this world. A light worth following. From this moment forward, you can count on me."

Aaron was momentarily at a loss for words. Before he could say anything, Captain Nolan turned away and joined the others with Gavril.

Verona cleared his throat, and Aaron joined them at the table with Roselyn, Sarik, and Braden.

"The beacon of light at the arena was you?" Verona asked.

Aaron swallowed and nodded and echoes of the Eldarin spoke in his mind. *We of the Eldarin, honor the one who is marked by Ferasdiam. Seek us out as our numbers are few and there are things you must know.*

"We saw the beacon from the tower," Verona said. "I think the whole city saw it. There is talk of a dragon descending upon the arena."

"Yes," Aaron said. "He didn't call himself a dragon, but referred to himself as the *Eldarin*. He said that they honor the one who is marked by Ferasdiam."

"The Eldarin?" Verona said. "I've never heard of them, but if they came to your aid then they are okay in my book."

Aaron smiled at the simplicity that Verona had categorized the world. "I have the travel crystals," he said, opening his pack revealing the horde of glimmering purple crystals.

Verona and Sarik reached in and took two of them out, studying them for a moment.

"Do you know how they work?" Sarik asked.

Aaron's mind screeched to a halt and he looked up in alarm. "No," he said. "I was so focused on getting them that I hadn't considered how they actually worked. I was hoping that Isaac would be able to help."

Aaron reached in and pulled out one of the precious purple crystals. He could feel the stored up energy trapped within the prism confines of the crystal. "It can't be that hard," he said.

Verona shrugged his shoulders and Sarik studied the crystal intently.

Roselyn muttered something under her breath. "Typical. First thing is first. What do we know about how these crystals work?"

Aaron called up the memory of his encounter with the Elitesmen at the airfield in Rexel, but he had been too preoccupied with survival and didn't have an inkling as to how the Elitesmen had used the crystal to teleport from place to place. His mind returned to the Feast of Shansheru, the celebration held in Shandara's honor at Rexel, where he had first danced with Sarah. She had held the crystal in her hand.

That's it!

"They require physical contact," Aaron said. "I remember Sarah having it in her hand the night we danced in Rexel."

Verona nodded, remembering, and Roselyn smiled at Aaron, reminding him of his older sister. "How romantic of you. What else did you see? We need more to go on than that."

Aaron thought about it for a few seconds. "They only have so many charges, but I'm not sure how many. I think since they are mainly used by the Elitesmen, or those trained similarly, then it has something to do with tapping into the energy in the crystal."

"We'll need to test this before you go traipsing off after the Drake," Roselyn said.

Aaron nodded. "Agreed. We need to get out of here tonight. We cannot linger."

Roselyn frowned. "Why?"

"I can feel her fading," Aaron said in a voice barely above a whisper.

Verona and Roselyn exchanged glances, but Aaron did not have time to wonder what had transpired between the two.

"I don't want to reach out to her here," Aaron continued. "We need to be away from the city. Can the ship be recalled to a place of our choosing?"

The others glanced at Roselyn who answered. "Just slow down. Take a moment."

"She doesn't have a moment," Aaron said loudly enough to draw confused looks from those around them. He cast his eyes downward. "I'm sorry. I know you're trying to help."

Roselyn nodded in understanding. "We will get to her in time. I haven't wanted to ask, but have you given any thought as to how to find her?"

He had thought about it constantly. "I can find her through the bond. She is somewhere in the mountain range near Shandara, at least she was yesterday. The Drake knows I will come for her. He is counting on it and therefore doesn't need to move around."

The group was silent for a moment, each taking some time for their thoughts.

"How did you get them?" Verona asked. "The crystals, I mean."

"Oh I went into the other tower to the central chamber after the arena. It seemed to be the place where they recharged all types of crystals."

Verona pressed his lips in thought. "And you made it out undetected?"

Aaron frowned. "Not entirely," he answered. "I met the High King, or rather, he found me in the chamber."

Their mouths fell open, except for Roselyn, who looked questioningly at all of them.

Aaron suppressed a shudder. The High King was powerful. "He is Ferasdiam Marked like me."

Sarik made the sign of the Goddess upon his brow, and Verona leaned in. "Ferasdiam Marked?" he asked, clearly trying to come to grips with this news. "I wish Vaughn were here."

Aaron nodded. "I wish Colind were here, too. If they knew, why wouldn't they have said something?"

"They couldn't have known," Verona said.

Roselyn sighed in frustration and said, "Comms device, gentlemen. Try to raise him on it."

Aaron cursed himself inwardly for not remembering. He brought out the comms device and navigated the small display to Colind's signal, but it was dull, as if his device was offline. Aaron held it up for Roselyn to see.

"That shouldn't happen," Roselyn said, checking her own comms device.

"Never mind about that," Verona said. "Tell us what transpired between you and the High King."

Aaron swallowed some water. "I tried to reason with him. I told him of the invading army and how Mactar is not loyal to his cause, but I'm not sure he believed me. He didn't seem to care about Mactar."

Verona's gaze narrowed. "Did you tell him about Sarah?"

The High King's dismissal of his daughter's life made Aaron clench his teeth, but he nodded and said, "He doesn't care. He said that she was my weakness. People carry no weight in his eyes other than the purpose they serve."

"Did you fight the High King?" Sarik asked.

"I was more concerned with getting away than fighting a battle with him. I had gotten what I'd come for."

"Indeed," Braden said, speaking up for the first time. "You could have struck a blow to cripple Khamearra and cut the head off the snake here."

Aaron met Braden's gaze. "The snakes in Khamearra have many heads. To be honest, I'm not sure it was a battle I could win and to die here in a battle not of my choosing wouldn't accomplish anything. I'm sure the High King and I will meet again."

Braden's eyes still held the fires of anger in them, but he nodded once.

"Where was Mactar during all this?" Verona asked.

"That is an excellent question," Aaron answered. "I don't know and I don't think the lack of his presence was by accident. While I don't know for sure, I can sense his handiwork behind the scenes." Aaron told them of his encounter with Rordan and how Rordan wouldn't tell him anything.

"I can only imagine the restraint it took, given your fondness of arrogant young princes," Verona said, but before Aaron could reply, Verona continued. "I know for whom your actions were dictated, but at some point you will be faced with a choice. Sarah understands that as well."

Aaron nodded slowly. "I'm not here seeking to wage old wars, but for her I gave them this one chance," he said, thinking of when Sarah had asked why everything must end in bloodshed. His mind drifted to their time in the forest where they had jumped to dizzying heights through the trees. She moved with the agility and grace of a swan gliding along a lake against the setting sun, while he stumbled and bumped into a few trees trying to keep up with her. He smiled at the memory, missing Sarah's playful nature and the way she challenged him. How his heart raced as he melted into her arms during the night of the choosing in Tolvar's camp, when she had set her laurel crown upon his head amid the firelight.

Aaron forced the memory aside as Gavril joined them and said, "I think if we have finished our business in the city then we should leave tonight. Tomorrow will prove to be more difficult to move about the city, and I doubt you want to wait idly until the evening."

Aaron looked around at all the members of the Resistance in the warehouse. He wanted to leave. He had to leave, but at the same time he felt a twinge of guilt as if he were abandoning these people. Aaron could feel Gavril's eyes on him.

"This is their fight, Aaron," Gavril said. "They have been waging it for many years."

"I know," Aaron said. "I just wish there was more time. That there was more I could do for them."

Gavril nodded. "You have done much more than you realize. You have given them a path, and with our aid, we will help them reach it. In one evening you've managed to put the Elitesmen off balance, and the fires of hope will blaze throughout this city and all the lands of Khamearra. You've shown the world that they are not unstoppable. That there are those who can oppose them. I think that should you return to this city someday, you will find it a much different place than it is today."

But at what cost, Aaron wondered, taking another look around at all the people. According to Nicolas, there were places like this warehouse throughout the city. The people cast glances in his direction, but they all looked determined.

Gavril reached out to him, and Aaron turned back to him.

"Freedom is never given," Gavril said. "It is won. These people know this truth. They have bled for it and will continue to fight for it."

Aaron's gaze never left Gavril's. The old soldier from the Hythariam home world knew firsthand what it was like to lose freedom in the name of tyranny under the guise of necessity. He was no stranger to true oppression, unlike Aaron, who had never had to cope with it, but only learned of it through history books. Gavril was right. This was their fight, and he had contributed a verse to their battle song, but he couldn't sing it for them.

"It's time for us to leave," Aaron said, and the others around him slowly rose, each choosing of their own accord to stand with him. He nodded appreciatively to each in turn, and he knew that the debt he owed his friends was something that, in his eyes, could never be repaid. They would never call it a debt or view their actions as something owed. They simply stood together in unison with him on this path, wherever it would lead them. The burden of leadership fell heavily upon his shoulders, as it would on anyone's, but Aaron was coming to accept it as he never had before.

CHAPTER 19
PRINCES & KINGS

Colind stood on the deck of the Raven, watching as Rexel's airship yard grew smaller. They were heading toward a neutral meeting place between Rexel and Zsensibar, escorting Prince Jopher in hopes of winning support from his father the king. The boy had grown much according to Cyrus. Aaron's influence no doubt.

There were six airships with them, bringing their total to seven. All had been upgraded with the help of the Hythariam, and the newly promoted Admiral Nathaniel Morgan of the Free Nations Army. Morgan was using their little trip as an excuse to put the airships through their paces and practice coordinating attacks and maneuvers. Prince Jopher had taken to sailing the skies and had requested to study under the admiral, to which Morgan agreed while joking about needing more help in the kitchens peeling potatoes. Jopher's face grew red with embarrassment, and Morgan had commissioned the young prince as an officer in the army.

The Free Nations Army was composed of troops from Rexel and

its neighboring kingdoms, as well as former Shandarians, with more people joining every day. Colind and Reymius had often spoke of uniting the kingdoms while allowing for their independence. The Safanarion Order had made some progress toward this, but the people of Safanar hadn't been ready before the fall of Shandara. Now, almost twenty-five years later with the power of the High King and the Elitesmen running virtually unchecked, their eyes had opened to the fact that their world would have been a much better place had Shandara not perished.

Colind let the echoes of a gloried past go and focused on the now. He wasn't sure how Zsensibar's King, Jopher's father, would react to his son's enlistment into the military. He hoped they could win their support, as the kingdom of Zsensibar held the second-largest army in their part of the world and mines rich in metals and raw materials that they would need. Being located south of the Waylands, the home of Rexel, afforded Zsensibar to be able to avoid most skirmishes with the High King. Cyrus had told him that Zsensibar's army was well trained despite the questionable practices observed in the kingdom. They practiced a harsh class system of government that left most common people little more than indentured servants. While they didn't outright call them slaves, they could be nothing else in Colind's mind. The Hythariam would be reluctant to share their knowledge with them, and Colind knew Aaron would never approve, but they needed Zsensibar's support. He could see how easily their efforts to save Safanar from invasion could be thwarted if the nations of this world didn't unite.

292 | ECHOES OF A GLORIED PAST

Colind felt the bottom drop away from his stomach as the ship rose higher into the air and dodged to the side. Tersellis, the Hythariam ambassador, referred to the coordinated airship maneuvers as drills. Well, these drills were going to cause his breakfast to spew all over the well polished deck, which wouldn't help his legendary status in the eyes of the crew.

The enhancements to the ship had included smaller maneuvering engines that helped steer the airship with precision. While the airships could never maneuver as precisely as what the Hythariam's had in Hathenwood, they were a marked improvement over what previously existed.

The heavier fore and aft engines propelled the ships forward. With the additional engines, more yellow crystals were put in place to allow the airships to remain in the air despite the heavier load. Tersellis hinted at future airships that didn't require a cell or balloon to keep the ship in the air, but with the timeframe they had, he doubted that any would be ready in time. There were caches of weapons throughout the ruins of Shandara that had not seen the light of day since before the fall, and Colind hoped there were things there that they could still use. Anything that could give them an edge. Iranus was investigating the ruins of Shandara, but he suspected they needed Aaron to actually open the weapons caches.

Colind lifted his eyes to the west where half a world away, Khamearra lay, and within its capital city, the Heir of Shandara. He kept his frustration in check because part of him felt that he should be by Aaron's side, but they all had a part to play and his required him to be here at this moment. Still, he found it increasingly unsettling that Mactar was out there and he yearned to seek him out. They had unfinished business, and he counted it a fair trade to give his life up to take out Mactar. Safanar would be better off without him. Then there was Tarimus, his son. Almost nothing remained of the boy, Tarimus, but he was still his son, Colind admonished to himself. No amount of time or deeds done would ever change that. But unlike before the fall, he saw the evil that had been in Tarimus. His imprisonment left him with little else to do, and Colind had lost count of how many times he cursed his own foolhardiness for denying the truth before his eyes. Tarimus had always been power hungry and ambitious, but his intentions had been aligned with the Safanarion Order, which was the preservation of this world. He could blame Mactar for bringing Tarimus into his web, but deep down he blamed himself. He was Tarimus's father, and whatever failings were part of his son held an undeniable connection to himself. Even now, after all that had happened, Colind still struggled to think of something that he could have done differently that could change what Tarimus had become. In the end, he knew that the path of 'what ifs' would lead to nowhere, but he still couldn't help wanting to know why. The only way he would get any answers was to face his son again. The thought of facing Tarimus burned like acid in his mouth. It was his duty to bring Tarimus to justice for the part he played in the destruction of Shandara. Tarimus's dark betrayal by aligning with the High King and Mactar, causing the death of thousands of Shandarians, was left to him to address. Better himself than Aaron. He owed Aaron that much at least.

"My Lord Guardian," Jopher said behind him.

Colind turned to see Jopher in a blue officer's uniform standing proudly before him. There was not a hint of the youthful arrogance in his eyes, only the confidence and character one has through achievement, which commanded Colind's respect.

"My Lord, Prince," Colind replied.

"Please, no 'My Lord,'" Jopher replied. "I'm just Lieutenant Jopher of the Free Nations Army."

Colind suppressed a smile. "As you wish, Lieutenant."

Jopher nodded. "The admiral wishes for you to join him on the observation deck off the wheel house."

"I am, of course, at the admiral's service," Colind answered and gestured for Jopher to lead the way. "How are you settling in to your new role?"

Jopher walked ahead, addressing Colind as he went. "Honestly, My Lord Guardian, I love it. Never before have I felt part of something. To be a member of a team. Doing my part, knowing that others depend upon me, and that I in turn depend upon them to do their duty."

Colind smiled at the boy's eagerness and wondered how many other princes could benefit from the disciplined training that Jopher was receiving. Aaron had unknowingly started him on this path. Why not include princesses as well? It would not do to discriminate based upon gender, Colind mused, and he made a mental note to make the recommendation to Cyrus and Morgan later on.

"No need to be so formal with me. You can simply use 'My Lord' and do away with all this 'My Lord Guardian' business," Colind said.

Jopher nearly tripped looking back at him and decided a nod was better than trying to speak, but then said, "As you wish, my lord."

The deck of the Raven had its usual goings-on with members of the crew doing their utmost to ensure that this trip went smoothly. They had a reputation to uphold, as they were the first ship to be upgraded, which paled in the comparison to them actually journeying to Shandara and back again. Colind glanced to the other ships in close proximity. The sailors appeared significantly smaller at this distance, but they moved with the same sense of urgency. Perhaps the discipline of these so-called drills do affect the performance of a crew. It had been a lifetime since he'd had to lead men in such a fashion and his skills were a bit rusty, to be honest. He was a man out of time, and in quiet moments, he wondered if he would ever really find his bearings in a world that had clearly moved beyond him. None of the old faces were there. He missed his dear friend Reymius all the more after learning what the Drake had done to them. Knowing that Cassey was still caught in its web. Iranus said that there was nothing left of the Lady Cassandra, his dear friend Reymius's wife, as she had been fully assimilated by the Nanites. Had Reymius known what had befallen his wife, Colind doubted he would have left even with what had happened to his daughter, Carlowen. They just didn't know what would happen at the time. Reymius must have believed that Cassandra had died to protect them.

"My Lord," Jopher said, and Colind looked up. "It is just through here," Jopher finished, and they came to a gray door. Jopher opened the door and waited for Colind to enter.

Admiral Morgan looked up from a table strewn with maps. His gray hair was tied back and he wore his blue officer's uniform, its gold bars upon the shoulders shone brightly. Morgan gave a nod to Colind and looked at Jopher. "Thank you, Lieutenant. Please remain outside until I call you back in," Admiral Morgan said.

Tersellis, Vaughn, and Garret were already in the room, along with senior officers that he didn't know.

"We should make the meeting point in a little under an hour," Morgan said.

Colind's eyes widened in shock. He knew the new ships were fast, but didn't really expect the improvements to yield what would normally have taken at least a day or two by airship, to be condensed into an hour.

"Impressive," Colind said.

Morgan's neatly trimmed gray beard lifted into a half grin. "I thought you'd appreciate that, my lord."

Colind felt a slight shudder beneath his feet and saw the clouds outside the windows begin to move quickly by.

"We've engaged the new engines," Morgan said proudly. "The crystals powering them are fully charged and will remain so on a day like today. With the help of our Hythariam friends, the stored capacity of the crystals will allow us to operate at full power through the whole night and much into the next day, if needs be."

"That's how they should work," Tersellis said. "I expect that we may see better performance, but we won't know that until we test more."

"Understood," Morgan acknowledged. "Colind, are you able to advise us on how best to deal with the King of Zsensibar?"

With Cyrus remaining at Rexel, this left Colind the most senior among them to deal with the king. Before his imprisonment, he had dealt with many princes and kings.

"I'm going to continue to follow suit of the young Lord of Shandara," Colind said. "I'm going to be direct, as I don't have time to be drawn into long negotiations with the King of Zsensibar." Colind finished and again found his gaze drifting toward the window.

Vaughn frowned. "What is it?" he asked.

They all glanced out of the window and then returned their gaze toward Colind.

Colind had sucked in his bottom lip. "I'm not sure. I'm growing more worried about the group in Khamearra. We have not heard back from them in over a day."

Tersellis brought out what the Hythariam called a comms device. "We know they are still alive and are in Khamearra," he said, nodding to the device.

Colind frowned. "I'm glad the dots are where they should be, but I know something is not right in here," he said, pointing to his heart. "When we finish with Zsensibar, I aim to make a detour to Khamearra if I need to."

The room grew silent, and Tersellis put the comms device away.

Morgan spoke first. "We can head to Khamearra now if you believe they are in danger. I'm certain we can calculate the best speed…"

Colind held up his hand. "I don't know if they are in any more danger today than they were yesterday. It's a feeling I have, but I don't want to take away from our efforts here, and what you need to be doing has to be done back at Rexel."

"How will you get to them in time?" Vaughn asked.

"Trust in that this old man still has a few tricks up his sleeve. And I assure you that I can get there faster than any ship if I must."

The people of Safanar took his claim at face value, but he could tell the Hythariam were doubtful.

"Iranus sent me a message earlier," Tersellis said. "They've been exploring the ruins of Shandara and marking places of interest. There is a lot of ground to cover and the Ryakul frequent the area in coordinated patterns, as if the beasts are on patrol."

"That's because they are under control," Garret said grimly. "The Drake has some measure of control over the Ryakuls. The only thing that seems to break the Drake's control is when there are dragons in the area."

Tersellis's brow furrowed in thought. "Why is that, do you think?"

Garret shrugged his shoulders. "I'm not sure, to be honest, but it sends them into a frenzy. We've seen it first hand, during our last journey on board the Raven."

"So all we need are some dragons to help us with the Ryakul

problem," Tersellis said.

Colind shook his head. "The dragons are creatures of great intelligence and have roamed Safanar long before man ever did. They are worthy of our respect."

Tersellis held up his hand. "I meant no offense, but if they are already natural enemies why wouldn't they help us?"

"It would seem that way wouldn't it," Colind said. "The dragons' numbers are few now. I'm not sure they would help us even if they wanted too. Did Iranus say anything else about Shandara?"

Tersellis nodded. "They were able to confirm the state of the barrier, and Aaron was correct. The barrier is deteriorating fast. Something twists the landscape down to the core around that place and it is spreading."

Vaughn frowned. "Spreading? What do you mean?"

Tersellis was about to answer, but Colind cut him off. "What he means is that the barrier is tethered to this world and Hytharia. The shield upon the barrier on our side is tied to the energy that binds this world together. But the drain and the state of Hytharia is shifting things out of balance. Aaron was right. Time has indeed been growing short."

The men in the room looked grimly back at one another.

Admiral Morgan cleared his throat. "We're still here, and we will rise up to meet this threat."

Colind smiled inwardly, applauding the admiral. "What about the object heading here from the heavens?"

Tersellis met all of their gazes. "Three months. Whatever it is will be here in three months."

"Is there no way we can figure out what it is?" Vaughn asked.

Tersellis shook his head. "They are working on it, but there is no doubt that the object is heading directly toward this planet."

"All right, gentlemen. We have three months, and we need to make every minute count," Colind said and then he nodded his head toward the door.

Morgan called for Jopher to enter the room.

The young prince entered the room, and Colind smiled kindly, motioning for him to join them. Jopher couldn't have been more than eighteen years of age. Perhaps a year older than that, but certainly not more. So young… They all were, including Aaron. *This war will be fought primarily by the young.* The thought tasted like copper in his mouth, but he kept the bitterness from his bearing.

"We've called you in here, because we're heading to meet with your father," Colind began. "I'd like for you to give us your perspective on whether he will join our cause." There, he had said it. He was asking for a son to pass judgment on his father, and while he didn't like it, Colind knew that this was something Jopher would have to face.

Jopher took a long swallow and glanced around the room.

Morgan stood up. "It's okay, son. We understand this will be difficult for you," he said soothingly, putting the young prince at ease.

"Thank you, sir," Jopher said. "Please know that this son of Zsensibar will not abandon his post, nor will I sit idly by while our homes are being threatened."

Colind nodded. "I never had any doubts as to where you stood. It's your father and his advisors that I'm wondering about."

Jopher thought about it for a moment. "He will be shocked and most likely won't believe you. That is until you present him with proof. Then..." Jopher paused, thinning his lips. "Then he will press his advantage, because he will know that you need our kingdom's—apologies—*nation's* help to fight the Hythariam and perhaps the High King. It will be difficult to convey the gravity of the threat."

Colind was impressed with Jopher's summation of their situation. "Very accurate, and your honesty is much appreciated."

"I would like to speak with him before you go to negotiations," Jopher said. "I need to try to explain the things that I've seen."

Colind watched as Morgan shared a proud glance with Vaughn and Garret. "That is perfectly reasonable and will happen, I assure you."

Jopher eyes turned cold for a moment. "And if he doesn't listen then I will lead whoever will come from our homeland to aid this fight."

Colind barely kept his mouth from hanging open and shared a glance with the others. Jopher spoke for the first time as a true prince, a ruler, a leader without a trace of the imperious boy playing at being a man.

"I sincerely hope it doesn't come to that," Colind said. "That is not my intention for bringing you here. Fathers and sons should be able to work together. Would you like to know a secret?"

Jopher looked confused for a moment, but nodded.

"Sometimes men or fathers, kings in particular, can be the embodiment of stubbornness," Colind said with the barest hints of a smile. "Even Admirals," he said dryly, sending a glance toward Morgan, which drew a smile upon Jopher's face. "But I think you will find that if you speak with your father as you've spoken here before us, with the same conviction, that he may be persuaded to our cause. But you must be patient."

Jopher beamed at the compliment. "Yes sir," he said. "There is one more thing."

Colind nodded for Jopher to continue.

"There are practices from my home that are hundreds of years old and looked upon with disdain from the other nations," Jopher said. "I know how we are viewed by nations such as Rexel. We are tolerated because of our strength. Being tolerated for fear's sake is not how any nation should stand. Genuine respect should be held in the highest esteem not only between people, but between nations."

"Well said," Morgan nearly shouted, and the men around the room nodded in approval.

Aaron, if only you could see the seeds that you've sown in this young man bearing fruit, Colind mused.

Their brief moment of celebration was interrupted by the sound of alarms blaring throughout the ship. Morgan sprang toward the door and Colind followed.

They entered the wheel house.

"Admiral on the deck," cried the guard at the door.

"Situation?" Morgan asked.

"General alert, sir," replied one of the sailors. "We're coming to the meeting point and have the royal envoy of Zsensibar in our sights."

"Excellent," Morgan replied.

Colind surveyed the panoramic view from the wheel house windows. They were moving so fast that he looked back at Admiral Morgan in concern. "Should we slow down?"

Admiral Morgan grinned. "Let's make them sweat a bit first," he replied. "Hoist the colors," Admiral Morgan ordered.

Colind heard the order repeated, and after a few moments, watched as dark blue flags appeared toward the bow of the airships and on either side of their flanks. He squinted his eyes and felt them widen in shock as he recognized the flag of Shandara. The dragon emblem grasping a single rose in his claws in white upon a dark blue background. There would be no guessing as to the allegiances and ideals that the Free Nations Army was committed to.

"Signal to the other ships to reduce speed to one quarter," Admiral Morgan said.

The order was repeated and confirmed with militaristic discipline. Within one minute, all the airships had slowed down and approached the mutual meeting place with the Zsensibarians. The king brought a token force of a few thousand men, but had only two airships hovering over a field nearby. Colind could already see that the army on the ground was mobilizing in preparation for their meetings. He whispered a silent prayer to the

Goddess for patience and wisdom to be visited upon them all this day.

The Raven was the flagship of this squadron and descended toward the ground, while the remaining six airships maintained their altitude. They staggered approach so no one airship would be an easy target for the army on the ground. Morgan, it appeared, was not taking any chances.

"Shall we, My Lord Guardian?" Admiral Morgan asked, gesturing toward the door.

Colind nodded, and they headed out on deck, where they were joined by the Hythariam ambassadors, Vaughn, Garret, and Jopher, along with thirty soldiers. The soldier's armor gleamed in the sunlight and were accented with blue to match the sailor's uniforms.

A large tent had been setup between Zsensibar's army and the airships with a small force of soldiers near the tent. A white flag whisked in the air under a gentle breeze. They descended the gangplank and Colind suppressed his urge to reassure Jopher when he noticed the young prince's hands fidgeting. But he soon regained his composure, with his shoulders back and his head held high.

Tersellis walked next to Colind. "I've left one of my men on board the Raven in case this meeting doesn't go well. He will monitor through the comms device."

"Let's hope we don't need them," Colind replied.

"I second that," Tersellis said, and he looked around. "This is a tense group."

"With good reason," Vaughn said, coming up next them. "Dealings with Zsensibar have always been a fragile thing."

"Why is that?" Tersellis asked.

"They are a powerful kingdom with rich natural resources," Vaughn replied. "Their geographical location has allowed them to avoid most wars between the kingdoms, because they can fight without worrying about another kingdom coming in behind to pounce. They've allied with the High King in the past, but I'd say within the last ten years or so, that bond has been deteriorating."

Tersellis nodded in understanding, but did not say anything more.

As they neared the tent, they were greeted by a group of Zsensibarian soldiers, and one held up his hand.

"I am Captain Amir, and upon behalf of his exalted Royal Highness, King Melchior Nasim, I bid you welcome," Captain Amir said, bowing his head respectfully.

Admiral Morgan bowed back. "I am Admiral Nathaniel Morgan of the Free Nations Army and may I introduce to you My Lord Guardian Colind of the Safanarion Order and Tersellis Ambassador of the Hythariam."

Captain Amir bowed respectfully to each in turn, but his eyes widened at Colind's introduction.

Morgan spoke again. "We are also joined by Prince Jopher, who has been commissioned into the Free Nations Army," Morgan said, and Jopher stepped up from the group of soldiers.

Captain Amir's eyes widened, and then he immediately went to his knees. "Your Royal Highness."

Jopher stepped up. "Rise, Captain," he said. After the Captain came back to his feet, he continued, "Please take me to my father."

Captain Amir regarded Jopher for a moment as if he hadn't heard him correctly and Colind wondered if it was because Jopher had used the word 'please.'

"At once, Your Highness," Captain Amir said.

"Now we wait," Colind said, watching as the two headed toward the tent. The soldiers of Zsensibar split between dividing their gaze upon himself, the airships behind them, and the golden-eyed Hythariam—Tersellis and his bodyguard.

The minutes dragged by, and Captain Amir returned to them. Shouts came from within the tent, and a soldier came out running and whispered something to the Zsensibar Captain.

Captain Amir cleared his throat and narrowed his gaze toward Colind. "His Royal Highness, King Melchoir Nasim, requests your presence. Guardian, if you will follow me."

"One moment if you will, Captain," Tersellis said quickly. "I'm afraid that if your king wishes to speak with us, he will need to join us out here and not in the tent."

Captain Amir barely suppressed a sneer, but Tersellis kept on going.

"I am an Ambassador for my people, the Hythariam. Are we not two nations meeting upon this neutral location under a white flag of truce?" Tersellis asked.

Captain Amir considered this for a moment and then nodded. "Yes, Ambassador."

"Well then, if my understanding of two such nations meeting

upon a neutral field is correct and we are not in the providence of King Melchoir Nasim, then he must join us out here if he wishes to speak with this envoy," Tersellis finished respectfully.

Colind silently applauded the cunning ambassador and watched as the Captain struggled with the fact that Tersellis's astute knowledge of Safanarion customs between two nations upon the field put his king clearly in the wrong, and had unwittingly insulted another nation.

"Perhaps the king has been misinformed," Colind said. "Doubtless reuniting with his son, the prince, proved to be a compelling distraction. Wouldn't you agree, Captain?"

Captain Amir regained his composure and nodded. "My Lord Ambassador, please accept my humblest apologies. I will inform the king at once that the neighboring kingdom of the Hythariam are in fact here upon this neutral field."

"Thank you, Captain," Tersellis replied earnestly.

The captain inclined his head respectfully and walked stiffly back toward the tent. Colind couldn't fault the captain's attitude as he was following the orders of his King and historically subjects of Zsensibar's crowned king didn't fare too well when questioning his orders.

The weather was considerably warmer here in the south and sun was shining. Colind took a moment to rejoice in the sun's caress upon his face. After being imprisoned for so long in the shadows, he often found himself being taken aback by the simplest of things. Colind focused himself as the tent flaps were pulled back and King Nasim's retinue exited.

The court that the king of Zsensibar brought to the field was significantly smaller than what Colind had remembered since he last dealt with Nasim, who had been a much younger man at the time. King Melchoir Nasim stood tall among his people, aided in part by the traditional elongated crown that spiraled above his head. The jewels inlaid in gold gleamed and reflected the brilliance of the sunlight, giving a slight aura surrounding the head of the king. His long beard curled down to his chest, adorned with gold beads. Nasim wore light mailed armor under his ceremonial robes and a black handled sword at his side in the traditional curve. The king strode from the tent, taking in the scene before him, but his gaze gave nothing away as it focused upon Colind.

Colind bowed his head respectfully to the king of Zsensibar, and their small party followed suit. "Your Highness."

King Nasim's dark eyes studied him for a moment and then bowed his head slightly. "Guardian of the Safanarion Order," he said softly, which was in contrast to his broad shoulders and well-muscled arms. The king was in perfect fighting shape despite being well into his fifties.

"Peace be upon Zsensibar, Your Highness," Colind replied formally. "May I introduce to you Tersellis the Ambassador of the Hythariam Nation."

The king's eyes strayed to the Hythariam, and Tersellis inclined his head enough to show respect, but not enough to imply subservience. The Hythariam were proving to be very good negotiators indeed.

"Peace be upon the Hythariam," the king replied and then added, "and to the Safanarion Order."

"Thank you, Your Highness," Colind replied.

King Nasim returned his dark eyed gaze to Colind. "My son has told me of a fantastical journey into the cursed kingdom of Shandara. To be honest, I almost had him shackled for telling such lies."

Colind felt Admiral Morgan stiffen behind him and hoped that his normally ornery nature when it came to his men was kept firmly in check. The king's eyes scanned their small group and lingered for a moment upon Vaughn and Garret.

"I can see this does not meet with your approval," King Nasim said. "Seeing the legendary guardian of the Safanarion Order has given me pause in my immediate reaction to the situation surrounding my son. Speaking of which, I do not see Prince Cyrus among you. As my son was in his keeping, I would have thought he would be present upon this field and face me himself."

Most of the soldiers with them were originally from the Rexellian Corps and stiffened at the blow to their crowned prince.

"Please, if I may," Tersellis said quickly. "There are things that I wish to speak to you about that will shed light to the absence of our friend the prince, and I humbly ask you to allay any bad feelings until after you've heard what we've had to say."

King Nasim took a few moments, considering what the Hythariam had said, and with his nose in the air, nodded once.

"Prince Jopher will be present at these proceedings," Colind said, and it was not lost upon anyone nearby that he had addressed the king without his honorific title.

The king's eyes bored into Colind's unyielding gray eyes, but Colind's will was like granite and would not yield to the Zsensibarian king.

Tersellis broke the silence again, "Please, Your Highness, your son was with the party that trekked into Shandara and freed Colind. It makes sense to hear his account firsthand, as he will have much to add."

After a few moments, the king turned his thunderous gaze to Captain Amir and nodded toward the tent. Less than a minute later, Jopher strode from the tent at a quick pace and came to a stop between the two factions with his father, the king, upon one side and the Free Nations Army upon the other. He bowed respectfully toward both and coolly met his father's gaze.

"What ideas have you infected my son with that he does not stand with his kingdom?" King Nasim asked.

Jopher looked uncertainly toward his father and then back at Admiral Morgan, who gave him a nod that was not missed by the king. Jopher moved to his father's side.

"I would know your name," King Nasim said.

Morgan stepped forward. "My Lord, I am Admiral Morgan of the Free Nations Army. The airships you see behind me are a small squadron under my command."

King Nasim's eyes narrowed. "Free Nations Army?"

"Yes, Your Highness," Tersellis answered. "Allow us to explain," he said, gesturing toward Colind, Vaughn, and Garret to step forward.

The soldiers at the king's side stiffened at the movement of so many men near their ruler, but Nasim seemed unimpressed.

"Very well," King Nasim said. "Continue."

Tersellis nodded for Vaughn to begin. Vaughn stepped up and told the king about meeting Aaron and how he was the only surviving descendant of the house Alenzar'seth. Vaughn spoke of their travels to Rexel and beyond, and despite Colind knowing the tale of their journey that took them to Shandara, he was always a bit awestruck by its telling. Aaron had defied all the odds and survived his many encounters with the Elitesmen to get to him. As Vaughn spoke, he had Jopher offer his perspective on the events that they had both been a part of and Colind observed the grudging approval take root in the king's eyes when he looked at his son. There were more than a few times when King Nasim raised his brow at his son's bearing as he told his version of their journey. Jopher's account of his time with Aaron was filled with pure truth and he did not seek to diminish the events that involved him. Jopher even spoke of his time serving on board the Raven in the kitchens like a common servant, which led to his acceptance into the camaraderie of the crew of the Raven. Although the king's gaze took on a dangerous glint when it came upon Morgan, the admiral returned the king's gaze in kind and would not be cowed.

Tersellis cleared his throat and spoke of their actions after Shandara, and how they were working with the nations of this world to help stand against the invading horde from their home world of Hytharia and possibly the armies of the High King. At this point, the king almost rolled his eyes, but waited for him to continue. When Tersellis finally finished speaking, the silence carried on for minutes while the king collected his thoughts.

"Father," Jopher said, "I beg of you to please listen to these men and consider what they have said. I do not wear the uniform of the Free Nations Army to spite you or our home. I wear the uniform to help protect my home and stand with those who would protect this world. This is not an action I've taken lightly nor without a fair amount of thought, but I have sworn an oath."

King Nasim narrowed his gaze. "The best place to protect your home is from within our borders." The king held up his hand as Jopher was about to protest. "I have listened, as you have requested, and now I will speak my piece. The reason why Zsensibar thrives is because we have not been drawn into the wars of the north," the king said, nodding toward Colind and the others. "They would draw us into their war and make their struggles our own, but I assure you they are not."

King Nasim turned toward Colind. "You say this heir of Alenzar'seth is mighty enough to stand against the High King and the might of the Elitesmen? What are our assurances that he will not turn his power upon us should our goals not be aligned?"

The king's question drew blank stares from them, as none had ever pictured Aaron as the tyrant.

The king continued. "How do you know he will not turn on you as High King Amorak has done to you all? Better the enemy that you know than the one you would never see coming. I would have thought the lessons of Shandara's fall would have taught you that."

The king's questions stunned them all to silence until Jopher at last spoke. "Do you trust me, Father?" Jopher asked quietly.

The king turned back toward his son. His gaze taking his measure. "This is not a matter trust, my son, this is a matter of what is best for Zsensibar, your home."

"I am your son," Jopher said. "I stand among your many heirs to your throne, but I say I am your son with pride as a son should before his father. I would ask that you hear me when I say that your worries where Aaron is concerned are unfounded. He is not and never will be like the High King or the Elitesmen. No matter how much power he attains. It is simply a matter of who he is. He walks his own path and asks nothing of anyone else that he wouldn't do for himself. In fact, I would daresay that Aaron would prefer to do most things himself to prevent his companions from coming into harm's way."

Jopher's statement drew knowing smiles from Vaughn, Garret, and Morgan, which was not lost upon the king.

The king turned his disapproving gaze back to the others. "The young are often easily impressionable."

"Normally, I would agree with you in that regard, your Grace," Colind said. "But on rare occasions such as this, the impressions have the right of it."

Tersellis cleared his throat. "Your Highness, if I may," he began and took out the device he had used to convince the other leaders back in Rexel a few days before.

The king held up his hand and his soldiers took a menacing step forward with their hands upon their swords.

"I think not, Ambassador," the king said. "At this point I will not be swayed by any magical displays you've used to persuade the other kingdoms to your cause."

"Father, please," Jopher began, and the king silenced him with a withering glare.

"A son should know his place," King Nasim said.

"A king should know when to listen," Jopher replied tersely.

The air solidified between them, and in one swift motion, the King spun, striking Jopher with a gloved fist sending him to the ground.

The soldiers, some of which had been sailors who had served with Jopher on the Raven, moved forward, but Colind held up his hands to hold them in their place. While the king had his back to them, the Zsensibar soldiers did not, and Colind didn't want this to turn into a blood bath.

Jopher regained his feet, and the king closed the distance between them in a single stride. "A son should know better than to question the will of his father," he said and raised his fist to strike Jopher again.

Colind watched as Jopher fluidly stepped inside the blow and pinned his father's arm behind him, holding it roughly in place. The king's guards clenched their swords, but waited for the king's command to draw them.

"A son maybe," Jopher said eyeing the guards. "But it is the duty of a prince to stand for what is best for his home even when its King is too stubborn to listen. The threat to this world is like nothing you've ever seen before. None of us have. We cannot cling to our methods from the past if we are to have any hope for our future."

Jopher released his father's arm and stepped away, putting a small amount of distance between himself and his father, but stood resolute, waiting upon the wrath of the king in whatever form it would take. The Zsensibar soldiers stood frozen, waiting the king's word. The king's chest rose and fell as the only visible signs of the rage building inside. He glared around him and as he was about to unleash the full armament of his rage, a screech pierced the sky as the clearing around them filled with answering cries of Ryakuls emerging from the surrounding forests.

Colind heard the blaring alarms from the airships behind them following the roars of the Ryakuls. How had the Ryakuls gotten so close without anyone noticing?

"Treachery!" the king screamed.

Two of the Zsensibar soldiers charged forward with crossbows raised. Colind brought his arms up, poised to lash out, but Jopher swept their feet out from under them, calling out an apology as he did so.

"We're under attack," Admiral Morgan barked, then he turned toward the king. "If we can coordinate our efforts, we may survive this."

The king glared back at the Admiral, taking his measure and then gave a single grim nod.

"Get back to the ship," Colind ordered. "I will do what I can from down here."

Admiral Morgan looked as if he were about to protest, but thought better of it and ordered his men back to the ships.

Colind glanced at Garret. "You should head back with the others."

Garret's bushy gray eyebrows raised in amusement despite the Ryakuls closing in. "Like hell I will, My Lord. I stand with the head of the Safanarion Order."

Colind turned to see Jopher standing before his father, surrounded by a wall of spears. At their approach, some turned and leveled their spears in Colind's direction. He'd had enough and swept his arms out in front of him, opening a hole in the lines of men straight to the king.

"Go on, lad," Colind said to Jopher. "They need you up there. I will look after your father."

The king looked about to protest, but was startled by the roar of a Ryakul plummeting down upon their position.

Colind clawed his hands to his side, summoning an orb of crackling energy like liquid lightning, and thrust his hands out, sending it streaking blue into the black tusked maw of the closing Ryakul. He followed up with another orb, which burst through the Ryakul's black leathery wings. The soldiers formed their lines with spears and shields establishing the front ranks. Arrows flew and the Ryakul crashed into the ground, howling as it came.

The Zsensibar soldiers closed in to finish off the dying beast, and Colind turned back to the king, who nodded back grimly. They were allied for the moment, but he knew he must keep a wary eye upon the king.

"Cover their airships," the king ordered his men, gesturing beyond Colind. "They need time to move into position to cover us."

Stubborn and prideful King Melchoir Nasim may be, but once on task, he quickly adapted to a situation while keeping in mind all available resources, regardless if they were his own or not. If they were to survive this attack, they needed to work together. Garret stayed near his side and drew his sword as Colind scanned the sky. There were ten Ryakuls, each the size of a large building, swooping down upon the Zsensibarian army. Their black hides swallowed the light and their saber tusked maws ripped soldiers apart indiscriminately. The tips of the Ryakuls wings were adorned with blades and each swoop down from the sky above was accompanied with a harsh screech that ended with men being cut down where they stood. The Zsensibar troops were quick to adapt to the Ryakul attack pattern and less men lost their lives to those cursed wings. The troops used their long spears to good measure so when a Ryakul did swoop down upon them, they extracted a heavy toll upon the Ryakul's armored hide.

Five of the airships closed in, with the Raven bringing up the rear. Five Ryakuls launched up into the air, with one being shot down in a hail of explosive tipped arrows from the lead ship. Of the five Ryakuls upon the ground, four remained alive, while the others changed their tactics and resorted to brute strength, butchering the lines of men before them.

The Raven broke off from the formation, gaining speed, and the remaining four Ryakuls in the air pursued relentlessly. The great airship listed to the side to compensate for the sharp turn it was making and the agile Ryakuls easily followed.

Colind watched as the other airships pursued the Ryakuls, and even from the ground he could see the giant crossbows ready to fire from the bow of the ship. The ground shook beneath his feet catching some of soldiers around them by surprise and causing them to stumble. The ground flew away from Colind's feet as he was swept up into the air and then came crashing down to the earth. A Ryakul leaped over the Zsensibar soldiers to get to him. The saber tusked maw growled viciously as it closed in and the breath seized in Colind's chest. Off to the side a lone voice cried out, and the king dug his spear into the side of the Ryakul's head, catching the beast by surprise.

Colind looked up to find King Melchoir Nasim himself reaching down to pull him back onto his feet. The Ryakul shook its head and roared with the heft of the spear sticking out at an odd angle. Colind drew in the energy causing the ground to crack beneath the Ryakul's feet. The great winged beast sank into the earth, falling off balance as it scrambled with its claws to regain its footing.

The soldiers bellowing their war cry converged upon the beast, slaying it as the very earth beneath its feet kept it rooted in place.

"Thank you, My Lord Guardian," the king said, stepping to Colind's side. "I know the Safanarion Order and Zsensibar haven't always seen eye to eye, but today we fight as one."

They both watched as the Free Nations Army airships lured the more nimble Ryakuls into a chase and were shot down by the other airships, but they did not get away completely unscathed. Some of the airships had taken damage, but all remained in the air.

Despite the bravery of the Zsensibar ground troops, they sustained heavy losses. The field was littered with many of the dead, as the Ryakuls were adept killing machines and held little value to their own numbers. The battle was fierce in its intensity, but over almost as quickly as it had begun, with more than one Zsensibar officer glancing in awe at the Free Nations airships.

The king grimly surveyed the carnage around him, as nearly a third of his troops lay dying amid the Ryakul corpses.

"Your airships are impressive, My Lord Guardian," the king said.

"We would not be your enemies, Your Highness," Colind said. "There is a very real threat to this world. None may simply stay to the side and allow it to pass unscathed. The kingdoms that stand alone will be among the first to fall."

The king met Colind's gaze and nodded. "There are forces at work here beyond a random Ryakul attack. Never before have I seen so many attack at once."

"In this we are agreed, and is a taste of things to come," Colind said. How could anyone have known about their meeting here, and who could have moved fast enough to ambush them? They had assumed the Drake was preoccupied with Sarah's assimilation, but perhaps they were wrong not to keep a closer eye upon its whereabouts. Colind shuddered at the thought of what Mactar could do with the power to command the Ryakul.

Curses, Colind thought to himself. *I'm needed elsewhere.*

The Raven heaved into view, dark and majestic, cutting through the billowing smoke. Colind watched as Jopher leaped down from the gangplank followed by the Hythariam. Jopher ordered a group of soldiers to help with the nearby wounded. The king's eyes showed relief that his son was alive and Colind saw the grudging respect that came when a father recognized that his son was becoming a man in his own right.

Jopher ran over to them and stopped when he saw that they were safe. Following the relief in Jopher's eyes was anger glistening in his gaze as the king came before him.

The king raised his hand as Jopher began to speak.

"You've shown great courage, my son. Both on the field of battle and off," the king said. "Worthy of a Prince of Zsensibar and worthy of its future king."

The men around them came to stand still as a hush swept over those nearby.

"Kneel," commanded the king.

Jopher looked uncertain for a moment, but then did as his father commanded. The king drew his sword and placed it upon Jopher's shoulders.

"Do you, Jopher Zamaridian Nasim, accept the mantle of heir to Zsensibar's throne. To henceforth strive for the preservation of her greatness and defend the independent rule of our kingdom and her patrons?"

"I swear," Jopher said.

"Then rise, first among my sons," the king said and turned

toward his soldiers. "Men! I give you my heir. His blood is my blood. His will is my will. Acknowledge your future king."

The soldiers across the field sank to their knees and spoke in thunderous unison, "Jopher Zamaridian Nasim, our future king!"

The soldiers repeated their acknowledgment twice more and Tersellis came next to Colind and quietly asked, "What just happened?"

"The Kings of Zsensibar take many wives, and from their offspring, can select any as the future ruler of that kingdom. Our young friend is among the youngest in a long line of would be heirs and has been put first. Once the King makes his selection known, he cannot simply take it away again," said Colind.

Tersellis nodded and inclined his head in Jopher's direction.

Jopher rose up. "You honor me, Father."

King Nasim shook his head. "No, this day it is you who honor me."

"Father, it is my intention to stay with the Free Nations Army," Jopher said.

Colind noticed how Jopher announced his intention without indicating that it was a want, which was a testament to how much he had grown.

The king frowned for a moment. "We can discuss it along with the many things we need to discuss with this envoy."

Colind's focus drifted away from the conversation, setting his attention northward. He felt the faint stirrings amid the currents of energy up there. A presence that echoed as if from a great distance caught his attention that he had never felt before. He felt his gaze narrow, peering beyond the clouds toward Khamearra, allowing his augmented sight to see beyond those of ordinary men. He rode along the currents, leaving his body behind, and the sky turned dark as night fell upon this part of Safanar. There were few among the Safanarion Order blessed with the sight, and he was among the last. His skills had grown rusty from his imprisonment and he struggled to remain focused, but there was a vibrant presence just beyond his senses. The night darkened around him until a great white beacon of light blazed through the night sky.

The power of the Ferasdiam!

Myths and legend told of the power of Ferasdiam Marked and their ability to call upon the Eldarin, which was what the Lords of Dragons called themselves. Colind felt his mouth open many miles from where he was. The beacon flared brilliantly, pulsating in the rhythm of Aaron's lifebeat. It could be no one else as Aaron alone held the power within him. Colind searched the sky to see if any of the Eldarin would answer the call. The dragon lords had long faded to myth with many doubting their existence.

There was a flash of golden light fading to green as the answering call of the Eldarin pierced the night. A dragon lord hovered above the beacon, its light reflecting off its golden hide. After the barest of moments it winked out of sight, moving at speeds too fast even for him to track, and plunged headlong into the city below.

The *Eldarin* answered the call. Colind was so awestruck that his focus unraveled and he felt himself pulled back to his body. He felt himself collapse to the ground, and Garret was at his side holding him up.

"What did you see?" Garret asked, knowing full well what Colind had been up to.

Colind reigned in his racing thoughts and looked back at Garret, blinking away his confusion. "Something wonderful," he whispered.

Colind stood up. They were mostly alone, with soldiers still moving about and the airships hovering behind them.

"The others are speaking in the king's tents," Garret said. "I told them we would be along when you returned."

"Garret, Aaron has summoned the *Eldarin*," Colind said.

"What?" Garret gasped. "I thought they were a myth."

Colind shook his head. "They are not. I saw one and it was magnificent beyond words."

Garret smiled and Colind couldn't help but join in. "I need to leave."

"What do you mean?" Garret asked, the smile leaving his face.

"I need to travel to the north," Colind answered. "Faster than our airships can travel. Something sets itself against us, and I can guess that the Drake has somehow gleaned our plans and sent the Ryakuls to attack."

Garret frowned. "How would it know what we were doing?"

"I cannot begin to guess at what the Drake is capable of, but I know commanding the Ryakuls is among them," Colind answered. "If others knew that it was possible to command them, then they will seek to press their advantage."

Garret's brow furrowed in thought. "By others you mean Mactar."

Colind nodded. "I have to seek him out. If Zsensibar would join our cause, it will be in Tersellis's hands now."

"How will you even find them? You need help. Let's use the Raven to come to Aaron's aid," Garret said.

"Aaron's in trouble?" Jopher asked, coming up behind them. "I'm coming," he insisted.

Colind suppressed a groan. "I can't take you with me."

Garret narrowed his gaze. "How will you find them?"

"I will follow the currents of energy," Colind replied. "This is not something either of you can do."

"Let us take the Raven. She is the fastest ship and besides, once Jopher informs Admiral Morgan of your intentions, he will head that way anyway." Garret nodded to Jopher who turned around and ran back toward the tent.

"Subtle, Garret. Very subtle," Colind said with only a hint of annoyance.

"You and Aaron suffer from the same affliction of late, believing that you need to do these things all by yourselves. We are a team. When we get closer you can always charge off ahead and beat us there, but perhaps if we leverage our assets we may glean some intelligence on the way," Garret finished.

Colind's mouth curved in a half grin. "Didn't Vaughn say something about old dogs learning new tricks?"

"It was Verona, and I'm not as old as you, but you can see the wisdom in my point, otherwise you would have just charged off,"

Garret replied.

Jopher returned with not only Morgan, but with King Nasim as well as the others. Colind explained that they needed to leave immediately based upon what he saw unfold in Khamearra. Tersellis was silent for a moment until one of his Hythariam bodyguards whispered into his ear, and he nodded.

"We've finally gotten word from Gavril," Tersellis said. "They've succeeded in Khamearra and after they regroup he expects they will be leaving the city."

Colind shared a look with Garret and Vaughn. Aaron would only quit the city after he had gotten what he came for, and that meant he had the travel crystals in his possession.

"Thank you, Tersellis. Did Gavril report anything else?" Colind asked.

Tersellis shook his head, but something in the Hythariam's golden eyes told him there was more he wasn't saying.

Colind turned to the king. "Your Highness, it appears that some of us need to leave sooner than expected. I hope you will consider carefully what you've been told. We would very much like to call you an ally and friend in the dark days ahead."

Tersellis held out a small comms device and offered it to the king. "You can use this to reach us with your answer."

The king took the device and Tersellis proceeded to give instructions on its use. They headed back to the ships, save Jopher, who stood before his father waiting.

Father and son regarded each other for a moment before the king inclined his head. Jopher's eyes lit up and headed back toward the

Raven. The king smiled proudly, which was quickly overshadowed by the worry in his furrowed brows. He turned toward his staff and began issuing orders, taking long purposeful strides through the camp.

Admiral Morgan signaled to two of the airships to head back to Rexel and report in while the remaining four airships would head north toward where they suspected the Drake lay in wait.

King Melchoir Nasim did not commit himself to the Free Nations as of yet, but he had allowed Jopher to return with them, and that was a good sign. Colind doubted whether the king could have actually stopped his son, short of taking the lad into custody, which would not be wise. Morgan assured the king that Jopher would be under his command and that he would look after him. Colind knew that Morgan held no love for the Zsensibar king, but had in fact grown fond of its prince and heir apparent. He joined the Hythariam who consulted their devices and helped pinpoint their heading. Colind would use his own skills to make corrections, because in his experience technology could only get you so far, but he hoped it would be enough.

CHAPTER 20
DEMON'S TAUNTING

They had left behind the smoky capital city of Khamearra, using their travel crystals as they went. Mactar was able to leave a few key messages for Rordan to find should he survive the night. He really wasn't sure what Rordan would do, but if he was smart and could follow the breadcrumbs he had left behind, then he may yet be of some use to him. Darven had remained silent and quietly followed him. Darven was a good apprentice, never asking endless amounts of questions, and when it came time to follow orders, he did so quickly. The value the former Elitesmen brought was in his ability to act without being specifically told what to do, and he had proven on more than one occasion that he was someone dependable.

It was still nighttime, though the further east they traveled the sooner dawn would arrive. They were in the Waylands, using its centralized location to quickly observe the goings-on near Rexel. Prince Cyrus had become the spearhead uniting the forces behind the Heir of Shandara, and Mactar was impressed with the progress they were making in preparing for war. They just happened to be on the wrong side, which accounted for everyone not serving his purpose. He had wanted to stop to take a quick look around before proceeding further east to the Shadow Lands, as they were known today, but for others they knew it as Shandara. The Ryakuls had always concentrated in that area, and Mactar surmised that the Drake was somewhere within Shandara's borders.

"Are you sure the High King didn't require our assistance?" Darven asked.

"I'm certain of it," Mactar said. "Besides, what we're doing is more important."

"And what is that exactly?"

"The Drake can control the Ryakul," Mactar answered. "And we're going to try to figure out how it does that."

Darven gave a dubious frown. "There has got to be more to it than that."

The same qualities that Mactar appreciated in Darven also came at a price, and that price was he being required to reveal more of his plans than he would have preferred. He should have expected nothing less from Darven.

"Something has always puzzled me about the Ryakuls, but I've never had the time, nor inclination, to give them my full attention," Mactar said. "They restricted themselves to the borders of Shandara, but have recently ventured further and further from its borders. If one were able to control them, then they would be a force to contend with on any battlefield. They could turn the tide of wars, even with the elusive Hythariam."

"Mactar, the Hythariam are not so elusive anymore, and they have aligned themselves with the Alenzar'seth. Many have flocked to his banner at Rexel."

"Indeed," Mactar said. "In that you are correct, but—" He stopped himself, unsure whether he should share the knowledge he had kept hidden for so long. Darven, he noted, simply waited patiently. "They are not the only Hythariam out there."

Darven narrowed his gaze. "What do you mean, not the only Hythariam?"

"You know the Hythariam first appeared on our world about eighty years ago?" Mactar asked, and when Darven nodded he continued, "Things were very different then."

"Hold on a minute," Darven interrupted. "Are you saying that you were there when the Hythariam first came to Safanar?"

"Not exactly," Mactar answered. "I was among the first members of the Safanarion Order."

"The Safanarion Order!" Darven gasped.

Mactar watched the barrage of thoughts play through Darven's face. "It is true, I assure you. Although we didn't call ourselves that in the beginning, and the only person to remember is Colind."

"But that would mean you are over a hundred years old," Darven sputtered.

"There are ways to slow down aging," Mactar replied mildly.

"Yeah but—" Darven began.

"Let's not get caught up in my age," Mactar said. "Just trust in the fact that I was there when the Hythariam first came to our world. I was witness to the barrier when it first came to being. The Hythariam possess powerful knowledge of undreamed potential with a vast array of weapons and soldiers. Most believe the Drake to be demon spawn, but nothing could be further from the truth. The Drake is quite literally not of this world."

"What world is it from then?" Darven asked.

Mactar's gaze grew distant. "What world indeed," came his faint reply.

"Do you know why the barrier went up in the first place?" Darven asked.

"Not entirely," he lied. "There was some type of falling out with the Hythariam. I don't know how the Alenzar'seth created the barrier, but that is not why I'm telling you this."

"Fine," Darven said. "Keep going."

"I suspect that the Ryakuls have something to do with the Hythariam," Mactar said. "I always have, but have never had anything to prove the claim. Regardless, if the Drake can somehow control the Ryakul, then I want to observe how it's done and, if possible, take that control for myself."

Darven nodded. "I see, but what do you plan to do with the Ryakuls if you are able to control them? I doubt the Drake will sit idly by while you take away something that up until now was solely within its dominion."

"The Drake will only attack if it perceives us as standing between its main objective," Mactar said.

"Which is?" Darven asked.

"The annihilation of the Alenzar'seth," Mactar replied, keeping his own bitterness from his voice.

"Just so I'm clear on what we're doing," Darven continued, "we're to sneak into the den of the Ryakuls and observe how the Drake controls them?"

"That about sums it up," Mactar replied and felt a small chill slink across the back of his neck.

Darven's frown deepened as he stared off to the east. "I wonder how the Ryakuls numbers have grown so much of late."

Mactar schooled his features. "An excellent question, and truth be told, they are not of Safanar either."

"How do you know this?" Darven asked, but was answered by Mactar's contemptible silence.

"He fills your head with half truths," a raspy voice whispered.

Darven drew his sword and scanned the area, poised to attack anything that would dare threaten them.

Mactar seized the energy around them, giving in to his reaction to Tarimus's voice.

"I heard it that time," Darven said. "Come out, Tarimus."

They were greeted with a faint raspy laugh that despite himself had sent shivers down Mactar's spine. Tarimus was back in phase with the world and yet remained so aloof.

"Your master will betray you Elitesman," Tarimus taunted.

Mactar cast out around him, quickly finding where Tarimus hid, but he was gone in an instant.

"Show yourself!" Darven shouted. "How does he move around so fast?"

Mactar felt Darven draw the energy into himself and charge off

332 | ECHOES OF A GLORIED PAST

into the trees quicker than any normal person could see. He aligned the energy within him, allowing his solid form to dissipate, stretching so that he appeared like smoke. The essence of Mactar rose to the tree line and followed his Elitesman apprentice.

Darven charged off, seeking the demon spawn Tarimus. The Grand Master of the Elite had awarded him the rank of Adept because he was so gifted in his ability to use the energy around him. The rank, much like the Order, held little in the way of keeping him within the confines of its practices. It was no mere happenstance that he alone was able to break free of the Elitesmen Order and survive in recent memory. He moved quickly, striking out on a path very few could discern, let alone follow. He gained on Tarimus, who moved in and out of phase dotting the path before him. Darven discerned the pattern of his movements and seized the travel crystal, merging his energy with its own and surged ahead predicting where Tarimus would reappear.

He collided with the specter as they both transitioned back into phase.

Darven had his sword out before him, with its single edge catching fleeting glints of the fading moonlight.

Tarimus slowly rose to his feet and pulled back the hood of his cloak, revealing pasty white skin stretched over a completely bald head. Eyes of inky blackness regarded him.

"All right, Elitesman," Tarimus said, drawing his dark blade that hissed free of its sheath. He brought both his hands up, holding the blade ready with his feet planted shoulder width apart.

Tarimus brandished his dark blade, slicing the air around him. Then held it ready behind him as he beckoned with his other hand.

Darven, poised on one leg, angled the sword over his head in observance of the ancient sword forms. For the span of seconds, they stood unmoving, embracing the stillness around them, then Darven charged. Their blades met, ringing out in dawn's early light, signaling the beginning of their deadly dance. The two masters moved through the field, each testing the other's strengths, and assessing any weaknesses.

"You are very good," Tarimus said, breaking off the attack. "But you can never stand against the Alenzar'seth."

Darven swung his sword again, and Tarimus easily danced away.

"Elitesman, you don't even know when you are outclassed. Trust in that you will meet your end by the Alenzar'seth's hand. He knows you were there that night."

"Let him come," Darven said, and he remembered throwing the dagger that took the life of Aaron's mother. Killing was nothing new to him and many had come seeking vengeance. None had succeeded.

"I give you this message. The master you serve will betray you as he has done to all the others that stood at his side."

Darven dashed forward, seeking to cut through Tarimus's twisted face, but his sword only sliced through the air as Tarimus melted away before his eyes. He cast out with his senses, but he was alone.

After a few moments, Mactar appeared behind him.

"Darven, Tarimus seeks to drive us apart. He is bent on vengeance. I'm the one he wants."

Darven sheathed his sword. "Then why all the games? Why not just strike out? He had the element of surprise."

Mactar was silent for a moment. "Tarimus was my prisoner for many years. I know what he wants. He desires to see his victims squirm, putting them off balance so by the time he strikes they are so frozen with fear that they cannot fight."

Darven glanced around them. A blanket of mist covered the ground with the approaching dawn.

"What else did he say?" Mactar asked.

Darven looked pointedly at Mactar, tilting his head to the side. "He said you would betray me."

Mactar's lips curved into a sardonic grin. "You see, he seeks to put us off balance."

"I have no illusions when it comes to your intentions," Darven said. "I am here because you find me useful and I follow because of the knowledge you have."

"Then we know where we both stand," Mactar replied. "Come. We head to Shandara," he said, walking away.

Darven caught up to him easily. "About that. Travel crystals will only get us so far. They don't work in the actual city of Shandara."

"You are correct, but we don't need to get to the city," Mactar said. "Not this time at least. The Drake is not in the city, but somewhere in the northern mountain ranges. And the travel crystals do work in Shandara, but they are dangerous to use there.

We can't blindly use the crystals to travel there, but we could travel there by sight."

"You mean to travel to a place within our field of vision," Darven said.

"Precisely," Mactar answered and held up his hand. "I know we would drain the crystal, but as I have said, we can skirt around the borders of Shandara and gain the knowledge we seek."

Darven nodded. "Let's go then, but there is one thing that does bother me."

"What's that?" Mactar asked.

"How does Tarimus keep finding you?"

"That is another excellent question," Mactar said. "When I figure it out, I'll be sure to let you know."

Darven lips curved into a half grin and he nodded. They each brought out their travel crystals and headed north.

CHAPTER 21
THE ELDARIN'S PLEA

The cloaked Flyer class SPT silently eased away from the city, much to the ignorance of its inhabitants. Captain Nolan had seen them off and vowed to Aaron that he would do his best to keep the peace. Aaron wished him well and meant it. The De'anjard presence in Khamearra had proven to be something quite special and he hoped to return to them in the future. He rolled his shoulders, loosening them, and sagged into the cushioned seat of the Hythariam Flyer that changed its contours to match his body. Aaron sucked in a deep breath and exhaled while stifling a yawn.

"When was the last time you slept?" Roselyn asked.

Aaron raised his head slowly. "Probably the same time that you did."

"You need rest," Roselyn said. "We all do."

She was right. This journey was catching up with them all. He saw the same bone weary exhaustion mirrored throughout the Flyer. He turned back to Roselyn, whose golden eyes never left his, and nodded.

"Probably best to just agree with her," Verona whispered when Roselyn moved just outside of earshot.

"I am tired," Aaron said, feeling his shoulders slump further with the admission. "But we're so close. Each moment we delay..."

"I know, my friend. I know," Verona said, almost dozing. "Wasn't it you who told us on the deck of the Raven to take a moment to center yourself. Well, this is your moment. Recover your strength. Even working with the energy as we do takes a toll upon us and is not a substitute for actual rest. You won't be any good to Sarah when we find her if you can't think straight."

Aaron smiled tiredly and felt his eyes droop a little. "Glad you were paying attention." He looked back at Verona. "You said when, not if. Thanks."

Verona snorted. "I guess I did. My friend, I've never lost faith in you. You will find a way through this, of that I am convinced. And I will stand at your side watching your back as you do."

He nodded at Verona, sat back, and let his eyes close. Aaron settled his head back and released the breath he had been holding, allowing his mind to relax. He slipped into a dull, dreamless sleep.

A low-level alarm pulled him out of his slumber. He pushed his eyelids open and noticed that the others were all sleeping, save for the Hythariam, who were huddled at the front of the Flyer. Aaron wiped the sleep from his eyes and unbuckled himself from the seat. He had no idea how long he slept, but was sure it couldn't have been that long. He heard the Hythariam speaking in hushed tones as he came up and Tanneth silenced the alarm.

"What is it?" Aaron asked.

Gavril glanced back at him. "Proximity alarm. You're not going to believe this, but we have two dragons flying on either side of us."

Aaron looked at the screen. It was slightly opaque signifying they were still in stealth. The medallion grew cool upon his chest. Just as Gavril had said, there were two enormous dragons flying on either side of the Hythariam craft dwarfing it in size. The dragons were larger than the one that he and Verona had met when he had first came to Safanar.

"Can you come out of stealth? They know we're here," Aaron said.

"Are you sure?" Tanneth said, and Gavril nodded to him after glancing at Aaron.

"What's happening?" Verona asked, joining them and then looked down at the screen. His eyes widened at the sight of the dragons and his eyes darted immediately to Aaron.

"What do you think they want?" Gavril asked.

"Me, I think," Aaron said.

"Doesn't everyone," Verona grinned.

Both dragons had golden hides, but each had their own unique blend of colors with one gravitating more toward greens and the other, blues. The dragon with the bluish hues flew in front of them with a powerful flap of its wings. Aaron focused himself and his perceptions sharpened, seeing the shafts of energy gleaming from the two dragons.

"Do you see that?" Tanneth asked, pointing to one of the charts that sprang up on screen. "That's the energy reading from the dragon. I've never seen so much come from any life form before."

"We should follow them," Aaron said.

The dragon changed course, turning slightly, and Tanneth followed easily. Once the dragon was satisfied they were following, it tucked in its wings and streaked ahead of them. Tanneth increased the flyer's velocity to catch up. The dragon spun in the air, dodging past some tall trees, and Tanneth performed the same aerial stunt matching the dragon. The contest continued for a few moments and then a mountain range loomed ahead. The Flyer hugged the earth and the treetops zipped past them. Despite not feeling any of the inertia they should have been feeling while flying at these speeds, Aaron held onto the seat in front of him just the same.

"They're so fast," Sarik said, joining them. "I've never seen a dragon fly like that. He is not even flapping his wings."

Aaron reached out with this senses and felt the same presence he had felt at the arena. "These are the Eldarin."

Gavril eyed him for a moment, his brows raised in silent questioning.

"The one in front of us is the same dragon that came to my aid in the arena," Aaron said. "It knows I'm Ferasdiam Marked."

"Sir," Tanneth said, and Gavril turned to the front. "We're reaching the limits of the Flyer's ability for atmospheric flight. We cannot go much faster, but I believe they could," the blonde Hythariam said gesturing in front of them. "I think they are testing our abilities."

Gavril nodded. "Stay on course, Tanneth." The Hythariam colonel looked back to Aaron. "I'll be honest, we've never encountered these Eldarin before. Not even during the time of Daverim or Reymius."

"They told me their numbers are few and that there are things we need to know. They helped me against the Elitesmen. I think we should see what they want," Aaron said.

Both of the Eldarin flew ahead of their ship, momentarily disappearing over a mountain peak. The Hythariam flier quickly closed the distance and as they crested the peaks, they were all shocked into silence. Nestled amid the mountains was a valley seemingly carved from the mountains themselves. The surface was flat, but as they got closer they could see the smooth stonework and columns circling the great valley. The Eldarin landed near the center, and Tanneth circled over. The ground was adorned with dragon emblems mostly faded with the passage of time. There were several archways large enough for the Eldarin to easily pass throughout the valley.

Aaron didn't see any roads or trails leading to the valley. "You can only reach this place by climbing the mountain or flying in. I don't see how people would be climbing here unless they already knew of the place."

"Taking us in," Tanneth said, navigating the Hythariam Flyer to land before the two Eldarin.

Aaron was first to step out of the craft and was awestruck by the sheer size of the Eldarin. With the rune-carved staff in hand, he briskly walked out in front of the Hythariam ship and was quickly joined by the others. The Eldarin sat back upon their haunches, lifting their heads to a height equivalent of a four-story building. The vibrant intensity of their gaze made Aaron feel stripped bare, as if there was nothing he could hide from them even if he wanted to. A low rumbling sound echoed throughout the valley. Verona, Sarik, and Braden could be heard muttering a prayer to the Goddess. Aaron took a purposeful step forward, but inclined his head respectfully.

"Thank you for joining us, Ferasdiam Marked. Normally we would only commune with one who is marked by fate, but we will let our voices be heard by those who travel with you," the Eldarin said in unison.

Aaron turned to the others, who nodded back to him that they had understood.

"Thank you for helping me before," Aaron said. "To be honest, I didn't know I was calling anyone."

The two dragon lords eyed each other, appearing to communicate without speaking at all. Then they turned their gaze upon him, sweeping him in a torrent of energy.

"We have heard of you through the passing of one of our children. You were there at the moment of his transcendence," the Eldarin said. "You feel the lifebeat and know of the wrongness of the fallen ones."

Aaron swallowed, absorbing the unspoken words, taking in the Eldarin's juxtaposed voices inside his head.

"The fallen ones?" Aaron asked.

One of the Eldarin tilted his head to the side and an image of a Ryakul sprang before them. The black skin stretched over bat-like wings with its saber tusked maw opening like an enormous cave. The armored tail ended in a spike. Aaron clenched his teeth. The Ryakuls were the enemy.

"You see. You sense the wrongness of the fallen ones."

Aaron steeled his emotions while he searched for the meaning of what the Eldarin were trying to convey to him.

"The Ryakuls attack dragons," Aaron said. "They are the enemy. They serve the Drake."

"No, Ferasdiam Marked," the Eldarin said. *"The fallen ones are also our children. Their songs grow dark as they descend into madness."*

"Your children," Aaron gasped. His mind reeled, trying to force the pieces together, and at the same time refused to believe. The Ryakuls were once dragons. "How have your children fallen?"

The Eldarin's powerful gaze shifted behind him to settle upon the Hythariam. Gavril, Roselyn, and Tanneth's golden eyes widened in shock.

Gavril stepped forward. "With respect. We have not caused any of your kind to fall."

The Eldarin shifted their gazes to Aaron. *"One of their kind spreads a sickness that changes what was once beautiful and vibrant into something hideous. They are the fallen."*

Aaron turned to Gavril. "The Drake is of Hytharia. Who is to say that this is not something it could have done?"

Gavril's eyes grew distant as he considered, and then he shrugged his shoulders and shook his head.

"The Ryakuls attack us on sight," Aaron said, turning back to the Eldarin. "The only way for us to stop them is to kill them, but if you know of a way that we could help them instead, then perhaps there is something that we can do to help you."

The Eldarin regarded each other for a few long moments before turning back to them.

"We know of no way to help the fallen ones. We seek to protect what is left of our children. They would answer the call of the Ferasdiam Marked and engage the fallen ones to their doom."

Aaron looked around him as he finally understood. The Eldarin were concerned with the preservation of the dragons. Their children. That he would call them into battle with the Ryakul and... He turned back to the others.

"We've always wondered where the Ryakuls came from and why their numbers had grown," Aaron said. "The Ryakuls are fallen dragons. Roselyn, do you know of any sickness that could cause something like this? I don't think this is the work of the Nanites."

"Why not?" Verona asked. "I'm not disagreeing, but I'm not sure why it couldn't be Nanites."

Some of the others nodded, save for Roselyn, who returned his gaze evenly.

"It doesn't fit with the timeline," Aaron pressed. "The presence of the Ryakuls predate the Drake by over fifty years. Do you remember Vaughn talking about the Ryakul Incursion and how they were driven back in Shandara. My bet is that there were no recorded instances of the Ryakuls prior to the portal being opened between Safanar and Hytharia. Something is changing the dragons, turning them into the Ryakuls. The two are ferocious enemies, but perhaps we've got it wrong." Aaron glanced at the Eldarin and then back at his companions. "The dragons have been fighting and losing a war for their very survival right under our noses."

"It could be anything," Gavril whispered, looking visibly shaken, his eyes darting back and forth. "Near the end we weren't able to follow decontamination protocols. Something could have gotten through. Some type of sickness…"

Aaron shook his head. "I'm not blaming you. But we need to find a way to help the dragons if we can."

"I don't know of anything off the top of my head that could cause this," Roselyn said. "I would need to return to Hathenwood and search through our repositories of knowledge. Maybe—" her voice cut off as she stifled a cry and looked up, addressing the Eldarin. "I will try to find a way to help your species. I swear it."

Aaron turned back to the Eldarin, feeling his throat tighten. "I'm so sorry."

Each of the dragon lords lowered their heads in acknowledgement.

"We of the Eldarin will always heed the call of the Ferasdiam Marked. You are the champion of the Safanarion Realm. Do not forget your purpose."

The dragon lords launched into the air with grace and majesty, seeming to float up beyond the push of their wings. The wind rushed passed Aaron's face, blowing his dark hair back as the Eldarin disappeared in a blinding flash of light.

"We caused this," Roselyn gasped, looking at Gavril, whose eyes were downcast in shame. "Perhaps it should have been our fate to die on Hytharia."

"No," Verona said firmly, before Aaron could say the same. "This is not your fault," Verona said gently coming before Roselyn. "You saw a way to survive, my lady, to live and your people took it. Would any of us have done differently?" he said, lifting her chin slightly so she would look him in the eyes.

"You couldn't have known this would happen," Aaron said.

Gavril looked up and the old soldier's golden eyes drew down in shame. "I fear this is as bad as it seems," he said softly, drawing all their attention. "On Hytharia there was such a beast that could spread a sickness through its bite. Most victims would die of the poison, but some did not. They changed. Mutated into a hybrid of the original host and the victim. These beasts were hunted to extinction on Hytharia, however the venom was preserved. This was long before I was born, before we knew our planet was in danger. I first came across the venom during my time in the military. There was a secret special corps established for the enhancement of our soldiers. The program had been long shut down, as with the invention of the Nanites the venom was no longer required. We could enhance our soldiers without turning them into beasts."

"Who would have known about the venom? Iranus or any of the other scientists?" Aaron asked.

"Not a chance. They were just scientists and not associated with weapons research," Gavril replied. "This was strictly military and only the most senior of the military would have access to this knowledge."

"You think this was a weapon," Aaron said. "But how?"

Gavril sighed and took a long haunted glance at the sky. "Before the barrier went up there was fighting here on Safanar. General Halcylon did get some troops across before the barrier closed completely. Perhaps one of them brought it across, or was enhanced with the venom."

Aaron frowned, trying to remember what he saw when he looked through the barrier in Shandara that linked Safanar to Hytharia. The land was desolate, but there was something massive on the other side. A heavily muscled creature with wild yellow eyes beating its claws against the barrier. He blinked away the memory and looked at Gavril in horror, who nodded back grimly.

"You were there when the barrier first went up," Aaron said. "Were there dragons at this battle?"

Gavril looked to be swallowing something vile back down his throat and nodded slowly.

"We didn't realize." Gavril said.

"That's right, you didn't," Aaron said. "But now you know, so now we can do something about it. We must find a way to help the dragons."

"You don't understand, Aaron," Gavril said. "There is no cure for this. The change, once infected, is permanent. The only way is to exterminate all of the Ryakul on Safanar."

Roselyn pulled away from Verona. "It is not enough that we doomed our home world, but look at what we've done to yours," she said and ran off away from the others.

Aaron looked at Tanneth, who quietly shrugged his shoulders. "I was born here. Safanar is the only home I've ever known."

Aaron nodded and watched as Verona slowly closed the distance between himself and Roselyn. When he caught up to her, he simply stood to the side not saying anything for a few moments, and then slowly reached for her. Roselyn turned and buried her head in Verona's shoulder.

"She was a little girl when she came through the portal to this world," Gavril said. "I'm not sure what she remembers of Hytharia, but she is a healer at heart. Knowing that something we made could cause this…"

A searing pain burned across Aaron's chest, dropping him to his knees. He could hear Gavril call out to the others, but it all sounded muffled. The skin on his chest felt like it was being torn open, causing him to cry out. Aaron gasped for breath and pulled down his shirt, but his skin was untouched. The pain lanced across the dragon tattoo as if something was pulling his heart out of his chest.

Oh, Sarah…

He focused himself, calling the bladesong in his mind, and his perceptions sharpened. The lifebeat of the others pulsed around him with glistening clarity, but coming from his chest was the translucent line of energy that had been there since he had healed Sarah's mortal wounds at the hands of her brother Primus.

The pain came again and the line blared red for a moment before turning back to normal. He had to find her now before it was too late.

Aaron drew away from his physical body and heard Verona's voice as if from a great distance telling the others to wait. He hadn't followed his connection to Sarah this far for fear of causing her more pain, but he had to risk it. He needed to find her. Time was running out.

The land and the sky streaked by as he followed the connection, heading east from where they were. He crested over a mountain peak to a valley crawling with Ryakul, as if the ground below were in constant motion, stopping him in his tracks. Below him was a dark sea of black-winged spawn of what were once majestic dragons. The Ryakuls were much smaller than the Eldarin, but what they couldn't account for in size, they more than made up for in numbers. All was strangely quiet, as in this form he couldn't hear anything, but he could imagine the snarling Ryakuls as they shifted their positions. The Ryakuls appeared extremely agitated and frequently snapped at anything close by, including others of their kind.

A large figure stood upon a plateau amid the Ryakuls. The Drake stood poised, surveying the area with one of its arms abruptly ending in a stump from where his swords had severed the hand that held Sarah at its mercy. Even from this distance the smoldering yellow eyes appeared as liquid steel and the black armor held a purplish hue in the sunlight. The Drake's pale alien face gazed up to the sky and despite what Iranus had told him, Aaron was having difficulty believing that the creature had once been his grandmother.

Several of the Ryakuls clawed and bit at each other, snatching the Drake's attention. The Drake brought up its arm and a small display appeared. The effect on the Ryakuls was immediate as they fell writhing in pain and bowed their heads submissively. On a lower plateau, a dark figure curled into a ball with a lone Ryakul standing watch. Aaron closed the distance to Sarah and hovered over her. Her pale skin held black splotches where it was exposed to the cold mountain air. Her arms were clutched around her middle and her eyes were shut tight. He dared not go any closer lest he lose all control and reach out.

Having Sarah's exact location, he began to pull back to his body. The world streaked by until he slowly opened his eyes. Verona knelt next to him, offering him some water. Aaron nodded his thanks and stood up.

"I know where she is," he said. "East of here, less than twenty miles away."

"That's great," Verona said. "Let us be off then."

"We need a plan," Aaron said. "The Drake has a nest of Ryakuls all over that mountain. I don't think we should charge in, as much as I would like to."

"He's right," Gavril said.

"How did Sarah look?" Roselyn asked, her eyebrows drawing up in concern.

"Not good. I don't think she has much time left," Aaron said and described the dark splotches on her skin and how she was curled up into a shaking ball.

Roselyn put her hand on Aaron's shoulder. "She fights. The

Drake has not won yet. Have hope."

Aaron nodded and sighed in relief, unclenching his fists. Seeing Sarah like that, with the Nanites doing their worst, had all but sucked the hope from him.

"Do you think the Drake can detect the ship?" Aaron asked.

The Hythariam regarded each other silently before Gavril answered. "No. If we're cloaked then we are completely hidden."

"The Drake is controlling the Ryakuls," Aaron said. "But I think that if we agitated them enough it would break whatever control it was using over them. We need to draw some of them away while I go and get Sarah."

The others considered what he had said, save Verona. "My friend, I know the first thing you want to do is to rescue Sarah, but if we don't handle the Drake then I think your rescue attempt may be doomed to failure."

"The Drake is not going to sit idly by once our presence is known," Gavril said.

"I propose that we split our efforts into two teams," Aaron said. "The first team will stay with the ship and engage the Ryakuls, drawing as many as they can away from the mountain, clearing the way for the second team. The second team, with myself, will attempt to rescue Sarah and if the Drake— No, when the Drake makes its move, then we take it out."

"A good plan," Gavril said. "There is just one thing I don't like about it. We don't know how Sarah will react when she sees you again."

Aaron looked up in alarm, but waited to hear what Gavril

meant.

"The Nanites have some control over her," said Gavril. "She may not want to be rescued even if part of her does. She may fight you or any of us that tries to help, but most especially you, Aaron. Seeing you is going to be traumatic for her."

Aaron sucked in his bottom lip considering. "I know. We'll need to capture her."

"What about the travel crystals?" Verona asked. "Do you know how to make them work?"

Aaron's jaw clamped shut in frustration and shook his head. He had probed the travel crystals, but didn't know how to key them. He had hoped to speak to the Elitesman Isaac about it, but never had the chance.

"Sarah knows how to use them. I'll need to reach her," Aaron said.

They were all silent. No one wanted to ask the obvious question of what he would do if he couldn't reach Sarah, but the question was self evident in all of their gaze.

"She is still in there, despite whatever her appearance may be," Aaron said. "I have to believe that there is still a part of Sarah that hasn't been tainted by the Nanites. That is what I'm fighting for."

Verona cleared his throat. "I've said it before, but I feel that I can speak for all of us in that we'll be at your side to see that you at least get to try."

"About the two teams," Gavril began. "I will be with you on the ground, which leaves Tanneth and Roselyn to pilot the ship." Gavril glanced at Roselyn who nodded back. "Sarik, would you join them on the Flyer? I have two reasons for asking this. First, should the ship become damaged and need to be abandoned, then Tanneth and Roselyn will stand a much better chance at surviving with your support. Second, you've shown a keen aptitude for the Flyer's systems and I would like Tanneth to begin showing you how to pilot the ship."

Sarik's eyes darted to Aaron, who nodded encouragingly to the young man.

"I will do as you ask," Sarik said.

"Thank you," Gavril replied.

"So that leaves the rest of us to go on the ground with you, Aaron," Verona said.

Aaron took a moment to consider his next words. "Okay, but if you can avoid it, don't engage Sarah."

Verona and Braden looked at him as if he said the most obvious thing in the world.

"Fine," Aaron said. "If you do, I may be too preoccupied with the Drake to save your sorry asses." This drew chuckles from all of them and they replied in kind. He was glad for the momentary reprieve.

"About the Drake," Gavril continued. "I'm hoping to help even things out."

"How?" Aaron asked.

"The Drake used Hythariam technology against you in your last encounter, which put you off balance," Gavril said. "I will help nullify this threat. Are we agreed that the Drake will need to be destroyed?" Gavril leveled his gaze at Aaron.

Verona and Braden looked at Aaron questioningly. They did not know the Drake's true identity.

"I have no illusions about the Drake," Aaron answered and then faced the others. "Before we left Hathenwood, Iranus revealed to me that the Drake was created using my grandmother as the Nanite host. The previous Drake had infected her at the fall of Shandara. To the best of my knowledge, Reymius had no knowledge of this."

"He didn't know," said Gavril. "None of us did until it was too late. We believed that Cassandra had died in Shandara."

"She did," Aaron replied solemnly.

Gavril sighed, giving a single nod. "By the time we realized what was happening, the Drake all but disappeared."

"I think the Drake is more vulnerable now than before," Aaron said.

"How so?" Verona asked.

"We need to think like a machine," said Aaron. "The Drake's current form is proving to be ineffective, hence it is focusing on switching hosts and doing nothing to repair its current body. I saw that it never repaired the severed arm from when it took Sarah. So we're agreed we take out the Drake and move to capture Sarah."

The others nodded and Roselyn stepped away, heading toward the Flyer, saying she would be right back.

"Here is what I'm thinking we should do, and I'm hoping you'll tell me if this is too crazy," Aaron said and laid out the plan he had been formulating in his mind. It didn't take long as his plan wasn't all that complex, but he kept certain pieces to himself.

"Verona, I need to speak to you alone for a moment," Aaron said.

The others headed back toward the ship, giving them some privacy.

"Here we are, my friend. Again," Verona said.

Aaron grinned in spite of himself. "Indeed. There is something I need to tell you that I won't be sharing with the others. I will face the Drake only because I don't think we can get Sarah out without alerting it. I don't know how this is going to go and I've often heard it said that the best laid plans can sometimes go to waste once a battle starts." Aaron looked at the others for a moment. "If I can get to Sarah and get the travel crystals to work, I intend to head back to Shandara."

Verona's eyes widened. "But the crystals... They won't work in Shandara."

"That is correct, but they can get me near the city and near the barrier, as well. I've felt the imbalance there and believe that I could reach Shandara where others would fail." Aaron said. "I will only do this if there is no other choice and I wanted you to know so you can find us."

Verona nodded grimly. "I understand. I wish we had Colind's counsel for what we're about to do."

Aaron returned his friend's gaze, hoping that fate would deem them worthy of a kind hand in this, but either way, this business would be finished today. He just hoped they were all alive by the end.

***

Mactar and Darven crouched low amid a tree line's edge before the steep incline of a mountain teaming with Ryakuls. They had been there only a short while and saw that the Drake could, in fact, have some measure of control over the ferocious beasts. The control was barely tenable at best with the Drake's attention focused on maintaining the perimeter. They crept as close as they dared, and had a clear view of the plateau upon which the Drake now stood. It kept looking back at the other plateau where two Ryakuls now sat poised. The other Ryakuls appeared more agitated. Mactar couldn't recall ever seeing so many of the beasts in one place. Fighting among the beasts broke out frequently, which were suppressed when the Drake would activate a device upon its wrists.

Mactar utilized his skills to provoke the Ryakuls so he could focus upon the actions the Drake took to control them. He focused himself, seeing the many lines of energy, but what he was looking for was more subtle. A glowing display appeared above the device on the Drake's wrists. It was pulsing brightly and even with his heightened perceptions, he could barely make out the strumming sound in a freakish rhythm.

The affect on the Ryakul was almost instantaneous as their attention became fixated upon the Drake. Mactar winced at the screeching sounds piercing his ears, and several Ryakuls immediately took to the skies.

Mactar glanced back to Darven, who nodded, indicating that he had seen as well. He was about to speak when a loud boom shook the ground beneath their feet. The Ryakuls on the mountains flapped their wings, sending hundreds of whooshes through the air. A golden ship sped through the clouds and disappeared. Darven looked at him questioningly, and while Mactar had not seen a ship like that in over twenty years, he knew who had access to such technology.

"It's the Hythariam," Mactar said softly. "The Heir of Shandara is here."

"He's not the only one," Tarimus hissed from behind.

***

The Hythariam Flyer, while a superb ship, was only one ship, which limited their options for approach and reconnaissance. Aaron and the others set down on a narrow ledge of a rock face toward the far side of Ryakul Mountain.

Verona coined the phrase "Ryakul Mountain" and was proud of his vocal eloquence in naming the previously anonymous peak. Regardless, the name stuck with all of them.

"This seemed like a better idea while we were on the ship," Verona said, and Braden grunted in agreement.

"You wanted to come." Aaron grinned slightly. "You could try jumping." While both Verona and Braden could tap into the energy around them, and had accomplished some pretty impressive things with it, they could not jump like he and Sarah could. Back on the Raven before they had reached Shandara, Sarah had told them it would take time. However, the shield that Verona and Sarik were able to create was quite intriguing, and he was sure would come in useful in the future.

"You will be fine," Aaron said. "Tanneth used one of these to follow me through Khamearra when we learned of the attack on the inn. If we weren't about to head into a battle, I'd think the gliders were fun and would join you."

Gavril was helping Verona and Braden strap a glider to their feet. There were two rods upon the ground and Gavril was showing them how to activate the glider through the comms device now strapped to their wrists. At either points of the rod, discs large enough for them to step upon unfolded, forming an oval. Verona and Braden stepped onto the discs and metallic bands extended over their feet, securing them in place.

"Now listen carefully," Gavril said, stepping onto his own glider. "You key in the sequence I've just shown you. Not yet, Verona, just listen first." After Verona put his hands down, Gavril continued. "It's really quite simple. The glider will respond to your movements. If you raise both your knees then the glider will rise into the air. Lean to either side and you will go in that direction. The same also applies to backwards and forwards. Here, watch, I will show you."

The glider at Gavril's feet hovered about a foot off the ground. He brought his knees up and the glider pushed his body into the air. Gavril leaned to the side and the glider followed. The more he leaned the greater the speed.

Gavril spun in the air and returned back to them. "Just push down and straighten your legs to stop moving up or whatever direction you are moving. The glider's systems will respond to you. Once you step on and activate them, they record your weight and adapt to your movements, but you must be careful. There are some safeguards to prevent you from falling, but if you persistently lean too far forward and can't get your feet back under you, you will crash."

"Crashing would be most unfortunate," Verona agreed.

"We just need to use these to go up the side of this mountain. I don't expect you to go into battle on them. When we reach the plateau at the top, just hover over the ground and deactivate the glider through your comms device," Gavril said.

"What happens if the comms device gets damaged?" Verona asked.

"Now *that* would be most unfortunate," Gavril said and the old soldier's face lifted into a grin. "The comms devices are quite durable I assure you, and will not break easily. Let's try rising into the air and coming back down quickly before we make our ascent."

Braden muttered something about flying only being for the birds, but keyed in the sequence into the comms device and his glider hovered in the air. He was joined by Verona, who was unable to keep the smile from his face.

"Class is over. We've been made," Aaron said snapping their attention as a lone Ryakul flew around the corner, appearing as startled to see them as they to see it.

"I'll distract it. You get up the mountain," Gavril said and flew off to meet the oncoming Ryakul.

"Let's go," Aaron said, and he jumped into the air, aligning the particles in the air to push him higher than any strength enhanced jump could take him.

Verona and Braden began rising into the air. Slowly at first, but rapidly gaining speed and closing the distance between them. They were both warriors with excellent balance, which they used to their advantage as they glided up the mountainside.

Aaron landed high above them and waited for his friends to catch up. Gavril was dodging the Ryakul with an aero acrobatic display that he wouldn't have thought possible, even on a glider. The Ryakul's head was fixed upon its prey, and it instinctively flew wherever it led.

The Hythariam gliders were more agile in the air, making the Ryakul seem clumsy as it tried to follow. Gavril fired golden plasma bolts into the Ryakul from his pistol.

Knowing that the Ryakuls were once dragons made him slightly sympathetic toward the feral beasts, but it was only because they were the shadowy reflection of their purer self. Aaron turned back to Verona and Braden and gasped as Verona lost his balance. Braden stuck out an arm to steady him, and they both reached where he was unharmed. They continued to climb, reaching another plateau. Aaron turned to see Gavril blind the Ryakul by shooting out its eyes and the dark beast spun away, plummeting toward the ground.

Gavril caught up to them easily just as the roars of hundreds of Ryakuls echoed off the surrounding mountains. Tanneth had uncloaked the Flyer to draw their attention. Verona, becoming more comfortable upon the glider, drew his bow with an arrow ready and continued to follow them. Aaron kept his jumps small and precise so they could stay together at first, but the closer he got to the top, the more the distance grew between them.

Knowing that Sarah was so close, he couldn't help it.

They crested the ridge and settled down low to look at the other side. The air was a sea of black flapping wings as the Ryakuls pursued the Hythariam Flyer as it streaked across the sky like a golden bullet. Aaron turned toward the left, focusing in on the Drake.

The Drake was watching the Flyer as it streaked across the sky and immediately spun, heading toward another peak. Aaron scanned ahead and saw two Ryakul keeping a watchful eye around them.

Gotcha. So much for the plan...

Aaron pointed. "Sarah is over there," he said, grasping the small curved ax from his belt.

"Go," Verona said, "We'll be right behind you."

Aaron gathered the energy around him and the runes on the staff flared to life. He fed the energy into his muscles and launched into the air. He pushed forward, gliding with the wind, and heard the screeching howl of the Drake below him. The Ryakuls snapped their heads in his direction. He unleashed the ax as he bounded off another peak.

The ax streaked silver across the sky, demolishing the Ryakul's head, and its great body slammed down upon the ground as Aaron landed in front of the remaining Ryakul. He dodged the snapping jaws of the Ryakul's saber-toothed maw. The Ryakul swiped with its poisonous talons, barely missing him.

Aaron drew the Falcons, and as the blades kissed the air, notes from the bladesong surged forth within him. He spun and dove into a roll, avoiding another swipe of the talons. Aaron brought up the blades, anticipating another strike, but at the last second the Ryakul spun, sweeping out with its armored tail. Aaron launched into the air, cutting through the Ryakul's hide as he went.

The dark beast roared in pain and sought to overwhelm Aaron as it crashed down upon where he landed. Aaron dove to the side and sliced behind the Ryakul's forward leg, bringing it down. He danced to the other side, cutting through the hamstring of the Ryakul's remaining front legs.

Aaron darted out of the way as the beast swayed and crashed down on its side. One of its wings flapped uselessly as it tried to regain its footing. Aaron circled and drove both his blades into the long neck and black blood spewed forth from the dying beast.

He pulled his blades clean and felt something grab his backpack and swing him away. Aaron tumbled and skidded to a halt inches away from the plateau's edge. He glanced at the dizzying heights of the drop off down below and sprung back to his feet. He nearly stumbled at the sight before him.

Sarah stood with her sword held at the ready. Her eyes glowed yellow, and the black blotches almost completely covered her exposed skin. There was no recognition in her baleful gaze, just a surety of the murderous intent in her eyes.

"Sarah!" Aaron called. "It's me."

Sarah cocked her head for a second and shook it violently.

Aaron was about to step forward when he saw the Drake pull itself over the ledge. The Drake's howl sawed through the air, and Aaron felt the ancestral blood within rise in protest. He dashed forward, closing the distance to the Drake, and brought down his blades in a crushing blow toward the Drake's outstretched arm. The dark swirling armor solidified as his blades made contact and the impact jarred his bones.

The Drake was over seven feet tall. Its great body pulled back, and then an armored fist planted firmly into Aaron's face, sending him flat upon his back.

Aaron shook his head to clear it, losing his focus. The Drake punched hard.

The Drake's eyes peered into Aaron, and then turned its attention to the stump of its left arm. The surface of the arm bubbled up, forming an armored twin of its other arm.

Aaron charged forward, but the Drake shot its hand forth and something rippled through the air, knocking him off his feet and pinning him to the ground. There was a cry behind him as Braden leaped off the glider and landed in front of him, driving the Shield of Shandara in front of them both. The crushing force that kept him pinned to the ground stopped. Aaron came to his feet and saw the glint of metal from the corner of his eye. He spun and his blades met Sarah's. He kicked out with his leg, knocking her off to the side, and turned back toward the Drake.

The Drake leveled its staff and fired upon Braden. The bolt of energy bounced off the shield, but the force of the blast sent Braden sailing through the air and over the edge. Aaron cried out, and Gavril zipped past him over the edge, chasing Braden.

Aaron seized the bladesong and the crystals in the Falcons flared anew. He swept out with his blades, sending out an arc of energy and knocking the Drake back. An arrow flew past Aaron, but bounced harmlessly off the Drake's armor.

"Behind you!" Verona cried, and Aaron turned, bringing up his sword.

Sarah swung her sword at him and then advanced, raining down blows as she came. Aaron met each blow and yielded precious footing upon the plateau. He wielded the Falcons into the bladesong, probing out to Sarah, seeking out the golden core that was her true self and not that tangled mess of the Nanites. He locked her blade in his own and came face to face with her, feeling her ragged breath upon his face.

"Fight them, Sarah," Aaron whispered.

From behind him, Aaron heard Verona cry out, and he risked turning to see that his friend had engaged the Drake in an attempt to give him time to reach Sarah.

Verona's arm hung loosely by his side, and the remains of the glider lay broken at his feet. The Drake hovered behind his friend, and Aaron dashed forward, moving with blurring speed. The twin blades on the end of the Drake's staff began to descend and Verona fell back. Aaron roared, thrusting both his glowing swords in front of him and skipping into the air. He twisted in midair to bring the Falcons down into the Drake's chest; his momentum carried them both over the side to the depths below.

Aaron struggled against the Drake's powerful grip as the wind roared passed his ears. The Drake howled in pain as they bounced along the side of the mountain and several Ryakuls pursued them.

Aaron released his hold upon one of his swords and rained

down blows upon the Drake's face with his fist. A dark form swooped underneath them, breaking their fall, and jarred his senses as a Ryakul flapped its bat-like wings to steady itself. Aaron brought his feet underneath him, planting them upon the Ryakul's broad back with the Drake in between and pushed away. His swords twisted free of the Drake, and the pain of it forced the Drake to release its hold upon him.

Aaron was surrounded amid a sea of roaring Ryakuls, tangling themselves up as they each tried to snap at him. He dodged one saber-tusked maw and used his feet to bounce off another. His swords dripped with the black blood of the Ryakuls as their poisonous talons tried to tear at him. He leaped to the back of another Ryakul, plunging his swords into its back, and held on tightly as the beast spun. His white-knuckled grip was locked around the hilts of his swords, but as the Ryakul spun, the blades cut deeper into the beast's hide. The Ryakul leveled off and Aaron saw the golden Hythariam Flyer try to reach him, but it was blocked by the sheer number Ryakuls throwing themselves at the craft. Aaron glanced behind him and then launched himself into the air, pulling his swords free as four Ryakuls, with one carrying the Drake, converged upon the already injured one carrying him. The Ryakuls began to tear their brethren apart, but Aaron was safely away.

He landed upon a ragged cliff and watched the Ryakul tear apart one of their own. He had to force the bile back down his throat. Perhaps it was the knowledge of what the Ryakuls truly were that clawed away at the walls of his heart, or the knowledge that death was the only remedy that could be afforded to the dragons afflicted with this disease. The Drake's call rallied the Ryakul. They dropped the lifeless corpse and closed the distance toward him.

The Drake leveled his staff and fired. Aaron leaped into the air, narrowly avoiding the blast, and charged at the Ryakuls. The beasts' putrid breath invaded his nostrils as he sailed by, lashing out with his blades and slicing deeply into one's hide.

Aaron scrambled off the side of the beast to land upon the back of another. The Drake leveled his staff at him, but as it was about to fire, a blue bolt of energy slammed into it from the side. Small bolts of energy spread across the Drake and the smoking staff fell from its hands.

Aaron looked up seeing Gavril rise up from behind the Drake upon his glider. He nodded grimly toward Aaron.

The Drake pulled back on the Ryakul, forcing it to fly higher. Aaron drew in the energy around him and pushed, launching himself into the air and gaining on the fleeing Drake. The armored tail of the Ryakul was in front of him and he latched on, dragging the beast off balance. The Ryakul crashed onto a mountain plateau and Aaron tumbled away from the tangled mess of tooth and claw. He regained his footing, shaking his head. The Ryakul lay dying with some of its limbs moving feebly, until they stopped altogether.

Aaron glanced at the sky around them, hearing the roar of airship engines at full burst. Streaking into view were four airships firing giant crossbow bolts into the Ryakuls that swarmed the sky like insects.

The body of the Ryakul on the ground heaved and the Drake came out from behind. The Drake's armor sent sparks into the air as it moved and was hanging off in a few places. The two holes in its chest from Aaron's swords had not reformed. The Drake tried to key something into a panel on its arm and screeched a yell into the air, but the call that had previously commanded the Ryakul fell upon deaf ears as the beasts scattered.

The Drake tore the useless panel from its arm and tossed it aside. It cocked its head toward Aaron and for the briefest of moments, the smoldering yellow eyes diminished. Then the beast howled in rage and the yellow eyes flared anew as it charged.

Aaron brought up his swords, easily avoiding the blows of the Drake. He lashed out, cutting through the armor in multiple places. The Drake's attacks grew more feeble and Aaron could sense something growing beneath the surface of its very skin. He cast out, probing with the energy toward the Drake. It was dying, and the Nanites required a living host to survive. A small white light flared faintly from the Drake's dark form as it fell to the ground

***

Tarimus…again!

Mactar was at a loss as to how Tarimus had tracked them down again and he hadn't been able to get a clear shot at him. He and Darven decided to split up using the travel crystals. The Ryakuls flew in a frenzy, attacking anything that moved, which included snapping at other Ryakuls. One of his gifts was that of an impeccable memory and having observed the Drake's call, Mactar knew that it was something he could duplicate. The call however, was only half of the means used to control the Ryakuls, with the other half tied to the device upon the Drake's arm. Mactar watched as the Drake pursued the Heir of Shandara in his rather impressive acrobatic display, leaping from one Ryakul to the next. Ferasdiam Marked indeed. He could quite possibly challenge the High King, but not yet. The boy still thought of himself as a man and not one touched by fate.

The Drake was fading, and despite himself, Mactar's gaze was locked upon the battle before him. None of the Alenzar'seth before had stood against the Drake. They all perished one way or another. He engaged the travel crystal to a spot not fifty feet from where Aaron stood over the fallen Drake. He cloaked himself in such a way as to avoid notice, and judging by the state of the Heir of Shandara, he would not looking for him. Mactar quietly waited and listened to what unfolded before him.

***

"Who...are ...you?" the creature that had been the Drake asked him, struggling to get the words out.

"I'm Aaron," he answered. "Carlowen's son."

The deformed figure of the Drake's face crumpled in pain and grief as it whispered his mother's name. Aaron eyes widened as he realized that some part of his grandmother was still in there.

"Reymius?" his grandmother asked.

Aaron shook his head slightly. "He protected us. My mother found happiness and Reymius took comfort in that."

Cassandra's eyes still glowed yellow, and her face was twisted into something beyond human, but Aaron could tell that the Nanites's hold upon her was fading.

"He didn't know. He thought you had died," Aaron said, trying to give what comfort he could.

Dull yellow eyes searched his as her body spasmed in pain, and she glanced up to the plateau where Sarah was. "She is still in there. She still fights for you."

Aaron felt the tears fall freely and unclenched his jaw to speak. "How can I save her?"

His grandmother's eyes closed and she drew a shallow breath.

"Please," Aaron pleaded. "Can you tell me how to save her? She is my heart...my soul...my everything."

Aaron leaned in as his grandmother struggled to speak, silently begging that fate would allow her to give him this one last message.

"What...wouldn't...you...do?" The last words spoken by his grandmother ran together in a great sigh that he could hardly make out.

The remnants of the Drake collapsed to the ground and the crackling energy infused into the armor grew silent. He softly laid his grandmother's head onto the ground and watched as her body dissolved before his eyes. The Nanites that had once been so vibrant, doing their utmost to carry out their task, required a living host to survive, and without them, what was now his grandmother's body came apart, fading away to dust. Aaron unclenched his teeth and howled in frustration. His eyes drew up toward the plateau where he had last seen Sarah. He gathered the energy around him and launched into the air, heading toward Sarah with the echoes of his grandmothers last words in his mind.

What wouldn't you do?

CHAPTER 22
THE REACHING

Mactar dropped his shroud and bent to pick up the broken panel the Drake—Lady Cassandra—had discarded. Hearing Aaron speak to the beast yielded nuggets of information that he was ignorant of, and even now his mind raced to catch up with their implications. He stuffed the panel into the folds of his cloak, then someone grabbed him from behind.

Mactar's breath caught in his throat as he felt his body thrown like a rag doll to the ground. He came to his knees and erected a barrier between himself and his attacker. He shook his head, still disoriented, when a flash of light appeared. Darven emerged with his blades ready. Mactar reached out with bands of energy, locking them around the dark cloaked figure in front of him, and dropped his own barrier.

There is no escape this time, Tarimus.

Tarimus drew his dark blade and met the Elitesman. Mactar's bands of energy locked Tarimus in this realm, but he was still free to move about.

Mactar summoned an orb of energy poised to strike, but the two blade masters kept moving. He could take them both out, but Darven still had his uses.

The Ryakuls were scattering and the airships were closing in on their position. The sharp clang of steel hitting the ground snatched Mactar's attention, and he saw Darven being held up by the throat in Tarimus's grip.

Mactar's hand shot forth, sending the orb directly into Tarimus's back and causing him to stagger. He shot another one, but it disappeared into Tarimus's outstretched hand.

Tarimus rose to his feet with an evil knowing smile upon his face.

"Come reap what you have sown, Dark Master," Tarimus spat.

Mactar drew deep within himself, summoning so much energy that the air around them seemed about to ignite. He would squash this rodent once and for all. Gritting his teeth, he charged forward shooting a bar of molten energy toward Tarimus, not caring if Darven would get caught in the blast.

The beam of energy stopped abruptly a foot away from Tarimus, flailing off to the side by a shield of immense power, surprising them both. The backlash could be felt where he stood. Mactar turned to see the face of a dead man standing behind him.

"Father!" Tarimus howled.

Mactar smirked at Colind while engaging the travel crystal, leaving the mountaintop behind.

***

Colind clamped down on his anger for not taking out Mactar

when he had the chance. He was here for his son. What was left of him.

Tarimus turned and dragged the Elitesman to his feet, drawing back his blade to strike. The Elitesman fumbled with his travel crystal, which dropped to the ground.

"No!" Colind commanded and clamped bonds of energy upon Tarimus's wrists. "Let him go, Son."

Tarimus strained against his bonds, growling to the point of sounding more beast than man.

"I want a river of blood to flow, starting with him," Tarimus said, his black eyes narrowing menacingly, striking fear into the Elitesman.

"A river of blood has already been unleashed. Don't add to it," Colind pleaded. "The Elitesman is nothing. Let him go."

"I gave you the Alenzar'seth heir," Tarimus spat, still struggling against the bonds.

"You gave me nothing," Colind said. "You used him to free yourself from your prison."

Colind watched as his son strained against the bonds, his limbs shaking. He felt a great weight shift down in his stomach and a lump grow in his throat. The boy his son had been was gone. There was nothing but a monster before him, twisted and evil. Responsible for countless deaths and who showed no signs of stopping.

Colind held the bonds firmly in one hand and slammed down with the other, causing Tarimus to drop the Elitesman. He held no love for the Elitesman and more than likely the man would die in the near future, but what he fought for was a small redemption for his only son. He sent a shroud of energy that washed over his son, binding him. Tarimus's core was twisted from being trapped between realms. There would be no redemption for his son, only a father's regret for his failure.

"You've always catered to them," Tarimus spat. "The Safanarion Order led by the rulers of Shandara were always first in your priorities."

"Your childish tantrums brought about the destruction of one of the greatest kingdoms this world has ever known," Colind said. "You allied yourself with Mactar and the High King. You let the snakes into Shandara and look what it got you. They used you and when you were no longer useful, they found another way for you to serve. They betrayed you."

"You betrayed me, Father. My only joy all these years was knowing that you were imprisoned just like me. The mighty Safanarion Order pushed into hiding and your precious Shandara brought down by me. Your world burned and I wanted you to burn with it."

Colind released the bonds, having the shroud firmly in place prevented Tarimus from going anywhere. The rage and murderous intent washed off his son in waves, almost staggering Colind in his tracks. He couldn't change that which would not change.

"You're going to have to do it," Tarimus howled. "Yourself. If you want to stop me, you're going to have to kill me. I will never stop. You can't stop me!"

Colind raised his hands and his thunderous gaze bored into Tarimus's black demonic eyes. "Your mother and I brought you into this world, and I'm glad that she never had to see what you've become." Colind glanced to the sky, asking silent forgiveness for what he was about to do. Sometimes the evil was just too great and there were too many lines crossed that even the love of a father couldn't overcome.

"Tarimus, you've broken your solemn oaths to the Safanarion Order and knowingly murdered thousands of people, bringing this world to the brink of collapse. As the head of the order, I will carry out the justice that should have been visited upon you all those years ago." Colind pulled his hands apart, tearing Tarimus's essence into pieces, and felt his own broken heart shatter in his chest. Tarimus thrashed and screamed for a moment before dissolving into the tiniest specs with only echoes trailing their wake.

I'm sorry, Colind kept thinking before he collapsed to the ground, cursing the fate that made him judge and executioner of his only beloved son.

***

Aaron landed upon the edge of the plateau to see Verona doing his best to avoid being killed by Sarah. Braden was there using only his shield to keep Sarah at bay.

Aaron pulled two travel crystals from his pack and lightly tapped them together. The crystals rang their tones through the air, stopping Sarah in mid-swing of her swords.

"Let her come," Aaron shouted, retrieving the rune-carved staff.

Smoldering yellow eyes bored into him, and Sarah's golden hair rippled like a pendant upon the wind.

"Come and take it," Aaron whispered, leading Sarah away from the others. Verona would fill them in on the rest of his plan when they regrouped.

The purple travel crystal held her attention, and while Aaron knew the untarnished part of Sarah was still locked away inside, he hoped he wasn't too late. She turned to look at the others and poised as if she was about to charge off after them. Aaron closed the distance and blocked her path, forcing a crystal into her hand.

"Use it," Aaron said. "I know you are still in there."

Sarah stared at the crystal in her hand, appearing confused, and flung the crystal away, shaking her hand free of it.

Aaron seized the bladesong inside and forced another crystal into Sarah's hand. He reached across their connection, feeling the woman he loved huddled inside the dark recesses of her own mind, not willing to trust anything, including him. Especially him. Aaron pushed every memory he had across the link. From the first time he saw her outside that small town, to when they danced at the Feast of Shansheru in Rexel.

"Fight it, Sarah!"

He could see her golden core flare momentarily, struggling to break through the sea of blackness. Still Aaron pressed with everything he had, pouring every last look, touch, and breath across, sparing nothing. The sword she held came to rest at her side.

"It's now or never," Aaron said. "Use the crystal."

Aaron could feel her golden core grow dimmer, at last succumbing to the might of the Nanites.

He was too late. She couldn't break free. Sarah was fading.

"Just reach out," he pleaded, cursing himself.

The blackness completely tainted everything, smothering her golden core until the light all but ceased. Then the slightest of shimmers waved through, pushing against the darkness. The travel crystal flared in her hands, and Aaron instantly seized it with his own and then felt himself be sucked in. The world pulled away from his feet and he sank into the purple abyss.

They emerged alone somewhere in a forest. Sarah blinked her eyes, and for a moment they returned to her normal shade of blue. She looked at Aaron in surprise for a few precious seconds before doubling over in pain. When she looked back up at him, her eyes had returned to yellow.

Aaron seized the travel crystal and kept a firm grip upon her arm. He sent a slight tendril of energy into the crystal and built a picture in his mind of a place along the borders of Shandara. The affect was immediate and the ground fell way from their feet. They emerged at an abandoned campsite. The remnants of the bonfires were still there.

"Oh, Aaron," Sarah said, clearly recognizing where he had taken them.

It was working. Using the crystals was resetting the Nanites.

No sooner had the thought came into his mind did Sarah collapse, writhing upon the ground. Aaron brought out the comms device and keyed in the sequence to shut down the

Nanites.

Nothing happened.

Aaron keyed it in again, but Sarah cried out in pain.

He grabbed Sarah's arm and used the travel crystal again.

The world faded around them as he picked another place. As soon as they emerged, he brought out the comms device and tried again.

Sarah's eyes searched his and they both waited with baited breath. The Nanites eventually reasserted their control, but it took longer. He grabbed Sarah's arm and activated the crystal, setting a frantic pace of traveling from place to place, and using the comms device to try to shut down the Nanites.

He lost count of how many times he used the travel crystals, going to every place he could think of, but aside from slowing the Nanites down, they always returned. The command sequence given to him from Roselyn wouldn't work. Sarah gained a few minutes before the Nanites resumed their task, slaves to the perverted constructs of a malicious military machine. The likes of which he was powerless to fight. Each time the Nanites took control, the pain she was in shredded the walls of his heart.

Aaron clenched his teeth and growled. He had expended all but a few of the travel crystals with nothing to show for it. Despite himself, Sarah saw defeat in his eyes, and no matter how many times he tried, he couldn't free her of the Nanites.

What wouldn't you do?

His grandmother's last words spoke in his mind.

He pictured one last place and the dark forbidden land that had haunted him since he learned of its existence was brought to the forefront. The travel crystal flared anew and Aaron fed in more energy. They emerged into the land of twilight and the barrier separating Safanar from Hytharia shimmered in the air near them. The crystal cracked in his hands and turned to dust.

"Please," Sarah said weakly. "Let me go, Aaron."

"No," Aaron said. "I have one more crystal left."

Sarah winced away from him. "No, I can't take it anymore. You have to let me go," she groaned, gasping in short breaths. *"Please…"*

Aaron looked on helplessly. He had been sure that teleporting with the travel crystals would reset the Nanites, releasing their hold over her, but they were killing her instead. Aaron caught her as she collapsed to the ground, her body jerking in convulsions. He held her steady until they passed, dividing his gaze between the woman he loved with all his heart and the barrier that kept the Hythariam horde at bay.

What wouldn't you do?

He extended his senses to the barrier and saw for the first time the shafts of energy plunging down into the earth. He was tempted to follow them to their source, but Sarah called to him weakly.

"You mustn't," she gasped. "Don't sacrifice this world for me, Aaron." She looked up helplessly at him. Her eyes alternating from beautiful blue to baleful yellow with both breaking his heart. The Nanites were gaining control again.

"Oh, Sarah," his voice croaked, barely above a whisper. "This world means nothing to me without you."

"You have to do it," she said with her hand reaching toward the knife at his belt.

She wanted to die. The fight was leaving her as the Nanites resumed control.

"No!" Aaron cried. "I've got to save you. There has to be a way!"

Sarah looked up at him in a moment of clarity and her eyes retained their stunning shade of blue. "You already have, my love," she whispered.

Aaron held onto her tightly, tears streaming down his face. He could feel the Nanites working inside her, carrying out the will of the Drake, slaves to their programming. They couldn't be reasoned with and were a foe that he could not defeat.

There has to be a way, his mind raced, trying to find an answer.

Like a beacon he called through the bladesong, a thought sparked into his mind.

It couldn't be? Aaron glanced at the barrier.

He gently held Sarah to his chest. At any moment, the Nanites would take over and Sarah would become the Drake, continuing the cruel cycle that had killed the Alenzar'seth for trying to protect their home.

He called the bladesong in his mind, drawing upon the power that held the barrier in check. The barrier and the portal to Hytharia were bound together and one couldn't exist without the other. He couldn't force the Nanites from her system or she would die, nor could he command them to shut down, but he could give them what they wanted.

Aaron pressed his lips upon Sarah's, kissing her, and opened himself up. He aligned his lifebeat to hers and called to the Nanites, which were already working frantically to carry out their grisly task of assimilation.

Don't give up, Sarah, he thought as he fed his energy into her. As if sensing his thoughts, he felt her resist the Nanites with renewed vigor and opened herself up to him. His energy merged with hers until either source was indistinguishable from the other, but Aaron knew. His connection to Sarah was like a symphony opening up in his head with each instrument playing a chord of his lifebeat. The Nanites paused in their work, seeing a whole new entity open before them, and they rushed to assimilate. As they raced into Aaron, he closed them off from Sarah. To the Nanites, it would appear as if parts of Sarah went dark, like a lost limb, and were no longer accessible. As they left Sarah and came into Aaron, she became stronger, her body beginning to recover.

Aaron felt his own strength draining, as the last of the Nanites entered into his system, and he closed his connection to Sarah off entirely. He pulled his lips away from hers and collapsed to his knees.

"What have you done?" Sarah cried, grabbing him with both her hands. Her eyes shone with that brilliant shade of blue, like liquid lightning, and the shade of her creamy skin returned to its proper color.

She was saved.

"The only thing I could do, my love," Aaron whispered, and doubled over.

Sarah cried out his name.

Aaron shook his head to clear it. The Nanites were like tiny pinpricks invading his field of vision. Then he rose up through sheer force of will and swept her up in his arms.

"There's no time," Sarah whispered into his ear, repeating it over and over.

With each gentle breath of her words caressing his ears, he felt his heart shatter to pieces, and reform because she was saved. That was all that mattered to him, as he held her tightly in his arms.

"We've loved a lifetime's worth, and I wouldn't change it for the world," he whispered.

He released her and stood up, his body responded stiffly as the Nanites invaded his brainstem, vying for control. He stumbled closer to the portal that separated the worlds of Safanar from Hytharia, unbuckling his sword belt. He reached into his shirt and removed the medallion, letting both fall to the ground.

"What are you doing!" Verona cried, finally catching up to them. He held a travel crystal in his hand. Colind and Braden were on either side of him.

Aaron was mere inches from the barrier's threshold and turned back to look at Sarah one final time, leaning heavily upon the rune-carved staff.

Tears were streaming down both their faces and their breaths came in gasps. Sarah's getting stronger while his grew weaker.

"What I must do," Aaron said. "Goodbye, my friend."

His vision took on a yellowish hue as the Nanites gained more control over him. Pain, like hot lightning, lanced through his limbs. He lifted the staff and the runes glowed faintly to his touch. He slammed it into the ground, which gave way enough for the staff to stand on its own and bonded it to Shandara as the barrier had been.

Aaron released the bladesong in his mind, revealing to the Nanites that they were in a new host. There was an immediate spike in activity as per the protocols Aaron had surmised they must take. For the briefest of moments he regained full control of himself while the Nanites reset. He gripped the cylinder in his pocket. It was the keystone accelerator that allowed him to come to Safanar.

There is no other way, he told himself and looked at his friend, his brother in everything but blood.

"Take care of them, Verona," Aaron said, and looked back at Sarah as she struggled to her feet.

"Remember me," he said and brought his hands up to the barrier, severing the tethers that kept it in place. With one final look back at the others and a world he had grown to love, he fell back through the portal to the echoes of his friend's denial, and Sarah crying out his name in his wake.

Aaron slammed into the rocky ground that bit into his skin. Sparks rained down on him and he stumbled away. He saw the portal shimmering in the air between two metallic columns, with bolts of electricity running along them. Thick cables connected the columns to large pylons that gave off an azure glow.

The portal flashed and more sparks rocketed from the top of the columns. Aaron dove to the ground, covering his head, as the columns exploded, plunging the area into darkness. The smoggy air burned his lungs and Aaron looked around him as he felt the Nanites crawling inside his skin, gaining their bearings. After a few moments, the yellowish hue retreated from his vision as the Nanites shut down. He struggled to his feet, and his eyes burned, tearing up, and he couldn't stop coughing. The air was hot upon his skin. He wrinkled his nose in a futile attempt to block the stench of the thin air around him.

Aaron fell to his knees, gasping for a breath of air that would not come. Stars like tiny pinpoints of streaking light closed in on his vision. He fumbled through his pocket, grasping the keystone accelerator. The ground shook with the stomp of many footsteps surrounding him. He forced his eyes to open, blinking rapidly. Despite his blearily eyed vision, he saw that he was surrounded by dark figures, each holding some type of rifle leveled at him in their armored hands.

Aaron could hear shouting in a harsh language he didn't understand. He pulled out the keystone accelerator, desperate to open the way back to Safanar. Rough hands pulled him to his feet, knocking the keystone accelerator from his grasp. An armored fist slammed into his stomach, expelling the remaining air from his lungs. Another figure stepped closer, leveling his weapon at Aaron's head. They studied his face and seemed confused by the way his glowing yellow eyes faded to his normal brown color with hints of gold at the edges.

With the Nanites completely shut down, their primary

programming complete, Aaron felt his strength return. He was thankful that the Nanites didn't have any self-destruct mechanism built in upon completion of their prime directive. Something the Hythariam military had overlooked, apparently. They had expected the Drake to return. The ground shook violently underneath him, distracting his captors. Aaron seized the moment and twisted free of the men holding him, sending them sprawling. He squatted down, preparing to jump toward the keystone accelerator, when he heard the snap hiss of a rifle being fired. A net of light collapsed around him, pinning his arms to his sides, and Aaron fell to the ground, helpless before the Hythariam.

One of them spoke in that same language that he couldn't understand as another came to him, slamming a clear mask over his face. The leader spoke again, and he understood one word. Halcylon. They were going to take him to the dreaded Hythariam General that Iranus had warned him about. The one who wanted to conquer Safanar, but had been thwarted by Aaron's ancestor, Daverim. Unable to hold his breath any longer, Aaron sucked in some air through the mask and became light-headed. With his consciousness beginning to wane, he felt himself being dragged across the rugged landscape of a planet that was supposed to have been destroyed years ago, but appeared to be in its final death throws before oblivion.

Epilogue

"No, Aaron!" Colind screamed.

Verona was helping Sarah to her feet. She clung to him, crying out Aaron's name.

"We have to get to him, Verona," Sarah cried, struggling to step forward, but Verona held her back and looked at Colind.

Colind nodded and waved over the others from the Flyer.

"Please, my lady," Verona said to Sarah. "Wait here," he said, and left her with Roslyn.

"Quickly now," Colind shouted.

They charged forward, and a shrieking sound came from the portal, as if something were pressing against it from the other side, and then it disappeared.

All became silent as they skidded to a halt where the portal had been a moment before. The darkened land around them seemed to breathe a sigh of relief, already growing brighter in the sunlight.

"Can we open a portal back to Hytharia?" Verona asked, breaking the silence.

Gavril shook his head grimly.

"Is there no other way?" Verona pressed. "Colind?"

Colind's mouth was hanging open. "I... I don't know."

"We have to get him back," Sarah said, leaning upon Roselyn for support.

Verona immediately came to her side. "We will, my lady."

"He was right there," Sarah cried. "We have to get him back," she said again, collapsing, only to be caught by Verona. Braden came up and lifted Sarah's unconscious form into his thick arms.

Gavril blinked away his shock. "We don't have the equipment here."

Verona shared a look with Colind and the others.

"We need to return to Hathenwood," Colind said.

Verona's gaze drew toward the rune-carved staff. The vibrant glow of the runes faded to a whisper of what they once were. He leaned down, retrieving Aaron's swords and medallion, but as he came before the staff, he paused for a moment and glanced at Colind.

Colind focused on the staff. "Let's leave it for now. There are bonds of energy tethering it to the ground. It might be Aaron's link."

"To where?" Verona asked.

"To Safanar," Colind said.

"Right then," Verona said. "Sarik, I want you and Tanneth to stay here standing guard until we return." The others gathered around him and with a nod to Colind, the group disappeared.

***

Iranus stood in a room with his eyes locked upon the main display of the command center. From here, they could oversee Hathenwood, but also receive communications from the various satellites they had in orbit around the planet. He currently had all the satellites in range locked on their deep-space satellite, which tracked the object that Aaron had cleverly surmised existed.

"Confirmed, sir," the tech said. "Repeat, confirmed; the object has changed course."

Iranus grimly studied the main display as it mirrored the tech's console, giving voice to a fear that all the Hythariam at Hathenwood had hoped to escape. They tracked the trajectory of the incoming object, and it was indeed from their home world. The object had just changed course, denoting some type of intelligence guiding the craft.

"Acknowledged," Iranus answered.

He had hoped the boy had been wrong, but it was confirmed. Hytharia was catching up to them all and time was running out.

ACKNOWLEDGEMENTS

As with any big project, the author is only the tip of the iceberg in taking a huge pile of words and transforming them into something worth reading.

First I have to thank my editor, Jason, thank you for all the feedback and words of encouragement. Commas are now my friend.

Next up is my family, you've all been the cornerstone to my foundation. To my children, who with silent demanding, dared me to be better than I thought could be.

Then there are my "beta readers," Milosz, Phillip, and Tim who despite their busy lives, helped put the final touches on the book and provide an excellent sanity check for the story as a whole. Thank you so much for you time and support.

Finally, never last or least, my wife. Thank you for your love and support and help in making this story what it is today.

ABOUT THE AUTHOR

Ken Lozito has been reading Epic Fantasy and Science Fiction nonstop since the age of eleven. After devouring most of Piers Anthony's work at the time he moved onto authors Robert Jordan, Melanie Rawn, Terry Goodkind, David Weber, and more recently Brandon Sanderson to name a few. He was bit by the writing bug at an early age when he realized he kept focusing his search for particular types of stories that held elements he liked. Then decided to put all the elements into his own story.

Say Hello!

If you have questions or comments about any of Ken's works he would love to hear from you, even if its only to drop by to say hello at KenLozito.com

One Last Thing.

Word-of-mouth is crucial for any author to succeed. If you enjoyed the book, please consider leaving a review at Amazon, even if it's only a line or two; it would make all the difference and would be greatly appreciated.

Discover other books by Ken Lozito

Safanarion Order Series:

Road to Shandara (Book 1)
Echoes of a Gloried Past (Book 2)

Made in the USA
Lexington, KY
05 December 2016